Catherine Kenny was born in England to a large Irish family that migrated to Australia when she was twelve. She always wanted to write, but working and raising three children left her little time. Upon her retirement, she completed several writing courses at U3A. Thus her first novel, "Nobody's Child," has emerged.

Dedication

My sincere thanks to my wonderful U3A lecturer Ron Selmes,
for his guidance and unfailing encouragement.

Catherine Kenny

NOBODY'S CHILD

AUSTIN MACAULEY PUBLISHERS™

LONDON • CAMBRIDGE • NEW YORK • SHARJAH

A CIP catalogue record for this title is available from the British Library.

ISBN 9781787100732 (Paperback)
ISBN 9781787101760 (Hardback)
ISBN 9781787100749 (E-Book)

www.austinmacauley.com

First Published (2018)
Austin Macauley Publishers Ltd.
25 Canada Square
Canary Wharf
London
E14 5LQ

Acknowledgments

Sincere thanks also to my dear friend Noel, for his unfailing faith in me, who has patiently proofread my manuscript several times.

With sincere thanks to Ron Selmes, my excellent U3A lecturer (University of the Third Age) for his professional guidance and unfailing encouragement.

PART ONE

IRELAND

House of
Dromgoole

CHAPTER ONE
IRELAND

They said it was the screams of the child, ringing through the huge stone manor cast high on the crest of the wild cliffs on the West Coast of Ireland that had awoken them all that cold December morning. A bitter Arctic wind, gusting in from the sea, a frost thick and white spread upon the earth.

The screams, first awaking Molly Joyce, the elderly housekeeper in her rooms off the kitchen therein. Then echoed on down to awaken the workers in the bleak thatch-roofed cottages of the neglected estate, huddled, as though for comfort, about the ancient stone church in the valley below.

"Screams loud enough to awaken the sleep of the dead!" the alarmed workers whispered, drawn to their dark cottage windows in the pre-dawn light to peer up at the massive bulk of the house towering above. "Screams full of madness, just like the master," others dared say, speaking of Bran Dromgoole and the child few had seen but knew was there.

"The Mystery Child," brought to the house under cover of darkness some twelve months before and kept hidden from view like the shameful thing they believed him to be. A seven-year-old idiot, they'd heard, who jumped at every shadow and spoke not a word. The responsibility of whom, had fallen to the sole care of Molly, the Dromgoole's trusted employee for the past forty years, who in their opinion had gone overboard and wouldn't let the child out of her sight. Reluctantly revealing his name was Rory, "Miraculously found," she had piously added, "by the grace of God and the good Monsignor O'Leary, in an orphanage up in the Heathen North." Then she'd clamped her mouth shut on the subject, refusing to reveal the one crucial detail they most wanted to know: "Who" the child actually was? Or more to point "Whose" he was? Yet at the same time almost certain they knew.

11

"Holy Mother of God…" Molly gasped, when torn from a deep snoring slumber and hurriedly casting the sign of the cross over her wildly beating heart, while wondering what in God's name had been sent to try them now.

And it seemed sent to try the child in particular. For though Molly's head was still bound up with sleep, it was clear enough to know she wasn't dreaming and that the screams were as real as the fear mounting in her and coming from the child. The beloved child whom the master had entrusted to her care and of which she had sworn to protect with the last breath of life she had in her.

Yet perplexingly, the screams seemed to rise far distant from the child's makeshift bedroom across the hall from her own, into which she had lovingly tucked him the previous night. Her blood running cold as the screams persisted, for suddenly they chorused the high-pitched howling of dogs and pinpointed his location precisely, the master's solitary quarters in the otherwise deserted North Wing of the house. The place no other servant but Molly now dared venture, the place that the child had come to dread above all other.

How he had come to be there, to have suddenly found the courage to abandon his bed in the middle of the night and wend through the big dark house alone, was beyond Molly's understanding, courage he'd so dismally lacked only hours before.

"Mother of God, protect him," she murmured, clasping her hands tight to her chest in her fervent plea.

Yet it was not for the child's physical wellbeing her concerns lay, aware there were none there within that would harm him, herself and the child, the only ones that the master's troubled mind now permitted to reside therein. Her greatest concern was for the child's mind, and the unknown psychological damage his being where he was – and at that particular time, could be doing to him?

In so far as she could see it could set him back years. Undo the small progressive steps he'd so gradually made that she'd so secretly gloated about, claiming their credit, convinced that her common sense approach to what ailed the lad, had been right after all and beginning to pay off.

But now, with the screams echoing so wildly about her, she began to doubt her judgement and to question if she'd been wrong after all. Recalling the damning predictions of the orphanage psychiatrist with some measure of guilt, who had given the child little hope of recovery or leading a normal life. Predictions she had openly scorned as a whole heap of claptrap at the time they could well do without. Convinced that all the child needed to put his mind right, was a loving and stable environment, which she believed that she could – at least for the moment, provide.

And the truth of the matter was he *had* been progressing since placed in her care little more than a year before. Tiny steps by professional standards she granted, yet gigantic strides according to the measure of her own: No longer did he wet his bed or plead to sleep in hers or scream out in the night from the horrors of his past like he used to, but now slept the whole night through in his own bed alone.

Even speaking to her now – whole conversations! As though the wind-up key to his voice box had been de-rusted and oiled and in good working order again. And he'd even let go of her apron strings and ventured to places beyond her sight! Exploring the old house for instance – or at least the South Wing of it, and not two days past he'd even ventured outside to romp and play with the master's dogs, where miracle of miracles she'd even heard him laugh! Progressing up until now that was – or at least up until yesterday.

Yesterday… Dear God in heaven, whatever had she been thinking of? Yesterday the kind of day she wished she could return to and replay its scene all over again – or better still, scrub it right off the slate of life! Recalling, with ever-increasing feelings of guilt, the visit she and the child had embarked upon to the very same place only hours before.

Three p.m. sharp it had been, the grandfather clock in the vast entrance hall confirming the hour, chiming up about them as they mounted the North Wing stair. The house veiled in drab winter light and nursing a harsh winter's chill. The wind in the rooftops howling a dirge that surely portended what was to come?

Patting herself smugly on the back at the time she had been, applauding herself for yet another small victory she believed she had won – getting the child to overcome yet another of his fears and accompany her to the master's sickbed at last. For the master was nearing the end of his days and pleading for the child to come.

13

Succeeded? Huh! Her play of good intentions had gone horribly wrong and backfired in her face. She should have known better. Not pushed the child so hard or been so quick to blow her own trumpet, but recognised the truth for what it was – that he had only gone with her to please only her! His saucer-like eyes in his dear little face saying it all as he'd looked uncertainly up at her, his slight young body holding back, even as his feet took him forward, and clinging so tightly to her hand, one could have thought it permanently glued there.

The visit ending almost before it had begun. A few brief moments at the master's bedside – barely time for the terrified child to flick his eyes over the ailing old man in the bed, before the terror he'd tried so hard to suppress had arisen and overpowered him! A pitiful whimpering issuing from a wound deep within that the world could not see, and trembling so violently from the agony of it that she'd ushered him harshly from the room, convinced at the time that that was the end of that! That regardless of the master's dying wishes or anyone else's, a team of wild horses and Sampson himself, could not wield enough power to drag the child back!

"An' who could blame him," Molly murmured, struggling to raise her five-foot rotundity from the bed as the events of the child's unhappy past gathered darkly again in her head.

He had come to her bound up with fear. Sucking fear in with every breath of the troubled young life he took and exhaling fear out. Fear of practically everything she could lay her mind to, but especially fear of death and the dark and the nightmares these two things incurred. Cowering beside the master in the back seat of the car, hugging all he possessed in a brown paper parcel tied up with string. Later to discover another piece of string holding his ill-fitting britches up, and yet another dangling a battered green bauble about his neck.

But oh, how she'd taken to the lad, taken him straight to her heart – as he had taken to her.

He'd even reached out and taken her hand, instinctively trusting, sensing her kindness and aware from the moment she'd wrapped her loving arms around him and held him close to her sweet-smelling breast that he was in a safe place at last. Certain he'd arrived at the gates of heaven, that heaven itself had opened its doors and taken him in when she called him her "Dear Sweet Lamb" and "Precious

One." Lapping her love up, starving for it and loving her back in return, loving everything about her from her soft grey hair and warm pink skin to her homey smells of violet soap of turf-fire smoke and fresh pan bread. Convinced he'd been lucky two times over when The Dromgoole had come to the orphanage and brought him back here to Molly, as though he'd dipped his hand into the lucky dip barrel at the fair and brought up two parcels tied together for the price of one.

"Aye, an' who could blame him," Molly repeated, pursing her lips and contorting her kind round face to an unaccustomed scowl, understanding first hand from whence the child had come, having been in a place not unlike it herself in a time long ago. Yet quick to acknowledge that her own experience had been but a spit in the sea compared to the trials this innocent child had been put through. And quick to acknowledge also that from the moment she'd looked into his soulful green eyes or spied the little shamrock about his neck, she had known who his mother was. Known, beyond a shadow of a doubt that he was a Dromgoole through and through, returned to his own. And as such she was honour-bound to love and protect him till her dying day. Vowing anew as she reached through the darkness and switched on the light, that whatever new burden the Lord in His wisdom was to put upon the child this day, she'd be right there beside him, loving and protecting and bearing the load with him.

But suddenly the screams reached a more anguished pitch, spurring Molly to greater action. Sparing not a moment to recover her slippers from under the bed, only to grab her gown from its foot and throw it about her as she rushed through the kitchen and out into the hall. The screams seeming to climax there, to gather and bounce off the great end walls of the house and reverberate back through her as she pattered barefoot the familiar route back down the hall.

Confirming that the child was not in his room in her passing, nor was he found in the vast entrance hall, or treading the steps of the great oak stair entwined about the massive round tower at the house's core and rising to the cold empty floors of the North and South Wings above.

Her breathing laboured on attaining the first floor landing of the North Wing, the dreaded wing, the ill-fated wing and the oldest part of the house. The place of the tragedy of so long ago when the

15

beautiful mistress had fallen to her death! Or was it the place of a deed more sinister – as the isolated community persisted to believe? The screams and the howling ceasing abruptly then, leaving only their echoes quivering about her in the dim morning light that alarmed her even more, her superstitious mind spinning into overdrive and imagining the worst.

"Arragh!" she exclaimed, scornful of her thoughts and sniffing loudly as she hoisted the robe more closely about her. "You daft old cow... 'Tis *you* who's flipped *your* lid an' scattered *your* brains all over the place! The poor little mite's just heard your tread on the stair, that's all – or plain worn himself out with all of his screamin'."

She was feeling pretty worn out herself at this point of time, aware like never before of the sixty-six years of her age upon her and weary to the bone of the never-ending troubles this family had always incurred. Troubles, they seemed to draw unto themselves like a magnet, troubles, which, whether she liked it or not, she'd always got dragged into the middle of and somehow became responsible for.

Praying now that the two alienated daughters, Caeli and Josephine, would soon be found and persuaded to return and shoulder their responsibilities themselves and lift their burden from her. Daughters, with troubles known to all and troubles known to none, who'd departed their father's house many years before and never returned since. Not a day had gone by when they'd not been in her thoughts or a night they had not been in her prayers, but especially the firstborn Caeli... For Caeli was special to her... As close to her heart as if she had sprung from her very own womb. Praying hardest of all that her precious Caeli would be soon found and persuaded to return – now that their father was soon to pass on, for it was him who had driven her away.

Desperately now, she wanted to be gone from the house with its tragic past and dark family secrets, to be rid of the problems this family had heaped on her far too long. To gather her few belongings and the damaged child and the master's dogs and go hide in the cottage that the master had promised would be hers one day. To bolt its doors on the world and be left in peace to enjoy the delight of the child in the time she had left. To do as she pleased when she wanted to do it, or if she so wished just sit in a chair and stare into space and do nothing at all. Yet all too aware that her wishes counted for nought in the scheme of things. That there were things to be done and she would toe the line as she always had and do whatever it was she was required to do.

Determinedly now, she stepped in the direction of the master's quarters in the dreaded North Wing, inhaling deeply of the musty stale air as she went in the hope of clearing her head. Aware like never before that something of great consequence had occurred and that she would need every ounce of her wits about her if she was to cope with what lay ahead.

Around to the right the master's rooms were located, at the front of the house overlooking the courtyard and wide panorama of Dromgoole lands sweeping north and south and inland as far as the eye could see.

It was even darker in this wing, dustier, mouldier and, neglected, as though abandoned to a state of perpetual mourning. Its heavy dark draperies always closed and forbidden to be opened, denying even the faintest glimmer of light or life to filter in. The balcony to her left encompassing the dark silent void of the Great Hall below into which mistress had fallen some twenty-three years before, its obscure vaulted ceiling, spanning the whispering heights of the vacant floors above.

Would it ever reveal its secrets, she wondered. Would she ever learn the truth of the events that had taken place there on that terrible Boxing Day of long ago? Would it answer the timeless question ever on her mind: Had her mistress and her very special friend and confidant, Maureen Dromgoole, been pushed to her death by the master – as the community so steadfastly believed? Or had it been the tragic accident that he and the authorities had claimed it to be?

Yet pushed or fallen, Maureen Dromgoole was but a memory that haunted Molly still, unable to dispel its tragedy from her mind. Still seeing, in her mind's eye, the mistress lying so dead upon the Great Hall's stone floor; see the green of her riding habit, the tan of her boots and her glorious copper hair fanned out about her broken neck. The painful images clicking before her eyes when she least expected them, click – click – click, like the pictures of a magic lantern show. The same tragic images assailed her now, as they always did when she came up here to this part of the house, images that taunted her reason and gave her no peace. For not only did the scenes from that long ago past return again and again upon the screen of her mind, but also their terrifying soundtrack returned too – the mistress's screams echoing up from the Hall as she fell.

The master's suite directly opposite the place she had fallen, its doors standing open and from somewhere within she could hear the child again. A strange sort of whimpering sound now, remindful of an animal trapped in a cage and scared half to death, forcing Molly's already hurrying gait to an ungainly trot.

With heart in her mouth Molly entered into the private sitting room furnished with rich silken draperies and the Fine French furniture of her mistresses' elegant taste. Not a thing had been changed; everything remained exactly as the mistress had left it at the time of the tragedy all those years before. An inner arched doorway, screened with a dark velvet drape, leading directly into Bran Dromgoole's lonely bedchamber…

"Holy Mother of God…!" Molly gasped on crossing its threshold and switching on the light.

CHAPTER TWO

LIATH CAISLEAN

The house had been built for one Turlough Dromgoole, two centuries before, a towering grey-stone mansion rising from the isolated cliffs on the West Coast of Ireland and overlooking the more protected waters of Raggemorne Bay with the vast expanse of the Atlantic Sea stretching beyond.

"Liath Caislean" (Lee-ath Kosh-lawn), the house had been aptly named, words meaning "grey castle" in the old Gaelic tongue. For that was the name hewn deep into the massive stone lintel spanning the doors of its entrance and beneath it in Latin, Anno Domini 1779 – the unhappy year of its birth?

Apt in the sense that Turlough had been a middle-aged widower hailing from Dublin with an infant son named Finn, and deeply in mourning at the untimely death of his beloved young wife. A loss it was said Turlough never got over and that he pined for his beloved for the rest of his days, that he'd turned his back not only on his friends and the bright lights of Dublin, but on life altogether, never to set foot from his gloomy retreat again – even in death! The old stories claiming his earthly remains were in the house still, entombed beneath a stone in the Great Hall's floor! The stone engraved with a shield and the word "Valhalla" – Turlough's "Valhalla" – his hall of the dead! The legend long ago become the accepted reality; for no tombstone had ever been found in the graveyard below that bore Turlough's name.

Originally, the house had comprised of the North Wing and round tower only, the South Wing added several years later – obviously to accommodate the family of Finn. For as far back as anyone could remember, the individual wings had been known as "Turlough's" and "Finn's" respectively, with both sharing the one entrance hall built around the base of the huge round tower.

Externally, the wings were identical; three storeys of dull grey stone tucked under grey slate roofs that spread either side of the conically-capped tower like sleek bird's wings, and from a distance, the house had often been likened to a giant bird of prey poised on the clifftop ready for flight.

Within was a world of constant chill and creeping shadow, its stout stone walls and narrow mullioned windows, allowing in little warmth or light, its maze of winding stairways and passageways, an endless stream of draughts and questionable noises. For deep in the bowels of its rock foundations dwelt the gawping void of a cave that heaved and sighed like some giant mortal thing with every thrust and suck of the tides, bringing a sense of heartbeat to the house and of an eerie presence ever lurking in its shadows. The rear of the house lay bare to the sea. The rest enclosed within high stone walls.

Yet this had been "home" to the Dromgoole clan for two hundred years, passing in unbroken line from father to son. Within its walls the fruits of their loins had been thrust into life, and from where, in the due course of time, their allotted measure of life duly spent, their earthly remains had been trundled down the hill to unite with their forebears in the ancient sod of the graveyard below. The very essence of the house seemed to personify everything that the Dromgoole's stood for: Powerfully built, roughly hewn with few social graces and proudly acknowledging an ancient Viking heritage. The walls of "Turlough's Great Hall," in the original North Wing, were hung with the Dromgoole's ancient Coat of Arms and the weapons of Viking antiquity, its towering vaulted ceiling with iron candelabra, and at its furthermost end, a massive stone fireplace stood, above which a life-sized portrait of Turlough Dromgoole was hung. Its ornate gold frame looking completely out of place amid the rugged setting, yet the image of its content, the wildly rugged, yet undeniably handsome middle-aged man with watchful black eyes gleaming down from the painting like polished beads of jet, looked completely at home – in spite of his dandified garb of the day: tight white breeches, red brocade jacket and ruffled lace at throat and cuff. The image disturbing when it first caught the eye, for it was the mirror image of Bran Dromgoole, the present master of the house today, whose portrait hung alongside.

"We all have our lookalikes," most were apt to say, yet it was not only in looks that the resemblance laid. Bran Dromgoole's book of life reading like edition two of his ancestor Turlough's two hundred years before him. For not only did he share the same strong physique and brooding dark looks as Turlough, but certain characteristics and major events in his life as well; the most amazing event being that they'd both lost their wives to an early grave by breaking their necks in a fall! Liath Caislean to become for Bran what it had been for Turlough two centuries before him, a refuge from an outside world grown too cruel to bear; Bran as fated as Turlough had been to walk the same halls and windswept track along the ridge of the cliffs, with *his* visionary love ever at his side.

Sparse gatherings of gorse and bracken crouched in the dips and hollows of that well-trodden track that cold December morning, stiffly frozen and brittle enough to snap. The frost covered land sweeping inwards, sprouting winter-bare trees and the shadowy shapes of the cottages and outbuildings of the estate. The revered stone chapel seeming to float in its mist-filled hollow, time-weathered gravestones and Celtic stone crosses floating about it.

No glimmer of light was yet to be seen through the house's shuttered windows. No human sound to come echoing now from its towering grey stone walls. It was as if it was a place suddenly deserted, relinquished to time and that time itself was frozen in the moment and holding its breath, in spite of the obvious signs of life: Peat smoke streaming from two of its chimneystacks, and the powerful headlamps of Doctor Tom's four-wheel-drive swinging hard through its wrought iron gates.

The cottages in the valley were in darkness too, yet Doctor Tom was intensely aware of life therein, that his every move had been watched since he'd entered upon Dromgoole land way back at the gatehouse. The twitch of a lacy white curtain, the slit of a door pulled ajar, the palpable silence that said they were listening, regardless of the inclement weather and ungodliness of the hour. Convinced that some highly refined telepathic communication system existed between them, informing them minute to minute of all that was going on, and would continue to do so until his eventual return to confirm what he knew they already knew, that their master Bran Dromgoole, "The Dromgoole" of the notorious Liath Caislean Estate on the west coast of Ireland, was dead.

For Doctor Tom knew his community well, having lived there all his life and delivered most of them into the world. For many a confidence slipped between feverish lips or the deliverance of a newborn to its mother's breast, or the ultimate passing from this life to the next. Sacrosanct secrets, he was as bound as any priest to keep. Knew, that on the whole, they were good God-fearing people, yet as heartless as a sack of stones when it came to their master Bran Dromgoole. Certain they'd spare not a moment of their time to pray for his soul, but condemn him to eternal damnation for the terrible wrong they believed he had done.

For hadn't they heard it straight from the horse's mouth? Or at least from the mouth of Bridget O'Brien, the gossipy middle-aged spinster maid, who'd happened to be lingering in The Great Hall below at the time and the only eyewitness? Heard that the master and the mistress had been above in their rooms arguing "fit to kill" and that the mistress had come tearing out onto the balcony in a terrible state with the master "hot on her heels."

"Trying to grab hold of her he was," Bridget had said, relishing her new-found celebrity and recounting the tragedy as many times over as anyone cared to listen with the same dramatic sweep of her arm: "Pushed by the master over the balcony right above me head up *there!*" she would say, "and landed at me feet down *here!*" regardless of the official finding of "Accidental Death."

He was also aware – as they too were aware, that for the first time in two hundred years there was no son to inherit the estate; only daughters, and two estranged daughters at that. Certain their only concern would only be for themselves and for what was to become of them now that their master was gone, for most had been born and bred on the estate since the time of Turlough and knew no other way of life.

What if the daughters refused to return? He could hear them ask, and was the final chapter of Dromgoole's – and of themselves at Liath Caislean?

For even though they had come to despise Bran Dromgoole, they still felt inherently close to the family, that the family belonged to them as much as they belonged to it. Weeping long and hard over their mistress's tragic passing twenty three years before, as though she was one of their own.

And they'd wept again, when twelve months later a series of events was to occur that was possibly even more tragic than the one before. Again involving the Dromgooles, so again involving

22

themselves and again making headlines across every newspaper in the land:

Mysterious disappearance of local lad, Daniel O'Halloran…
Danny Boy lost at sea…
Where has young Danny O' disappeared to…
The Dromgoole of Liath Caislean brought in for questioning…

Nor was the juicy detail suppressed that the said young man and the sixteen-year-old daughter of the house, Caeli Dromgoole, "had something going on" and more than eager to leap into the marital bed. Neither was the relevant fact concealed either, that her father "The Dromgoole" was dead-set against it.

But things had gone from bad to unbelievably sad when the even more tragic news came to light that the retarded fourteen-year-old Meegan Dromgoole had drowned in the waters of Raggemorne Bay below the house, and the tabloids had sunk to an all-time low.

Suicide of Distraught Younger Daughter… one headline cruelly ran.
Teenage Love Triangle Claims Second Victim… sensationalised another.
House of Evil… screamed a third, promoting the scandal to the worldwide press.

Even the tragedy of the mistress's death the previous year was not left to rest, but dragged up again; questions asked then asked all over again, somehow linking the events of the past to those of the present.

The official verdict "Lost at Sea," handed down the day of Meegan's funeral. The chief coastguard, Paddy McGraw, puffed up with importance, looked everyone straight in the eye and swore on a stack of bibles that after days of searching the waters of Raggemorne Bay, not a trace of Danny or his personal belongings had been found, in spite of the fact that the wreckage of his little yellow yacht "Sea Nymph," had been washed ashore not two miles beyond Raggemorne Harbour from whence it had launched.

The community convinced of a cover-up, that "The Dromgoole" knew more than he was letting on about in his determination to keep Caeli and the young man apart.

Suspicious of Paddy McGraw's testimony and his hasty departure for Italian shores; for hadn't they seen him huddled with

Bran in Rafferty's bar several nights before and slipping a long fat envelope inside his coat pocket? And again they found their master guilty, though guilty of what they were never quite sure.

But no one had been the least bit suspicious of Caeli's hasty departure, every last one of them hearing of the scene up at the house on the family's return from the little girl's funeral. Heard how the master had completely lost it that day, accusing Caeli of not only being the cause of her little sister's death, but the cause of Danny's death too, and even of her mother's tragic passing twelve months before. Even going so far as to say he rue'd the day she'd been born, and literally pushed her out of the house with not a penny to her name.

Barely sixteen Caeli had been when cast upon the world to fend for herself, undoubtedly torn between love and hate and mourning her loved ones lost. Unbeknown to her then she was carrying Daniel's child at the time, and if rumour was correct and Daniel's mother Zita O'Halloran to be believed, she'd been forced to marry some Dublin businessman she did not love who had taken her and the child abroad. Whereas Zita, by all accounts, appeared to be in no state at all over the loss of her only issue, flying off to America "for a holiday" the very next week.
"Scheming," was the best the community could say of Zita, distrustful of her "Wild traveller's blood," with more up her sleeve than her arm?

But twenty-three years had passed since then, and Caeli's reasons for leaving common knowledge to them all – cast from the house by her vengeful father.
Whereas the youngest daughter Josephine's mysterious departure just eight years ago, had puzzled them all – at least until the "Mystery Child" had appeared on the scene. For Josie was the spoiled precocious one, her father's favourite, who could do no wrong in his eyes and stood to gain everything?
Odd that she'd left then, especially in the manner in which she had – simply snuck away during the night following her grand eighteenth birthday celebrations in Turlough's Great Hall, with word to no one. The Hall ablaze with music and light; the band come all the way from Dublin.

From all accounts she'd appeared deliriously happy, danced every dance with every adoring young man in the room yet showed favour to none. Astonishing them all at her likeness to her mother in her portrait that night; adorned in an identical golden-tulle gown especially made for the occasion, and fashioning her hair in the very same style.

"The spitting image," everyone said, as though she'd stepped down from the painting itself.

An empty bed and the beautiful gown a crumpled heap on the floor come the morning, all to prove she had been in the room at all.

The community first thinking an elopement had occurred, swearing she had glowed like a woman in love, until all the young men who had been at the ball were duly present or accounted for.

Her mysterious departure remaining as such until the orphan child Rory had arrived at the house twelve months before. Obvious to all he was Josie's unwanted child, her castoff bastard son. For the numbers added up, as they'd added up for Molly and the pieces of the puzzle slotted neatly into place. Josie gone about eight years… the child past seven… But also like Molly, they hadn't a clue as to who the child's father might be.

But Josephine Dromgoole knew his identity only too well. Someone she had trusted implicitly who had come to her room and entered her bed in the deep of the night. Sick to the core at the unspeakable deed he had done to her, stripped her of her nightie and her innocence and the cherished dream of marrying the man she adored, certain he would never want her now. Nor could she have stayed and given him the chance to say otherwise, unable to look into his clear honest eyes and see the shame of the deed reflected in her own. How desperately she had wanted to run to Molly, to bury her head in Molly's soft breast and unburden it all. To feel Molly's comforting arms around her assuring her everything would be alright, while knowing in her heart nothing would ever be the same again. For the reasons that prevented her going to Molly were too close to home and too shameful to reveal. Nor could she have gone and confided in Dada – especially not Dada. His poor befuddled mind so confused, he would never have understood. Away with the fairies most of the time, poor Dada was, lost to the happier memories of his past.

Like a woman possessed, she had fled in fear and revulsion from her father's house to the early morning train that would take her north into Ulster. The only clear thought in her head: To get as far away from Him and the house as fast as she could.

CHAPTER THREE
MR. SHAW

"I thought there was murder committed, Mr. Shaw," Molly tearfully blurted out, shaken to the core, when phoning Eugene Shaw at his Dublin home to inform him of her master's passing – for Eugene Shaw was not only Bran Dromgoole's lawyer but also his closest life-long friend. The words tumbling from her lips in a highly emotional stream of brogue and homebrewed colloquialisms, informing him that the master had suffered a massive heart attack earlier that morning and lay "As dead as a doorknob" above in his bed.

"An' what with the child screamin' blue murder at the top of his lungs, sayin' – Lord save us all, Mr. Shaw – that he'd killed The Dromgoole dead as dead!

"An' hadn't the dogs gone mad 'n all, prowlin' an' howlin' about the bed? They sure put the wind up me! Honest to God Mr. Shaw, I thought it was herself in disguise come for the master – the feelin' of death so strong in the room."

"And who's the "herself" you'd be speaking of Molly?" Mr. Shaw blandly inquired, knowing full well what her answer would be.

Her response was one of incredulity, as though she was speaking to a halfwit,

"Why, who but herself the Banshee Mr. Shaw, an' certifiable I was. They could have sent the wagon for me there an' then an' I'd have gone aisy – an' that's only the half of it!

"It was the child's screaming that woke me" she continued, having taken a deep breath and attempting to recount the early morning drama in a more coherent and correct grammatical manner, respectful of the refined and well educated gentleman she was speaking to, for she had the tendency to drop her "d's" and "g's" when she got in a state. "And, I nearly had a fit there and then in me bed," she enunciated. "But by the time I'd discovered he was not in his room and had climbed the stairs to the master's quarters, he was gabbling on like an omadhaun with his eyes rolling back in his head, saying over and over that he'd killed The Dromgoole – just like he'd killed his mammy and daddy and little babby sister... And meself all alone here in the house, what with Jamjo off in London and the girls not due 'til ten."

After much probing, it became apparent to Eugene Shaw, that the child had gone alone to Bran's room in the North Wing of the house sometime during the wee small hours of the morning, on account of a dream he had dreamt in which Bran had died. Recounting the dream enfolded in Bran's arms when the fatal heart attack had actually struck, and Rory's dream had become a reality before his very eyes.

"'Twas as terrible a thing as ye'll ever see in all your born days, Mr. Shaw," Molly continued, relapsing into old habits and scarcely pausing for breath, "Seein' the child locked in the master's arms in his pose of death... Glory to God, Mr. Shaw, it sure shook the stuffin' out of me, an' no easy task to pry the lad free, I can tell ye... An' I can't begin to imagine the terror that the poor little mite must have been feelin', for death an' dyin' are the things he fears most. An' I fear for his sanity all over again, that it's more than his traumatised mind can bear." Adding, before Mr. Shaw could get a word in edgeways.

"An' 'tis no consolation I can bring the lad either, though I keep tellin' him 'twas never his fault. He's altogether lost his senses, Mr. Shaw. Just keeps gabblin' over and over that he's killed The Dromgoole – just like he killed his family before. An' me biggest worry is that he'll regress right back to the state he was in when he first came here among us, an' all the good that's been done will be undone."

Molly breaking down herself at this point of time, overwhelmed at the thought of such a calamitous thing occurring.

"Molly, get a grip on yourself," Mr. Shaw called anxiously into the phone, alarmed at the elderly housekeeper's distress. "We're depending on you!" Yet for some unclear reason, his well-meant words made her bawl all the more.

Patiently, he waited for Molly to gather her senses about her. The trifling seconds stretching to the eternity of minutes and still he waited, for he wasn't about to rush her or breathe another word that might upset her any more than she already was. And he flinched when the fog-horn sounds of nose-blowing finally trumpeted down the line.

He had all the time in the world where Molly Joyce was concerned, her unfailing loyalty to his closest friend's family for the past forty years had earned her his utmost respect. Visualising the plump little woman in all her despairs in the massive old house alone, stoically bearing the burdens of her master's demise and the traumatised child and the dozens of things that would have to be done. Doubting not for one moment her ability to handle the situation, certain she would cope with whatever came along as she somehow always had. Aware of how much the Dromgooles had depended on her over the years, and in his opinion, depended too much and taken her for granted. But he was also aware of how much the Dromgooles meant to Molly, how she had come to regard each and every one of them as her own flesh and blood, and no less the troubled child who'd been thrust upon her without warning twelve months before. And aware also of how much she loved the child and how eagerly she had taken him to her heart. Claiming he was no trouble at all but a sheer delight, and treating him like the grandchild she had long yearned for but was never likely to have. For her only son and offspring, James Joseph Joyce, at the mature age of thirty-three, showed not the slightest interest in marriage or the company of the opposite sex.

And well she might, Mr. Shaw thought now, nodding his head in agreement with his thoughts. She above all had earned that right. That she'd done more for the Dromgooles and their children over the past forty years than any employee was ever obliged to do.

And a forty-year relationship was a long time in anyone's book. Forty years turned the pages of life right back to the time when they were all young and in their prime, and also to the time when his best friend Bran Dromgoole had married the girl of his dreams and broken his heart.

Molly was a bride herself back then, arriving at the Dromgoole's infamous household with her new husband Pat from the highly refined and respected manor of Lord Declan's estate. Molly engaged to fill the vague position of cook-cum-housekeeper – a huge step up from her previous position of assistant cook. But a definite step down for Pat, downgraded from the prestigious position of Lord

Declan's esteemed butler, to fill the lesser and equally vague position of Bran's personal manservant, cum anything else that was required of him. For the likes of a butler was never required at Liath Caislean.

Mr. Shaw had made it his business back then – being Bran's closest friend as well as his family lawyer, to personally check the couple's backgrounds out. Pat's credentials exemplary, as Mr. Shaw had expected them to be: Respectable parents, high achiever at the village school and employed by Lord Declan for the past fifteen years, whereas Molly's revealed a life far from a bed of roses. Also employed by Lord Declan as a lowly scullery maid since the age of ten, having come from an orphanage as Rory had, and perhaps thus explaining – at least in part, her close affinity to the child. But Mr. Shaw didn't know the half of it.

By Molly's own admission, those early years had been harsh years indeed, for she was altogether too outgoing for her own good and slow to learn her place. Yet incredibly, she looked upon those years as being the most fortunate years of her life and even considered herself blessed to have been there. "For wasn't it there," she would purr in her soft Tipperary brogue and wearing her heart on her sleeve for the whole world to see, "that I met me handsome Pat?"

Consequently, Molly had blossomed at Liath Caislean, free of the strict social confines of the Aristocratic Upper Class to be herself at last, her warm friendly manner drawing everyone in, but none more so than her mistress, Maureen Dromgoole.

To Mr. Shaw's mind, riding the rollercoaster of time to life back then, he could clearly understand how the friendship between the once social butterfly and the servant girl with the heart of gold had come about. Maureen, so starved of companionship in the isolation of Liath Caislean, that Molly's unfailing kindness and genuine concern could not have failed to draw her in.

But what he failed to understand then, and still did to this day, was why Maureen had chosen to marry Bran in the first place instead of himself? To hide herself away in Bran's gloomy old house in his world of isolation on the brink of nowhere, when she could have married him and lived in his elegant home in Dublin, and availed herself of the high social life Dublin had to offer, that would have eagerly gathered her celebrity in?

For, much to his surprise, she had actually accepted his latest proposal of marriage on her return from London and he had been over the moon, believing he had won her heart at last. Only to have her change her mind the following day when he'd taken her to Liath Caislean and introduced her to his best friend Bran. One look at Bran and it had been curtains for him – all over red rover.

Her sudden change of heart had not only broken his own but baffled him too; unable to comprehend why the acclaimed "Songbird or Ireland," who'd thrived on bright lights and celebrity, had been drawn to Bran and his lonely world right from the start, as though it and Bran were the answer to her prayers.

The friendship between Molly and Maureen growing even closer the night Maureen had gone into an unexpectedly early labour and Molly had been summoned to attend her until young Doctor Tom arrived. But by the time Doctor Tom had got there, Caeli had already been born into Molly's loving arms and claimed a place in her heart forever.

And wasn't it God's honest truth now, Mr. Shaw thought with a wry twist of his mouth, acknowledging again what he'd acknowledged many times in the past, that over the years Molly had been more of a mother to the three Dromgoole girls than Maureen ever had. For it had always been Molly the little girls sought to dry their tears or soothe their childhood woes away, and Molly they'd wanted to tell them stories and hear their prayers and tuck them into bed at night, for the children adored her and would have it no other way.

But then everyone adored Molly, for there was something about Molly that drew everyone in. Something that twined around your heart and made you feel warm and safe and precious inside. Her genuine love and unshakeable faith in mankind perhaps that brought out the best in her fellow man? Recalling one of Molly's pearls of wisdom (and Molly had one for every occasion), written in capitals on a piece of cardboard and tacked inside the downstairs lavatory door – where, Molly assured him that sooner or later it would catch everyone's eye. "IF YE CAN'T SAY SOMETHING NICE ABOUT SOMEONE – BEST YE SAY NOTHING AT ALL!"

Yet even the pure-hearted Molly had been known to take exception to her rule. Ferociously loyal to her beloved Dromgooles, she could tear strips off any poor unsuspecting soul who happened to say one derogatory word against anyone of them, springing to their defence like an alley cat.

And by God, Mr. Shaw thought now, the hairs on the nape of his neck standing on end, having seen the whole five feet of her in action with her arms akimbo and blue eyes blazing, she presented a very formidable adversary indeed.

"I'll have ye know, Mr. Shaw," her voice piped down the line interrupting his thoughts, "that Doctor Tom has given Rory some green-coloured medicine to quieten him down, an' that I've coaxed him into the little sittin' room an' tucked him up all snug an' warm before a fire, where I'm hopin' he'll fall asleep."

"Ah, good, good... But you must keep him calm, Molly," he added anxiously. "For he's not strong, you know." His ill-chosen words as ill-received and coming back to bite him before barely said.

"You're tellin' *me* that!" she spluttered, "*me*, who's cared for the child since the day he came here among us! Do you think it's altogether a fool that I am, that I need *ye* to be tellin' *me* the state that the poor child's health is in? It's the plight of *him* an' what's going on in *his* head an' not the master's dyin' that's upsettin' me so, for the master was old an' it was his time. But the child is young with his whole life before him an' must be convinced that he isn't all bad – that he isn't to blame for the terrible things he believes he has done.

"What a cross for anyone to bear, Mr. Shaw," she continued, sounding quite cross herself, "let alone a seven-year-old who believes that he's killed his whole family an' now killed the master as well. So I'll be thankin' ye not to be tellin' *me* how fragile he is – I'm all too aware of that already!"

He cringed at the sharpness of her tongue, regretful of his words and hastily sought to console her,

"Yes, yes, of course you are, Molly, and I meant you no disrespect, none whatsoever, merely suggesting you keep the lad calm." Proposing, before she could rebuke him further, that she ring the tower bell in the courtyard and get the O'Brien twins to come up early and a few other women besides, adding that she'd be needing more help than that "useless pair" could give her this day.

"And for goodness sake, Molly, go make yourself a good strong cup of tea and put a nip of whisky in it, for we can't have you cracking up on us now, can we?

But Mr. Shaw's well-meant instructions fell on deaf ears. Molly's priority, to attend to her dead master's needs. Only to find on returning to his room that Rory had also returned and was standing by the bed with his mouth wedged open in a silent scream that would scream inside him for a long time to come.

CHAPTER FOUR

MOLLY

"Arragh… Forty years!" Molly expelled on a sigh, her thoughts spinning off on much the same tangent as Mr. Shaw's had been, referring to the time she had spent in the house and wondering where the forty years had gone. Forty years of ups and downs and memories good and bad. Forty years of secrets… "Forty years," she repeated, sounding incredulous, as though the thought of time passing had never crossed her mind before.

The cup of tea at long last a reality and placed on the scrubbed kitchen table before her, and for all outward appearances at least, she was again in possession of her bustling capabilities and some sort of order restored to the house. Orders despatched left right and centre to the middle-aged spinster twins Biddy and Bridget O'Brien and to several other women from the valley called in for the day.

And young Kieran – old McGinty's youngest – God bless him, had arrived there unbidden, to give her a hand to prepare the master for his wake and subsequent burial.

Yet if the truth was known, Molly was far from being in possession of anything, every minute of her sixty-six years bearing down on her like a ton of bricks. Her mind in turmoil over the death of the master and the worry of the child and what was to become of him now that the master was gone.

Sipping the tea gratefully, she glanced around the sparkling kitchen where the greater part of those forty years had been spent with a great sense of pride, knowing she had done her best and served this family well. Then, with a strong sense of ownership, she cast her eyes over the great oak dressers lining its walls, laden with plates and bowls and soup tureens shining back at her like dear old friends, then raised them heavenward to the huge iron pot rack that hung from its rafters, dangling an array of black iron pans and gleaming copper pots.

34

"What stories they could tell if they could all speak," she muttered to herself, thinking of the countless meals she had boiled and baked and served on them. The ordinary three-times-a-day meals, the special occasion meals, the soothe-and-make-better treats and the treats she had made for no reason at all, simply because she was who she was and loved to spoil them all – not forgetting the bread she had baked and the jams she had made and the countless pots of tea she had brewed in between.

"A lifetime of cookin' and carin' for other people," she muttered again, "with hardly a minute to meself – let alone take me off on that holiday Pat promised to take me on one day." Still dreaming of the once in a lifetime trip to Paris that she and her late husband Pat had planned to take.

The romantic cruise along the Seine under the bridges of Paris – just like the words of the song her Pat used to sing to her, *Sous les ponts de Paris*... To climb to the top of the Eiffel Tower... To kneel in prayer in the great Notre Dame and give thanks to the Almighty for the many blessings He had bestowed on them – the holiday of a lifetime to create special memories to tuck into their hearts and reminisce upon in their old age.

"Forty years of me life servin' this family," she muttered again, "An' I'm already old... Waitin' for life to happen when it's already passed me by."

A blushing bride she had been at the time she had come, arriving at the isolated Liath Caislean Estate on the West Coast of Ireland with her new husband Pat. The rooms off the kitchen to become their home and the only home they had known. Apprehensive of the rumours that had preceded them and wondering what in Heaven's name they were getting themselves into? For they'd heard their new master, Bran Dromgoole, was a bit of a strange one, antisocial, ill-mannered and ill-bred, and more than a little bit cracked in the head, and were therefore relieved to find him reasonably normal and a newly-wed too. The in-house gossip quick to inform that his bride was Maureen O'Sullivan, the famous "Songbird of Ireland" no less, that it had been "Love at First Sight" and that the master had proposed to her the very same night they had met – even though – scandalous as it was, she had been engaged to his best friend Eugene Shaw, the prominent Dublin lawyer, at the time!

Her sudden change of heart and impromptu marriage, had puzzled Molly, unable to comprehend why such a talented and exquisite creature, nearly half her husband's age, should have chosen to marry the coarse Bran Dromgoole and live in his dismal old domicile in the first place at all, when she could have married the refined and highly respected Eugene Shaw and lived in his grand home in Dublin and been treated like a queen among the high social life that Dublin had to offer.

To Molly's mind, everything about the marriage seemed wrong for the mistress, not only the gloomy old house and its wild isolation, but above all Bran Dromgoole himself. In her estimation he wasn't half good enough for her and that she deserved better. Feeling the mistress had bargained with the devil and sold herself short and sensing in her a lost soul with a story to tell and badly in need of a friend.

All being revealed the night Maureen had gone into an unexpectedly early labour with her firstborn daughter Michaela (Caeli), and Molly had been summoned to attend her until the new young locum, Doctor Tom, arrived. But by the time Doctor Tom had got there, the tiny black-haired infant had already been delivered into Molly's eager arms and captured her heart forever; whereas Bran, her father, had coldly closed his and shunned the exquisite child from the start, that he'd taken one look at the beautiful newborn – whose stunning violet eyes seemed to be staring straight back into his, then he'd stormed from the room without so much as a word or a glance at his wife.

Something about the innocent child had upset him greatly. Something that had riled his blood and stirred up old memories he would rather forget. He hadn't liked her eyes. Above all he'd hated her eyes. Deep violet-blue eyes… He'd seen eyes like hers before. Haunting eyes that haunted him still… Caeli had immediately begun to cry – as if even then she had sensed his rejection of her.

The infant was almost forgotten in the emotional upheaval that followed. The mistress hysterical, Doctor Tom overly attentive, trying to calm her, shocked at her husband's brutish treatment and unable to hide his own adoration of her…

But it was Molly who'd attended to Caeli's needs. Molly who'd bathed and dressed the beautiful child and put her to suckle at her distraught mother's breast. And Molly who'd remained with her mistress the whole night through, sharing deep personal secrets and making promises that were never to be broken, bonding the unlikely pair as the closest of friends for all time.

The second daughter Meegan was rejected in much the same manner as Caeli had been, for Meegan was a great disappointment in her father's eyes. For Meegan, though she strongly resembled her father, had entered the world three months too soon and created special problems of her own.

How different the scenario when a whole nine years later, daughter number three arrived on the scene. Trumpets blared and a choir of angels sang. Bran had been over the moon and couldn't have been happier with the perfect, exquisite, green-eyed, copper-haired Josephine, the image of her beautiful mother. A Godsend, thought her mother. "A charmer," said her father, for right from the start, little Miss Josephine Dromgoole had managed to do what his other two daughters had failed to do – completely enslave his heart.

The rhythm of the house gradually began to shift and the care of the children to fall more on Molly. And she came to look upon the three Dromgoole girls as babes of her own and as precious to her as her own son James Joseph was, showering them all with the same loving care. And to Molly's mind, they were the best of times, the times she would cherish deep in her heart till the end of her days.

But then there were the bad times, the worst of times that would haunt her just as long. Like the time when the mistress had fallen to her death into Turlough's Great Hall, and the time when twelve months later, precious young Meegan and Caeli's young man had drowned in the sea and the master went mad and cast Caeli out.

Pat had been urging them to leave back then, all for packing their bags and moving on. For Pat was a peace-loving man who hated conflict of any kind and protective of Molly and their son to a fault.

But Molly's tongue had been persuasive; her argument for remaining one Pat knew he couldn't win – the possibility of Caeli returning and Molly's need to be there for her. Aware of the promises Molly and the mistress had made to each other on that night of long ago, and how much Caeli meant to her, that the girl was as close to her heart as if she had borne her herself and not their employee's daughter at all.

"And besides," Molly had added, adding fuel to fire, hell-bent on staying no matter what and aware that the argument was already won, "what sort of a creature would I be if I was to break me promise I made to the mistress all those years ago... That I'd be there for her children – as she would've been there for mine, if our roles were reversed and some tragedy had befallen' me!

"God rest her soul, Pat, an' forgive us all, the poor woman would turn in her grave if I was to leave an' turn me back on our dear little Josephine! For it wasn't just Caeli I vowed to be there for the night the beloved child was born, but for all the Dromgoole children that were to follow as well! An' Josie's just a babe," she added, plucking at the strings of his heart, "barely four years old with not a soul in the world to watch out for her!"

So they had stayed, despite Pat's constant urgings to be gone, the weeks stretching into months, the months into years, waiting for Caeli's return. Another Christmas, another spring with the whole of creation bursting with life and still she hadn't come. But Pat's life ebbed away. They had waited too long. And Molly knew there'd be no moving on for her now. That Liath Caislean would remain her home – or her prison, for the rest of her days.

As for the mistress's death, it was hard to get over and put from her mind and get on with her life in a normal manner, in her thoughts first thing in the morning and in her prayers last thing at night. A strange occurrence if ever there was one. Strange in the sense that the calm gracious creature the mistress had so normally been, should have been anything less that day, for she'd never been one to lose control or get worked up over anything. But worked-up she had surely been that day, evidenced by the shouting heard right through the house. Something untoward had taken place up in their rooms in Turlough's Wing that day; something that the master had said or done that had sent the mistress tearing out onto the balcony in a terrible state to meet with her death.

"Like a madwoman," Bridget had added to her repertoire, her story becoming all the more incredible with every telling. "Wrenching and writhing away from the master as though she couldn't bear for him to touch her! And then himself like a madman – but twice as bad, sort of grabbin' hold of her here around the throat, and the next thing I knew, over she came."

Molly could not believe Bridget's dramatic allegations, even though she was aware that Bran Dromgoole could be cruel – as evidenced by his on-going ill-treatment of Caeli from the moment she was born. Yet unable to believe he had suddenly become the violent evil madman that Bridget had made him out to be and deliberately push his wife over the balustrade and down into The Great Hall to her death.

"Arragh... If only they'd written," Molly sighed, saddened by the girl's lack of contact over the years. "Just dropped me a line to ease me mind and let me know they were alright." For she'd wept long and hard over their absence and wondered where in the world they were, and hoped they'd found happiness wherever it was.

Muttering again under her breath – as she was increasingly apt to do, and swearing – as she was not, that since their mother's passing there'd been "bugger all" happiness to be found around there.

Blame of which, she laid fair and square at the master's feet. Firmly believing he had failed his daughters to be what a father should be – their strength and protector. And again in her opinion – as humble as she thought her opinion to be, he had failed the mistress as well and held him responsible for whatever had occurred in their private quarters in Turlough's Wing that day. For the mistress had never been one to pick fights, just the opposite! To Molly's mind she'd kow-towed to the master too much, as though atoning for sins of the past and still had a huge penance to pay?

And for what it was worth, she believed he had failed young Danny O'Halloran too, that things were not as they were said to be, that the official finding "Lost at Sea" did not ring true. Recalling the scraps of hushed conversations overheard by the master when speaking on the phone or the reversed cryptic notes absorbed into the blotter on his desk or the memos screwed up in the wastepaper basket to be burned in the fire. But above all, the abiding sense of something left unsaid that hung forever in the air.

But her strongest and most tangible suspicion was the mysterious visitor who'd been coming to the house in the dead of night for years. Aware that he entered the house via the cave and the secret door that led into the master's office directly above. Sensing the intruder's identity when she'd nearly collided with him one night and that a grave injustice had been done. Wanting to warn others of the deceit, but loyalty sworn to the mistress on the night

Caeli was born, held her to silence. And besides, who'd have believed her anyway, an old uneducated servant woman? But her thoughts were her own to think as she pleased, and she knew what she knew.

Almost desperately she wanted to be gone from the house now, to cast off its secrets and sins and be free of the never-ending responsibilities it demanded of her, to take some time-honoured time-out to stop and smell the roses and simply be plain old Molly Joyce again. Hoping against hope that the girls would soon be found and persuaded to come home, yet aware that even if they were, there was no guarantee they would want to come back – especially not Caeli. Unable to imagine the beloved girl ever wanting to set eyes her on the place again – let alone set her foot in its door! All too aware of what had driven her away.

And for all she knew, Josie might feel the same way, especially if the child she had born and cast from her as a vile and unwanted thing, had been conceived in her room on the night she had fled? Yet that made little sense, for Josie could never have known she was carrying a child at the time. There had to be something more?

As far as Molly could see, they just had to find Caeli and persuade her to return – now that her father was gone. For Caeli was the smart one who could sort all their problems out in a flash, the strong-minded one who could gather the sad little band of Dromgooles that were left and unite them as a family once more.

For apart from the worry of what was to become of Rory if Josie refused to come back, there was also the worry of the house and what was to become of it. All too aware – as the community was aware, that for the first time in two hundred years there was no son to inherit the estate and perpetuate the family name.

Bending her head low to the bare kitchen table before her, her hands clutched reverently to her breast, she uttered a prayer to the Heavenly Father as bald and as simple as any prayer could be.

"Dear God in heaven," she fervently pleaded, "Will ye please tell me Caeli it's time she came home?"

PART TWO

AUSTRALIA

CHAPTER FIVE
AUSTRALIA

December, brought the official season of summer to the huge island continent of Australia, enveloping its states in a vastly differing array of atmospheric conditions. Bushfires raged in New South Wales and up in the Victorian Dandenongs, a cyclone was hovering in the Arafura Sea threatening the northern city of Darwin, and in the states of South and Western Australia, torrential rains were bursting the riverbanks and causing floods, to name but a few; while in the southeast corner of Queensland where Caeli Morgan lived, ongoing drought and heatwave conditions were the long-range forecast from the Bureau of Meteorology.

"So what else is new?" Caeli murmured, shrugging her shoulders and thinking they were stating the obvious, unable to imagine the hot steamy conditions of sub-tropical Brisbane ever going away. And yet another season of drought was the predicted lot for the Cockies of the Darling Downs and the vast cattle stations out west. Another season of cracked red earth and dried up riverbeds where mighty rivers once coursed their flow. Faded eyes doomed to peer beneath faded hats as generations before them had peered in the timeless chain of seasons past, scanning the clear sweep of sky for the merest sign of relief: A splotch of a rain-cloud perhaps, or the hint of a storm on the shimmering horizon, or the sight of brolgas dancing on the plains – for according to Aboriginal Legend, dancing brolgas brought rain. Finding nothing to encounter in the endless arc of blue but the blinding furnace of the sun, and the only dance being danced on the cracked red earth was the frenzied rumba of heat.
The residents of the City of Brisbane and its sprawling outer-lying suburbs were longing for a downpour of rain to revive sagging spirits and quell the dust, for nothing but a token torment had dribbled from the azure-blue skies in many long months. The levels

of the Queensland dams were alarmingly low and water restrictions were in full force – water being the most precious commodity to the "driest continent on earth" and every last drop metered out.

How paradoxical this Motherland Australia was. Serenely beautiful one day, lulling her children to a false sense of security with her mild winter's weather and balmy songs of spring: *She'll be right mate… Everything'll be apples…* yet a ruthless creature of raging fire and passion the next, turning in an instant to reveal her savagely brutal guise.

Yet this was the faraway land of milk and honey. The bright "New World" Caeli's late husband, Malachi Morgan, had dreamt of entering many years before, seeking a new beginning and a better way of life for her and the illegitimate son of another man's seed he had chosen to name as his own. A young nation by world standards, founded on convict labour a mere two hundred years before, its "mixed-bag" population lured from every corner of the globe and every walk of life with its promise of equal opportunity and "giving a bloke a fair go." The huge sunburnt island of heat-crazed vistas and endless horizons, that Malachi had believed to be his destiny and contrasted so sharply with the moist green lands of the small Emerald Isle he had left behind.

But "destiny" was not of Malachi's making. "Destiny," having mapped a different course for him in a time long ago that would snatch him away in the blink of an eye and leave Caeli to enter his dream land alone. Alone that was, but for the infant son of Danny O'Halloran's seed suckling hungrily at her breast, and the then unknown quantity of Malachi's daughter evolving to life in her womb.

Her home was distinctively termed a true-blue "Queenslander." A sprawling timber and iron-roofed residence built on the banks of the Brisbane River, circa 1903, by some rich English gentleman who'd appropriately named it "Rivergum House" on account of its glorious river location and the prevalence of river-gums sweeping its banks. Its high-ceilinged room's featured the original VJ walls and filigreed breezeways above its doors, its ceilings, intricate pressed metal, a luxury of a bygone era, and characteristic French doors that opened to wide, shady, wrap-around verandas. A cool grey décor paid ultimate compliment to the up-to-the-minute white-leather lounges and dark brooding antiques, and in general, it suited the sweltering Queensland climate exceedingly well.

The rundown property purchased "for a song" several years before, but by the time she had refurbished and coaxed it into the latter half of the twentieth century, it had wound up costing the proverbial arm and leg.

But let it be said here and now that where Caeli Morgan was concerned, there were no half measures. She was an all or nothing – a do it right or do it not at all sort of person, thus a stunning butterfly had emerged from a peeling brown chrysalis of years of neglect. Some glossy magazine having described it as: "The perfect integration of old and new… A delightful blending of the pioneer charm of the past with every convenience the modern day world had to offer." claiming it a triumph to the new "Business Woman of The Year." A far cry by anyone's standards from the humble, tumbledown shack she'd been forced to endure on her arrival in Australia.

Indeed she could not have settled for less. Promising herself when money had been exceedingly short and life a constant struggle to survive, that when good-fortune *did* come her way (and determined she was that it would) that only the best would be good enough for her and her children.

The stifling humidity of the hot Brisbane night had steeped its population in a slather of sweat, permitting only fitful bouts of restless sleep. To rise from their beds with bodies weary and tempers frayed before the day had barely begun with one universal thought in mind – they were in for another stinker!

"Holy Dooley… Another hot one…!" Caeli muttered irritably, kicking the damp sheet aside as the first light of dawn nudged the smoke-filled sky, feeling decidedly cranky and out-of-sorts.

For the night had been an especially trying one for her. The little sleep she'd had, fraught with the nightmare that had plagued her nights for years and never failed to terrify her. Yet for some inexplicable reason, it had seemed even more terrifying to her *that* night and its aftermath still crawled like cold claggy snails all over her back. The nightmare concerning events back in Ireland some twenty-two years before when she'd been forced from her father's house and eventually leave Ireland altogether.

The nightmare that entered her dreams almost every night now that she had come to accept it as a normal part of her life, despite the passage of so many years and the thousands of miles put between.

The smoke from the bushfires down south still lingered in the hot moist air like an unwelcome visitor refusing to leave or be ignored, and she raised the mosquito net and swung her slender legs to the floor and switched the bedside radio on, anxious news of the New South Wales fires and the plight of her fellow countrymen presently caught in their grip. It was good news at first. The learned voice of the announcer sounded quite cheerful, claiming the fires were now under control, and Caeli sighed with relief, for Kevin, her twenty one year old son, who was studying to become a vet, was down in the Coonabarrabran district of New South Wales with some of his uni mates, seeking hands-on experience with the local country vet. And even though he had rung her the previous night to assure her he was not in any danger – unless the wind took a violent swing to the west, he'd not eased her mind one little bit. Ever mindful of how quickly conditions could change in this vast sunburnt land.

As it turned out, her fears were soon proven right, as another newsflash cut through the strains of Nat King Cole…

> *Pretend you're happy when you're blue.*
> *It isn't very hard to do…*
> *And you'll find happiness without and end*
> *Whenever you pretend…*
> *Remember anyone can dream.*
> *And nothings bad as it may seem…*

Oh, but it *was*! Unimaginably bad! A thousand times worse than bad! The fires in the Dandenongs were sweeping out of control! The announcer's voice was out of control too, near fever-pitch as he spoke the words Caeli was dreading to hear.

"Human Casualties Found!" A young family of four trapped on a lonely mountain track, their remains fused as one in the burnt-out shell of the family car. Still, it got worse. "Dozens of properties destroyed… Grave fears held for a missing fire-truck and its volunteer crew…" But it was early days yet.

For those who'd lost everything, the heart-wrenching task of starting all over again would begin, thankful to God that they and their children had survived. Time to sift through the ashes in the hope of recovering something of the old to link them to the new, something to build a new dream on, no matter how damaged or insignificant that something might seem.

A heat-crazed cup from grandma's inheritance perhaps, a sentimental trinket more valued than gold, a child's singed toy, a trike, a wheelbarrow, anything at all was considered a prize. Rebuild their ravaged homes along with their ravaged dreams in the hope of recapturing the essence of that which was lost. For the land was a constant, the land remained. No time for whinging or wallowing in self-pity – that was not the Australian way. Just band together and roll-up the sleeves and get on with it mate, and in dinky-di Aussie tradition, give it another go! But for others it would be the end of the line, financially and emotionally wiped out.

Abruptly, she switched the radio off, feeling quite sick.
Not a breath of a breeze rustled a leaf or rippled a curtain as she padded barefoot through the silent Sunday-morning house, a strange sense of stillness walked with her, a morbid expectancy that all was not well and that an ill-wind was rising, the feeling so strong that goose-bumps rippled her flesh.

"The lull before the storm," she murmured prophetically. Yet even as at the words left her mouth and hung in the hot humid air about her, she could never have imagined how true they would turn out to be.

Her head was throbbing when she arrived at the kitchen, feeling badly in need of a cup of tea. She filled up the kettle and switched it on and heaped two teaspoons of loose-leaf tea into a small one-cup pot while anxiously waiting for the water to boil.

Memories from the past still spun in her head and predominated her thoughts, clearly hearing Molly calling back through time as if she was standing on the rooftops of Liath Caislean… 'A watched-pot never boils, lass!'

Thinking again how strange it was that the past should have such a hold on her this day.

Scalding the tea the second the water boiled and straining it into a fine china mug and somehow swallowing two aspros down with the first scalding sip, hoping to banish the headache, the dream and the sickening thoughts of the young dead family from her mind. But doggedly they remained, like loyal cobbers, lodged between dreams and reality and disinclined to be shifting on anywhere.

Right from the start the day had not augured well, having sensed something ominous simmering in the air from the moment she'd opened her eyes. Her senses to prove alarmingly right, for it would turn out a day she would come to regret many times over in the days that lay ahead, despite the unexpected sliver of joy that would slip in among its evil intent. A day that would cause her to question the devious nature of mankind and to ask herself why, why that lot back there in Ireland just hadn't left her alone?

For the moment had come for the chimeras of the past to gather about her and carry her back; the disturbing dreams of the night born of the certainty it was so.

CHAPTER SIX
CAELI

At thirty-nine-years of age, Caeli Morgan was stunningly attractive still; despite the years of hardship life had flung her way. She possessed a raw sensuality she was unaware she had, which the male of the species found wildly attractive. Yet conversely, her cute pert nose had a no-nonsense tilt to it and her wide generous mouth a don't-mess-with-me set that warned them away. Her jet-black hair was as sleek and glossy as a raven's wing, her eyes an incredible violet-blue, her body slim and supple and radiated good health and vitality, and from a distance she had often been mistaken to be a young girl. It was only on closer observation one could see she was not. For apart from the fine embryonic lines that crept from the corners of her amazing violet eyes, the real give-away was the world-weary look in their unswerving gaze, a flicker of something that spoke of old pain that was totally disturbing and made those who cared and knew of her past, feel the need to protect. And there was something in her manner even harder to define; a hunch of shoulders, a tilt of head when things of her world were not going right, as if to say: "So, what did you expect, a bed of roses?" completely out of sync with her normally forthright manner.

For all outward appearances, Caeli Morgan was the epitome of modern day woman who had it all, totally in control of her life, juggling single parenthood and the growing business empire she had built of her own volition, with apparent ease and undeniable success. Friends and associates alike viewed her with a mixture of envy and awe. To the few who knew her intimately, Caeli Morgan had "done it hard" and was of the opinion she deserved everything she had. Aware she had begun her business venture with practically nothing to her name, yet succeeded against the almost insurmountable odds of being a near destitute teenage widow with two babies to support, when she'd literally stumbled into her first modest dress shop in the heart of the City of Brisbane, and that it had taken her many more years of dedicated toil to expand it to the not-so-modest, seven trendy boutiques she now owned today.

Yet to mere acquaintances who knew nothing of her past or her struggle to achieve the success she had, she was considered "Lucky."

"Lucky, lucky, *lucky* Caeli Morgan," they would say in voices dripping envy, believing everything she had, had been handed to her on a silver platter. For apart from the obvious seven boutiques – six in and around the City of Brisbane simply named "Caeli's Fashions," and the latest on the buzzing tourist strip of the Gold Coast – managed and suitably named "Holiday Romps" by her nineteen-year-old daughter Liz ('In keeping with the Gold Coast's legendary holiday mood Mum…') she also owned "Rivergum House," a sprawling riverside mansion on the outskirts of the city, and the very latest top-of-the-range Mercedes Benz.

"Caeli Morgan the beautiful," they would say, "Caeli Morgan the smart," for the new "Businesswoman of The Year," presented a very self-satisfied face to the world, exuding the impression her life was ideal, whereas in reality, nothing could have been further from the truth. Inside, Caeli Morgan was haunted by her past and falling apart.

As for luck… luck didn't enter the equation at all, despite her being born with the proverbial silver spoon in her mouth. Unaware she'd been forced from her father's estate in Ireland, when only sixteen, penniless and pregnant with her dead lover's child and dependent on strangers to take her in. Everything she had accomplished, she'd accomplished herself, fought tooth and nail for. And it could be said of Caeli Morgan, that at the relatively young age of not yet reaching her fortieth year, she had amassed a small fortune and done very well for herself.

The early years being the hardest: her husband of but a few months duration, Malachi Morgan, having unexpectedly died of a heart attack on the ship en route to Australia, thus leaving Caeli no choice but to enter the unfamiliar land at the bottom of the world alone. Life had been an eternal struggle to simply survive back then. Yet a struggle she had won, triumphed over even, despite her father's obvious wish to destroy her.

She showered, and dressed in scanty white shorts and white cotton top, rescued *The Sunday Mail* from the hydrangea bush at the bottom of the drive beside her front gate, planning a leisurely Sunday-morning read on her rear veranda overlooking the river. The shaded tranquil setting her favourite thinking place and the early hours of the morning, her favourite time of day. Its quiet seclusion amid the sheltering overhang of trees encouraged her thoughts to flow freely, whether pondering the great mysteries of life or the mundane complexities of the everyday. But right from the start, it was proving to be a cow of a day and her thoughts all twisted and tangled in a tightly knotted skein. For apart from the dreams and the horror of the bushfires, Sebastian Templeton – her so-called "special" friend, had turned decidedly "un-special" after dinner the previous night. Their parting, unpleasant to say the least, spiked with infantile tantrums and wild accusations that revealed a side of him she had never seen before and quite frankly a side she never wished to see again, and she was still reeling from the shock of it.

Had the night abated his anger, she wondered. Had it soothed his damaged ego and made him regretful of his childish actions and ill-chosen words? Hoping he'd tossed and turned as much as she had and arisen repentant with the sharp sting of guilt on his mind, and turn up today apologetic and at least remain friends. Yet she was pretty sure he wouldn't. Sebastian wasn't the type to apologise to anyone – especially not a woman, and she doubted she would ever see him again.

With a shrug of her shoulders and a tilt of her head she murmured resignedly under her breath, "Well If that's how you want our relationship to end… So be it, Sebastian Templeton, so be it." Resolving – at least for the moment, to put him out of her mind and into the "discuss with Liz later basket," Liz, being her nineteen-year-old daughter who lived on the Gold Coast and was driving up later for lunch.

"Be there around twelvish, Mum," Liz called gaily into the phone the previous afternoon. "And oh, Mum… Is it OK if I bring a friend…?"

"But of course…"

"A rather special friend…"

"No prob! You know me… The more the merrier I always say… I'm surprised you even asked." Bemused by her daughter's offbeat manner and the mystery riding her voice, a holding-back-yet-bursting-to-tell-all sort of voice that immediately sparked her interest.

"Anyone I know?" she had casually asked, dying to know if this 'special friend' was a he or a she.

"Well yes, you do… Well sort of…" Liz replied, deliberately hedging. "At least you have met him once…" Promising on a happy laugh to reintroduce them the following day and hanging up the phone before Caeli could pry any further.

"Well, that's one question answered," Caeli retorted, smiling smugly to herself. Liz had definitely said "him" that she had met "him" once before, and said it in a manner that left no doubt in her mind that this "him" was far more than just a friend. Immediately jumping to the conclusion that romance was in the air and that her beloved daughter had fallen in love.

But in love with whom, was the question now burning upon her mind. For even though she'd been told she had met "him" before, she hadn't a clue as to who this "him" could be, becoming more intrigued with every passing moment, and anxious for lunchtime and her daughter to come.

With a bit of luck, Kevin might land on her doorstep too and complete her small family trio, her big handsome son with his usual roaring appetite and the inevitable bag of laundry in tow. Tired of smoke-filled country towns and sleeping it "rough" in a tent, having "gone bush" down Coonabarrabran way with two of his uni mates. Three eager beavers, hungering for hands-on experience with the local country vet.

"Heaven help the poor vet," she muttered with a grin.

Still, whatever eventuated would be no bother, thanks to her housekeeper Dot, Dot being the absolute treasure who kept her house gleaming and the weekend fridge chock-a-block. "Enough food to feed the army – should the army drop in," was Dot's standard weekly attempt at humour, followed by a list of supplies Caeli knew off by heart: Cold chicken, ham, coleslaw and salads, fruit, ice cream and chocolate – not forgetting the crate of chilled bubbly.

"Oh and I mustn't forget those prawns," she mumbled disgruntledly, remembering the parcel of "Kings" Sebastian had bought fresh off the trawlers on their way home from dinner last night. The memory rekindling the anger that still seethed within her.

And she added more forcefully: "No... I mustn't forget Sebastian's damn prawns!"

The sun was a blinding blaze above the horizon now, dispelling every last vestige of the dawn. The lawns, streaked with elongated fingers of shadows reaching through the trees, prompting Caeli to think of more positive things, like hosing the garden for instance.

It looked breathtakingly beautiful in the early morning light, thanks to Harry King, her gardener. Brilliant bougainvillea trailed the pergolas in profusion, exotic perfumed jasmine and honeysuckle wandered the line of the sloping picket fence. For Harry was an aborigine, born in the shadow of Uluru some seventy-something years before with an inborn affinity to the land and everything he touched seemed to burst into life? His entire working life spent on the vast cattle stations of the outback, until recently retired to the suburbs to be near his only offspring Mable, a slick Brisbane Solicitor and her adored tribe of "grandies."

"Come to the big smoke, missus," he had laughingly told her while his watery brown eyes blatantly yearned for vast open spaces. His body reed thin, his sun-baked skin the texture of bulls-hide burned to a crisp, a battered Akubra, stained with years of sweat and red outback dust, a permanent fixture upon his head. "My father," he told her and spitting on the ground, "a bloody white fella Englishman," from whom he'd inherited nothing but his once-fair hair and right royal name.

All around the morning chorus was rising; all manner of birdsong trilled the air, while around a hidden bend of the river, a small motorboat could be heard, chug-a-chugging like a heartbeat, its sound growing louder but not yet in view.

"How I love this time of the day," Caeli whispered, cocooned in her haven of peace and tranquillity, a treasured "time-out" from the humdrum reality of her work-a-day-world and the ever-increasing demands on her time, perceiving it the perfect time to reflect and gather her thoughts and plan her day. For she was by nature, a dyed-in-the-wool creature of habit, her life methodically organised and governed by the old platitude that everything had its time and place. And she firmly believed that each new day was a precious new gift, a chance to cast an imperfect yesterday aside and begin anew. So even today – albeit a Sunday and her one day of rest, it was not to be squandered. The simple inspirational verse she had learnt from her mother as a very young child, once again running rote through her head:

Today you come to me so new,
 And with you comes the chance to do,
 The things I'd not done yesterday,
 Oh please don't let me waste this day...

Mondays were hectic. Come hail, rain or high water, Mondays were always hectic, and the following Monday promised to be no less. A shipment of stock was due to arrive from the Sydney and Melbourne warehouses for her steadily expanding business, and that meant an extra early start. Pretty party garments, ordered for the oncoming Christmas Season when everyone demanded something special to wear, and guaranteed to walk out the door as soon as they hit the rack.

Come New Year – the Christmas break behind them, the fashion houses would again fling wide their doors with a whole new range to woo buyers from home and abroad. Establishing the cardinal rules that millions of women the world over would blindly follow. Rules that determined the colours and styles and lengths of skirts to be worn that season – maxi, midi, mini...? Or if slacks were in vogue (had they ever gone out?), or if bras were designed to minimise or enhance, or lift and divide? Hard-core buyers with a wealth of experience from some of the biggest establishments in the land would descend on the showings like vultures, eager to view the latest trends and visually devour everything in sight.

Caeli had no delusions of grandeur amid such illustrious company. Aware of her menial status, that even though she was now the owner of seven boutiques, she was still considered "small fry" and a very small cog in the ever-changing fashion wheel. Yet right from the start, from the time of her tentative inauguration into the glamorous world she had stumbled into as an eighteen-year-old fledgling and the proud owner of one small and very out-dated shop slap-bang in the heart of Brisbane mortgaged to the hilt, there had been no other option for her, smitten by the world of fashion for life. *One small shop slap-bang in the heart of Brisbane, mortgaged to the hilt...* "God," she murmured, shaking her head in disbelief, overwhelmed at the magnitude of the task she had taken on back then and how enormously it had changed her life. For with the opening of her latest acquisition, "Holiday Romps" on the fabulous tourist strip of the Queensland Gold Coast and managed by Liz, she had almost become a household name. Thanking her lucky stars to have Liz on board in the business with her, for Liz was a born natural and had taken to the Fashion World like a duck takes to water, having an instinct for fashion that could never be taught. Every garment she had ordered had virtually walked out the door! "My lucky sixth sense," Liz had explained blithely brushing her mother's praise aside.

Caeli was more than delighted with her daughter's performance and was planning to send her on the next buying trip alone. Grinning broadly at the prospect, trying to gauge what her reaction would be. Probably shock-horror, she imagined. For even though Liz was approaching twenty, and two years older than she herself had been on *her* first buying trip alone, she acknowledged the experience could be far more daunting for Liz. For Liz would be buying for *seven* boutiques, whereas she had been buying for one! Yet she trusted her daughter's judgement implicitly, having no doubt that Liz would more than cope, for she already had her favourite designers in mind.

Aware of Liz's undisguised admiration for two up and coming young fashion gurus that had recently burst on the fashion scene: Maggie Van Ander and Anthony Laporio, the pair having created a sensation of megalithic proportions and walked away with armfuls of awards right from the start.

Liz's personal preference leaning towards the latter, the young man's creations, who, in Liz's opinion, was nothing short of brilliant and convinced he'd become an iconic name in the fashion world (and if she had her way, in her world too).

He had brought out the label "Sir Zac." His forte being beautifully cut classical lines reminiscent of a bygone era, which was not only surprising in one so young, but even more so when one knew of his background. His roots Italian goat farmers, but now-third generation graziers on a vast cattle station out west, and he proudly admitted he was a dyed-in-the-wool country bumpkin who'd barely set foot in a city. And it could be said of Anthony Laporio (and often was) that this affable blonde, blue-eyed hunk of a man with skin the colour of roasted coffee beans, looked somewhat out of place in his trendy up-to-the-minute designer clothes and Italian shoes. That he'd look more at home in jeans and an Akubra wielding a branding iron and squinting into the sun. But Liz couldn't have cared less what

Anthony Laporio wore... She'd adore him in anything (or in nothing at all), she naughtily thought.

While in startling contrast, the oh-so-chic, dark-haired Sydneysider, Maggie Van Ander's creations were knocking 'em dead in the aisles! A second-generation Aussie of Dutch heritage, Maggie's creativity had born the label "Zaneline," which suited her creations exceedingly well. Announcing that her frilly, brilliantly coloured concoctions were for "the young at heart" which quickly became her catchphrase, emblazoned across shiny-black carrier bags in a rainbow of colours. Her target, she said, was the young of all ages; the blithe-spirits of the world that refused to take life too seriously with their zany, fun-loving approach.

"Absolutely perfect for the Gold Coast Mother," Liz had oozed, trying to curb her youthful enthusiasm and appear the more discerning and highly sophisticated professional.

As it turned out, Liz had again been absolutely right, taking delivery of her first "Zaneline" order and selling the lot in a matter of days and scrambling to re-order more! The beautiful kaftans and wraps and little bits of nonsense, which Caeli was reluctant to stock for the more conservative city clientele, suited the fun-seeking holidaymakers on the Gold Coast to a tee! Thus Caeli had no doubt that when given free rein it was to these two juvenile pundits that Liz would first beeline, putting them right at the top of her shopping list.

In spite of the earliness of the hour, the sun held the scorching intensity of high noon in its rays, drawing Caeli in under the sheltering overhang of trees. Eucalypts and Jacarandas and Poinciana's spread their shade, entwining their branches unwaveringly in the still morning air, as though stricken with palsy.

One small shop slap-bang in the heart of Brisbane... she mused again, *mortgaged to the hilt...* and wiping the inevitable sweat from her brow, allowing her mind to wander back to the time she had purchased the small, old-fashioned camphor-smelling shop from her oldest and dearest friend Joyce Tufnell. Joyce and her husband Bill, the elderly couple who had lived next-door to the modest timber cottage she had rented on arrival to this land, and the first and only neighbour to knock on her door with batch of scones and a welcoming hug. And what incredible neighbours they had turned out to be, for they'd hit it off right from the start. The childless couple had been horrified to learn of Caeli's plight, that she had lost her husband on the journey to Australia with a six-month-old baby to care for and another one on the way and had immediately taken her under their wings and fallen naturally into the much-desired role of doting grandparents.

As for the business, the timing was right. Sixty-five-year-old Bill about to retire, and Joyce as keen as mustard to unload the small business she had owned for years and retire with him. A sort of a role-reversal had transpired in which Caeli, who was desperately in need of an income to support herself and her children, was to take over the business for a nominal fee, while Joyce and Bill would care for her children during the day. The arrangement had worked out exceedingly well, as though it was meant to be.

How young and inexperienced I was back then, Caeli thought now, barely eighteen, with two precious babies depending on me. For it had been a huge gamble back then, risking the modest sum of Malachi's legacy on a business she knew nothing about. But, to her credit, she'd remembered his number one rule for succeeding in business. "Remember the three 'P's' Caeli," he had said – "Position – Position – Position!" The old fashioned shop was slap-bang in the middle of Queen Street!

The ins and outs of actually running a business, she learned the hard way – trial and error – the too many errors almost wiping her out. Joyce, her ever-reliable backstop, taught her every trick of the trade and dragged her up by her bootstraps when the going got tough. But even more importantly, Joyce had been her friend. For back then, friends had been few and far between to a questionable Irish teenage migrant with no husband in sight and two babies in tow. In fact, back then, more often than not, she'd been spurned!

But learn she did, inched along day by day, turning yesterday's failures into today's triumphs. For well she understood it wasn't a game she was playing, but the serious matter of survival, survival for herself and the children she adored. Determined not to fail… She could not fail… For every last cent she had was invested in it.

CHAPTER SEVEN
MEMORIES

Memories of Ireland and the nightmares of the night continued to plague Caeli's mind, causing her to wonder why today they should have such a hold on her. Why today, the tightly locked door to her past should be grinding ajar and beckoning her back. Even when out in her garden with the reality of life so abundantly warm and real and pulsating about her, the haunting memories continued to persist.

"Don't go there Caeli..." her inner voice cautioned, *"Let sleeping dogs lie..."* But the pull of the past was too strong and it was almost with relief that she succumbed to it and let the years fold away. Time slid on time like well-oiled doors slithering back the years, taking her back to another time, another place, to a life beyond knowing and loving and losing her Danny and Mother and Meegan. Back to the magical days of her innocent childhood when Molly and Granny Grainne had been the core of her world and so greatly influenced her life.

She had always been an early riser, regardless of season; springing from bed as the first gleam of dawn nudged the dark night sky. *Daughter of the Dawn...* Granny Grainne used to call her. *Daughter of the Dawn...* Granny Grainne... the adored old fortune teller who had lived in a hut deep in her father's woods where ancient evergreens spread eternal shade. "Daughter of the Dawn," she whispered now, recalling how special the words made the child in her feel. Even a blanket of snow spread pure and white upon the earth or the fall of early morning dew had not quelled her zest for life, eagerly treading board and stair while the rest of the house lay hushed and still. Only Molly to encounter in the welcoming kitchen, the delicious aroma of fresh baked bread abundant in the air, the fire in the hearth already ablaze with the big black kettle humming merrily on its hob.

Recalling too the many whispered conversations she and Molly used to share in the still-sleeping house, the early-morning kitchen their special meeting place. Sharing too, the simple delights of Molly's homemade bread – thick slabs toasted on prongs before the open fire and slathered with butter and jam and washed down with sweet milky tea.

"To warm the cockles of your heart, my lamb," Molly would purr in her soft Tipperary brogue.

How she'd loved Molly then, how she loved Molly still, regardless of time and reasons that had so cruelly kept them apart.

The dew lay heavy on the sweet moist earth when she'd fled barefoot through the kitchen door, eager to shed the shackles of the house and her father's undying hatred. Molly's anxious voice catching up to her ears as she'd opened the gate in the high stone wall: *Wait now... Put some shoes on, child... Ye'll catch your death of cold...* But Caeli never paused or heeded Molly's words, she was in a hurry, the stream of life was rushing by and would not wait for shoes! Beyond the gate lay her idea of heaven. Beyond the gate the path traced wild and ragged the ridge of the cliffs rising bold and grey and magnificent from the churning sea below. Beyond the gate, emerald fields rolled away inland and beckoned her down to romp wild and free, her young heart bursting with the sheer joy of life as only a child's heart can. There were stone walls to climb, leafy lanes to meander and a stream to follow gurgling deep into her father's woods to that special place... The enchanted place of her childhood dreaming... The soul of Granny Grainne's legends... The place of the ancient hawthorn tree...

"Don't go there Caeli... Don't look back..." her inner voice cautioned her again. *"Only fools look back..."* But she was heedless of her warming. For back there, in the swirling mists of time, she had glimpsed her heart and her soul. Back there, she had seen her beloved Danny O'Halloran, young and vibrant and passionately in love, and desiring her all over again.

And Granny Grainne was back there too. Granny Grainne, whom she had truly believed was her very own granny and loved with all her heart and had played such a significant role in her formative years. The blind old woman of traveller's blood with the milky-white eyes and an ancient crystal ball who claimed she saw everything. The hobbling fright of matted grey hair and tattered clothes, the maker of lotions and potions, spells and predictions, telling fortunes with such accuracy that they'd made your eyes bulge and your flesh crawl. Her image as sharp to Caeli's mind now as the damp mossy woods and the tang of the bracken and decaying woodland leaves, adoring the memory of her still, as she had adored in life in all her ragged glory. Sitting spellbound at the old woman's feet for hours on end, devouring the tales of the ancient folklore of Ireland and ever hungering for more. For it had been Granny Grainne who had filled her head with the legends of leprechauns and fairies and wicked hobgoblins that lived in the hawthorns and under the hedgerows, of the pots of gold at the end of rainbows and the magic harp of Tara's Halls, Caeli believing every last word to be gospel true.

Cross Granny's palm with a sixpence and your whole life she'd spread before you, like the handsome person you were going to marry and the number of children you were going to have and the fortune you would undoubtedly make. For a penny, she'd tell you the things you would rather forget, like your innermost secrets and sins that prickled your conscience and turned your face red; things between you and your Maker that no other living soul ought to know. She listened to the voices of Ireland, she said that rose from the sod and rustled the trees and whispered in the wind since the dawning of time.

But there were those of the village who feared Granny Grainne. Claimed she was a witch and possessed the unholy gift of pishogue and the power of "Pointing the Finger," that if her gnarled old finger sought you out, you were as good as gone. For hadn't she pointed at Brian Tierney and spat on the ground and cursed his name for having thrashed his young lad within an inch of his life, and hadn't he up and died the very next day?

"Beware him, child…" Granny had warned Caeli time and time again, her sightless white eyes peering deep into the crystal ball on the table between them. *"Beware the one you love most…"* The words always the same, never changing, *"Beware him, child… Beware the one you love most…"* Perplexing words that meant nothing to the child in her then; brushing them aside to later recall when life had turned cruel and Danny was dead, words that should have died with Danny. For Danny was the one she'd loved most,

loved with a passion bordering on madness like none other before him and none other since. The sensual black-haired Danny with the dancing black eyes who'd cast his own spell upon her.

Beware him child... Beware the one you love most... words as perplexing to her now as they had been back then.

Now, standing in her garden in the middle of an Australian heatwave, the hose spraying moisture upon the gasping greenery, the humidity popping perspiration from her every pore like spawning coral, she actually shivered, the past gusting over her like an icy polar wind. The vision of her beautiful dead mother arose before her then, riding her magnificent black stallion *Starfire* across the green fields of Liath Caislean, her glorious copper hair flying out behind her like streamers of fire trapped in sunlight, her beautiful face contorted with pain. Then her young sister Meegan appeared, as soft and gentle as a floating cloud, dressed in her blue velvet gown. Her skin alabaster-white, in stark contrast to her long black hair, her childish voice stuttering back from that memorable day of so long ago: *D-Dada's m-mean C-Caeli... D-Dada's m-mean...* Then Malachi Morgan appeared – her husband of but a few months duration and the father of her daughter Liz, brushing through her mind like a gentle apology, his love shining bright in his kind blue eyes. But then, to her utter dismay, her despised father pushed his way in, big and brazen and laughing manically, his eyes glinting with malice, his arms outstretched as though he would seize her, that she actually turned in her garden to shrug him away.

"The parade of the dead," she murmured with a shiver.

Then following them all, outshining them all, the most beloved of all, the vision of her beloved Daniel O'Halloran came, swaggering through her mind in the devil-may-care manner that was his and his alone.

How achingly boyish he appeared to her now with his lop-sided grin and beguiling ways. How the mere figment of him excited her still, her old hunger for him tearing through her once more, setting her pulses racing as they had in days of old and filling her with an unbearable longing.

For it had always been Danny. Danny from the very first moment they'd met. Danny then... Danny now... Danny forever... Memories, more physical than memories, shimmered through her and welled up inside her like blood-red wine filling a golden chalice, brimming and spilling about her in an overwhelming flood of desire.

Now, my beautiful colleen… Now I shall take you and make you my own… The erotic whispers of that bygone liaison swept through her once more, transporting her back to the moment in time and the place of their rising, encapsulating her and Danny as one on the soft green ring of the cool mossy grass that encircled the hawthorn tree deep in her father's woods. The sensations of that long ago liaison so overwhelmingly real that they surged through her once more like a powerful aphrodisiac made by the hands of the very Devil himself! Her response as urgent and wanton as it had been then: *Oh yes, my beloved Danny… Yes… Yes…! Take me… I'm yours…!*

Trembling now, her clothes clinging sodden to her skin, her legs buckled beneath her, forcing her down to a garden bench. Uncertain if her cries were ringing in the steamy Brisbane air about her or only in her head.

"What did I tell you, girl," her innermost-self berated, *"Didn't I warn you of the dangers of looking back…? Just couldn't let sleeping dogs lie, could you…? Now see what you've done…"*
She had trodden on graves – that's what she'd done. Walked upon hallowed ground and disturbed the ghosts' immortal slumber. Ghosts become so real, she could feel them hovering about her and brushing against her skin.

Yet, on looking around, all appeared to be normal. No bogey monsters lurked in the bushes or booed in her ear. The arc of sky still spread incredibly wide and impossibly blue overhead, the sun still blasted its blistering rays upon the earth, and the river, a scintillating ribbon of diamonds by then, still flowed on shushingly by, licking and lapping the banks in its passing. Birds still twittered and cooed and rustled the trees, a boat engine still spluttered and coughed around some sleepy bend in the river like a phlegmy old man, and Mother Nature still pranced so tirelessly on, flouncing her rainbow-coloured petticoats of the glorious summer's day, that it came as a shock for Caeli to realise that the phantoms of the past lived only in her.

CHAPTER EIGHT

SEBASTIAN

Sebastian Templeton was pushing forty, yet a bachelor still, despite having the drooling good looks of a Hollywood Movie Star that set many a female heart aflutter and wedding bells ringing in their ears. The kind of looks most other men would have gladly sold their souls to the Devil to own. And Sebastian Templeton knew it.

The relentless Queensland sun and capricious sea-winds having had their way with him and tempered his flesh to a deep walnut-brown and his blonde curly hair to a pale ashen gold. His long-lashed eyes, eyes to die for, harboured the shades of the sea from warm-water blue to cool aquamarine, as changeable as the ebb and flow of his moods. His body, a rippling washboard of bulging muscles and biceps, not, as one might expect from long hours of toil or workouts at the gym, but from years of hoisting sail and heaving to, for sailing was Sebastian Templeton's supreme love.

His lifestyle was an enviable one of the self-indulgent rich born to old family money. His bachelor pad a luxury penthouse on the northern bank of the Brisbane River, a fifty-foot yacht named *Manta Ray*, moored at its exclusive marina. The sleek, black-hulled, white-sailed vessel, as lavishly appointed as his apartment was, rigged from bilge-pumps to mizzen with every luxury his money could buy. Plus he had a sea-going cat named Sinbad and a live-aboard budding young artist-cum-crewmate of dubious talent, with the equally dubious name of Renoir, or Renni, Dubray, whom Sebastian had chanced upon meeting and was instantly attracted to in his whim of the moment, an art gallery.

With no serious commitment, Sebastian had become the proprietor of a thriving little gallery in the trendy inner-Brisbane suburb of Paddington, affectionately called "Paddo's," the gallery as affectionately called "Dabbler's Days." The ownership of which appealed to his stylishly "arty" instincts of the moment, patronising the work of several extremely talented artists – talent of which Sebastian had none, which in turn attracted a perpetual stream of wealthy clientele – wealth of which Sebastian had plenty. Yet despite his affluence and drooling good looks, Sebastian Templeton was far from content, tormented by the fact that the big four-o was looming and that time was rapidly passing, and the ever increasing feeling that something was missing in his life.

As fate would have it, Sebastian was also to meet Caeli Morgan by chance, an elegant Sydney fashion salon the fated venue. Caeli there on a buying trip with her daughter Liz, ordering stock for her Brisbane and Gold Coast boutiques, Sebastian's attendance of a more frivolous nature, namely the pursuit of one of the models.

He had slipped in un-noticed to the reserved aisle seat beside hers, her attention absorbed by Liz on her other side, discussing the glorious outfits the models were parading on the cat-walk and making vital decisions as to which suited the steamy Queensland climate and its laid-back way of life best. Sebastian, on the other hand, lolled indolently in the gold-brocade chair, thoroughly bored with the whole affair and becoming more and more interested in the dark-haired woman beside him, who incredibly, and annoyingly, continued to ignore him as though he wasn't there. She hadn't so much as glanced at him, for heaven's sake – that was the rub – to his way of thinking, the slight to his ego that increased his need to make his presence known.

"You come here often?" he had casually asked, glancing at the dark glossy hair half covering her face.

"Um…? O' yes, I do," she had absently replied, acknowledging his question with a slight turn of head and a flash of intense violet eyes. And well she might have responded further if it hadn't been for Liz's excited intervention tugging at her arm and demanding her immediate attention. For that one brief glance had given her quite a jolt, unprepared for the presence of such a stunningly good-looking middle-aged man seated beside her.

"Ooh, isn't that positively fab, mother!" Liz had gushed, genuinely impressed and jabbing her pen in the general direction of the garment in question. "So chic – and the colours are divine! No, not that one… The silky one with the longer line… We'll order it in every colour – if you agree, that is," yet making note of the order

64

regardless, whether her mother agreed or not. "And those pants-suits positively slay me – perfect for evening wear. No, not those mother... Yuk! Boooring! The bright-coloured crepes with the padded shoulders and cute short jackets... Fab! Fab! Fab! Perfect for the Gold Coast and all that glitteratzi up there..."

Caeli's head was spinning at her daughter's enthusiasm and snap-confident decisions, instinctively selecting or rejecting garments like a seasoned pro, condescending enough to ask her mother's opinion, yet clearly taking the initiative and galloping on to the next.

Proudly Caeli watched her daughter, more than satisfied with what she saw and happy to allow her free rein. Impressed with her new maturity, with her phenomenal transformation from pony-tailed, tee-shirted student of fashion-design the previous year, to the beautiful confident and very fashionable young woman she had become today. For though this was Liz's first buying trip, she was proving a born natural and had taken to the fashion world as if she'd been patterned on a designer's table for it, her instinct of cut and colour beyond reproach.

Keenly they followed the Junoesque models; their long legs strutting, their generous lips pouting, their heavily painted eyes smouldering, the incredibly clear diction of the female compere holding the audience captive and focussing their attention precisely where she wanted their attention to be.

But Caeli's attention was becoming increasingly unfocused, and the man seated beside her the one to blame. Positive he was watching her now, and even worse, eavesdropping on her private conversation with Liz. And now, heaven forbid, he'd begun to fidget. Ants-in-pants sort of fidget, crossing and uncrossing his legs, and even more annoyingly, thrumming his fingers on the padded arm of the chair as though he was deliberately trying to irk her. Well he had succeeded! And she turned to him, ready to protest and give him a piece of her mind. Only to be met with a boyish, I-want-some-attention-too sort of look in his gorgeous greenish-blue eyes, and the reprimand died on her tongue.

Still, he had sensed her annoyance. Missed not the fiery glint of anger in her deep-violet eyes and even had the grace to appear embarrassed.

"Sorry," he'd said, grinning sheepishly and sounding as though he really meant it, revealing as he did a set of perfect white teeth. "Dreadful habit of mine," and by way of a lazy flick of his hand indicating the papers in hers, commented, "Looks like you put in a pretty big order there."

He had her full attention now. His body sprawled lazily in the chair before her, his right leg casually resting on his left knee, revealing the thick crepe sole of an expensive tan casual. Her trained eye noted his suit, it was expensive too. Designer Label, Italian, she thought, fine cream linen, the best of the best, the jacket casually unbuttoned over a pale-green-silk open-necked shirt. Even his voice was the culmination of culture, "The Gentleman's Club" tone of voice, deeply resonant and twanged at her nerve endings.

"Yum…!" She thought, suddenly wanting to know who this drop dead gorgeous man with the bored-to-death countenance was and so seemingly intent on knowing her business.

"You're not ordering then?" she had asked in an off-handed manner matching his own.

"Lord no!" was his incredulous reply. "Just filling in time… Waiting for someone actually…"

Again Liz interrupted, nudging her mother as the first of the eveningwear appeared: Gorgeous concoctions of whispering chiffon and rustling taffeta and shimmering satin, and the timeless reintroduction of the "Little Black Dress." Every eye in the elegant salon, glued to the catwalk as the compere announced the "Piece de Resistance" – the culmination of the parade. A gasp of sheer awe rippled through the crowd as an incredibly child-like beauty emerged in a breathtaking bridal-gown of organdie silk, her long blonde tresses trailing beneath a long filmy veil and she literally floated along the catwalk on the arms of two stunning male models in black tie and tails, her white- slippered feet seeming to never touch the ground, bringing the audience rising to theirs amid a thunderous applause and shouts of "Bravo!"

It was not until the music was silenced and lights of the catwalk dimmed and the salon almost deserted, that Caeli again became aware of the thrumming fingers and fidgety feet in renewed agitation. The prying man was still there and she couldn't help wondering why. But of course, he had said he was waiting for someone… Obviously one of the models… The gorgeous child bride, her bet, thinking he looked the type. Still, she had always prided herself on good manners and was feeling somewhat ashamed of the way she had brusquely cut him off. Turning to him then and flashing him her most brilliant smile, in the hope of making amends.

"Phew! Am I glad that's all over," she said, heaving an exaggerated sigh of relief, "for it can be a most arduous task you know – this buying business I mean. Demands a lot of concentration, for mistakes can prove costly."

He looked into the startling violet eyes of this woman, at the shaft of gleaming black hair so sensuously brushing her shoulders, at the generous curve of her mouth smiling almost too wide and vividly painted in letter-box red. She was older than the chicky-babes he was normally attracted to. Ancient by comparison, nearer his own age he guessed. But God, she was beautiful. Something about her got under his skin and attracted him intensely. Even her voice was a sheer fascination to him. Irish he thought, as lilting as a song with a do-as-I-bid-you-do ring to it. Surreptitiously he'd watched and listened to her the entire afternoon, becoming more and more entranced with every passing moment and unable to tear his eyes away. Barely noticing the sylph-like models drifting the catwalk or the beautiful garments they wore, determined to capture *this* woman's attention who had dared to treat him as though he was but a shadow and really not there at all. But it was he who'd become the captive, he who'd become the enslaved.

New emotions stirred within him. Forgotten ideals locked in the depths of his ancient genes that challenged him now to break free; ideals so foreign to his live-for-the-moment philosophy, to his toss-away relationships and cold ritualistic lover, that he was eager to taste of the different emotions and see where they'd take him.

Yet he wasn't looking for permanence – for ties that bind – for the happy-ever-after bit. Lord no! Just an amicable fling with a different flavour was all he was seeking, for he didn't believe in love or marriage. Marriage to him meant a chain around the neck and shackles on the feet, and love but an illusion, fairy-tale stuff. Yet automatically he turned on the charm in response to her words. His smile was a languid tug of the mouth that twigged latent memories within her of another man's smile way back in her past. A smile that possessed in itself enough charm to grant him a thousand pardons, a smile that assured him of getting his own way.

"Yes, I imagine it could be," he'd replied equably enough, "though I have to admit I'm an absolute dunderhead when it comes to the "Rag Trade." Are you buying for a department store or something?"

"Heavens no...!" she said, tossing her head back and laughing delightedly, "Much more modest than that I'm afraid! Definitely the 'Or Something,' my humble establishments north of the border in Queensland. "Caeli's Fashions" I'm known as. And hi, I'm Caeli Morgan," and politely proffered her hand.

He pulled himself up in his chair, unable to believe his luck – she was not only stunning, but actually nice! "Sebastian Templeton at your service," he said, eagerly grasping her hand. "I'm so very pleased to meet you, Caeli Morgan.

"But what a coincidence that you are from Queensland, Caeli, for I'm from the north of the border too!" Then chuckling deeply, seeing something humorous in what he'd just said, added (in a poor impersonation of John Wayne), "Don't we sound like a couple of ol' cowpokes, Caeli – crossing borders I mean. Did you happen to come on your horse?" making Caeli chuckle too.

"But on a more serious note... Your business here... Is it all finished? Can we get out of here and get a drink or something?"

The question was unexpected and pulled her up short and she fumbled her reply. "Well I... No... I'm sorry... I really can't leave yet – um Sebastian. There are details to finalise..."

"What utter nonsense, mother!" Liz, who'd been listening from the sidelines had then butted in, of the opinion that her extremely attractive and young-looking mother devoted far too much time to "business" and not enough to her currently non-existent love-life, and that it was time she got out of the rut and found herself a really hot man, and of the opinion this Sebastian guy sure filled the bill! In five seconds flat she sized up the situation, sensing a chemistry buzzing between them and deciding, in her busybody manner, to help things along. Without further ado, she ducked her head in front of her mother and saucily introduced herself. "Hi! I'm Liz Morgan – Caeli's daughter," she offered brightly, unconsciously mimicking her mother and also proffering her hand.

Immediately Sebastian rose to his feet, sensing in her an ally and revealing his taller than average height and gorgeous physique, and bowing gallantly, he took Liz's hand.

"Sebastian Templeton at your service," he said, his smile not diminishing for one single second. "How do you do, Liz Morgan – Caeli's daughter, I'm so pleased to make your acquaintance."

Liz chuckled at the whimsy and without further ado, decided to take charge.

"I know Mum is dying for a red, Sebastian; she said so not five minutes ago." Then turning towards her mother so Sebastian could not see, she comically raised her eyebrows and rolled her eyes, suggesting all sorts of ridiculous innuendoes.

"I can finish up here Mum," she said meaningfully, "I know what to do. And the experience will be good for me. So off you two go now and have a good time."

Caeli found it hard not to laugh at her daughter's busybody interference and her obvious attempt at matchmaking and even more comical facial contortions, thinking at times that her Liz was quite mad. But her timid response, "If you're sure you can manage..." was all Sebastian needed to grip her arm and whisk her away.

CHAPTER NINE
PARTING

That was how Sebastian and Caeli had met. Sebastian had literally swept Caeli off her feet. But three months down the track, his gold-plated charm was beginning to wear thin. His spoilt egotistical ways were coming to the fore and getting on her nerves, and she was planning to break the relationship off. Did she say relationship – as inferring there was some romantic connection between them? That was a laugh, for he hadn't so much as made a pass at her, for heaven's sake, and it was far from the romantic liaison she had hoped it would be. But even worse, he'd become a control freak, attempting to control every facet of her life. They had entered the realms of a war zone – Sebastian versus her at every turn. He even resented the time that she spent with Liz and Kevin, but more so the time she spent on her business and was urging her to sell.

He'd really overstepped the mark, for selling the business was something she had no intention to do. For not only was it how she made her living but it was also her life-blood, built of the sweat of her brow and an ocean of tears and a good twenty years of her life. A personal triumph arisen from her shattered young life and of which she was justifiably proud. It had even earned her a coveted place in the fashion world and in the business world too. Colleagues and friends alike, held her in highest esteem – even though most were unaware from whence she had come and how hard her coming had been. It was *her* achievement and hers alone. Asking nothing from no one, but especially nothing from *him* back there…

Yet as with all achievements, there had been a price to pay and the price had not come cheap. Recalling how back in those early days she had been near breaking point, both financially and emotionally. The incredibly long working hours taking their toll, stealing precious time she could have otherwise spent with her children, or perhaps even nurtured a personal relationship of her own? And her children had paid the price too: Rarely seeing their mother and deprived of material things that their friends took for granted. Never ceasing to amaze her how well they had turned out – two delightful well-adjusted young adults by anyone's measure.

"Sell, be damned, Sebastian Templeton!" she had muttered indignantly, for to her mind the business was as much her children's as it was hers; a constantly expanding empire for them to inherit one day, and she'd planned to break the relationship off over dinner the previous night at their favourite French restaurant high on a hill overlooking the waters of Moreton Bay. Yet she had put it off, not relishing the task, mellowed by the wine and the music and superb French cuisine, opting to tell him instead in the privacy of her home later that night. And thank God she had, for it had not gone down well. Sebastian had taken it worse than she had expected, visibly stunned by her words, the colour draining from his face and his jaw dropping open, and for many long moments unable to speak.

"B-but why, Caeli?" he'd eventually spluttered. "Surely you're joking… I thought our relationship went deeper than that – that we were about to get married?"

It was Caeli's turn to be shocked. "Married!" she'd exploded. "We've never spoken of marriage Sebastian; we've never been anything but friends! Why, you've never so much as grabbed me and groped at my body or kissed me passionately, let alone ripped my clothes off and dragged me to your bed!"

He screwed up his nose to express his distaste. "Don't be crude, Caeli, it doesn't become you. You're just being silly." He sounded annoyed, as though he was dealing with a difficult child. "Of course we're getting married… I absolutely took it for granted we were."

"Then you'll just have to absolutely un-took it," Caeli blurted back, "for I haven't the slightest intention of marrying you."

He took a deep breath and regained control and slipped an arm about her shoulders and in his most charming manner said.

"But darling, I've really grown to love you and thought you loved me…"

She too had calmed down.

"What twaddle you go on with, Sebastian dear… You know I care for you deeply, but that isn't love – at least not the marrying kind of love. I need someone who'll simply adore me and scatter rose petals at my feet and be adored in return, someone who'll be there for me through good times and bad for the rest of our days. And we'd be selling ourselves short if we settled for less."

"But – I thought you *were* that one…"

"Oh Sebastian," she replied, shaking her head and shrugging her shoulders in a helpless gesture, "stop fooling yourself. The relationship just hasn't developed that way – though I freely admit that when we first met I was hoping it would. For you are an extremely good-looking man Sebastian, and I was tremendously flattered by your attention, only too aware that there were any number of women who would gladly have stepped into my shoes. But there's no chemistry – no passion between us – or passion in you – or at least if there is, it isn't for me. You've more passion for your cat or your young artist friend than you've ever had for me…"

"What's that supposed to mean?" he snapped, looking startled. "That's how I am. I've always played it cool, but if we were married, I assure you that things would be different."

Again she shrugged and shook her head in a hopeless manner.

"They wouldn't, Sebastian, and we'd soon get on each other's nerves. We just haven't got that special something two people in love are supposed to have. Just accept we're not right for each other and move on…"

"But I need you," he persisted, his rich cultured voice reduced to an ingratiating whine. "I've never known a woman that I actually wanted to marry before. Don't do this to me, Caeli – now that I've thought it all through and made up my mind. Besides, what's wrong with a marriage based on good old friendship?"

She couldn't believe what she was hearing. "You've got to be kidding!" she said, almost screaming the words.

"You don't marry for good old friendship, Sebastian! I've more friends than I can poke a stick at and I don't want to marry any of them!"

He stared at her dumbfounded, demoralised by her rejection, and for one horrible moment she thought he was about to cry. Then something within him seemed to snap and fill him with rage, a black unreasoning rage.

How dare the bitch, he thought. No one had ever rejected him before – no one – ever! And certainly not a sheila – and a bloody Irish sheila at that! If anyone was ending anything, it would be him! For wasn't he the master controlling the game?

He sidled along the couch as far from her as he could sidle, a thunderous silence driving them even further apart. And Caeli watched in horror at the change that came over him, at the anger that filled him, anger that literally flared his nostrils and sparked little green specks in his eyes. And when he spoke, his voice was coldly accusing and made her shudder.

"You have led me on Madam... LED ME ON," he shouted dramatically, leaping from the couch and towering over her. "Made a fool of me when I'd made up my mind, when I'd decided to marry you and share my wealth with you and even my body... But now I shall only think of you with contempt – if I think of you again!"

"Sebastian... You're overreacting... This isn't the way..."

"Enough!" he had shouted, his anger overpowering his reason and stomping from the house like a spoilt brat. The slamming of the car door and its tyres screeching out onto the road, telling her he was gone.

She could only shake her head in confusion. At a loss to understand what had actually happened and where the charming Sebastian had gone and horrified at the person who'd emerged in his place. Yet somehow she wasn't surprised. Often suspecting Sebastian Templeton had problems complex and deep.

She had come to the bottom of her garden where river gums swept the water and bird life was abundant. Ducks dabbled in its shallows; shags dived beneath its surface making barely a ripple and bobbing up like corks several metres away. While through the brilliant arc of the cobalt-blue sky, ungainly pelicans soared, skimming the reaches and landing on its surface with unexpected grace.

"OK! OK! I'll get you some bread," she responded delightedly as the family of ducks waddled onto the shore and eyed her expectantly, as if to say: "Well we're here, where is it?" when deep in the house the phone began to ring.

"That'll be Liz" she murmured, galloping up the garden path and turning off the hose. "No – too early for Liz," she contradicted, for Sunday mornings Liz liked to sleep late. "More likely to be Kev..." she concluded. The ringing persistent, sounding urgent, and she bounded up the steps two at a time.

"Hello... Caeli speaking," she said, sounding quite breathless when she picked the receiver up, aware of the intake of breath on the end of the line, before the caller spoke.

She was both right and wrong, for it wasn't Liz, but neither was it Kevin or anyone else she knew. It was a stranger's voice that came back at her, rich and male and Irish to the core.

"Good morning," it said with professional reserve. "Would that be Mrs. Morgan? Mrs. Caeli Morgan, nee Caeli Dromgoole of the Liath Caislean Estate on the west coast of Ireland?"

Lord, how her flesh crawled as the words reached her ears, at the strong Irish accent and coincidence of the call. For the voice sounded strangely familiar and set alarm bells ringing in her head, feeling yet another ghost from her unhappy past had come to seek her out. Her guard was immediately up and her answer wary.

"Yes... That is my name... Caeli Morgan... And yes, I *was* Caeli Dromgoole..."

The response was not the response she was expecting to hear, but a response fair bursting with joy that took her by surprise.

"Good God!" it said, "Is that really you Caz... Dare I believe that I've found my darling girl at last? Been searching for you forever..." The highly accentuated brogue oozing genuine delight as the old childish nickname rolled off his tongue.

Overwhelmed at the outburst, she could not reply.

"Are you still there, Caz...? 'Tis me, your old pal, Liam Shaw speaking... Don't tell me you've forgotten me now – forgotten the boy who's seen you as naked as the day you were born?"

Inwardly she grinned at the memory, outwardly perhaps even blushed, for he had been naked too. Of course she remembered. How could she forget her dearest childhood friend or that hot summer's day when she'd been barely six and they had skinny-dipped together in the stream in the woods? His mother, the soft-spoken Jessie, his father, the prominent Dublin lawyer Eugene Shaw – her father's best friend and the most frequent visitor to Liath Caislean. Liam the younger son of two, the shy one with the gorgeous auburn hair and soft brown eyes who'd had a giant-sized crush on her all those years before. And if she were to be honest, she'd had a sizeable crush on him too – at least until Danny O'Halloran had come on the scene. Sifting through old memories, she attempted to equate the stammering unrefined youth of the past to the confident middle-aged man he'd so obviously become today, but failed to do so.

"Are you still there...?" the voice again asked, sounding anxious.

74

"Surely you've not forgotten me girl? 'Tis Liam," he repeated unnecessarily, "your old pal and Eugene Shaw's son, calling you all the way from dear old Dublin town!"

"Why, Liam," she said, desperately trying to gather her senses and finding her voice at last, yet unnerved to the very core at the coincidence of the call and familiarity of his tone.

"Of course I haven't forgotten. How could I forget," she added too brightly, "or that day at the stream when we were just kids, or all the other wonderful times we spent together? I'm just overwhelmed at hearing your voice after all these years." Yet thinking it decidedly bizarre that this very dear friend from her long ago past should have rung her *this* day, *this* day of all days when her night had been filled with the demons of that past and still shivered through her. For apart from the predictable "Nativity Scene" Christmas card she had received every year as regularly as clockwork from Zita O'Halloran, with its equally predictable message scribbled inside, this was the first time she had heard from another living soul in Ireland since the day she had left it twenty-two years before. Even thinking the coincidence went beyond bizarre, that some supernatural force was gathering and coming into play.

Yet "time" was to prove her intuitions spot-on, for the seemingly innocent phone call of but a few minutes' duration was to change her life and her faith in mankind forever. For Liam had informed her "with deep regret" that her father, Bran Dromgoole, "THE Dromgoole" of the notorious Liath Caislean Estate on the west coast of Ireland and the man who had openly despised her every minute of every day since the moment she was born, had just hours before died of a massive heart attack in his bed and that her presence was "respectfully requested" in Dublin for the reading of his will.

CHAPTER TEN

DECISIONS

"I'M NOT GOING, LIZ!" Caeli firmly stated several decibels louder than was warranted, frustrated at her daughter's constant urgings to be on the first available flight to Dublin. "AND THAT'S ALL THERE IS TO IT!" Adding in a softer tone – seeing the disappointment cross her young daughter's face, "I know you mean well, love, and I really don't expect you to understand, but I'M – NOT – GOING – FULL STOP! That phase of my life ended a long time ago."

"But Mum…"

"No buts about it, Liz," she added, slicing her hand through the air, indicating end of discussion, "for I see no point in raking over the past. It's all too painful, and as far as I'm concerned, it's dead and gone!"

"But Mum," Liz persisted, "that's precisely my point! It isn't dead, nor is it gone, but very much a part of your life and intruding more and more upon it every day!"

"Nonsense girl… Utter rubbish!" she retorted, reluctant to admit that deep in her heart she knew Liz was right. Admit that the same terrifying dream *had* filled her nights and encroached more and more upon her days, affecting her work, her play, her relationships… The dream that began way back in Ireland before Liz was born, when the love of her life, Danny O'Halloran had been lost at sea.

How her life had crumbled then. The dream finding her floundering in the depths of an endless ocean searching for Danny, to eventually see him in the watery distance entangled in swaying tendrils of weeds and holding her young sister Meegan tightly to him, both deathly white and as naked as the day they were born.

Desperately, she would call Danny's name but no sound would come. Wildly she would flay her limbs and attempt to swim to him, only to find the same swaying tendrils wrapped about her and holding her back.

Then strangely her mother would appear, as beautiful as she ever, a translucent white gown floating eerily about her, her gorgeous copper hair wavering in the current, her emerald green eyes luminous and sad.

"Danny's not here, Caeli," she would call in a voice sounding distant and surreal. "Go back, child... Go back... Danny's not here..."

Looking again, she would find Danny and Meegan gone and her father filling their place, huge and Neptunian garbed in a mantle of seaweed and laughing manically as he struck a golden trident upon the ocean's floor and created a whirlpool into which she was spun. Awaking then, drenched in sweat and screaming Danny's name. The dream was always the same, the outcome never changing.

"Please try to understand, love," Caeli said, attempting to sound reasonable, yet feeling far from it. "There is nothing for me back there. Everything I want is here in Australia with you and Kevin. This is my home now and you kids are my world, and I simply don't *want* to return to Ireland, even for a day! I see no sense in raking over the past, for what is done is done and best left alone."

Spacious rooms with dove grey walls seemed to echo her words in the silence that followed. Mother and daughter seated across from each other on white-leather lounges sipping iced champagne – for it had truly turned out to be a champagne sort of day. Tony Laporio, the brilliant young fashion designer whom Caeli had indeed met once before, the "surprise guest," the "someone special" Liz had mentioned on the phone and brought home for lunch. The handsome young man was obviously more special than Liz had let on, for he'd asked Liz to marry him and she had accepted and already wearing his ring. This brand-new future son-in-law discreetly removed to the garden, tactfully leaving "two strong-minded women," to thrash out some family matter of seemingly great importance to them and of which he was wise enough not to buy into. Those "strong-minded women" were eying each other across the space between them now, pondering their next move. The tinkling of ice in the champagne flutes and the whirring of ceiling fans overhead, the only sounds audible in the room.

Liz was the first to break the silence, trying a different tack. Firmly believing her mother should return to Ireland, if only to attempt to lay the ghosts of her past to rest.

"Mum," she began tentatively, "I really think you ought to reconsider, after all, he was your father. And when you come to think about it, he really must have cared for you more than you believe he did, or he wouldn't have made you a beneficiary of his will, would he?" She paused, trying to gauge her mother's reaction to her well-intended words, not wanting to push her too hard. But when only a tight-lipped silence came back, she continued along another vein.

"And remember, he was our grandfather... Not that we ever knew him or anything like that... And I'm absolutely positive that Kev would be of the same opinion as me, and tell you you should return to Ireland too – if Kev were here that is."

"But you're missing the point, my love," her mother at last responded, unable to hide the bitterness in her voice. "I don't *want* to be his damned beneficiary! I don't *want* a single solitary thing from him – now! He's dead, Liz, and it's far too late for sugary feelings and making amends – if that's what he's trying to do!

"Too late!" she repeated ruefully. "Too many years of silence have passed – and you know what they say about silence – that it breeds resentment and contempt! And by golly, I sure resent him and find him contemptible for what he has done, and I'll never be able to forgive or forget that he threw me out...

"God, Liz, I was just a kid, barely sixteen with practically nothing to my name and ignorant of the world beyond Liath Caislean. So believe you me, my darling girl, when I say I want nothing from him now! Even when a very young widow and you kids were just babes in my arms and I desperately needed a dollar or two, I never went begging to him!"

Liz could see she was getting nowhere fast; her mother's head tossed haughtily back, her chin defiantly jutting out.

"No, Liz," Caeli continued, "I've survived without help from him all these years, so I'll be damned if I'll accept anything from him now – not that I expect there'll be much to accept, and in my opinion, whatever there is should go to Josie. She's the one he loved – the bright shining star in his eyes, who has stayed by his side all these years."

"Be that as it may, Mum," Liz persisted, surprised at her mother's dogged resistance and thinking it likely she was wasting her breath. "Regardless of what you consider to be right or wrong, surely you must see that you still have to go, for it's not the inheritance that's the issue here. Whether you accept or reject whatever your father might or might not have left you is of no concern to me, that's your decision entirely. What *is* my concern is the past you're not facing up to. The past that's consuming you and encroaching more and more upon your life every day, preventing you living a normal existence! You've even come to regard all those horrible nightmares you're having as *normal?* For heaven's sake, Mum, return to Ireland and to Liath Caislean and at least talk to Molly, for its obvious your regard for Molly hasn't lessened with the years. Perhaps if you talk things over with her you might get some answers and some sort of closure and put your demons to rest?"

She could see her mother's agitation mounting and quickly added.

"Now don't get me wrong, Mum, I'm not suggesting for one single moment that it's going to be easy, or that you'll not get hurt a whole lot more than you already are, or that those horrible bogymen of your dreams will magically up and disappear. All I'm suggesting is that you return to Ireland and give yourself a fighting chance, that you go and confront those demons of yours head on, and force them back into the past where they jolly well ought to be!"

Caeli was stunned by her young daughter's words, words that made infinite sense and wise beyond any nineteen-year-old's words should allow. And they twigged at her conscience and made it impossible to deny their ring of truth. For it was true she was as powerless now as she ever had been to dispel the dreams, regardless of the mountains of pills and professional counselling she had received. And also true that the dreams were recurring with ever-increasing regularity, practically every night now, and more often than not, remaining like an itchy second skin about her, to taunt her throughout her working day.

She knew she was being pigheaded, refusing to see how returning to Ireland could possibly help to oust the dreams. Surely the opposite was true? Surely by returning to the place of their rising would bring them more vividly alive? Indeed, how could she ever hope to dismiss them completely, when they portrayed the people she loved? That it made little difference whether she returned to Ireland or not, for it would never bring those loved ones back. Long ago she had accepted their passing. What she could not accept – now or ever, was the futility of it all and the manner in which they had died.

"No, Liz, I just can't do it!" she again burst forth, shaking her head vigorously, emphasising the depth of her feelings. "I feel too bitter when I think of the lives ruined and the lives lost because of *him*. So much grief and suffering... And for why, I ask, for why? It all seems so pointless to me and I'll never understand it if I live to be a hundred!"

A morbid silence descended between them. Liz, acutely aware of her mother's pain; old pain, deeply embedded pain, hard to shift pain, and she desperately sought the right turn of phrase to soothe and ease it from her.

Rising, she went to her mother's side and knelt at her feet and clasping her hands, looked earnestly into her mother's eyes.

"I don't mean to lecture you, Mum," she said, "but you've always told us kids to face up to our problems square on. 'Bring them out into the open' you used to tell us, to take a step back and look back in, so that we might see them more clearly and cope with them better because of it. Now I'm saying the same to you. For as I see it, by returning to Ireland after such a long absence, you'd be doing just that – looking back in and giving yourself a golden opportunity to bring those dreams out into the open and see them for what they are – nothing but jumbled memories of events that happened a very long time ago. Don't let them destroy your life, Mum – destroy you. Go back to Ireland and tackle them head on – as you've always told Kev and me to do, and get them out of your hair once and for all."

Caeli was speechless, wondering from which well of wisdom her daughter's words had sprung, words that made her feel immeasurably humble, undeserving, yet incredibly blessed. Words that even though they stung at her motherly pride, she had to concede were true. She *had* taught her children to face life square on, to be their own keeper, that life didn't always play fair and followed its own fickle set of rules and that one had no choice but to play the hand they'd been dealt and carry on regardless of one's station in life. How hypocritical she must appear in her daughter's eyes now, preaching ideals from a soapbox she didn't practice herself. For it was easy to preach. Any half-witted dingbat could preach, open their mouths and let their idealistic mumbo-jumbo tumble out. It was putting it into practice that was so darned hard.

She did not reply... could not reply... thoughts of her late husband Malachi Morgan, predominant in her mind. Recalling *his* wisdom and unfailing kindness – traits he'd so generously passed on to his daughter, the likeness between them clearly evident to her now.

Rising, she kissed her daughter's troubled forehead and stepped out onto her high rear veranda where glorious jacaranda bows reached in and lent their shade, strewing the last of their incredible violet-blue blossoms over the deck and across the lawn right down to the water's edge.

The panorama of the river and the jagged skyline of the buildings beyond danced crazily in the heat; the young man, Tony Laporio, the future son-in-law she had known for little more than an hour, lingered discreetly on the small wooden jetty, hands thrust deeply in stylishly baggy trouser pockets, head as deeply bent in thought.

Probably wondering what sort of a mob he's getting himself into, she mused, liking what she saw, liking his open honest face and clear hazel eyes and impeccable manners. Aware he had walked in on some family crisis – namely the subject of the telephone call from Ireland earlier that morning, informing her of her father's passing, and discreetly bowed out. This stranger of the morning she'd now taken to her heart.

Her thoughts were distracted by her neighbour's cat, a disdainful ginger tom unimaginatively named "Ginger." The animal purring about her legs with sheer pleasure as she bent and stroked him, then leapt onto one of her veranda chairs with inimitable feline grace, to laze his day away. While further down river in the park on the opposite bank, kookaburras laughed raucously, cutting through the strains of Slim Dusty's rendition of *"The pub with no beer"* blasting from the ferry berthed at its jetty, its cargo of day-trippers descending its gangway and calling to each other in gay holiday mood. "Bosom buddies of the moment," she mused, never likely to cross each other's paths again. While into her garden, a brilliant wave of rainbow lorikeets soared, to feast upon the seeds and honey she put out for them every day.

"God, how I love this country," she murmured, more speaking her thoughts than talking to Liz. But love of this country had not always been her sentiment. There had been a time she had truly hated it, convinced it had as little to offer her as she had to offer it. Arriving in Sydney Harbour aboard a migrant ship from Ireland some twenty-two years before and more than a little bit out of her mind, her new young husband Malachi Morgan having suddenly died en route, a seventeen-year-old widow going on seventy and having no choice but to disembark and enter this foreign land alone. Alone that was but for the six-month-old son of another man's seed suckling hungrily at her breast and the unknown quantity of Malachi's daughter growing to life in her womb

Lord only knew they were tough times back then, immeasurably tough, everything about the land appeared alien and unfriendly to her then. The stifling intensity of its heat, the blinding brightness of its sun, the unfamiliar sounds and vibrant clotted hues of this rich sunburnt country like none she'd experienced before, feeling homesick for the cool green plains of Ireland and her late husband's protection before she'd even stepped ashore.

She had also pined for Molly... Lord, how she'd pined for Molly, her family's beloved old housekeeper who'd been more like a mother to her than her own mother had been.

And she had also pined for Josie, the adored four-year-old sister she'd been forced to leave behind.

And though reluctant to admit it, she had pined for the ease of life on her father's Irish estate with its bevy of workers both indoors and out, believing the door to that life had been closed to her forever.

Then why was she now being lured back?

A "testing time" she had come to think of those early years as, a time to sink or a time to swim. A time to draw deep of her innermost-strengths and test the mettle she was made of. For well she understood, even back then, that it wasn't a game she was playing, but the serious reality of survival, survival for herself and the children she adored.

She had found it harder than hard to survive on the pittance Malachi had left her – a mere five hundred pounds and some old-fashioned jewellery forfeited from the pawn-shop in Dublin. But the jewellery had proved more valuable that she had imagined and had enabled her to purchase the small dress shop that her friend Joyce

Tufnell had owned in the heart of the City of Brisbane, for Joyce was eager to sell and retire with her husband Bill. And Joyce had made it easy for her, proposing she care for Caeli's children during the day, take them to nursery school in the mornings and pick them up mid-afternoon. For she and Bill had come to adore her children almost as much as she did, delighted to adopt the role of the doting grandparents they had longed to be. And though she was totally inexperienced at the ins and outs of running a business, Caeli had jumped at the chance and given it a go.

And by God, I succeeded, she thought, as goose-bumps of pride rippled her flesh. Not done too badly for me and mine. And not one single penny did I ask from *him* back there... Nor was one offered.

Liz came quietly to stand at her side, a silent comforting presence in her agony of indecision, and reassuringly slipped an arm about her shoulders, as the predictably compassionate words fell from her lips.

"I'm sorry if I've hurt you, Mum, if I've pushed you too hard. I didn't mean to. It's just that I truly believe it's important to say what I feel and be honest with you, for in the long run, I only want what's best for you. And these nightmares of yours are worrying me silly. They're occurring far too often and you really must do something about them.

"That's why I've been pushy, Mum, for I honestly believe that returning to Ireland will be best for you in the long run – though I'm certain you can't appreciate that now. I know it will be hard, that you'll be stirring up all that bad stuff you've been trying so hard to forget. And if you're really dead-set against going, so be it, it'll make no difference to Kev and me. We love you just as you are – nightmares and all.

"And I know I speak for Kev too," she added, "when I say we're behind you every inch of the way – whichever way you decide to go that is."

Again Caeli felt humbled to the depths of her being, awed at her daughter's understanding and more than a little ashamed of herself. Thinking again how much like her father, Malachi Morgan, Liz was, that she'd not only inherited his wisdom and kind caring ways, but his looks as well. The same delicate features and diminutive stature, the same fine blonde hair and cornflower-blue eyes, whereas her rollicking big son Kevin was just the opposite.

At twenty-one, Kevin was a towering six feet four, precisely the height his father, Danny O'Halloran had been. He also had the same jet-black hair and midnight-blue eyes like Danny's, eyes that sparkled with the same devilish fire. "As different as chalk and cheese," she could imagine her mother saying of her children.

Her voice held the quiver of tears when at last she spoke, but tears for whom or for what was beyond her understanding. The only thing she felt certain of at that particular moment in time, was that the rush of emotion that engulfed her now was not for her father's passing, dead or alive, she'd be wasting no tears on him. Perhaps they were tears for loved ones lost and the unjust manner of their passing? Or perhaps they were tears for time wasted and the futility of what her father had done?

Turning back into the room, she returned to the sofa, her energy spent, Liz followed closely, like her guardian angel, to sit by her side.

"You're absolutely right, my love," she said at last. "Of course I must go. There's no avoiding it. How foolish I've been."

"Oh, Mum, please don't – don't," Liz implored, seeing her mother's face streaming with tears. "I can't bear to see you cry. I'll do anything I can to help you, truly I will, I'll even go with you if you want me to. Though I honestly believe I'd be more help to you here – keeping an eye on the business and such…

"But hey," she added, as though suddenly struck by a brilliant idea, "why not get Kev to go? He's a free agent at the moment and I know he would jump at the chance, for he's absolutely gaga about Ireland and everything Irish of late. Reading up on its history… Researching the Dromgoole family tree and the ancient Vikings… He even has thoughts of practicing there when he gets his degree, don't you know."

No, she didn't know. Kevin had always been a bit of a dark horse, but more so of late and had made no mention of any such plans to her. But though surprised and a little offended at being shut out, she didn't labour the point. Now was not the time.

"No… No my darling," she responded instead, taking a deep breath and dabbing her eyes and flashing her daughter an uncertain smile. "We'll leave Kevin out of the picture for the moment. Besides, he's still down in New South Wales doing his veterinary thing and I'd hate to deprive him of that." Not mentioning that the journey to Ireland was a journey she preferred to make alone, that returning to Ireland was an immensely personal thing for her in more ways than one. For besides having the past to contend with, there was now the future, Liam's phone-call from Ireland that morning, having caused that. For he'd given her the feeling he was still in love with her, that there was unfinished business between them – *I've found you at last... Been searching for you forever...* Words that rekindled some old spark within her from way back in their youthful past. And that excited her. "And I wholeheartedly agree you'll be more help to me here," she added, "supervising the businesses and such... It takes a load off my mind."

Liz was delighted at her mother's trust and eager to prove she was worthy of it.

"I'm so glad you have faith in me, Mum," she said in all sincerity, "and I promise I won't let you down. But hey, aren't we forgetting Holiday Romps? Who's going to manage that while I'm up here in Brisbane? For as clever as I am, I can't be in two places at once, though I've often wished I could. Just wiggle my nose like Jeannie on TV does and transport myself from one place to another in a flash... That'd be a lark!"

"Huh! I think not, my girl! And have you popping up behind me and scaring me out of my wits? No thank you!

"But seriously, love... As for Holiday Romps... I'm sure Mabs can manage for a week or two. You did say she was extremely capable?"

"Yes, I did. And she is. Extremely is the word. No worries there. It's just with the holiday season in full swing and Christmas only weeks away; I don't think it's fair to leave Mabs short-staffed as well as having the added responsibility of managing the place too."

"Then we need more staff... At least one more to replace you... What about Mab's daughter Sally? Didn't you say she was looking for a summer job and itching to get her foot in your door?"

"Yes, I did, and I think she'd be great too. She's just completed year twelve and is also planning to do Fashion Design like Tony and I did."

"Well, there's your answer... Problem solved... Give Sally a go. And if she's half as good as Mabs is we'll have nothing to worry about, will we. OK?"

"OK!"

"That's settled then... Mabs on the Gold Coast and Sally the extra... You here in Brisbane... What more could I want? And I'll be back before you can say Jack Robinson – or at least before Christmas…"

"Yahoo! Good on ya, Mum!" Liz hollered, her youthful exuberance getting the better of her and planting a big smackeroo on her mother's cheek, not imagining for a moment how wrong her mother could be. "I just knew you would go… Knew you wouldn't let all those horrible things that happened to you yonks ago get the better of you. And you don't have to worry about the business, Mum… everything'll be apples – no prob!"

Caeli laughed heartily, as much from relief – now that the decision to travel to Ireland had been made, as from her daughter's wacky behaviour and striney turn of words. Feeling incredibly light-hearted now, as though a huge burden she'd been humping around for a very long time had suddenly been lifted away.

Finally admitting to herself that it was a journey she should have embarked upon years before and one probably vital to her wellbeing – and perhaps even her sanity, ever mindful of the mad Dromgoole genes and the tales of her loony old ancestor, Turlough Dromgoole.

But she also admitted – though strictly to herself, that Liam Shaw's voice on the phone had been the primary inducement that had swayed her decision to return, arousing old memories deep within her and forgotten feelings she was eager to explore. Curious about him; anticipating what? Hinting at what? Promising what? His words repeating over and over like a drumbeat in her head and throbbed in her pulses – *I've found you at last… Been searching for you forever…*

"And don't forget you can always call on Aunty Joyce," she added distractedly. "If there's anything you can't handle, that is."

Already visualising herself winging across the great oceans and continents of the world before reaching that tiny green speck of an island that had once been her world.

The land of her birth and her dotty Irish forebears – the rough-hewn Dromgooles – her father's people of ancient Viking blood and the man she had come to despise above all other.

Yet reminding herself it was also the land of her mother's people too, the respectable O'Sullivans and renowned horse breeders of County Kildare.

Wondering again, as she had wondered many times in the past, how her well-bred mother had come to marry such a rough and callous brute as Bran Dromgoole. Reluctant to admit that all that she was stemmed from the alliance of the unlikely pair, that she was half him and half her mother and bound to them both and Ireland's ancient creed for time ad-infinitum, whether she liked it or not.

"Mother, for heaven's sake, will you stop worrying!" Liz cut into her thoughts, misinterpreting their content and again rolling her eyes in feigned exasperation. "I'm sure there'll be no need to call on Aunty Joyce… Trust me. For as much as I love her, she's getting too old and too doddery to be of much help anyway…" Then added in a softer tone that she understood how hard the decision had been for her mother to make and that she admired her enormously for having made it.

"But hey," she now said on a lighter note, "now that you *have* decided to go, be positive about it, hey Mum? Try to recapture some of the happier times you spent with your sisters when your mother was alive. They're the memories to dwell on and hold close to your heart, for as far as I can see, all the others are just excess baggage and not worth carting around for the rest of your days."

Again, Caeli felt immeasurably humbled at her daughter's wise council and wondered from which ancient gene her wisdom had sprung. Certainly not from hers – or at least not from hers at the moment! Her behaviour like that of a petulant child to say the least and her daughter's like that of a wise and caring adult – daughter teaching mother the rudimentary lessons of life!

Conversely the years overrode her thoughts and made her feel older than her thirty-nine years should allow. The events of the day having forced her hand, bringing the past rushing back with crystal-clear clarity, demanding at last to be met.

"Ah, my darling," she said with a sigh, "I'm sure you are right. And yet…" The sentence left hanging.

How could she put into words the overwhelming feeling that all was not well and bad things lay ahead, that she was entering troubled waters and would come to regret her decision to return to Ireland at all? The feeling so strong, that icy cold shivers shimmered through her that no amount of logic or the blistering heat of the Queensland sun could dispel?

"Well, you just remember one thing, Mum," Liz gabbled on brightly, waggling her finger in time to her waggling head, totally unaware of her mother's feelings of impending disaster. "Regardless of what lies ahead and the decisions you make, Kev and I will be here for you ALWAYS."

"Always…" How the word jolted through her. It was meant to bring comfort but rang hollow. She was wary of "always," promised "always" before and put her trust in it and it had broken her heart. Yet at that particular moment in time, it was precisely the word she needed to hear.

Flashing her daughter her most brilliant smile, she responded graciously. "Thank you, my darling… But go find your handsome Tony now, before he considers us too weird a mob to get mixed up with and decides to do a bunk! I'm going to ring Qantas."

It wasn't until very late that night, when stretched between cool percale sheets and verging on sleep after fluking a flight via Heathrow to Dublin a few days hence, that Sebastian Templeton re-entered her mind. Amazed she had completely forgotten to mention his ludicrous behaviour and assumption of marriage to Liz, but even more so to mention their very nasty breakup of the previous night. In fact, since Liam Shaw had rung her from Ireland that morning, all thoughts of Sebastian Templeton had clean left her head.

PART THREE

DUBLIN

CHAPTER ELEVEN
THE RETURN

Caeli was shivering as she stood at the tenth-floor window of the luxury hotel suite overlooking the rain-washed rooftops of the grand old city of Dublin, certain that icicles had crystallised her blood, despite being wrapped in the feather-down quilt from the bed and the central heating thermostat telling her "cold" she could not possibly be. Yet cold she was, right through to her bones, due, she supposed, to the dramatic climatic extreme she now found herself in – Ireland's exceptionally cold winter, versus the sweltering heatwave conditions of Queensland in Australia from whence she had come.

The hotel, an American conglomerate as modern as tomorrow and tritely named "Angel Inn." Its garish flashing multi-coloured Neon, an obscenity to the City's refinement, wooing the weary traveller with the equally trite slogan, "Stay at the Angel for a bit of Heaven." Its chrome and glass structure sticking out like a sore thumb amid the sedate red-brick Georgian buildings that Dublin was renowned for. Within, it was hushed and padded, five-star rating, "sumptuous" the key word and reeking of wealth.

Pedestrians scurried in the rain-washed street below like an army of ants beneath a sea of bobbing umbrellas. Green double-decker buses and all manner of vehicles honked and vied for position on the broad thoroughfare. The bleakness of the scene, contrasting sharply to the brilliant pigmentations of the scorched red earth of her adopted land at the bottom of the world, and she was feeling homesick for it already and longing for the heat of its sun to bite into her flesh.

Yet despite the rain and the cold and her reluctance to be in Ireland at all, there was something about Dublin that had fired her blood. Something in her ancient genes, perhaps, she hadn't counted on? For not only was Dublin the proud capital of the Irish Free State, the home of Dail Eireann, Trinity College and Molly Malone, it had also evolved from a small Viking village at the mouth of the River Liffey some twelve hundred years before. And it was also from where her dotty old ancestor Turlough Dromgoole had departed a mere two hundred years ago, proudly claiming a Viking heritage, destined to live out his life mourning the loss of his beloved young wife in the grim isolation of his "Liath Caislean" – his "grey castle" – his "self-imposed prison," that rose from the wild western cliffs of Ireland and the fateful waters of Raggemorne Bay.

Hugging the quilt more closely about her, she turned from the window shivering still, uncertain if she was shivering from the cold or nervous anticipation of the ordeal that lay ahead – namely the meeting with her family's lawyers, the highly esteemed Eugene Shaw and Sons.

The huge bouquet of flowers, delivered to her suite that morning, once again caught her eye: Blood-red roses, deep-purple irises, golden-yellow tulips – a brilliant burst of summer to the winter of the room, correctly assuming them products of a hothouse.

For the countless number of times, she reached for the accompanying card, "To friendship renewed, Liam Shaw," it read. Five commonplace words bereft of emotion remaining unchanged no matter how many times she read them, yet persistently searching their content for more.

Some secret message within its message... Something to convince her she had not been mistaken when Liam had phoned her in Australia, that she'd not read something into his words that simply wasn't there – *I've found you at last... Been searching for you forever...* Words that had ultimately swayed her decision to come, and not the words of her daughter's wise counsel at all.

Yet the message on the card remained blatantly unchanged no matter how many times she read it. There was no cryptic message to decipher. No hidden promise of anything other than renewing old friendship. And the flowers, nothing more than a courteous gesture from her father's firm of lawyers and old family friends.

The only thing she was certain of at that particular moment was that she wasn't certain of anything at all, but feeling a bit of a dill flying halfway round the world on the strength of a whim, expecting something intimate and eternal still existed between them. Unable to dispel the increasingly awkward feeling she was making a fool of herself and reaching for something that simply wasn't there, or poking a stick at a hornet's nest and about to get stung.

Committed to meeting her family's lawyers in Dublin now and heaven forbid, even return to *Liath Caislean,* the house of her father she had long ago vowed she would never return to again, if only to put the ghosts of the past to rest and see her beloved Molly again.

For it certainly wasn't to mourn her father's passing she had come, nor of the hope of inheriting something from his estate. Reaffirming again the vow she had made before she had come, that she wanted nothing from him. "

The phone in her room buzzed into her thoughts with all the refinement of a bee in a bottle, and the dulcet tones of the hotel receptionist crooned in her ear. "Good morning, Mrs. Morgan. This is Teresa O'Malley from reception speaking."

"Yes, Teresa. And good morning to you…"

"I wish to inform you your car has arrived, Mrs. Morgan, awaiting your convenience at the front entrance foyer." The car, compliments of her father's lawyers, pre-arranged to pick her up at ten.

She glanced at her watch. Five minutes to. "Thank you, Teresa. I'll be down directly."

She viewed the forthcoming meeting with the Shaw's apprehensively, for not only had they been the Dromgoole's family lawyers since the year dot, but also their dearest and closest friends. A friendship that reached beyond the Grandfather's Dromgoole and Shaw to their fathers before them, a friendship that endured to the end between her father – the late Bran Dromgoole and the present patriarch of the Shaw's – the esteemed Eugene Shaw, himself. Consequently, there was an intimacy bred into the relationship that Caeli was not looking forward to facing, a familiarity that tore down private barriers and permitted one to pry, aware that by profession, Eugene Shaw was an expert at this.

To talk about old times – particularly those relating to her father, was something she did not want to do. Time had not applied the balm of forgiveness, nor healed the wounds of the past. Yet the principals of good manners and respect for one's elders had been paramount to her upbringing, imbued into the very essence of everything she was from the day she'd been born and no less expected of her now. So if Eugene Shaw was in attendance in his office that day, (uncertain he would as she believed him retired) and chose to reminisce and rake over the coals of the past, then common courtesy demanded she respect and respond accordingly and endure what she must.

Slipping a caramel coat over black woollen slacks and turtle-necked sweater, then donning a burgundy beret and matching scarf, she glanced at her image in the mirror. "Hmm... not bad," she conceded, smiling uncertainly at the petite reflection bedecked in the unaccustomed bulk of clothing, staring back. Her intelligent violet eyes glinted determinedly, concealing the misgivings she was feeling inside. Totally convinced she had made a massive blunder by returning to Ireland at all, that she'd let silly romantic notions get the better of her reason and read something into Liam Shaw's words that simply wasn't there. Having no choice now but to see the meeting through, determined she would play it cool and conduct herself in the well-bred manner that was expected of her and of which she no less expected of herself. That she would politely refuse anything her late father might have left her and hot-foot it back to Australia on the first available flight; grabbing a black leather handbag to match her knee-high boots, as she rushed out the door and headed for the lift.

Freezing winds assailed her as she stepped outside from the warmth of the foyer, and she gasped at their force and hugged the coat more closely about her.

"Would that be yourself now, Mrs. Morgan?" asked the dwarf of a man who'd magically appeared at her side.

She nodded a stiff-lipped affirmation and said something that sounded like "Ya" – her whole body shivering and bunched up tight. "I'm Hugh, at your service, Mrs. Morgan" he offered, respectfully tipping his cap.

"Mr. Shaw's man," he further explained; a glint of amusement entering his beady black eyes at the sight of her quivering state.

"H-hello H-Hugh... Isn't it f-freezing?" she managed to mumble through chattering teeth as he bundled her into the black limousine.

The beaming, red-nosed gnome of a man chuckled gleefully.

"Sure 'tis a lazy wind we're having the day, Mrs. Morgan – goes right through you – altogether too lazy to go around...

"But wasn't Mr. Shaw after telling me now, that you'd be feeling the cold – 'coming up from that blazing hot place that she lives in down there?'

But we'll soon have you all snug and warm, Mrs. Morgan," he added brightly, tossing a chequered woollen rug over her legs and closing the door, then slipped behind the steering wheel with the sprightliness of a five-year-old and switched the ignition on.

"You make it sound as though I've come up from the fires of hell, Hugh," Caeli called companionably to him as the warmth of the rug and the car seeped through her. "Just like the mythical phoenix rising from the bowels of a fiery pit!"

He guffawed at that.

"That's a good one, Mrs. Morgan, The mythical phoenix rising from the bowels of a fiery pit... I must remember to tell himself that one now... It will tickle his fancy no end..."

He was still chuckling – as indeed that seemed to be his natural state as he effortlessly pulled the purring limousine through a minuscule gap in the traffic and out into the mainstream flow.

"But I swear to God, Mrs. Morgan, they were Mr. Shaw's very words," he called back to her – 'Coming up from that blazing hot place that she lives in down there...' And that I was to mind to keep you warm."

"Well, I wholeheartedly agree with that, Hugh – keeping me warm that is. For I feel like a waddling penguin with all the clothes I've got on and I *still* feel cold!" feigning an exaggerated shiver to emphasise the point.

"Sure your blood's gone all thin living down there in all that heat," he commented, "but a few pints of the Guinness will soon put it right and thicken it up in no time at all."

Caeli was enchanted with the little man, enchanted with his looks and his blarney and his ease of manner – familiar yet not offensive. Though his brogue was not local, detecting the harshness of the north in it that clearly marked him an Ulster Man. Somewhere in his fifties, she surmised, and though smartly clad in a tailored grey suit and a matching chauffer's cap, she could easily imagine him dressed in a green elfin suit. For as well as being a bit on the plump side, his eyes twinkled mischievously in his round ruddy face, bringing to mind the wizened old elves that dotted her garden back home.

"How is Mr. Shaw these days?" she enquired, feeling slightly thawed and more at ease. "Is he keeping well?"

"Ah, well now," Hugh replied, glancing at her in the rear vision mirror, "He is and he isn't so to speak... He has his good days and his bad... But as Mr. Shaw so rightly points out, it all gets down to one's frame of mind at the given moment.

"Take this morning now for instance, 'tis a prime example... His arthritis usually gives him the divil of a yip in the morning and I get him out of bed and help him bathe and dress. But this morning he was up bright and early and rearing to go before I even got there, claiming he felt better today than he's felt in ages – which I could only put down to yourself arriving

"And while we all tend to coddle him because of his dicky heart, he tells us to stop worrying because it hasn't stopped yet! So all in all I have to say he's not too bad, Mrs. Morgan, not too bad at all for a man of his years."

Caeli felt confused, but thought she got the gist of what Hugh was trying to say, that a positive mental attitude was the crux of the matter and the key to it all. Yet Hugh had alarmed her, reading between the lines that Mr. Shaw was not a well man, concern for the old family friend she used to call "Uncle," evident in her reply.

"He doesn't sound too well to me, Hugh... But then I tend to think of him as he was when I last saw him twenty-odd years ago and I forget he's getting old."

"Ah so, Mrs. Morgan, we're all getting old... Life's a terror of a thing and won't hold still for any of us and is fast catching up with us all..."

The conversation ending on that rather glum note as the car swung into wide O'Connell Street and came to a streamlined halt outside the offices of Eugene Shaw and Sons.

A sense of déjà vu swept over her then as she cast her eyes over the "Shaw Building," the feeling she was trapped in a time-warp and replaying an old scene. That mother and father were about to appear, to step out of her father's limousine – that had been black too, with young Meegan in tow, that mother would come and take her hand and lead her inside as she used to do. For though some things had undoubtedly changed, nothing immediately caught her eye, the building appeared exactly as she remembered it – five floors of red brick stability, with the same shamrock green trim.

As though on springs, Hugh sprung from the car to open her door, and clutching her elbow as he ushered her inside.

"Now, Mrs. Morgan," he said, sounding quite conspiratorial and tapping the side of his nose as though revealing a long kept secret. "Take the lift here to the fourth floor now, and Faith will take care of you after that." Then, with a tip of his cap and a wink of his eye, as magically as he had appeared, he was gone.

Faith will take care of you after that... Caeli screwed up her nose, contemplating the words, wondering if "Faith" was a person to be met, or the "faith" she might need to get her through the forthcoming meeting.

The "time warp" feeling remaining with her as she flicked her eyes over the familiar surrounds of the foyer. Noting the gleaming brass plaques that lined its walls, proclaiming the names of the illustrious company therein, and the curve of wrought-iron staircase twisting exquisitely up to the luxurious office suites above and down to the drab grey filing rooms in the basement below, everything oozing age-old wealth and stability and the lingering aromas of Brasso and Lavender Wax. The ancient wrought-iron lift to the left, clanging shut behind her when she stepped inside and began its creaking ascent to the fourth floor. Her confidence mounting as she alighted and familiar surroundings unravelled about her. The reception desk directly opposite it, where it had always been; the young receptionist looking expectantly up as the lift clanged shut and Caeli approached.

"Could this be 'Faith,'" Caeli wondered, suppressing a ridiculous urge to giggle. The "Faith" Hugh had said would take care of her, recklessly deciding to chance that it was.
"Good morning. You must be Faith" she said brightly, making more of a statement than a question. "I'm Mrs. Morgan, from Australia... I believe Mr. Shaw is expecting me?"

"Oh *yes*, Mrs. Morgan. Indeed he is, and good morning to you too and welcome!" Faith oozed. "And *yes*, Mrs. Morgan, I am Faith," politely rising to her feet with the inevitable Irish smile alighting her pretty young face.

"I do hope you've had a good trip, Mrs. Morgan," she continued. "Such a long way to come..." obviously well informed of the client's backgrounds. The enquiry perfunctory, expecting no reply, as none was given.

"Mr. Shaw is *so* anxious to see you, Mrs. Morgan," Faith further oozed, having advised him of her arrival via the rather old fashioned intercom on her desk. "He requests that I bring you in immediately... would you be so good as to follow me?" Faith lead the way down the hall on cherry red stilettos, her long brown curls shining and bobbing to their rhythm, then arriving at a dark panelled door, which Caeli recognised immediately, having entered it on numerous occasions in the past, Faith tapped lightly upon it before turning its gleaming brass knob and ushering Caeli inside.

CHAPTER TWELVE
MR SHAW'S OFFICE

It was Eugene Shaw himself who awaited her arrival at the offices of Eugene Shaw and Sons, the distinguished Attorneys at Law in the grand old city of Dublin, and Caeli was pleasantly surprised. Having convinced herself – because he was now in his seventy-fifth year and the same age her father had been, that he would be retired and one of his sons would be in attendance that day. Either Liam Shaw (she hoped), her close childhood friend and once budding sweetheart and owner of the beguiling voice on the phone, who had swayed her decision to come, and also the sender of the magnificent flowers to her hotel suite that morning, or Chester Shaw, the eldest son and senior partner of the firm.

He stood with his back to the window, his hands clasped behind him, his eyes unwaveringly intent upon the door. And he smiled with genuine delight and immediately started towards her the moment she entered, his hands extended in welcome.

His grooming was impeccable, as it always had been, from the top of his well-barbered head to the tip of his shining black shoes, every inch of him the elegant affluent gentleman she'd remembered him to be. Yet his tall frame was stooped and his well-tailored suit hung too loosely about him looking a size too big. And his once auburn hair – though still thick and wavy with no sign of balding, now silvery white, and his blue Irish eyes wore the weariness of time.

"Ah Caeli, Caeli… *Cead mile failte,* my dear – a hundred thousand welcomes to you," he enthusiastically gushed. "And what an absolute pleasure it is to see you again." Then, cocking his head to one side, he asked, "Or is it Mrs. Morgan I should be calling you now?"

"Definitely not...!" Caeli retorted with a happy laugh, as delighted to see him as he was to see her, her nervousness easing, as eagerly she grasped his outstretched hands.

"You've always called me Caeli, Mr. Shaw, and I couldn't imagine you calling me anything else. But the pleasure's all mine, I assure you. I am more than delighted to see you again," impulsively standing on tiptoe and kissing the old lawyer's cheek. Noting as she did how much he had aged and how deep the lines of time had etched into his flesh. The thought occurring to her then that had never occurred to her before, that the years must have been equally as cruel to her father, and turned him into an old man too.

"I was half expecting one of your sons to be here today," she said brightly, "for I thought you'd be retired, so finding you here is a double-delight! And may I say how wonderfully well you are looking, and if possible, more debonair than ever."

He positively beamed with pleasure. "Ah... But you flatter an old man my dear and I thank you for it," explaining, as he helped her off with her coat that he was indeed retired, but wasn't about to miss the chance of seeing her today for all the tea in China! "And yes my dear, thank God my health is not too bad, though the joints are a bit arthritic and this terrible weather helps them none. But I shouldn't complain, for I can still get about. And when one reaches my age, one has to expect a discomfort or two and be thankful for small mercies.

"But come now, Caeli, where are my manners!" he said, grasping her arm and leading her to a chair companionably placed to one side of his huge mahogany desk. "Come, sit yourself down and tell me all about yourself... And there's a fresh pot of tea and some cakes," indicating a huge silver tray on the corner of the desk with a jerk of his head.

"Peggy brought it in not two minutes ago." The tray, laden with a magnificent silver tea service and fine bone china, and the cakes on a two-tiered silver stand.

"Shall I be mother?" she asked.

He chuckled and nodded. "Please do my dear, so gracious of you, but just a spot of milk and two lumps of sugar in mine, if you please." Adding, while patting his stomach, "Must watch the figure, getting too paunchy you know," whereas just the opposite was true.

"But I must say you are looking extremely well yourself – and as pretty as ever, I might add, changed very little with the years. But how long is it now you've been gone – sixteen – seventeen years?"

"Heavens, Mr. Shaw, much longer than that! Nearer twenty-two…!"

He gasped. "Good God! Is it really that long? How time flies… And you've lived in Australia all that time?"

"Mostly – apart from the first year I lived here in Dublin."

"Ah yes… Australia…" he said, sounding wistful and ignoring her reference to Dublin. "A beautiful country I've been told. Had thoughts of going there myself at one time – when I was young and unattached… And have you been happy there, my dear?"

"Definitely…" she replied, passing him a cup of tea and a snowy white napkin then offering the cakes; cream-filled butterfly cakes, well-dusted with icing sugar, of which he took two. "*Extremely* happy," she emphasised, "for it's truly a beautiful country and a wonderful place to live."

"But how do you cope with all that heat and all those wild animals leaping about?"

It was her turn to chuckle at how misinformed he was, her spoon tinkling on the fine china as she delicately stirred her tea.

"Actually the climate is glorious, Mr. Shaw, practically summer all year round – especially in Queensland where I live. As for the wild animals you speak of, we rarely see kangaroos hopping about in suburbia, you have to go bush to see those, though the occasional snake or a lizard sometimes crosses our path." Adding, a little defensively, "Many of us Irish have settled there, you know, and I'm proud to call myself an Australian, it's been very good to me and mine."

"But I'm glad to hear it, my dear, for I've often thought of you over the years and wondered where you were and hoped you'd found happiness wherever it was. And I hear you have children… Two I believe, Kevin and Elizabeth. Is that correct?"

She shot him a glance of surprise. "Yes, it is." Wondering how he knew of her children, and thinking that the dreaded inquisition had begun. "How do you know I have children?"

He drained the last dreg of tea from his cup and dabbed his mouth with the white serviette before answering. "Through Zita O'Halloran of course…"

"Zita…!"

His reply took her aback, genuinely surprised. "What's Zita got to do with any of this?"

"Apparently quite a lot, for it was on account of Zita – and the information she so obligingly supplied us with, that led us to you."

"I don't understand…"

"It's really quite simple my dear. Zita came here soon after your father passed away – waiting on the doorstep when we opened the office that very same morning as a matter of fact – amazing how quickly news travels… And what a veritable fountain of knowledge she's turned out to be. Keener than mustard to spill the proverbial beans once she knew that your father was dead.

"And of course we've heard many rumours about you over the years. Heard you were married with children and supposedly lived in many different places abroad. Practically everywhere on the planet was mentioned – even Australia! All unsubstantiated here-say of course and leaked I suspect by none other than Zita herself.

"But then there's always been talk about you Dromgooles, hasn't there, my dear? The very nature of your father's position in the community enough to keep tongues wagging – especially in a community as small and isolated as yours… And very cruel tongues they have been at times too, I might add – though I'll not go into that now.

"The reality was that none of us had the foggiest idea as to where you were – until Zita O'Halloran came on the scene and unloaded her bags of enlightenment. Told us all we needed to know to locate you in five minutes flat, and more besides. She seems to know everything about you, which really surprised me, for she never let on she knew anything about you before. Not only did she inform us of where you lived and the names of your children, but she even cited your telephone number off by heart – hence my son Liam phoning you in Australia later that night."

"Ah… So that's how he found me…"

"To think" he continued, disregarding the remark, "that Zita knew all along where you were and deliberately kept your whereabouts from us. That really astounds me, but even more so because she kept all knowledge of you from your father and remained vindictive towards him to the end."

"That's the way I wanted it, Mr. Shaw," Caeli cut in, as though needing to justify Zita's actions. "You can't blame Zita; she was respecting *my* wishes and being loyal to *me,* for she's the only one in the whole of Ireland I've corresponded with all these years.

"And she *is* Kevin's grandmother," she reminded him, as though needing to justify herself. "Or had you forgotten that?"

Not adding that Zita had never so much as set her eyes on her only grandchild in the twenty-one years of his life, even though he'd been born here in Dublin months before she and Malachi had departed for Australia, giving her every opportunity to meet her only offspring's newborn son if she had so wished.

"I'm perfectly aware she is that, my dear, and to Zita's credit, she made it perfectly clear that was why she'd come – on Kevin's behalf. Claiming she had only her grandson's interests at heart and seeking nothing for herself from your father's estate, only the assurance that Kevin was acknowledged as his grandson and that he would inherit what was rightfully his – hence the disclosure of your whereabouts to us.

"I'm sure Zita saw it as no betrayal to you, Caeli. After all, we *are* your family's legal representatives and so very grateful to receive such information, for in the long run, it has saved us a great deal of time and effort.

"But by God, Caeli, what a bitter old woman she's turned out to be. Festering with hate, for Daniel was all she had, and she still holds your father responsible for his death and to my knowledge, she never spoke to him again since the day of the tragedy.

"But its water under the bridge now, isn't it, my dear?" he said dryly, as though he had said it a thousand times before. "All in the past and we must move on and think of the living – though I'll never be able to forgive her for meddling with other people's lives as she has.

"But then," he added, as though he himself was not without blame, "who am I to be Zita's judge and juror? Arragh! The pity of it all…"

They sat in silence for what seemed a very long time, Mr. Shaw's words dangling between them like a great leaden key, the key that unlocked the unhappy events of a time long ago. Events, that had not only affected both their family's lives, but spread like an ever-widening ripple on a pond to affect the lives of so many others as well.

Caeli's heart heavy, as she again recalled the wild winter's day her father had informed her that Danny's little yacht, *Sea Nymph,* was way overdue. Experienced again the sickening fear that had filled her then, as she'd watched from the tower room of Liath Caislean as the daylight was fading and an almighty storm was exploding out to sea, somehow sensing that even then Danny was lost to her forever, and she would never see him again. Seeing again, so clear in her mind, the flotilla of craft searching the waters of Raggemorne Bay and the army of volunteers combing its beaches when the storm had abated, yet not one single item of Danny's personal belongings had ever been recovered, even though the wreck of the bright yellow *Sea Nymph* had washed into an inlet not two miles beyond Raggemorne Harbour. A million yellow pieces scattered among the rocks like a spray of spring flowers, shattering every last hope he might still be alive.

Perplexingly though, Zita had shed not one single tear for her son. Even when the search was called off and he was pronounced "Lost at Sea," the grim news awaiting them on their return to the mourning house following Meegan's funeral. For Zita had claimed that without her son's body to mourn and weep over, she could never believe he was dead and therefore lay him to rest, but forever live in hope he might still be alive and walk through her door one day.

All of nineteen Danny had been, his life, like Meegan's, plucked away too soon by an angry sea. But Caeli believed, and would continue to believe until *her* dying day, that it was her father's scheming ways that had put them there.

Meegan's words, seared for all time like a red-hot brand in her memory, an eternal reminder of what she believed her father had done. Words, which Meegan had so innocently overheard while trapped in the tower room above Dada's office and the strongest confirmation of his guilt. Overheard Dada and Danny arguing, and Dada telling Danny he could never marry Caeli and must go far away.

Her hatred for her father surging anew in her breast at the memory, rising bitter like gall upon her tongue, and was therefore surprised that her voice sounded normal when she spoke.

"And I blame him too, Mr. Shaw," she said gently, exercising enormous composure, "And I blame him too…"

He could see the pain coursing through her, burning like coals in her eyes. See a trapped, wounded animal before him with nowhere to run. And his voice was full of compassion when he replied. "Ah, Caeli, Caeli, I know you do, I know you do," the morbid silence that followed, eventually broken by Mr. Shaw, changing the subject altogether.

"We must live for the present, my dear, and put the past behind us," he said, feigning a brightness he was far from feeling. "So tell me about these offspring of yours. Who are they are like – you or their fathers? Though from what Zita has told me, they resemble each other not one little bit. She tells me your daughter is a beautiful delicate blue-eyed blonde and that your son is as big and dark and as handsome as his father before him had been."

Here we go again, Caeli thought, the inevitable prying into my private affairs. Yet her manners proved better than her thoughts and her answer as polite as was expected of her.

"It's really a mistake to ask a mother to describe her children, Mr. Shaw, you should know better. For I fear I am the typical mother who sees her children through rose-coloured glasses, and would bore you to tears in two minutes flat!"

He chuckled. "So bore me."

"OK, I will. But remember you asked for it!

And yes, I wholeheartedly agree that in looks they have little in common and that my daughter is every bit as beautiful as Zita makes her out to be – how can I, as her mother, say otherwise? She's the image of her father Malachi, and fortunately, she has also inherited his lovely temperament too.

"And yes again, I also believe that my son is every bit as handsome as Danny was, and coincidentally Mr. Shaw, also like Danny, he wants to be a vet."

The raising of eyebrows conveyed Mr. Shaw's surprise. "Well I never…" he said, "That is truly remarkable my dear. So history repeats itself…"

"It appears so. Weird, isn't it? For Kevin has been crazy about animals as long as I can remember, claiming he was going to be an "Aminal Docker" before he could even pronounce the words. I suspected *Lassie* and *Skippy* on the television the influence at the time, and thought he would change his mind a dozen times over before he grew up. Obviously I was wrong, for animals have always been his passion, and becoming a vet the only profession he's ever considered, never wanted to be anything else."

Mr. Shaw indicated the teapot with a flick of his eyes and proffered his cup. "Carry on, my dear, don't let me interrupt. But would you be so kind as to pour me another? All this unaccustomed talking has parched my mouth dry."

Caeli poured the tea and offered more cakes with barely a pause. "My friends have always said he's the image of me, but then they never knew Danny, did they? The same black hair as mine, I'll grant them that, but that's where the resemblance begins and ends. For personally I see only Danny in him. To me, he is Danny incarnate."

She paused, her lovely violet eyes imbued with a dewy softness, as though they'd encountered some highly desired image way back in time. Then with a shiver running through her as though she would shake the image off, she reiterated, "Yes, he's his father all over.

"And he has Danny's build too, I might add – tall and big boned like Danny was. And he also has Danny's eyes, eyes so intensely dark blue that they sometimes look black...

"But wait, Mr. Shaw, I'm forgetting, I have photos..." Delving into her handbag and producing a yellow Kodak folder, which she promptly handed to him. "They're all fairly recent... I've just had them developed – for Zita."

Eagerly he spread them on the desk before him like a deck of playing cards, his spectacles perched to best advantage on the tip of his nose. His forthcoming questions giving the impression he was genuinely interested in every last detail of her children, but especially so in Kevin. Keenly she watched, for suddenly it seemed so terribly important to her that Mr. Shaw should like her offspring. Important that he'd glean from the glossy images the beautiful young people they had turned out to be, that they at least were one aspect of her life she had got so incredibly right. Proudly she observed Mr. Shaw observing her son and her daughter now, between morsels of cake delicately transported via silver fork to her mouth.

"Yes, my dear, I couldn't agree more." he said. Kevin *does* have Daniel's undeniable good looks. Yet I can definitely see the Dromgoole in him too. There's a lot of your father... Hence there's a lot of old Turlough there too."

"*Really...?*" The observation surprised her and she snatched one of Kevin's photos up and studied it more closely. "I'd never noticed..."

"As for your daughter..." Mr. Shaw went on, "What can I say? The photos speak for themselves and confirm there was no exaggeration on Zita's part, for she truly is a beauty, my dear. But not much of the Dromgoole..." he said, squinting and pulling the desk lamp closer to gain better view. "Definitely your husband's side of the family, as you've already implied. Yet I also see something of your mother there too..."

Again Caeli was surprised, and again she said "Really?" and again she snatched a photo up.

"I've always thought Liz to be Malachi's child through and through," she said. "For not only does she have his wonderful looks and blonde colouring and the same cornflower-blue eyes, but she's also been blessed with his kind disposition and his amazing wisdom too.

"Though I'd like to believe she has a little of me in her too? The same nose as mine I think, which I in turn inherited from *my* mother. Perhaps that is what you see?"

"Yes... Perhaps..." he said, sounding dubious... "Tell me about her."

"Well... What can I say without sounding biased?

"Though I honestly believe she's a very special person with the loveliest nature one could ever hope to find – and the wisdom of King Solomon thrown in to boot, which spooks me a bit.

"Even Kevin bows to her counsel – even though she's the younger of the two. For if he ever has a problem, it's invariably Liz he will seek before ever coming to me. Probably because I wasn't always there for them when they were growing up, due to the pressures of work, for Liz has always mothered him and is still very protective of him to this day – as he is of her. They're as thick as thieves those two..."

She returned her teacup to the tray. "And fortunately for me – *and* for my business, Liz also has a wonderful flair for fashion. Instinctively knows what to order and what will sell – which is a Godsend to me, for that's how I earn my living."

Ah yes, her living... He'd heard about that too.

She paused, seeing his hand go to his mouth and stifle a yawn.

"Now didn't I warn you, Mr. Shaw," she said accusingly, "that I'd bore you to tears, speaking of my children?"

He guffawed. "Not at all, my dear, not at all, I am truly fascinated, and it's obvious to me you are very proud of them, and rightly so! They sound like delightful young people, and it's my greatest wish that I'll meet them one day.

"Though I have to admit my mind was beginning to wander, thinking of what you were saying about Kevin and how much he resembles Daniel, and wondering if he was aware that Daniel is his father. Or does he believe he is Malachi's…?"

"Lord no, Mr. Shaw," Cacli cut in before the words were fully out of his mouth. "Kevin knows the truth. Both of them do.

"They know they have different fathers and that I was never married to Danny. I've never lied to my children, Mr. Shaw, but always been a stickler for the truth and putting the record straight right from the start. Believing it better they hear the whole truth from me, rather than some half-baked cock and bull story from a less reliable source. I've always encouraged an open and honest relationship between us."

"Quite right, my dear, I couldn't agree more."

"Before Malachi had ever asked me to marry him, he was aware of my relationship with Danny and the whole sorry Dromgoole saga from woe to go – much of which I might add, he had read in the papers. He was also aware of how much I loved Danny and how glad I was that I was expecting Danny's child. I held nothing back, Mr. Shaw. Yet in spite of everything, Malachi still wanted to marry me."

"He sounds a remarkable man."

"Yes, he was. But I only came to realise just how remarkable since his death and that I really didn't deserve him."

Her mind pricking with shame as she skimmed back over the few short months of her marriage to Malachi Morgan and how one-sided the love of that marriage had been. Failing to recognise or appreciate the wonderful man Malachi Morgan had been.

"He was a Godsend to me, Mr. Shaw," she continued. "He took me in and made me feel safe when my whole world had crumbled about me, and I hate to think what might have become of me if he had not.

"How I wish I had shown more gratitude and love for what he had done for me and the lengths he had gone to protect me. He was even prepared to raise my child as his own and insisted I name him as Kevin's father on the birth certificate. I think he believed it would make things less complicated – or perhaps less embarrassing for Kevin and me as Kevin grew up – you know how badly illegitimacy was frowned on back then?

"That was the nature of Malachi, Mr. Shaw, completely unselfish. Always putting others first and totally devoted to Kevin and me.

"I was devastated by his death and have thought many times since that if he had lived we could have been happy together, that we were good for each other, and it's my greatest regret that he died before he knew I was expecting his child. For he would have been over the moon about Liz, for he desperately wanted a family of his own."

Mr. Shaw was shaking his head and looking bewildered. "But – but – but my dear," he stammered, as though the words were stuck in his throat. "Are you telling me Malachi Morgan is dead – that your husband is dead – that you've been a widow and alone in Australia all these years?"

"But of course, Mr. Shaw. I assumed you knew."

"I had no idea and I'm shocked – truly shocked! Zita kept that from me too – and from everyone else that I know of. What happened, my dear? Tell me what happened?"

CHAPTER THIRTEEN

MALACHI

Tell him what happened? How simple the request, how commonplace the words, how difficult the reply, to cast her mind back and recount the events of that fateful day of so long ago, mindful of the pain and the guilt that recounting would bring. And at the end of the day, what was there to tell? Malachi had died pure and simple. Gone – kaput – end of story, his life snuffed out in the space of a heartbeat.

Was it important she fill in the bitter-sweet details and tell Mr. Shaw they'd been on a huge ocean liner en route to Australia to begin a new life together? Or to mention that the weather had been glorious and the Mediterranean sun had been bursting from the heavens and scorched their pale Irish skins to a bright lobster pink? Or inform him that the waters of the sea had been such an intensity of blue that it had pained the heart and dazzled the eyes just to look upon it? Or to say that they had been bobbing about in the ship's pool with Kevin gurgling delightedly in her arms and that she was beginning to feel safe with this man, comforted by his love and his strength and gentleness and beginning to believe he'd be with her forever?

She hadn't even been aware he had left the pool, for heaven's sake – distracted by the baby, let alone he'd collapsed and already lay dead on the sun-bleached deck but a few feet away. Dead! Deplete of life! Horribly and unalterably dead – just as Danny and Meegan and mother were dead. That he'd actually *died* while she was laughing and playing with her son in the pool! One minute he was there, living and breathing and loving her, and the next he was not – it was as simple as that! Another death she somehow had to live through and keep from going mad, another cold statistic to record in the ship's log.

She had clambered from the pool her heart full of fear, the cries of those gathered around him alerting her to the fact that something was dreadfully wrong. Roughly she had pushed in among them, disbelieving of their words, that her lovely young husband was *dead*! She had thrown herself upon him with the child in her arms and desperately kissed his lips and called his name, willing him to be alive and to open his eyes, thinking he could not possibly be dead when his body was as warm as the glorious sun-filled day. Eventually, they'd dragged her from him. Stranger's hands that prised open her fingers and legs that would hold him and refuse to let go, watching in horror as they carried his lifeless body away.

She cast her mind back even further still, to the day her mindless wanderings had led her to him. The day following Meegan's funeral it had been, and the day her beloved Danny O'Halloran was officially pronounced "Lost at Sea". And it had also been the day her father had unjustly cast her out with nothing but the clothes she was wearing upon her back. Vaguely, she recalled catching a bus to Dublin, but where she had gone or what she had done on arrival there, or the events of the following day, she had no recall.

Only when night was falling did she come to her senses and aware of the desperate state she was in. That she was cold and hungry and standing before a strange little shop in some unknown backstreet of Dublin.

Had it been chance or divine intervention that had guided her steps down that nameless street that day, for stumbling upon the pawnshop had without doubt been her salvation. "CASH FOR GOODS" and "GOODS REDEEMABLE," emblazoned across its window. The white painted capitals somehow jarred her to her senses and made her aware of her need of nourishment and protection from the cold. But the sum of her wealth was a few paltry shillings jangling in her coat pocket and the precious heirloom ring upon her finger. The emerald and diamond ring, passed down from mother to daughter since great-great-grandmother O'Sullivan's time and unexpectedly gifted to her the previous Christmas Day – the day before the terrible Boxing Day that had taken her mother's life away. It was almost as if her mother had known she was about to die, thus making the ring even more precious to her. Never once had she removed it from her finger, and she didn't want to part with it now. But her logical mind and sense of survival were greater than her sentiment, and she realised she had no choice but to pawn the ring, but confident she could "redeem" it when she found some form of employ.

Even now, to this very day, she could still hear the shop's bell jangling overhead as she opened the door and stepped inside. Still smell the dust and the agedness of the place in her nostrils; still see the jumble of goods cramming its shelves and the great bulks of furniture crowding its floor. But the thing that amazed her the most and quite puzzled her eyes was some sort of a cage at the rear of the shop with a real live man inside? His voice echoed hollowly about her as she'd stepped towards him, asking if he could be of assistance to her. But before she could reply, the room had begun to spin and the floor come crashing up to meet her, turning everything black.

The following days had rolled into one indistinguishable space of strange hovering faces and whispering voices, of warmth and floating softness, of sustenance and sleep. Eventually opening her eyes to look into the kindest cornflower-blue eyes she had ever encountered, the eyes of a stranger looking anxiously into hers, lines of concern, ridging his brow.

"Mrs. Ross! Mrs. Ross! Come quickly now," he'd called out excitedly at the sight of her fluttering lids, "the girl is awake!" A flurried Mrs. Ross – the young man's "daily," she was later to learn, had rushed into the room, drying her hands on her apron as she came.

Malachi Morgan the young man turned out to be, the proprietor of the little pawnshop she'd so providentially stumbled upon, who lived in a flat up above. The days ran into weeks and still she was there, unburdening the whole tragic story of her past to these two kindly strangers. And when it became apparent she was with child, there was no question of turning her out, for by then Malachi Morgan was deeply in love with her and begging her to marry him. Explaining that he had sold the business and planning to migrate to Australia and would she go with him and make a new start? She had accepted his proposal, seeing it as the answer to her immediate problems, though certain she wasn't in love with him, that after loving Danny, she could never fall in love again.

It had been her young son that had kept her from going mad upon her arrival in Australia, Kevin's total dependence on her, forced her to keep going day after day. Fulfilling his everyday needs became her most positive link with reality, but also the care and concern of the elderly childless couple who'd lived next door. The following months and her expanding body making it obvious she was again "with child" – Malachi's child, forcing her to snap out of her depression and get on with life. That soon she would have another mouth to feed, another precious life dependent on her.

Her voice was determinedly strong and straight to the point when she replied, invoking no sympathy.

"Malachi died on the ship en route to Australia, Mr. Shaw. He had a massive heart attack and was gone in an instant. There was nothing anyone could do."

Mr. Shaw was clearly shocked, his face turned ashen. "Dear God, no... I had no idea!" he said, "But wasn't he a young man, Caeli? And was he aware that he had a bad heart?"

"Well, yes he was – young, that is. Twenty-nine years old – though quite a bit older than me. And no, there was no indication he had anything wrong with him whatsoever. He'd passed all the medicals required of him before being allowed to migrate to Australia. His only defect being his gammy leg – his left slightly shorter than his right due to him having polio as a child – for which he wore a built-up shoe. But I later discovered his father had died at a similar age of a heart attack too, hence his being raised by an elderly aunt – his mother having died giving birth to him. And apart from the limp, he appeared to be in excellent health.

"But it was the suddenness of his death that shocked me more than anything, Mr. Shaw, for he was gone in an instant and I found that incredibly hard to come to terms with.

"Laughing and playing with Kevin and me in the ship's pool one minute, dropping down dead on the deck but a few feet away the next. It happened so quickly, and ironically, just like Danny, he left us without saying good-bye and we buried him at sea."

Mr. Shaw seemed greatly distressed by the news. "Ah, my dear," he said, "how cruel life can be. But I swear before God I knew nothing of this. Dear God had I known, I might have been able to help..."

"It's uncanny, isn't it, Mr. Shaw?" Caeli continued, ignoring the belated and unwanted sympathy. "How certain events seem to repeat themselves in life? For not only has the sea become Danny's grave, but Malachi's grave as well, the final resting place of both my children's fathers. Yet I'd always had a tremendous love of the sea. I felt it was a part of me and in my blood – on account of being brought up at Liath Caislean I guess, and swimming and sailing on Raggemorne Bay was my greatest joy. But it's become my most dreaded enemy now, and I never go near it."

"Did you ever remarry?"

"No. I've never met anyone I wanted to marry."

"Then why did you struggle on in Australia all these years alone? Why didn't you come home to Liath Caislean – or at least home to Ireland?

She grimaced and shrugged her shoulders in her habitual manner and her answer was wry: "That's another story Mr. Shaw. One to write a book about one day…"

CHAPTER FOURTEEN

LOYALTIES

Mr. Shaw was filled with admiration for the woman before him. In awe of her strength and indomitable spirit, the spirit that had enabled her to surmount the enormous setbacks she had so obviously encountered in her young life and go on to achieve the success she so obviously had. He understood that it could not have been easy being a teenage widow with two babies to support in a foreign land alone. And his heart went out to her, wanting to protect her, to be on her side. Outraged at Zita O'Halloran for keeping her whereabouts from him and from everyone else all these years, and outraged at Bran too for his treatment of her and for what he still had in store for her and would have him do. How he wished he could end the farce then and be honest with her, now of the opinion Bran had carried his resentment towards her too far and that it should have been buried with him when he went to his grave. Yet outrage he should have saved for himself, for his own silence and for the part he had played in the whole sorry charade – and for the part he was yet to play.

He remained silent for what seemed a very long time, wrestling with his conscience and loyalties of his own. Loyalties he owed first and foremost to Bran Dromgoole and Monsignor Timothy O'Leary. The three of them, born within days of each other and inseparable friends... Life-long friends... *More* than friends... Brothers! Closer than brothers even, a brotherhood of choice, sealed with their blood and spittle when they were mere lads in the cave beneath Liath Caislean. Entering the cave when the tide was low and the small beach exposed, climbing the rocky face of the cliff to the only entrance they had then known. The adventure dangerous and strictly forbidden, for the tides ran fast and they could have been trapped – had been trapped, thus making the adventure all the more memorable.

"Here, put your fingers on this rock," Bran, their undisputed leader, had commanded, brandishing a big rusty knife and spurred on by "Dutch Courage," a swig of the strong fiery liquid they'd discovered at the back of cave and gone to their heads. Cases and cases of fine French Cognac stacked high and dry. "And we'll cut our fingers and mix our blood and be real blood-brothers!"

"By God we will," Timothy O'Leary agreed, showing signs of his holy vocation even then. And obediently they had placed their small index fingers alongside Bran's, neither Tim nor himself daring to shrink from the task or challenge their leader's direction, Bran slicing through them with one foul sweep.

"Quick now, spit!" he had further ordered, as their fresh young blood spurted warm and red. And they'd spat on the blood and rubbed their fingers together along with the unbidden tears that spurted hot and stinging from their eyes, uniting their bodily fluids as one.

"One for all and all for one!" they had then hollered, swigging again the priceless French Cognac and clashing their three wooden swords on high. Three little boys fired with the spirit and the exploits of their fictitious heroes, defending Ireland and honour and vowing to come galloping to each other's aid forever, no matter what! Unaware of the rising tide that had forced them to drunkenly stagger to the rear of the cave in fear of their lives; relieved to discover the steps that led up to a door, which in turn led into Bran's father's office in the base of the huge round tower above.

"One for all…! All for one…!" The far-distant echoes resounded in Mr. Shaw's memory, reminding him of the loyalty he was bonded to keep unto death. The boyhood pledge they had honoured in childhood and carried into manhood.

He would have liked to have warned her, to have told her to be gone from this land as fast as she could and return to the place from whence she had come, to flee like the wind from the crucible of pain he knew was in store for her, to save her from the truths of the long-held lies that were soon to be revealed in the cruellest possible way – poured at his own hand from Bran Dromgoole's cauldron of hate. For the innocent-sounding proviso to Bran's will, contained a double-edged sword designed to draw blood. That it really made no difference whether she went or whether she stayed, the outcome would be the same and she would be the loser either way. The

116

wheels of Bran's sick mind having set the plan in motion long before his passing and nothing on earth could stop it now.

A sixteen-year-old child Caeli had been, protected from the outside world behind the walls of Liath Caislean when Bran had so callously thrown her out, and out at the cruellest possible time. For not only was it the day of her young sister Meegan's funeral, but it was also the day her young lover, Daniel O'Halloran, was officially pronounced "Lost at Sea" and the search for him called off – the news awaiting them on their return to the mourning house.

Bran really lost it that day, wracked with pain and guilt over Meegan's tragic passing and venting his anger on Caeli; unfairly accusing her of not only being the cause of her young sister's death, but of Danny's death too and even the cause of her mother's tragic passing twelve months before.

How ignorant she was of the truth behind the wild accusations and of the way of life beyond the walls of Liath Caislean. And ignorant also (as they all had been) of the seed of Daniel's son growing within her womb.

Yet in spite of everything, she had survived. Indeed, she had more than survived. For if Zita O'Halloran was to be believed, she had built a substantial business empire for herself in Australia.

'Seven dress shops, would you believe!' Zita had said, 'And more on the drawing board... Done well for herself, that one,' unable to hide the malice in her voice.

Clearly Mr. Shaw could see Caeli's worth. See her bright intelligence staring almost impudently back at him. And he thought with regret what an asset she would be to Liath Caislean, that given time, she would have surely undone the damage that Bran's sick mind had so damnably wrought – brought low the estate and shamed the family name.

"I think we'd both benefit from a fresh pot of tea, my dear," he said kindly, as he reached for the phone.

"No, not for me thank you, Mr. Shaw."

She was beginning to relax, to let her guard down, to feel that the "dreaded demons" she had so far encountered were nowhere near as daunting as she had imagined they'd be, and with a new sense of security, she settled back into the surrounds of the chair and appreciatively cast her eyes about.

It was a magnificent room... A gentleman's room full of gentleman's things, reeking of old family money and fine malt whiskey and old tawny port. Its décor warm and inviting: rich red carpet, gleaming mahogany furniture, floor-to-ceiling bookcases filled with leather-bound books, and red-shaded lamps casting a rosy glow over all. The room remained precisely as Caeli remembered it, having visited there with Meegan and mother and father, on many occasions in the past.

"I've always loved this room, Mr. Shaw," she confided with a sigh and an encompassing sweep of her hand. "There's something about it I always found satisfying, though I suppose that sounds silly to you, but I've always thought of it as a very *satisfying* sort of room."

"Hmm, satisfying, you say," he said, rubbing his chin thoughtfully. "That's a rather profound observation my dear." Yet he looked pleased and followed her lead and cast his own eyes about and nodded approval at what he saw. "Yes, yes, I couldn't agree more," he said, harrumphing loudly to clear his throat. "Satisfying" describes it well.

"The decorators wanted me to change it, you know. 'Modernise it,' they said. 'Jazz it up with bright colours and bring it into the twentieth century' – the cheeky young buggers! But I would have none of it, for it suits my personality the way it is – old-fashioned like me! A lick of paint to freshen things up and new carpet and drapes much the same as the old, was as far as I'd let them go. Not like young James down the hall... Now there's a modern-day man if ever there was one. Gone in for that pale Scandinavian stuff – Baltic Pine, I think it's called. 'Contemporary,' says James. 'Insipid,' say I. Flash-in-the-pan sort of stuff that won't last five minutes! And God save us all – bright yellow walls – buttercup – bah! Give me good old-fashioned conservatism any day!"

Caeli laughed heartily at his passionate outburst. "Good for you!" she applauded. "And I'm so glad you did, for I'd have been devastated if I'd come here today and found it all changed, for it represents a significant part of my past."

He looked at her with eyebrows raised. "Oh?"

"Didn't you know that I was in awe of the place as a child? All those books reaching up to the ceiling made me feel terribly small, and I'd fancy myself Alice in Wonderland shrunken in size in some magical place. And if I remember correctly..." she said, pointing to a cupboard in a corner, "you had a stack of children's books in that cupboard over there, including *Alice in Wonderland* and my favourite *Milly Molly Mandy* books as well. And as I recall, there was also a box of tiddlywinks and snakes and ladders and a few other games besides, your ploy, no doubt, to keep us children amused while you grownups conducted business.

"Though I assure you, Mr. Shaw, Meegan and I were always on our best behaviour, for mother used to bribe us with tea at Clancy's afterwards, if we were good."

"Ah yes, good old Clancy's," he murmured reminiscently. "Pulled down years ago, I'm sad to say. But your father and I had some rollicking good times there when we were young. They used to have a dance there every Saturday night in the ballroom at the back with a fantastic band playing the latest hits. And there was a big mirrored ball hanging from the centre of its ceiling that flashed prisms of light all over us as we danced below. God it was good. It's a pity things have to change and we have to grow old – especially if we look back on our lives with regret?

"But its futile looking back and regretting what is done, isn't it my dear?" he said, looking at her meaningfully. "For what's done is done and we can't change a thing.

"Though I daresay in hindsight we'd have done things differently if permitted the teeniest peek into the future... been wiser than barn owls in hindsight."

Caeli cringed back into the chair, feeling he was having a non-too-subtle jibe at her, yet he prattled on innocently.

"And speaking for myself, Caeli... Your father's passing has left an enormous void in my life that I know I can never fill. There's not many of us older generation left now, and I assure you he'll be sadly missed."

Caeli made no comment, but her guard was up, for speaking of her father was the dreaded path she had no wish to take and the last place on earth she wanted to go. Yet logically, if she genuinely wished to lay the ghosts of her past to rest, there was no other path she could take.

Mr. Shaw observed the beautiful woman before him, her arms folded defensively across her chest and crouching back into the curve of the chair like a scolded child. For that's how he saw her now – as a child – an incredibly vulnerable and wounded child, the anguish of the situation clearly evident in her amazing violet eyes.

How he wished things were different, that he could wave a magic wand or work a miracle and slip back in time and change certain things: Influence Bran's warped sense of justice and his treatment of Caeli and make him see she was an innocent party in all of this and not the one to blame. But it was too late for such thoughts; for Bran was beyond his influence now and in the hands his Maker, and would never have heeded him anyway. Besides, the way Caeli was looking back at him, boldly defiant, daring him to say one more word in Bran's defence, he knew he'd be wasting his breath to even try.

CHAPTER FIFTEEN
DISCLOSURES

"Your father's funeral was very well attended, Caeli," Mr. Shaw said, as gently as he could, aware of the ill feeling still burning within her, yet determined to have his say. "Crowded, in fact, for he'd become quite a hero among the young folk of the county, though I have to admit I was more than surprised at the number of them that turned up. Realising later of course that it was on account of the halfway houses and the workshops your father had established on their behalf."

He sniffed and pulled a handkerchief from his pocket and wiped his nose, giving her time to absorb the information he'd deliberately cast before her and make some sort of comment. But when none was forthcoming, he stuffed the handkerchief back in his pocket and continued.

"And I made sure he got the send-off he requested, my dear. 'A wake to end all wakes' was what he wanted, with gallons of whiskey and stout and fiddlers playing 'til the crack of dawn, which I thought, under the circumstances, was quite appropriate. So, as you can imagine my dear, we had quite a shindig at Liath Caislean that night and there were more than a few sore heads the following morning, I can tell you!"

Still Caeli said nothing. Aware she was behaving like a total idiot, yet incapable of rising above it.

Mr. Shaw fingered his pen and examined the nondescript object minutely, as though it was a priceless treasure retrieved from some ancient Pharaoh's tomb that contained the secrets of the ages.

"You do know of your father's charitable works, Caeli?" he said at last, frowning at her sternly, "of his assistance to the homeless youth of the community?"

She shook her head miserably. "No, I don't... How could I... We never communicated..."

"Ah Caeli... Caeli... How sorry I am that you've been so unhappy. But twenty-two years is far too long to be holding grudges. Perhaps if you'd stayed a little longer before scampering away and talked to someone – even talked to me, we might have been able to sort something out.

"For I am the first to agree that your father was unjustly harsh on you and sold never have said the things he did. But in my opinion, it was mainly the fault of his unbalanced mind that made him say them to begin with, and there were many times – in his more lucid moments, he expressed his regret. So believe you me, my dear, he was nowhere as bad as you've made him out to be."

Caeli shrugged her shoulders and looked aggrieved, yet the novelty of her father doing charitable deeds urged her to speak, for charitable deeds had never been his scene. But her words were uncharacteristically mean and sarcastic and unbecoming to her.

"If Dada set up all those workshops and halfway houses you speak of, Mr. Shaw, then he really *must* have been crackers!"

"Now, now, Caeli, don't say things you might come to regret," he admonished, wagging his finger at her and again frowning sternly. "For it wasn't until he found Rory that his eyes were opened to the plight of other young lads in similar situations closer to home, and was horrified at the number of youth living on the streets with nowhere to go and no skills to speak of and virtually unemployable, and many fell by the wayside.

"Rory was a good influence on your father. You could even say he brought him back to life and made him take an interest in the world around him again, for since Josephine left, he was unbearably lonely. He missed her terribly you know, for she was all he had, for he always was a bit of a loner and never one for making friends.

"Yet surprisingly he seemed to get tremendous satisfaction out of Rory and helping the homeless youth, and was really chuffed when someone he'd helped achieved some small success and turned up at the house to thank him personally.

"I also believe his charitable deeds were his way of making amends for what happened to Daniel and Meegan all those years ago. Fortunately his good work will continue – as indeed it would be a pity if it did not. For there's an annuity you know – but more of that later."

"Who's Rory?" she asked.

The question pulled him up short. Taking it for granted she would know all about the lad, about her sister's extremely traumatised child she had given away at birth. Traumatised, not only because of the sudden death of the family who'd adopted him, but even more so because of his unalterable belief that it was he who had caused them to die. Nor would she be aware of how brutally the child had been treated in a dozen different foster homes since. Coming to realise then, that there must be many questions she would need answers to, many blanks to fill in to cover the gap of her many years abroad.

"Rory was your father's legal ward, Caeli," he bluntly informed her. "A seven-year-old discovered in an orphanage up in Ulster by the good Monsignor O'Leary – You remember the Mons – Timothy O'Leary?"

"Yes, yes, I remember the Mons," she said impatiently, not wanting to go there, suddenly feeling sick and shuddering inside at the mention of the Holy Father's name. Remembering him for all the wrong reasons – the vile old hypocrite's wandering hands, and of whom she had kept her distance and avoided being alone with like the plague.

"But *who* is 'Rory'?" she repeated, sounding quite agitated and putting great emphasis on the 'who' in her search for the truth. "Who is he?" she again asked. "And how come Dada took this particular child in? Surely he as family…"

They were calm and incredibly trustworthy eyes that returned her stare. "Yes, Caeli," he answered evenly, "Rory does indeed have family, but as yet they are as unaware of his existence as he is of theirs. The child believes he's alone in the world and that your father was his Guardian Angel sent straight from heaven to rescue him and deliver him to Molly and to Liath Caislean. But to cut a long story short, he was an unwanted infant, put up for adoption as a newborn seven years ago. His mother an unmarried teenager, his father, the lass flatly refused to name."

"But why Dada…" Caeli persisted. "What connection is he to Dada?" Yet her intuition telling her she already knew.

"Because my dear," Mr. Shaw replied, confirming her instinct, "the name of that mother was none other than Josephine Dromgoole – your sister."

"Josie's child…!" she gasped, visibly shocked, even though the thought had crossed her mind. "Are you telling me that this Rory you speak of is my sister's child and therefore Dada's grandson?"

He could not help but smile at Caeli's gaping mouth and stunned-mullet expression. "Precisely, my dear, and also your nephew I might add."

"But didn't you just say he was put up for adoption? Where are his adoptive parents then?

"Killed in a car crash, I'm sorry to say. But thanks to your father and the good Monsignor, Rory is safely returned to the home of his forebears at last. So you see, my dear, your father wasn't altogether the hard-hearted ogre you've made him out to be."

Huh! That'll be the day, she thought, that he would always be the hard-hearted ogre to her, regardless of Mr. Shaw's efforts to slather him in whitewash and present him as Saint Bran Almighty! But she held her tongue, the bitterness she felt for him unchanged in her mind and her heart. Reluctantly recalling the big dark man who'd stood six feet four in his socks and never cast one kind word her way nor shown her the slightest affection since the day she was born. And little more had he shown sweet fragile Meegan either, her innocent retarded little sister who'd craved his affection even more than she, affection he'd so openly lavished on Josie.

"And his grave, Mr. Shaw…?" she asked, brazenly raising her face and willing back tears. "I take it he's buried with mother?"

"Oh yes, my dear, he is at that. That was also Bran's wish. They rest side by side 'neath the old copper beech in the graveyard, together once more," adding hastily, "As I'm sure that would have been your mother's wish too."

A far-away look entered his eyes as other-time memories drew him back, and his voice was full of yearning when he spoke again.

"What a beauty she was, Caeli – your mother, I mean. Broke many a heart…"

She could see he was lost to a time long ago, the past rolling over him like a mist in the valley, leaning back in his chair, his eyes locked on some faraway vision that was not hers to see. An old man absorbed in his young-man's dreams and mesmerised by the beauty of what he saw. Oblivious to her presence and his surroundings now, even when she reached for his cup and clattered it loudly on its saucer to regain his attention, and for one glorious moment his face seemed to shine, to shed its lines of age, permitting her to glimpse him young and vibrant and throbbing with life as he once had been.

"And that fine black stallion of hers… A magnificent creature, though I'm blessed if I can recall his name?"

"Starfire," she offered eagerly.

"Yes, that was it! Starfire – the bold black beauty! Arabian blood, I believe, though regrettably, my knowledge of the animals is miserably nought. But your mother's surely was not. It was she who brought horses to Liath Caislean from her parents stud in County Kildare, you know. And she bred many a champion in her day.

"I can still see her now, flying across the fields as though she and that horse were one. What a magnificent sight to behold: The black of the stallion, the copper of her hair sparkling like fire in the sun and the green of her habit. For green was her colour and enhanced her bewitching green eyes that were flashing like emeralds from the thrill of it all!"

He was on fire himself and his colour was high, his words clearly daubing the image of what her mother had been on the palette of her mind with the skill of a fine-artist's brush, that it came as a shock for her to realise that Mr. Shaw had been in love with her mother too, that his was one of the hearts he had claimed she had broken.

"It sounds as though you were an admirer of hers, Mr. Shaw," she said gently.

"Admirer…? Course I was! Me and half the lads of the county! For back then she was the prettiest colleen in the whole of Ireland with the voice of an angel! For there was something about her that made her standout from the crowd – apart from her singing I mean. Something that drew you in and bowled you over without her even knowing, for I'd swear to God, Caeli, she had not the slightest idea of the hold she had over us. We were like putty in her hands or moths drawn to a candle… And talk about fun…" for there was no stopping him now, "As God is my witness she was so full of fun that she literally sparkled with it.

"I even courted her once, you know, and believed I had won her heart, for she actually agreed to marry me would you believe. Back in the December of 1940 it was and she fresh back from London – for she sang for the British servicemen there. I proposed to her again when I picked her up from the ferry, and to my amazement, she said yes. I was over the moon, as you can imagine, and couldn't believe my luck, for I'd asked her a dozen times before and she'd turned me down every time.

"But it must have been the shortest engagement on record, for she broke it off the very next day when I took her to Liath Caislean and introduced her to Bran. For something seemed to click inside her at the sight of your father, for she set her cap for him right from the start and I knew then and there I was history."

Caeli was enthralled with what she was hearing, not wanting him to stop, her very silence urging him on, willing him to weave the magic that opened the doors to that world of long ago that belonged to him and her mother and father that she could not enter, only glimpse for a few stolen moments through the eloquence of Mr. Shaw's words. A world struck of innocence, of golden days when they were all young and in their prime and bonded together triumphant in their youth.

They were the cream of the land back then, the well-heeled Irish, cocksure and fancy-free with their college degrees and country estates. They had it all, far removed from the troubles of Ireland's past. Their futures stretching before them like a fantasy yellow-brick road that led to their very own castle of dreams, and they were foolish enough to believe it would go on forever.

"And her voice, Caeli... The sweetest sound I ever heard... 'The Songbird of Ireland' she was known as back then with the world at her feet. But she married Bran..." he added glumly, as though suggesting that had been the end of everything. "But did I ever tell you that she once sang *Danny Boy* just for me?"

"Really...? No, never..."

"Well she did! She even substituted Eugene for Danny, 'O Eugene boy' she sang. It brought tears to my eyes and tears to hers too, I can tell you.

"It was the very same night I'd taken her to Liath Caislean to meet Bran. She wasn't her old self at all at the time. Something had sapped her sparkle and filled her with melancholy – which I at the time put down to her being in London with all those bombs exploding and people getting killed all over the place. It was a bad time in all of our lives and I knew it had affected her deeply. She even mentioned to me how sorry she felt for the young British pilots in particular, never knowing if she would see them again, flying out over the Channel and few coming back... For so many didn't return...

"Ah, but again I digress… Back to her singing that beautiful song just for me…

"The acoustics in Turlough's Great Hall are amazing, Caeli, as you'll no doubt agree. Your mother's voice rang out as clear as a bell with the heart-wrenching words that you'd swear had been written only for her. We were all deeply moved, Bran more so than any of us. He couldn't take his eyes off her and proposed to her that very same night! And muggins me, the idiot who took her there and introduced them! But not long after that I met my darling Jessie…

"Hah! But enough of my reminiscing now," he snapped, as though he was suddenly embarrassed and annoyed with himself, remembering who he was and where he was and why he was there. Breaking the spell he had woven like snapping a dry old sally reed in two. "You'll be thinking me a sentimental old fool," he said. The change in him awesome, leaving no room to protest, to beg him to continue, to plead that she wanted to hear more. The warm blue eyes chisel cold now and his lawyer's tongue as sharp as a blade as he formally addressed her.

"Mrs. Morgan," he said, harrumphing again, "it is time we got down to business. We've digressed long enough."

He reached for a file to one side of his desk, then abruptly changed his mind and withdrew his hand. "Wait now," he said, rising to his feet. "First things first, for there's one other thing I'm obliged to do before we get down to the nitty-gritty of your father's will."

Her eyes followed him curiously as he went to a safe concealed behind a painting on the wall behind his desk, her gaze intent upon him, never leaving him for one single moment as he spun its dial and opened its door and extracted a buff-coloured envelope from within, noting his hands were trembling as he placed it on the desk before him, suddenly appearing so terribly old and unsure of himself.

"Caeli, my dear," he began, his voice quivering with emotion now. "I'm sure I have no need to remind you that our families have been friends for a very long time. Generations in fact… And in view of this long-standing relationship between us, I feel I can speak to you freely, purely as a friend – that is if you still consider me as such?"

"But of course I do, Mr. Shaw."

Still he hesitated, turning the envelope this way and that as if playing for time, time to reconsider perhaps, to return it to the safe

127

or to find the right words, the diplomatic turn of phrase that would not raise her ire? False words, part of the plan words, designed to bring this young woman back into the fold – where he now genuinely believed she should be, regardless of the other words soon to be said that would drive her even further away.

"About your father, my dear," he said gently. "Would it help if I were to tell you that he loved you very much and that he deeply regretted…"

"Don't! Mr. Shaw! Don't!" she protested angrily. "Don't patronise me with anymore of your Irish blather! I don't need you to be telling me how my father felt about me! I lived with his hatred every minute of every day I lived under his roof!"

He was taken aback at her reaction, shocked at the depth of her anger and the obvious hatred of her own, pushing his hands out before him as though he would stem its flow.

"Caeli," he said harshly, bristling in a rare show of anger himself, "at least have the courtesy to hear me out!

"God Almighty, girl, do you honestly believe that you were the only one to suffer – the only one to have pain and regret? Your father was no living saint by any anyone's rule of measure, but then none of us are – yourself included! He was all too aware of the pain and the suffering he had caused you, believe you me! But he didn't altogether get off scot-free, as you seem to think he did! He suffered too, and suffered too much if you ask me! Paid with loneliness and the sickness ever growing in his head until the day he died."

Mr. Shaw struggled to gather his self-control about him, aware he was overstepping the mark, the client/lawyer mark and taking liberty of old friendship. Chastising this woman before him as though she was the child he had known in that time of long ago and not the mature client about to inherit a fortune – if she had the fortitude to take it on that was, and he moderated his tone to a condescending plea.

"Your father… He wasn't a bad man, Caeli, just an ordinary human being with the faults and failings that scourge us all, and it couldn't have been easy for him when Maureen died, raising you girls alone. And believe you me my dear, it clear broke his heart when young Meegan drowned and Daniel was lost in the sea. I think he felt especially bad about Daniel because they had argued and he'd wanted to apologise. He had no wish to harm the lad Caeli, let alone be the instrument of his death, for he positively adored him.

128

As for his reasons for not wanting you two to wed? I really cannot comment on that. Perhaps he was being the overprotective father with only your interests at heart – as surely to God you will have to agree we parents tend to be when we believe our offspring are at risk? In my opinion, he did just that – overreacted. Sadly, my dear, you know the rest – know how it all ended so horribly wrong."

Caeli could not comment, for Mr. Shaw's words had lashed at her conscience and torn open old wounds, and again she crouched back into the curve of the chair as she had done before, and again she folded her arms defensively across her chest.

He was aware of her anguish, yet made no apology for what he had said, but patiently awaited her comment. But when again she remained broodingly silent and he realised none was forthcoming, he continued more gently.

"Your father entrusted this letter to my safekeeping several months ago when his health was obviously failing and his end was near, with the expressed wish that I hand it to you personally one day."

He eased himself out of his chair with apparent difficulty now, betraying the cruelness of the years and the pain in his joints as he slowly advanced towards her. And her heart went out to this dear old family friend who had ridden the highs and lows of life with her father, and remained unfalteringly loyal to him to the end.

"Caeli, my dear…" he said, standing before her, "By passing this letter to you, I fulfil my promise to my dearest friend in the whole wide world – your father Bran Dromgoole, with the expressed wish that I tell you, his daughter, that it comes from his heart with his undying love."

He held the letter out to her, yet all she could do was stare at it blindly through tear-filled eyes, her voice an unrecognisable rasp when she spoke.

"Why now, Mr. Shaw… Why tell me this now when he's dead and gone and it's all too late? Why tell me this now as if I should care, when the truth of the matter is that he hated the very sight of me! Why tell me this now, when never once in the twenty-two years since he'd cast me from his house did he try to contact me and tell me that himself! Never once did he drop me a line to even enquire if my children and I were alright! Why tell me this now, Mr. Shaw?"

He drew back aghast, shocked at the depth of her feelings and the hysteria riding her voice. "Ah, but you are quite incorrect there, my dear. Your father *did* write. I assure you he did. I remember the occasion distinctly."

"Well, I never received any letter! – And *I* remember *that* distinctly too!"

"Well, I can only assure you again that he did – though now that I come to think of it, I do seem to recall the letter coming back and your father being very upset about it at the time. 'Return to Sender' stamped across its envelope in that bold black post-office print. He'd sent it to some business establishment here in Dublin – Priory Lane, if I remember correctly, having received an anonymous tip-off in the form of a note that you were there and to later discover it was Malachi Morgan's address. I remember Bran brought the note here to this office to discuss it with me. I questioned its authenticity, suspecting it was yet another of the many cruel hoaxes he'd been receiving – *and* continued to receive to the end. But your father was of the opinion that he at least had to try regardless, so he sent the letter again. But when it was returned the second time, he concluded you were either no longer there or that you wanted nothing more to do with him. But I know he lived in hope that you'd find it in your heart to forgive him one day and that perhaps he would hear from you. But of course the years slipped by and he never did."

Her father had written? Had actually put pen to paper to contact her? Could Mr. Shaw possibly be right and she so terribly wrong, that she had misjudged her father all these years? She thought not. Yet the thought had disturbed her, the seed of doubt sown that put a whole new perspective on things – especially as it was to Malachi's place of business that the letter had gone. If that was the case, then why hadn't she received it? Suspicions of gentle Malachi Morgan entered her mind, to be instantly dismissed.

Tenderly, Mr. Shaw placed a hand on Caeli's shoulder; genuinely caring for her and regretful of the treachery Bran's instructions from the grave still required him to do. "Here, take the letter, my dear," he urged, "It may reveal some of the answers you are seeking. Tuck it into your bag if you can't bring yourself to read it now, for I know the day will come when you will."

Caeli stared at the envelope that this dear old family friend held out to her, subconsciously noting the buff of its paper and the black of its ink. *To Caeli, Acushla* it read in the unmistakable scrawl of her father's bold hand. How she wanted to believe he had written to her and attempted reconciliation, but the notion felt false and did not ring true. Yet she took the envelope from Mr. Shaw's hand regardless, and clasped it tightly to her bosom for several long moments before tucking it deep in the folds of her bag.

"Bless you, my child," Mr. Shaw said, by way of benediction.

CHAPTER SIXTEEN
REUNION

A light tap on the door and its immediate opening startled them both back to the present, glancing guiltily towards it as though they had been caught in some clandestine liaison. A round cheery woman breezed in pushing a tea-trolley laden with food, a very attractive, middle-aged man, following closely in her wake.

Caeli dabbed her eyes and arranged a semblance of a smile on her face, for although she'd not seen him in twenty-two years, she recognised Liam instantly.

"Ah... 'Tis Peggy with lunch," Mr. Shaw said, eagerly rubbing his hands together, "And Liam my boy," obviously relieved at the timely intervention.

"We thought you might welcome some nourishment now," Peggy retorted, with the familiarity of the long employed. "For 'tis half-starved you must be, being locked up in this room for more than two hours!"

"Well, if they're not, they jolly well ought to be!" Liam interjected good-naturedly, backing Peggy up, observing, yet not commenting, on Caeli's emotional disarray, "What with all the shenanigans we've heard going on in here!"

"Oh ay, Mr. Liam, they should and all!" Peggy chuckled, trundling the trolley to the side of the desk where Caeli sat. And if she too noticed Caeli's red eyes or ruffled state, she also made no comment but tactfully focussed her remarks on the menfolk: "So get that lot into you now" she ordered, with the intimacy bred of a long and happy association.

"Right Ho! The men responded affably, giving Peggy a rigorous salute. Peggy chortled, obviously satisfied, and gathered the tea things and trundled herself out.

"You remember Liam, Caeli?" Mr. Shaw unnecessarily asked as the door closed on Peggy.

"But of course I do. We were the best of friends and we spoke on the phone just a few days ago. And I believe I have Liam to thank for the beautiful flowers delivered to my hotel room this morning?" Turning to Liam with a million questions in her eyes, she proffered her hand, aware she had no choice but to raise her tear-swollen eyes to his. Warm, brown, melting sort of eyes fringed with coppery lashes searched deeply into hers with a million questions of their own, eyes that seemed to melt all over her and soothe her unease and convince her that she had been right after all to come.

She was completely beguiled by the man he had ripened to be. Everything about him seemed comfortable and pleasing to her eye, from his beautiful kind mouth stretched wide in a welcoming grin, to the lock of chestnut-brown hair that dangled on his forehead, begging to be stroked back into place. Even his casual attire: brown brogues, open-necked shirt and tweed jacket, spelt ease of manner – far removed from the awkward, unsophisticated youth of her memory forever dressed in shabby dungarees.

How he excited her. How the breath seemed to leave her body when he pulled her up into his arms, and for one overwhelming moment she thought he was about to kiss her on the mouth. But he took her hand instead and tenderly pressed it to his lips.
How the action unhinged her, something inside her seeming to come undone and ripple through her. Never before had a man had such an immediate knee-buckling effect on her – not even Danny! Her legs began to wobble, leaving her no choice but to cling to him as one breathless word gushed from her lips – "Liam!" Aware he was looking at her intently, feeling naked and vulnerable beneath his gaze.

"'Tis wonderful to see you again, my Caz" he whispered close to her ear, using the possessive "my" and the nickname he alone used to call her. The aroma of his aftershave invaded her senses, remindful of wild woodland ferns and cool rippling streams. "Sure I'd almost given up hope of seeing your lovely self again," he added, holding her at arm's length. "But by God you look sensational, girl!"

"So do you," she murmured, aware she was blushing and clumsily extricating herself from his embrace and groping blindly behind her for the arm of the chair, while wanting to stay in his arms forever.

Liam's colour was high too, and he was looking exceedingly pleased with himself. Aware of the effect he was having on her, and of the effect she was having on him. And he smiled a smile meant only for her, a triumphant sort of smile that promised a wealth of untold delights.

"Has Dad been taking care of you, Caz?" he asked, in a voice turned all husky. "Or is it filling your heart with sadness, he is? For I'd swear I saw tears in your gorgeous eyes when I entered the room?"

"Heavens no...!" she retorted too brightly, glancing at his father, "Uncle Eugene has been an absolute darling and kindness itself!"

"Well, I'm pleased to hear it, for I'd swear you were looking quite down in the mouth when I came through the door, and I blamed dear old dad for it." And turning to his father he pointedly said, "For now that we have her back here in Ireland, we don't want her running away again. Do we Dad?"

Mr. Shaw protested, saying that the passing of a loved one was never a joyful occasion. "But I give you my word that from here on in I'll bring nothing but smiles to her face.

"Now who's for one of Peggy's sandwiches?" he digressed, happy to change the subject and eagerly rubbing his hands together again. "I take it you're joining us, Liam?"

"I'd be delighted to," Liam replied, thinking there was no way on earth he was going to leave. "That's if Caz has no objection?" Yet he pulled up a chair beside her regardless. "Anyway, objection or not, I think I had better, for I distinctly heard the sergeant major order us to eat every bit!" And without further ado, he reached for a plate.

"Well, I'll certainly do my bit," Caeli announced, matching his frivolous mood. "We mustn't disobey orders now, must we? Besides, I'm so ravenous I could eat a horse!"

"You possibly will be," Liam retaliated. "Horse sandwiches with lashings of horseradish sauce, are Peggy's speciality. Yum!" he said, Licking his lips and rolling his eyes and making all three of them laugh.

Hungrily they devoured the simple yet succulent fare; slices of warm roast beef, horseradish sauce and crusty slabs of homemade bread washed down with more tea. Three old friends renewing old friendship and tossing old memories about, pandering to each other's need, playing the game of "remember when."

It was only the good times they wanted to hear, the happiest of moments brought back to mind that had bonded their families in friendship for generations past. Caeli coming to realise then, how deeply the breakdown of her family had affected their lives too, almost as much as her own. That perhaps Mr. Shaw had been right when he'd said she had been too hasty in turning her back on her family and friends. For it was only now that she was back on Irish soil she was coming to realise how much she had missed these warm friendly people, sharing memories that only the closeness of family and time-honoured friendship allowed.

A sense of belonging, of coming-home, came over her then, wrapping its arms around her like a warm Claddagh Shawl and thawing the fingers of cold that had clutched at her heart too long.

How could she explain this onrush of feelings born of the old to her daughter? How could she explain this onrush of love for these people and this land she had scorned for so long? Yet she somehow perceived that Liz already knew and had even anticipated it. Hearing her daughter's wise words resounding like a clarion call through her mind: *Find the good memories, Mum... They're the ones to hold onto and cherish...*

But would Liz understand the utterly overwhelming attraction she was feeling for this man, Liam Shaw, the tongue-tied youth of her memory she had barely spared a thought for in more than twenty years, who'd matured to the deliciously drop-dead gorgeous man she could hardly keep her eyes off today? Would Liz understand why her normally sensible and down-to-earth mother had flown halfway round the world on the strength of a whim – lured by something she thought she had read into Liam's words on the phone – '*Dare I believe that I've found you at last...? Been searching for you forever...*' and not on account of her level-headedness at all?

"How is Chester these days, Mr. Shaw?" Caeli courteously enquired, referring to Mr. Shaw's eldest son. "I suppose he's an old married man by now with half a dozen children of his own?"

"Seven, actually, my dear," he beamed, obviously pleased at her interest, for she'd touched on a subject dear to his heart. "And beautiful children they are – even though I say so myself!

"My Chester was lucky," he continued, needing no prompting. "He married the girl of his dreams, Mary Bourke from Carrick. But you'd know Mary… Wasn't she an old school chum of yours?"

"Mary Bourke! God yes! We were the best of friends at the Sisters of Mercy – though Mary used to say there was nothing merciful about them. 'The Unmerciful Mercy's' she used to call them – not that she was anymore merciful herself! A holy terror Mary was, forever skylarking and getting in trouble… She put the poor nuns through such hell that I almost felt sorry for *them*!"

Mr. Shaw guffawed heartily and slapped his knees in delight.

"That sounds like our Mary all right. And she's still full of devilment. Never a dull moment with Mary around! Ah, but she's a grand girl into the bargain Caeli, and a wonderful mother to the children. She does us all proud and makes my son happy. What more could I ask for? It's a marriage made in heaven if ever there was one. Would you not agree, Liam?"

Liam had been listening in silence, a look of sheer indulgence on his face, obvious he adored his father and quick to patronise. "Oh I would, Dad, indeed I would. They're as happy as larks all right!"

"And its seven beautiful grandchildren they've given me, *seven!*" Mr Shaw reiterated, "And every last one of them as smart as a lick!"

Caeli could see the pride in his eyes and hear it in his voice, only too eager to talk about those nearest and dearest to his heart.

"Seven! Holy Dooley," Caeli exclaimed, genuinely impressed. "But how on earth did such a little thing like Mary manage to bring seven children into the world, for we used to call her Midget Mary at school?"

He threw back his head and roared with glee. "Is that a fact now? She never told me that. But according to Mary, birthing a child is as easy as an apple falling from a tree – when the fruit is ripe, it will fall!"

"So tell me about them, Mr. Shaw," she encouraged, being a little patronising herself. "How many are girls and how many are boys and what are their names and their ages?"

"Well, Patricia is the eldest," he began, delighted to oblige. "All of nineteen she is, and the prettiest colleen you could ever lay eyes on in all your born days. Then come three boys, Eugene – named after yours truly," beaming and pointing to himself. "Then Pascal and Patrick and two more girls, Kathleen and Mary, and last of all, though by no means least, young Toby, who is six – or is it seven he is, Liam?"

Liam raised his hands and shrugged his shoulders helplessly.

"Lord, Dad, you've got me there. I leave all that technical stuff to you. You're the doting grandfather who spoils them all rotten! Though I seem to recall Toby was seven last month."

"Well then, Caeli," Mr. Shaw continued, giving her an impish wink, "as I was saying, Toby is seven. But Lord, don't ask me how old all the others are… I have difficulty remembering now. But the way I see it, if I can get Patricia and Toby's ages right, I'm home and hosed, for all the others fit somewhere in between roughly two years apart. And I've never been known to forget a birthday yet!"

"That's because the little blighters always remind you!" Liam cut in good-naturedly. "Those cheeky rascals have never been backward in coming forward when presents are at stake!"

Mr. Shaw guffawed again at what he knew to be absolutely true.

Caeli realised she was looking at a happy man, a man in his twilight years with a loving family around him, content with the blessings life had brought, and was therefore surprised to find her thoughts straying to her father and comparing his life to that of Eugene Shaw's. How empty and lonely it must have been without mother and Meegan and herself, she thought, and then having Josie's sudden disappearance to contend with too, that before the child Rory had come into his life, he'd had no one.

Glancing now at Liam, assuming all along he was a bachelor, the ghastly thought occurred to her then that perhaps he was not. That perhaps he also had a beloved little wife and seven adorable children tucked away in some haven of bliss? That perhaps she'd got carried away and read something into his words on the phone that was simply wasn't there, but a desire of her own imagining. Almost too afraid to ask, dreading what the answer might be.

"And what about your other son, Liam here, Mr. Shaw… How many grandchildren has he given you?" to be overwhelmingly relieved at his reply.

"Ah, bless my soul Caeli, Liam's not married. He's altogether too slow to catch a cold let alone to catch himself a wife! Though he assures me he'd love to get married one day – when the right colleen comes along…"

"Thank you, Dad," Liam cut in. "I'm quite capable of speaking for myself... But yes, Caeli, Dad is right; I *have* been waiting for the right colleen."

For several long moments he said nothing more, giving the impression he had said all he was going to say on the matter. Then, with a thousand questions hovering in his soft brown eyes, he again looked searchingly into hers, and in little more than a whisper, said.

"I found her once you know Caz; a long time ago when we were young, but regrettably she was infatuated with another and foolishly I let her slip away."

Instinctively, she knew he was speaking of her, of the time when Danny had come to Liath Caislean and she had been so besotted by him that she'd had no time for Liam Shaw anymore. With her heart thumping wildly in her chest and something turning cartwheels in the pit if her stomach, she whispered back.

"Then I hope you find her again... But be bold when you do and tell her how you feel, lest she slip away from you again."

Liam clasped her hand gratefully, understanding her double-edged words and their underlying meaning, and for one glorious moment they were lost to each other, as though they were the only two people to remain on the face of the earth. The moment shattered, by the intrusion of Mr. Shaw harrumphing again, deliberately drawing their attention.

It was meant to sound gruff and remind them of where they were and that business was the essential. Yet his following words fell paternally embracing upon them, realising what he had long suspected, that after all these years Liam was still in love with Caeli. That Caeli was the one he'd been waiting for, the colleen of his dreams...

"Now my dears," he said brusquely, yet not unkindly. "Time's a-galloping away and we really must get down to business. You will have to excuse us, Liam. There'll be time enough later for you two young ones to do your catching up."

"Yes, of course, Sir," Liam responded respectfully, rising immediately to his feet. "Dad – Caeli – I'll take my leave of you then."

Yet on reaching the door, he spun on his heel and without saying a word, returned to Caeli's side. And again, in that utterly unhinging gesture he had made before, he again took her hand and

138

pressed it to his lips. "'Til later then, my beautiful Caz," he whispered, "'til later..." and before she had time to recover her senses, he was gone and the room and her heart overflowing with emptiness.

CHAPTER SEVENTEEN

THE WILL

Alone again, Mr. Shaw resumed control. Gone was the proud family man, the sentimental old friend in lawyer's guise wallowing in memories of days gone by. Here was her lawyer, the head of the legendary firm of Dublin lawyers, the esteemed Eugene Shaw & Sons, the best lawyers in the land who'd represented her family since the year dot, briskly efficient and as smart as a whip. Again he reached for the pertinent file containing her father's Last Will and Testament, a sure, positive action this time, devoid of quivering hand or feeble hesitation. The file that held in its substance the power to up-end her world, which in turn would surprise, dumbfound and cause her to rethink her lofty ideal of accepting nothing at all from her father's estate.

Presuming there was little to receive anyway. Recalling Mr. Shaw having said that Liath Caislean had been "sadly neglected," equating that to mean "falling to rack and ruin." Reaffirming her belief – at least for the moment, that whatever there was should be left to her young sister Josie.

The moment now upon her when, for the first time in twenty-two years, she would be forced to listen to her father's words deciding the fate of his worldly possessions, albeit through the friendlier and more eloquent tones of Shaw's tongue.

"Your father's will is very straightforward, Caeli," the curt business voice cut into her thoughts. "Though all the legal jargon might make it sound complicated, I assure you it is not. But please, my dear, if any point is unclear, don't hesitate to intervene."

She nodded without making comment.

The preamble was brief and the body of the will soon read. Caeli listened in silence, becoming more and more astounded as its content unfurled.

To begin with there were several bequests to old friends and faithful employees who had served the Dromgoole family well at various times throughout her father's life. Molly Joyce (widow), who had worked and lived with the family for forty years, was the first to be mentioned, bequeathed a generous pension upon her retirement, plus a comfortable cottage on the estate within walking distance of the main house – at her disposal whenever she chose to move into it. There were also substantial annuities for several halfway houses and training centres for homeless youth in various parts of the country, founded by her father.

At the mention of this, Caeli could not hold her tongue.

"Really," she said, raising her eyebrows, notably surprised at her father's unexpected benevolence.

Then her sister, Josephine Dromgoole, was mentioned, bequeathed the family house in Dublin that had seen many family gatherings there, plus a generous sum of money and a portfolio of stocks and bonds in several blue-chip companies.

"But what about Liath Caislean, Mr. Shaw," Caeli again intervened, when no mention of it had been made.

Mr. Shaw raised his hand to silence her. "And to each of my grandchildren living at the time of my death, I bequeath One Hundred Thousand Pounds, to be held in trust until their respective twenty-first birthdays."

Here Caeli gasped at the sum and sought qualification, "One Hundred Thousand Pounds! – To each of them? I'm staggered Mr. Shaw. Does that include Rory?"

His blue Irish eyes stared deeply into hers, his forefinger poised on the relevant spot. "But of course, my dear. Why shouldn't it? For he is a Dromgoole, I assure you of that. I checked him out personally." Then turning back to the will, he continued to read in his dauntingly professional mien.

But it was the words he said next that rendered Caeli speechless, the very last words she had expected to hear. Words that sent her head in a spin and her pulses racing – that the bulk of the estate, consisting of numerous commercial properties throughout Ireland and several prominent ones right there in the heart of Dublin she hadn't even known her father had owned, plus a significant amount of cash and a portfolio of blue-chip investments similar to the ones Josie had inherited, were bequeathed to her!

She gasped with shock and leant forward in the chair, her jaw gaping open. But still there was more.

The supreme prize – the jewel in the crown of the Dromgoole legacy – the family home Liath Caislean and its ten thousand acres of rich grazing lands and all the buildings and chattels therein, had also been left to her!

"As you can see, Caeli," Mr. Shaw continued blandly, showing no sign of amusement at her stupefied gaze, "your father was no fool – as many liked to believe – especially in his latter years. Where business was concerned, he was always clear-minded – remarkably so.

However, the inheritance is not all cut and dried… There is a proviso…"

Wouldn't you know it? Caeli thought wryly, typical of Dada. Where Dada was concerned – at least in relation to matters concerning herself, there had to be a catch. A give-a-thing-take-it-back stipulation to run the smell of the riches under her nose before snatching them away!

Yet when Mr. Shaw revealed its content, it was not an especially daunting one. Indeed, it seemed remarkably mild to the point of being ludicrous, it merely required she reside at Liath Caislean permanently – permanently defined as ten months out of every year.

Her thoughts were in turmoil, unprepared for such an outcome and wondering what had been going on in her father's head to have left the bulk of his astonishingly affluent estate to her instead of to Josie? Her ideal of accepting nothing from him – assuming there was little to accept anyway, was now shot to pieces with wealth beyond imagining dangled like a carrot under her nose. It was a different ball game now with different rules that changed everything. Indeed, she was now asking herself if she had the right to refuse.

Her voice trembled when at last she spoke, but her question was straight to the point, speaking the thought foremost in her mind.

"But why did Dada leave the bulk of his estate to me, Mr. Shaw, and not to Josie? I am really confused, for quite frankly I expected to receive nothing from him at all. Neither did I expect there would be so much! Unaware he was so wealthy, and of a mind that whatever there was should be left to Josie.

"Yet I've always been aware that we Dromgooles were better off than any of the folk around us and that we lived in the biggest house and owned lots of land and had lots of people working for us. Beyond that, I just took everything for granted. It wasn't until I was forced to leave home and fend for myself and see how the other half lived that I began to appreciate how much we had." Adding, with a cynical twist of her mouth, "It certainly proved the old adage true – that one doesn't appreciate what one has until one no longer has it – or something like that."

She was gabbling on about irrelevant things and she knew it, unable to stop herself, scarcely pausing for breath. The shock of the inheritance sending waves of adrenalin pumping through her that made it impossible to contain her thoughts or hold her runaway tongue in check.

"But I can honestly say we girls never wanted for anything at Liath Caislean, Mr. Shaw," she went on, "at least not material things. And as I recall, we had some pretty important people staying at the house when mother was alive. Eamon De Valera the one I remember the most – as if I could ever forget, for Molly referred to the room that he slept in, as 'The De Valera Suite' forevermore. Even so, I can't pretend I'm not flabbergasted at the wealth of the estate, especially in light of your earlier implication that Liath Caislean was practically falling to wrack and ruin."

He chuckled wickedly. "Was that the impression I gave? I never meant to imply anything as drastic as that, only that it was looking a bit old and tired, a bit like myself you could say, and badly in need of a facelift! For your father could be a niggardly old article at times, reluctant to spend a farthing on the place either inside or out since your mother died, and we often had words. Though I've come to believe that the truth of the matter was that he was clinging to the past, attempting to preserve things just as they were when your mother was alive, and keep the old dream alive."

"So are you saying then that nothing's been done to the place in twenty-odd years?"

"Oh, I wouldn't go so far as to say *that*, Caeli... *Some* work's been done. A bit of plumbing... Electrical wiring... Repairs to the roof... And a few years back, he even had one of those newfangled stoves that work on bottled gas installed for Molly, whom, I might add, flatly refused to use it – for Molly can be every bit as stubborn as your father was when it comes to change. She dug her heels in good and proper. Said it was a dangerous thing that hissed at her like an ally-cat and was liable to blow up in her face at any old tick of the clock! And as far as I know, she's of the same mind to this day and continues to use the old one."

How accurately Mr. Shaw had summed Molly up and brought the image of the beloved old housekeeper so clearly to Caeli's mind, wholeheartedly agreeing with him that Molly had never liked change and stubbornly clung to the tried-and-true.

"But tell me, Mr. Shaw," she asked him again, repeating the question she had asked him just two minutes before. "How come Dada left the bulk of his estate to me, when I honestly believed he would have left it to Josie? Why me? I thought he would leave it to the Cat's Home in Cork before he'd ever leave it to me – he hated me so much!"

"Oh no, Caeli," Mr. Shaw protested, "Don't say such things, for I'm sure they're not true. I know he was never one for kind words or baring his feelings, but I'm certain that in his own way he loved you very much. Why, it was only a matter of weeks ago that he told me how bad he felt for not bringing you girls much happiness – especially you, Caeli, and how deeply he regretted what happened to Daniel all those years ago.

"As to the wealth of the estate… That comes as no surprise to me. Your family's been wealthy for centuries, thanks, I believe, to your ancestor Turlough and his trade in French Brandy – illicit as it may well have been and carried on by Finn and later generations too I believe, and possibly even by your father? For I know for a fact there's still cases of the stuff stored in the cave beneath Liath Caislean – which in itself must be worth a small fortune. I've seen it for myself, tasted it even, there in the cave when I was a lad," yet explained no further. "The Dromgooles have never been ones for flaunting their wealth or climbing the social ladder, in fact just the opposite is true. Bran in particular shunned that sort of thing. Damned anti-social, if you ask me, and the little socialising your parents did was due to the efforts of your mother and limited to a very scant circle of friends.

"But Bran was never tight-fisted when it came to the creature comforts of his family, for as you've just said, you wanted for nothing. And of course with Meegan and your mother gone and yourself and Josephine off in the world to God only knew where, there was little for him to spend his money on and the profits just accrued at an alarming rate.

"As for Bran himself… he virtually lived off the smell of an oil rag, for he rarely entertained and never went out, so much so that the locals have been calling him "The Hermit" for years, or more often than not "The Mad Old Hermit."

People can be cruel Caeli and words can cut deep. Though you can't altogether blame them, for he really did go mad on the day he threw all the servants out, and they're never going to forget or forgive him for that, for they *were* the servants! Though I suppose you've not heard of that one either?

She shook her head. "Not that I recall…"

Mr. Shaw chuckled. "Well you'd certainly recall it if you had, and if it wasn't so serious it would be funny. For he dismissed all the household staff one day – excluding Molly of course, in what was undeniably a fit of pure madness. He literally herded them out the front doors of the house like a herd of cattle, prodding them in their backsides with one of those spears from Turlough's Hall and a horned Viking helmet upon his head.

"He really flipped his lid that day, accused them of plotting against him and sniggering behind his back. Then he raced through the house shouting something about his "Valhalla" – just another example of the absurdity of his illness. Thank God no one was hurt, for those spears are real weapons and meant to be lethal. But he seemed quite normal the following day. Even asked where the servants had got to.

"Consequently, there's no live-in staff at the house anymore – apart from Molly that is, and she's hardly thought of as staff, but more like family, she's been there so long. And most of the rooms of *Finn's* have been closed off for years – just like the rooms of *Turlough's* have been since your mother's passing – apart from their private quarters of course, which your father continued to occupy until the end.

"But it was a hard time for Molly with no other servants to help her. She was running herself ragged and I had to intervene and tell her to bring in all the help she needed and be accountable only to me. And if I've said it once, I've said it a thousand times, that for the life of me I can't understand why she's stayed on at the place all these years? She should have been off enjoying herself for a change. But

I'm sure I have no need to tell you that she's a remarkable woman, Caeli."

Caeli was horrified, visualising the scene: Her father raving mad, herding at least seven live-in staff out the front doors, prodding them with a real Viking spear and wearing a real Viking helmet upon his head!

"God, I had no idea he was that bad," she said, "for regardless of the old family stories of Vikings and Turlough and the dreaded Dromgoole madness that I've been hearing all my life, I never quite believed them. Though Dada must have been well and truly bonkers," she added – again with a hint of sarcasm, "establishing all those halfway houses and training centres you spoke of, for charitable deeds was never his scene."

"You do him an injustice, my dear," Mr. Shaw objected. "He did more charitable deeds in his latter years than you'll ever know, for he believed, as the good book tells us, in hiding his light under a bushel. He had a pretty soft heart beneath that gruff exterior of his."

Now it was Caeli's turn to laugh... Her father soft hearted? Piffle! Hiding his light under a bushel? What light – he didn't have one! Tell me another, Mr. Shaw! Surely he was speaking of someone else? But she neither laughed nor voiced her thoughts, other than to utter a scornful "Humph!" Her opinion was not about to be changed by a biased old friend's coat of whitewash. But as Mr. Shaw suspected, her interest was aroused.

CHAPTER EIGHTEEN
CURIOSITY

"These halfway houses you've mentioned, Mr. Shaw," Caeli finally asked, curiosity getting the better of her. "How did they come about?"

He thought for a moment, unprepared for the question.

"I suppose it was on account of Rory," he eventually replied, "Learning of the hardships that Rory had endured before it was discovered who the lad was. Bran came to realise that being an orphan was a hard place for any child to fall, let alone a five or six-year-old, but especially one in that terrible excuse for an orphanage up there in Belfast! Having Rory to think of proved an excellent therapy for your father and eventually drew him out of himself and opened his eyes to the plight of others in similar situations, but especially those too old to remain in the orphanages and turned out onto the streets to fend for themselves. Bran's initial intention was only to put a roof over their heads and food in their bellies and nothing more. But with no skills to speak of, he soon came to realise that that was not enough, that they had little hope of improving their lot in life without some skills to earn themselves a living – hence the training centres and halfway houses. The whole project was an absolute lifesaver for the lads and a lifesaver for Bran too, I might add. It drew him out of himself and back into the world of the living and made him immensely proud in the end. Not that he was directly involved... He established a committee to supervise it all and ensure that the work would go on," adding hastily. "But have no concern for the cost of the project on the estate my dear, it makes hardly a dint in the coffers. More of a tax hedge if anything, though I assure you that wasn't Bran's reason for doing it."

He took a sip of the water he'd poured from a jug on the far side of his desk, before he continued. "As for the properties here in Dublin... Bran's owned them for years. Some he inherited from his father and several he purchased himself when he and your mother first wed. I know that for a fact, for it was me, who did the conveyancing.

"But here, Caeli," he said, rising and intending to proceed towards her. "I am truly remiss, for I believe congratulations are in order. In anyone's estimation you are now an extremely wealthy woman – provided of course you meet the proviso."

"Yes, there's that proviso, isn't there," she said thoughtfully, echoing his words. "But what will happen to the inheritance should I *not* comply?"

The question was unexpected and pulled him up short, causing him to splutter and sit down again.

"Not comply? Not comply? But of course you'll comply! I really don't see that as being an option!"

"Perhaps not, but what if it was?"

"Well, in such an unlikely eventuality, you'd forfeit everything pure and simple. Pack your bags and return to the colonies from whence you have come, none the worse or better off than you were when you came."

"Yes, I'm aware of that, that I'd be leaving empty handed. But what I want to know is w*ho* would inherit Liath Caislean and my share of the inheritance in place of me?"

"Ah, well now," he said, avoiding eye contact for the very first time and fumbling through unrelated papers on his desk. "In that unlikely eventuality, the inheritance is to pass to the eldest grandson."

"But wouldn't that be Kevin, my son?"

"I believe it would."

It was her turn to splutter and bring her forward in her chair again.

"Kevin? Kevin?" she repeated, genuinely taken aback and cocking her ear as though she'd not heard him correctly. "My son Kevin would inherit Liath Caislean in place of me, and not Josie?"

It was clearly an outcome she had not anticipated, assuming that if she rejected the inheritance, it would automatically pass to her sister Josie. But apparently that was not the case. It was to by-pass Josie altogether and go to her son Kevin.

For Kevin was indeed the eldest grandson. The grandson her father had never laid eyes on nor shown the slightest interest in doing so in his twenty-one years of life, the illegitimate son of

Daniel O'Halloran's seed, chosen above her father's favourite daughter as the new Master of Liath Caislean and wealth beyond imagining?

It didn't sit right. There must be some valid point she was missing. That Dada was playing some devious game and messing with her mind.

"But what about Josie, Mr. Shaw, what about Josie?" she cried, genuinely concerned for her sister's welfare and tapping her finger rapidly on the desk. "I've always assumed that Dada would leave everything to Josie – being his favourite daughter and all."

He raised his eyebrows at such a suggestion, as though it was an outcome he had never considered.

"Granted, he spoilt Josephine rotten," he said. "But when she just left him without an explanation and didn't even bid him goodbye, he was bitterly disappointed in her – or shattered is a truer way of putting it. And it only made matters worse when he later discovered she had borne him a grandson and given the child away. He never forgave her for that.

"But it was different with you, Caeli. He knew why you'd left and that he was to blame. So mark my words it was *you*, his firstborn he wanted to succeed him. Therefore it seems perfectly logical to me that if you don't want Liath Caislean and everything else that your father has left you – and you'll never convince me you don't, then I think it's only fitting that the inheritance should pass to your son. In my opinion, Kevin is an admirable second choice.

"But here now," he said, seeing her agitation mounting. "Aren't you jumping the gun and concerning yourself with something that isn't likely to happen, for you can't seriously consider rejecting the estate – at least not before you've given it a try?"

"Perhaps you are right, Mr. Shaw" she replied, sounding thoughtful. "It's far too early to be making decisions. And besides, I really need to discuss it with Kevin and Liz before I make up my mind. For ultimately, whatever decision I make, concerns them as much as it concerns me.

"Just the same I can't help feeling bad for Josie, as though being passed over for me wasn't bad enough. But being passed over for a nephew she's never even met… I should imagine she won't be jumping for joy, when she finds out."

"Have no fear for Josephine, my dear. She is by no means being "passed over" as you seem to think she is, but is well taken care of, and I guarantee there'll be no complaints from that quarter – when we find her that is."

"Yes, when we find her…" Caeli echoed the words. "No news yet, I suppose…?

"No, not as yet, my dear, but God is good, and these new leads we've received are far more positive than any we've received before and give us reason to be quietly optimistic."

"Well, that's encouraging… But where, might I ask, did these leads come from?"

Mr. Shaw looked a might uncomfortable and hemmed and hawed and sipped more water. "From Zita O'Halloran, my dear," he finally said, "the same source that led us to you."

"Zita…!" she again exclaimed. "What's Zita got to do with any of this?"

"Apparently quite a lot, for now that your father's passed on, she's turned out to be the veritable fountain of knowledge and is bending over backwards to spill the proverbial beans. For besides informing us of *your* whereabouts – for which we are eternally grateful, she also appears to know a great deal about Josephine's affairs as well and has supplied us with some pretty amazing information regarding your sister's whereabouts."

"What sort of information?

"Well, according to Zita, Josephine is a professional singer – must take after your mother, eh? And quite a famous one, it seems, who likely lives in London. For Zita claims she saw a write-up of her in some magazine starring in some musical in the West End."

"Then how come none of you here saw the article?"

"It's quite possible that some of us did – those of us who are into glossy women's magazines and musical reviews and such. But even if we had, it's unlikely we'd have recognised her. For again, according to Zita, you sister was wearing heavy stage-makeup and one of those feathery costumes they wear in those sorts of shows. Zita said she wouldn't have recognised her either if it wasn't for the name."

"Well, then again I ask, why none of you did likewise?"

"And again, even if we had, we still wouldn't have been any the wiser. For you see – again according to Zita, Josephine changed her name several years ago, which is probably why we've failed so miserably to track her down."

"Changed her name... Why would she want to do that...? No wonder she couldn't be found... Anyhow, changed it to what? And how come Zita knew all about it and none of you did?"

Mr. Shaw was way ahead of her, anticipating the question and flicking back through his diary and running a finger down a page. "Let me see now... Yes, here it is," his finger triumphantly stabbing the relevant spot, "Susan – Susan Sinclair... Josephine Dromgoole is now known as Susan Sinclair, and as you say, it's no wonder she couldn't be found.

"But as for Zita being so well informed... I asked her the very same thing, but her answer, as usual, was evasive. She muttered something about also recognising Josephine's picture on a billboard of some musical she was appearing in on one of her recent trips to America, and that she'd waited backstage to meet her and make sure it was her. But I get the feeling there is more to it than that. That Zita is being her usual cunning self and we can only hope she is telling us the truth."

Caeli grimaced. "Ironical isn't it, that we're all indebted to Zita O'Halloran?"

"Yes, I had the same thought. And you are quite right, my dear. Like it or lump it, we *are* indebted to her and in one way or another we have much to thank her for – though it gripes me to admit it.

"But there's much to despise her for too, for she's led us a merry dance all these years, withholding vital information from us all and your father. For she's harboured a lifetime of hate for him Caeli, and as far as I know, she's never spoke to him again, which in a way I can almost understand. What I can't understand is why she'd withhold the whereabouts of you girls from him when she's known all along where you were?

"Surely to God she must have understood the depth of his loneliness with you girls gone and your mother passed on, having lost her only issue herself? Yet, as I have already stated, we have much to thank her for too, and she's won my eternal gratitude for leading us to you and the Dromgoole grandchildren."

Caeli offered no comment, not as inclined to spring to Zita's defence as she had been before. Intuition telling her that Zita had played a most devious game all these years. Played them off against each other for the fools they most likely were, and that she had more than a little explaining to do.

Yet she was also aware that she herself was in no position to cast aspersions on Zita, for Zita had been obeying her instructions to conceal her whereabouts from everyone in Ireland, but especially from her father. Realising too late that there was much she herself could have done to right the wrongs of the past and bridge the gap grown so wide between them. That life was a two-way street and that she could have taken the first step and met her father halfway.

"So Zita knows about Rory then, knows he's Josie's son and who his father is?"

Mr. Shaw frowned at the thought. "Well she knows the lad's here, and I guess she has her suspicions about his parentage like everyone else. But I don't think she knows anything for certain, for if she did – knowing the nature of Zita, you could bet your last penny to a pound she'd have blabbed it all over the place. No, I think we can safely assume that Rory's paternity remains Josephine's well-kept secret."

"So, who *is* Rory's father then, Mr. Shaw?"

The question was direct, as was the look in his blue Irish eyes that calmly returned her stare. Trustworthy eyes… Believable eyes…

"That, I can honestly say I don't know, Caeli. I don't think anyone knows but your sister and the reprehensible blagg'ard himself, for apparently she refused point blank to name him."

"But Dada… Surely Dada had some idea?"

"Perhaps he did, but I doubt it, what with the state his poor mind was in at the time.

"It was me who instigated the initial search and engaged a private detective to find your sister, but what a disappointment he turned out to be – no Dick Barton, Special Agent, I can tell you! Though to give the man his due, he did track her north into Belfast where she'd apparently gone when she first left home, and to where, I might add, we later discovered Rory had been born. But after Belfast, the trail fizzled out. The private eye fellow claimed it was too easy for young folk to disappear these days, if so inclined, and I have to agree. The world's grown smaller since my day and there are too many places for someone to hide and too many do-gooders offering assistance left right and centre for them to do it, throwing money at them like confetti! Bah! Makes me wonder what this modern day world is coming to! Not that Josephine was short of funds... We long ago established she had plenty of her own."

"So when *did* she change her name then?"

"We can only be certain it was sometime after Rory was born, for Dromgoole is the name on his registration of birth."

"Be that as it may, Mr. Shaw, but I find it impossible to believe that my dear little sister would abandon her newborn baby, for she had the sweetest nature... That she'd actually hand him over to strangers she hadn't even met... That absolutely astounds me, especially as you say, she wasn't strapped for cash."

"Oh, she abandoned him alright. By all accounts she rejected the little fellow from the moment he drew his first breath. Refused to even look at him or hold him in her arms we've been told, and put him up for adoption straight away. The matron still remembers her as 'The Cold-hearted Fish' in a class of her own, and claimed she was being charitable when she called her that!"

"Well, all I can say is that she must have had a darn good reason for doing what she did, for I simply can't imagine my sweet little Josie – or any other woman on the face of the earth, for that matter, rejecting her child so completely if she had the means to keep him.

"The sooner we find her, the better, I say, and hear her side of the story."

"I couldn't agree more, and I have a man in London right now as we speak following Zita's lead. My brightest young associate with the nose of a bloodhound hot on her trail – now that he has a trail to follow.

"He was in London on business for the firm when we informed him of Josephine's new identity and the possibility she might be in London also. And being an old family friend, he requested permission to stay on and attempt to track her down. A request I might add, I was delighted to grant."

Caeli raised a questioning eyebrow again, "An old family friend you say...? You have me intrigued, Mr. Shaw..."

"Oh there's no deep dark mystery here, Caeli," he quickly assured her. "I'm sure you'll remember James Joyce?"

CHAPTER NINETEEN
JAMJO

"*Jamjo…!* Surely you don't mean *Jamjo?* Mr. Shaw" Caeli asked incredulously, "Molly and Pat's boy? That Jamjo is a lawyer and employed by you? That it's Jamjo who's in London searching for our Josie?"

He chuckled, amused at her amazement,

"The one and the same my dear, but why so surprised, I always knew he was bright and that given the opportunity he would go far. Thank goodness Pat and Molly recognised that in him too, for he'd have been sorely wasted in service like them."

"Well I never!" Caeli exclaimed, unable to hide her astonishment. "But how on earth did Molly afford to put him through university, for I hear she's been a widow many years."

He felt himself blush, reluctant to admit that it was he who was Jamjo's benefactor.

"Well, yes she has," he replied, sounding guarded, "But Pat – God rest his soul, was also a highly intelligent man who could have gone far himself given half a chance. And you know Molly… She's no dumb bunny either when it comes to summing life up – despite her lack of schooling. She's as sharp as a razor beneath that bustling motherly exterior of hers, and nothing gets past her. And it was she who told me how they'd scrimped and scraped and saved every penny they could from the day James was born to give him a good education and a better chance in life than they ever had. But all of their scrimping and scraping has surely paid off."

"So you think highly of him then?"

"Indeed I do! To say he is brilliant is an understatement, and I consider my firm most fortunate to have him. Especially in light of the well-known fact that several other prominent legal establishments right here in Dublin have been trying to steal him away from me. Offering him more money than I ever dreamed of at his age and tantalising fringe benefits, such as holidays abroad and a posh new car. But for reasons that escape me, he's turned them all down and stays loyal to me.

"His mind is so quick, Caeli," Mr. Shaw prattled on, extremely proud of his secret protégé. "Anticipates things before I ever do and sees things in people that I never see, which I find quite intimidating at times, having been a lawyer myself these past fifty years and believed myself a pretty good judge of character. But James outshines us all.

"He has what you might call a sixth sense, or what we Irish like to term as "being here before," which in all sincerity is nothing to be scoffed at. I for one am of the belief that such people exist and that our James is the primest example I've ever come across in my life.

"But I hasten to add that he's also one of the finest young men I've ever come across too. He's a wonderful son to Molly and does her proud and absolutely worships the ground she walks on, and returns to Liath Caislean almost every weekend with arms full of presents and spoils her rotten. And I'm sure I've no need to tell you how proud Molly is of her 'Grand Lawyer Son.' Though for the life of me, I can't understand why he's never married."

"I know exactly what you mean," Caeli replied, bobbing her head in agreement with her words, as Molly's serious little black-haired son with piercing steel-blue eyes returned to mind. Eyes that even at the immature age of ten, had been strangely disturbing and given her the feeling he knew what she was thinking, as though he possessed the power to switch on a light inside her head and read her every thought.

"I've heard the same said of Jamjo many times before," she continued. "The folk of the village were in awe of him, and even though just a child, they respected his every last word and treated him as though he was as wise as King Solomon and as old as Methuselah and not a child at all.

'An old head on young shoulders' my mother used to say of him, for he always was such a serious little fellow, but oh such a likeable one. And I for one am not in the least bit surprised that he's never married... Had it fixed in *my* head that he'd enter the priesthood one-day."

Mr. Shaw looked at her thoughtfully, evaluating her comments and rubbing his chin as though rubbing a five o'clock shadow. "Now that's an interesting thought to ponder Caeli," he said, winking and grinning wickedly. "If Jamjo possesses all of those mystical powers that everyone credits him having, then we've certainly got the right man in London tracking your sister down – would you not agree my dear? Now *he'd*'ve made a damn good Dick Barton..."

Caeli nodded distractedly and he could see he had lost her, her thoughts spinning off on another tangent, trying to visualise the fully grown woman Josie had become, but failing to bring such an image to mind. The only image that would dance across the memory and tear at her heartstrings, was that of the adorable four-year-old sister with the bouncing copper curls and sparkling green eyes, she'd been forced to leave behind.

"How come Zita knew so much about Josie but never mentioned it to me?" she eventually asked. "I find that quite strange, Mr. Shaw, especially since Zita and I have been corresponding all these years on account of Kevin being her grandson. For all I knew, Josie was still living at Liath Caislean with Dada."

"I have no answer to that, my dear, though I've a pretty good idea why she'd want to keep such information from your father – pure vindictiveness!" The remark stretching into a long and thoughtful pondering as they both tried to comprehend Zita O'Halloran's actions; selfish, spiteful actions beyond comprehension, and the silence eventually broken by Mr. Shaw changing the subject altogether.

"When are you going to Liath Caislean, my dear?"

Caeli shrugged, relieved to abandon the subject of Zita, that she'd had quite enough of Zita for one day. To put it in bald Aussie terms, she'd had a "gutful" of Zita, believing she had known her son's grandmother well, but now of the opinion there was much about Zita she did not know – and much it would seem that no one else knew either. Mentally agreeing with Mr. Shaw that Zita was indeed a devious creature and not to be trusted and definitely covering something up. And that left a very bad taste in her mouth.

"Well, I'd hoped to be on my way this afternoon. I've hired a car, but considering the weather," indicating the rain lashing at the windows with a toss of her head, "I think I'll return to the hotel and have an early night and head off tomorrow – weather permitting."

"Capital idea... Very sensible, my dear...

156

"But would you like me to accompany you? Being the semi-retired gentleman that I am, I've heaps of time on my hands and would consider it a privilege to do so.

"Besides, it can be horribly harrowing driving on one's own in weather such as this, and the roads will be unfamiliar to you, being gone so long. And I'd feel less concerned if you had someone else along, for it's such a long way…

"Or alternatively, we could go in my car and have Hugh drive us…

"Or perhaps," he added, as though suddenly struck with a brilliant idea, "you'd prefer younger company? Would you like me to ask Liam to accompany you? For I'm certain he'd be only too happy to oblige."

Oh yes! She wanted to cry, that she'd love to have Liam accompany her, that she'd love to have Liam accompany her to Liath Caislean or to anywhere! Inwardly thrilling at the thought of being alone with him in the confines of the car, sitting so close that their bodies almost touched, inhaling the manly odour of him, feeling his warm brown eyes melting all over her, burning with desire and wanting to make love to her then and there in the car. Outwardly she blushed at her shameless thoughts yet revealed nothing of them in her contained reply.

"Thank you, no, Mr. Shaw. For as much as I'd appreciate your company or that of your son's, I really must decline. For I look upon returning to Liath Caislean as something of a pilgrimage for me, a deeply personal journey that I feel I must make alone.

"As for the distance being long… Why, it's just a hop, skip and a jump down the road, compared to the distances we travel in Australia."

He waved his hand dismissively, and if he felt spurned, he gave no indication of it.

"I understand completely, my dear. Say no more."

"But what can I expect when I get there, Mr. Shaw?" she now wanted to know. "Shall I find the house empty or what?"

"Well, technically it is, though I can almost guarantee Molly will be there with the red carpet rolled out and a choir of angels singing the *Hallelujah Chorus* to welcome you home. For she knows you are back in Ireland and coming sooner or later, and is very excited about that – gives me the impression that you were her favourite."

"Don't tell me that Molly's still there, Mr. Shaw?" Caeli questioned with a frown, "that she is still working at the house?"

His reply was illogical.

"Ah me now, she is and she isn't so to speak. Technically, she's living in the little cottage that your father left her for her retirement – moved in right after his funeral as a matter of fact. Got it into her head that after all the years she's been living in the house that it wouldn't be right to remain there with the master dead and gone.

"And of course she took Rory with her – there'd be no parting the pair. He's like family to her now and I dread to think how she's going to react if he's ever taken from her, for she positively adores the lad – as he adores her. His little face literally lights up at the mere sight of her, as though the sun and the moon and all the stars in the heavens above, shine out of her at once, and since your father's passing, they've been inseparable.

"It's a bit of a circus you know," he continued with a chuckle. "The locals are comparing them to a pair of wandering Travellers, traipsing back and forth between the house and the cottage several times a day with the dogs ever bounding at their heels. So I can almost guarantee that Molly will be there, standing on the doorstep with her arms open wide no matter when you arrive. Shall I give her a tinkle and let her know you are coming?"

"No, don't, Mr. Shaw," Caeli hurriedly replied, "I'd prefer to surprise her and just turn up, for if she knew I was arriving at any given time, she'd get all in a dither and fuss. Though it's me who's surprised that she's still there at all!

"Why, she must be well into her sixties by now, and far too old to be running a house as big as that – not to mention the added responsibility of caring for a child. At her time of life it is she who should be taking it easy and someone taking care of *her*! God only knows she's worked hard all her life and deserves it."

"You're quite right about that, my dear," Mr. Shaw said in full agreement. "But you know Molly; you can't tell Molly what to do. She only hears what she wants and does what she pleases regardless. So you'd be wasting your breath to suggest she retire and take it easy.

"I suggested as much just a few months ago – to my eternal regret. She just about bit my head off and told me in no uncertain

158

terms to mind my own business! That she'd work as long as she could and stop when she couldn't help it!

"But don't be too concerned about her "working" as such," he added, emphasising the word by inverting his fingers in the air, "She's more like the mistress of the manor these days. Brings staff in when she needs them and delegates royally, as though she was born to it, the place being her home for so long."

"Well I'm pleased to hear that," Caeli replied, feeling a tad relieved, knowing the house to be a monstrosity.

"The upkeep on the place must be horrendous!"

"Not as much as you might imagine, my dear, for there's no live-in-staff anymore, not since the time Bran went off his head and threw them all out, though the O'Brien twins go in almost every day."

"But what about Rory, who helps her with him?"

"No one… There is no question of delegation or interference of any kind when it comes to the child. Molly does everything for him and is very protective of him. Overprotective, if you ask me, won't even let the wind blow in his face!

"Never lets him out of her sight from the crack of dawn until he's tucked up in bed at night, for she insists he's her responsibility until his mother is found and brought home. Though I've heard tell of late, he's been off exploring the house on his own, and that's a huge step forward, and that he's even ventured outside to the kitchen garden to play with your father's dogs, which is progress indeed!"

"Obviously not mother's dogs…?"

"Bless me no! They're long since gone and pushing up the daisies. Though I'm blest if I can remember their names?"

"Dougal and Shara," Caeli murmured, speaking old memories aloud.

"Hah, yes! Dougal and Shara! Pure-bred Irish Red Setters – though I dare say this pair is related?"

"And what about Jamjo, Mr. Shaw, doesn't he object to his mother having such a huge responsibility of caring for a child at her age – and a very troubled child at that, as you've led me to believe?"

"Surprisingly, James is all for it, for he dotes on the lad as much as Molly does. Says if he makes her happy, then he's happy – not that she'd take a blind bit of notice if he were to say otherwise!

"As for the child's state of mind... Molly insists that it's nothing that love and the security of a permanent home cannot cure – and she could be right. She says he's improving day after day and that he's no trouble to her at all but a sheer delight and makes her feel ten years younger.

"Personally, I think she revels in playing the role of the doting grandmother she's long wanted to be. And I daresay Rory is the closest she's likely to get for a very long time – if ever!"

"So Jamjo's a bachelor then?"

"Oh yes, he is at that, and a confirmed one I'd say. A bit of a shy one when it comes to the ladies – not that there's any shortage of ladies wishing it were otherwise. For he's a remarkably good-looking young man, Caeli, dark and handsome; reminds me of that film star Tyrone Power – my Jessie's heartthrob a few years back – though you've probably never heard of him? And he's also a gentleman into the bargain.

"Molly brought him up well, and it truly amazes me that he's not been snapped up long ago. For I know for a fact there's a colleen right here in this office who literally worships the ground he walks on. And a gorgeous colleen she is at that that any young man would be proud to take home to his mother. But he pays her no heed, and I honestly believe she could pass him in her petticoat and he'd not bat an eyelid or notice her at all.

"But back to the subject of the house... As I've said before, I can almost guarantee that Molly will be there standing on the doorstep and waving a flag of welcome, no matter when you arrive. And if you are planning to stay – and I sincerely hope you are, then she'll bring in more staff and open the place up and have it sparkling and shipshape in no time at all.

"But for the time being, we thought it expedient to leave things idling along as they are so to speak, until we knew what it was you were planning to do."

Caeli ignored the obvious probe. Indeed, she could not have answered it even if she had wanted to, no longer having a clear-cut vision as to what her future plans would be.

The proposed quick trip to Ireland to lay the ghosts of the past to rest and the speedy return to Australia, now decisions of the past and long gone from her mind. The astonishing fact that the bulk of her father's surprisingly affluent estate had been left to her when she'd expected to receive nothing at all, having changed all that.

Her mind was in a quandary, betwixt and between, to accept or reject, and doubly so in light of the knowledge that if she refused, it was to bypass Josie altogether and go to Kevin, her own illegitimate son.

An outcome she had never foreseen for one single moment and it had not gone down well. Feeling she was missing some pertinent point that was staring her straight in the face and somehow being duped.

"But yes, now it comes to me!" Mr. Shaw suddenly announced, snapping his fingers and swivelling his chair and opening a drawer at the far side of his desk. "Something I knew I had to remember but struggling to recall."

Caeli watched him, intrigued.

"Keys!" he announced. "Keys to the kingdom in here somewhere… Yes, here they are!" triumphantly jangling a great bunch of keys above his head then sliding them across the desk to her.

"But don't ask me which key fits what, for I haven't the foggiest."

"Keys…?" Caeli quizzed, frowning and a hunching her shoulders feeling somewhat bemused. "What on earth do I want with keys?"

"Keys to the Kingdom – the Kingdom of Liath Caislean, my dear, at Molly's insistence I might add.

"I told her it was unnecessary, but she was adamant, insisting – as only Molly can, that it was only "proper" for the new owner of Liath Caislean to at least have the keys to unlock its doors! And," he added with a chuckle, "she also said it was in case she wasn't home – that she'd taken herself off on a cruise around the world. And Molly of course, has keys of her own."

The thought of unworldly Molly going anywhere – let alone on a cruise around the world, made Caeli chuckle too, for Molly was a "homebody" through and through who had never been further afield than the city of Dublin in her life.

"So be it," she said, dropping the weighty bunch of keys into her bag with a clunk and rising from the chair, proclaiming the meeting had come to an end.

"I guess we have covered all we can cover, for the moment, Mr. Shaw."

Mr. Shaw arose also, following her lead and gallantly assisted her on with her coat. Warmly, she thanked him, and again reached up and kissed his cheek, adding that they'd undoubtedly be meeting again in a few days' time when she'd made her decision.

"But surely there is only one decision for you to make?" he persisted.

Again she ignored the probe, thinking him too anxious for her to commit. Unwilling to reveal how utterly confused she was feeling at the unexpected outcome of the day, and that she definitely needed more time to think.

Companionably, he linked his arm through hers and led her out into the hall.

"You've brought an old man much happiness this day, my dear," he said in all sincerity, "albeit not under the happiest of circumstances.

"And please," he added, ushering her into the lift, "don't hesitate to call me if I can be of further assistance to you."

Her reply was as equally sincere.

"Thank you, Uncle Eugene, I shall certainly do that." Overcome with a sudden rush of love for this old family friend, calling and waving to him as the ancient wrought-iron-gate clanged shut and the lift began its creaking descent.

"Good-bye, Uncle Eugene... Good-bye... Good-bye..."

Yet as the chill of the lift-well gathered about her, his words seemed to take on new meaning and echo menacingly about her now: *"Surely there is only one decision for you to make..."* She shivered, suddenly filled with terror, imagining she could hear her father's voice echoing in among them: *Bind yourself to Liath Caislean and to me, Caeli...For if you don't, I will take your son...*

"Damn you to hell, Dada!" she cursed none too softly in the small descending space as the reality of the legacy began to hit home. Increasingly aware that if she accepted the inheritance, she would indeed be binding herself to Liath Caislean and bowing to her father's will. And if she rejected it, Kevin, her son, most certainly would not, and therefore, in one way or another, Dada *would* take her son, proving that even from the grave he still had the power to wield his vengeance and manipulate her life.

Yet as confused and betrayed as she was feeling, she could not deny that Kevin would be an admiral second choice.

162

Visualising her big handsome son – the image of his dead Irish father Daniel O'Halloran, wrapped in the Dromgoole mantle as Master of Liath Caislean. Kevin, who, unbeknown to her until a few days before, had planned to abandon Australia and replant his roots in the land of his forebears as soon as he got his degree.

She could even visualise his newly-painted portrait hanging in the Great Hall alongside that of her father and their ancestor Turlough. Startled to realise how much alike the three men were. Three almost identical men with coal-black hair and jet-black eyes and pale Irish skins… A likeness she had never noticed before, yet a likeness clearly evident to Mr. Shaw.

His words screamed into the creaking void about her and now and spun like a whirlygig in her head: *Meet the proviso, Caeli… Meet the proviso…* But at that particular moment in time, she didn't believe she could.

CHAPTER TWENTY
RETURN TO LIATH CAISLEAN

The huge stone house on the ridge of the cliffs was again caught in the grip of winter, a howling wind gusting in from the sea, and an icy rain bucketing down from solid grey skies as though it would never stop, overflowing its gutters and drain-pipes and gushing like a river down its steep drive.

It was up this drive that Caeli Morgan now climbed in the sporty little car hired in Dublin, navigating the final leg of the journey back to the house of her father, the house she had vowed she would never enter again.

It looked bleak and unwelcoming in the distance, glimpsed from the gatehouse two miles back. Its grey slate rooftops angled sleek and wet either side of its huge round tower and strongly resembled the giant bird of prey it had often been likened to.

Old McGinty, the gatekeeper, had been standing in the rain with the gatehouse gates flung wide as though he'd expected her arrival, and permitted her entry with a silent salute.

The village of rain-sodden cottages gathered about the ancient stone chapel in the valley, looked bleak and sodden and unwelcoming too. The whole estate appeared sadly neglected. The outbuildings in need of a coat of paint, the stable doors hanging half off their hinges, the stables themselves gaping and empty, the fences broken and leaning and in need of repair.

No pure-bred horses grazed in the meadows or stared from the stables as they had in her mother's day. No smiling faces appeared at the windows or called out in welcome or waved her on.

But she knew they were watching, and wondered what they were thinking behind their firmly closed doors.

Would they accept her as their Mistress, she wondered, a woman to rule over them and the first Mistress ever. Would they open their arms and their hearts and welcome her home and kill the fatted calf and rejoice in her return? Or would they turn their backs and treat her with same contempt with which they had treated her father?

The rusting iron gates at the top of the drive also stood open, as if they too were expecting her coming and eager to gobble her in. The bleak gravel courtyard beyond, bereft of shrub or tree, enfolded its rain-washed arms about her as she swung the car wide around the central bell tower and drew to a scrunching halt at the steps of the house's main entrance.

A sense of foreboding overwhelmed her then as she stared up at the massive stone structure before her having the uncanny feeling it was staring straight back and appraising her as much as she was appraising it.

How she wished she hadn't returned to the house now. How she wished she had followed her instincts and remained in Australia and not come to Ireland at all. How she wanted to drive back through the gates and be gone from this place just as fast as she could. Her hand trembled as she reached for the ignition and turned the motor off, her emotions swinging like a pendulum, between curious anticipation and nervous dread.

Too many bad memories haunted the house that dominated her dreams and encroached upon her days and gave her no peace. Yet reluctantly, she had to admit there were good memories there too, the memories her Liz had encouraged her to find. *Find the good memories, Mum...* The memories when her mother, the beautiful Maureen O'Sullivan from County Kildare had been alive. For the house had been her home too, and in which Caeli and her sisters had been born, and two hundred years of Dromgoole ancestor's before them as well.

Surely her mother and these gone-before relatives had instilled some sense of themselves into the house; surely they'd instilled some sense of themselves into her that made her feel irrevocably connected to them and the house for all time? Then why did she feel like a stranger at its door? An unwanted intruder to be sent on her way who did not belong – had never belonged, that it had never been her world as much as it had been theirs? For unlike her, they had stayed and raised their young and written their page in its book of life before passing on to their place in eternity, every last one but Turlough, recorded in the chronicles of the gravestones lined up in the graveyard below.

For wasn't that all that life amounted to, she thought philosophically, sitting quiet and still in the warmth of the car with wind and the rain roaring without; a beginning and an end, a birth and a death, with a short span of life in between? Sort of like a sandwich, she had heard it likened to, with every kind of filling known to mankind crammed in between and served without fanfare or favour to rich and poor alike until consumed to the very last crumb. Envisaging these ancestors here about her now, hovering, watching, and calling to her in the toss of the wind: *"Caeli, come home... come home..."* gaining their hold and tugging her back?

"Good God, girl, get a grip!" she rebuked herself harshly, spooked by her thoughts and hugging her coat more closely about her. Telling herself it was only the elements she could hear, the wind and the rain gusting about her and the wild winter's sea thrashing the face of the giant granite cliffs upon which the house stood.

Yet the house and its lands and all it entailed were now hers for the taking, if she so wished. Every stone of its massive grey structure... every acre of rich grazing land... every blade of its green Irish grass... She had only to comply with her father's surprisingly mild, yet confusingly strange condition and return to this world of yesteryear – a world that had nearly destroyed her.

Yet she had to admit she was tempted, while the temptation itself was repellent to her. For acceptance meant going back on her word and breaking the vow she had made to accept nothing from her father's estate, that it would be sheer hypocrisy to do so when she believed he was responsible for Meegan and Danny's death – and for all she knew, for her mother's death too. Yet she had to concede – now that her father was dead, that the truth of her mother's passing might be lost to her forever. As might the reason why Liath Caislean and the bulk of her father's affluent estate been left to her, when all along she had believed it would go to Josie and she would get nothing. Why so generous to her now, when in times of dire need as a teenage widow with two babies to support, he'd offered not a penny?

It just didn't sit right. Favouring her now just didn't make sense. He had hated her, but adored Josie. There had to be a catch. Some devious turn of his sick mind that she couldn't get *her* mind around, completely divorced from material things.

There was no sign of Molly and the promised smiling face waiting at the top of the steps to greet her. No red carpet rolled out or flag flying or even a porchlight to shine out in welcome. Only the wet bedraggled courtyard closed in around her as the bitter grey day succumbed to a cold wet dusk.

"Where are you, Molly?" Caeli called feebly, when after five minutes Molly hadn't appeared, terrified at the thought of abandoning the car and battling the elements and entering the massive dark house alone.

Coming to realise how much she was depending on Molly to be there for her, as Molly always had.

Shocked to learn Josie had abandoned their father that she had mysteriously disappeared eight years before. Having taken it for granted that Josie – being her father's favourite daughter and all, would have remained loyally by his side; but even more shocked to learn that Josie had also abandoned her new born child.

The mystery of Josie's baffling departure had only begun to unravel with the discovery of Rory, her abandoned child, in an orphanage up in Ulster just twelve months before. Apparent to everyone then, that Josie, like Caeli, had borne an illegitimate son.

But everyone knew who had fathered Caeli's son Kevin – Daniel O'Halloran, the vagabond son of the traveller woman Zita O'Halloran. Whereas no one on the face of the earth seemed to know who had fathered Josie's son Rory.

Casting her mind back, she wondered again why her father had gone to such lengths to keep her and Danny apart. Thinking again how strange it was that no trace of Danny or his personal belongings had ever been found, when the wreckage of his little yellow yacht, *Sea Nymph,* had washed into a cove not two miles beyond the harbour. Yet even stranger still that Danny had gone out in the boat in the first place at all with foul weather brewing. He knew better than that. He was known to be an excellent sailor, respectful of the elements and "My Lady Sea," having sailed the waters of Raggemorne Bay on countless occasions in the past. And she thought it unlikely she would ever learn the truth of what had taken place on that storm-filled day of long ago and fulfil her daughter's wise council: *Face up to your past, Mum… Confront your ghosts head on and put them back where they jolly well ought to be…*

Well, here she was, not only back on Irish soil but back at Liath Caislean, the place of their rising, attempting to do just that – to confront her ghosts head on and put them to rest once and for all. Supposedly there on account of her daughter's wise counsel and logical reasoning, yet admitting to herself that it was for a totally illogical reason she had come – the lure of Liam Shaw's words on the phone and the expectation of what lay behind them! Unable to put the words from her mind – *Dare I believe that I've found you at last...? Been searching for you forever...* But especially the manner in which he had said them, persuasively, seductively, that had strummed up old feelings and plucked at some deep forgotten chord in her heart.

Their re-acquaintance in his father's office the previous day had not disappointed, but allayed her fears and confirmed that her instincts had been right to come after all, that the youthful dalliance that had once surged between them surged between them still.

So engrossed in her thoughts of Liam and his whispered promise he would come to her soon, that she'd failed to see Molly descending the wet unlit steps until the car door flew open and a beam of flashlight and two cold canine noses thrust in about her.

"Is that really yourself, Caeli?" a strong Irish brogue called from the obscurity of the background, "that me darlin' girl has returned to me at last?" And lo and behold, there into the dim flush of torchlight emerged Molly, struggling to control a pair of Irish red setters and a big black umbrella, threatening to turn inside out.

"Molly – you're here?" Caeli said in a voice full of wonder. "I thought the house empty – no lights."

"Arragh... No power...! The weather...!" Molly countered above the wind. "An' of course I'm here... Where else am I likely to be when me darlin' girl was comin' home to me at last?

"But come away in now, lass, before ye catch your death of cold or the wind takes me sailin' off to China!" Then slapping the dogs sharply on their rumps with the equally sharp command to get inside, she practically dragged Caeli from the car.

"But mind those puddles now lass," she cautioned, "an' stay close to me," placing a protective arm around Caeli's shoulders and huddling her in under the flapping umbrella. "They'll freeze the toes off your feet in two seconds flat!"

And so it was that Molly and Caeli ascended the steps of Liath Caislean together. And together, with only the slightest of hesitation on Caeli's part, they stepped over the threshold and back into the world of yesterday.

CHAPTER TWENTY-ONE
FRIENDSHIPS RENEWED

It was only when inside the dimly lit hall that Molly hugged Caeli to her, unable to contain her joy a moment longer.

"Oh lass, lass, how it does me heart good to see ye again," she fervently cried. It's been far too long an' I'd almost given up hope. But you're here with me now and that's all that matters. But get out of those damp clothes now an' away to the kitchen with ye, for there's a big roarin' fire and a pot of me best…" But before the words were rightly out of her mouth, a strong gust of wind snatched the great oak doors and slammed them shut with an almighty bang, making both women jump. "The Lord be near me," Molly uttered, as she turned and slid the bolts.

Caeli delighted in Molly's quaint ways and rich Irish brogue, feeling the strain of the past ebbing away and a sense of peace nudging in – peace she'd not felt in a very long time.

"As you were saying, Molly…?" she prompted with a grin. "A pot of your best…?"

"Me best mutton stew lass – with your favourite mint dumplings on top."

"Oh Molly, Molly," was all Caeli could say, overcome with emotion and hugging the beloved housekeeper to her as though she would never let her go.

Realising how much she had missed Molly, how her feelings for Molly, who had shown her nothing but love and kindness as far back as she could remember, were as strong as they had ever been.

The past swept over her then, warm and welcoming, making her feel like a child again seeking the comfort of Molly's arms.

Tears she could no longer contain welled up in her eyes, brimming and flowing as great gulping sobs tore brokenly from her, achingly sweet in their bitter release.

For it was Molly's arms and not her mother's that had always been there to protect and comfort her. Molly's arms that had cradled and soothed her first infant cries from the moment she was born, and Molly's voice that flowed over her now as it had flowed then, a sweet forgotten balm more powerful than any apothecary's potion, soothing both her body and her soul.

"Oh Molly, Molly, I've never cried..." Caeli sobbed. "In all these years, I've never been able to cry – not since mother..." The following words smothered in the violet-smelling softness of Molly's ample breast.

"Whisht now, whisht now lass, your Molly's here an' Gods in his heaven an' all's right with the world..."

There, in that vast cold hall of Liath Caislean, its twin-oak-stairs entwined about the massive stone tower at the house's core to the whispering heights of the dark empty floors above, the mustiness of time and her father's neglect creeping into their nostrils, the ancient house creaking and groaning like some giant mortal thing, Molly held her beloved Caeli to her and tenderly kissed her tear-stained cheeks and rain-dampened hair, as though she was her precious young charge all over again.

"God love ye child," Molly soothed in her soft Tipperary brogue, sounding as anguished as Caeli so obviously was. "Cry it all out now, my lamb, your Molly's here... Cry it all out..."

The tears that flowed so freely brought Caeli no shame. Here, she was not on show to her stylish friends in her riverfront mansion or her successful business acquaintances in the elegant fashion salons of Australia. Here, she was out of sight of those who would judge her harshly, envious of her success and ignorant of her struggle to achieve what she had. And ignorant too of her past that would give her no peace and was tearing her apart. Here, she could shed her worldly façade and bare her soul and be plain old Caeli Dromgoole again. For regardless of the ill-will that existed between her and her father, and the vow she had made to never re-enter his house again, she had to admit that here was home because here was Molly, and Molly had no time for façades or pretence of any kind – plain honest Molly, who knew her better than any other living soul, and probably even better than she knew herself. For Molly had known her from the moment she had drawn her first breath and sprung from her mother's womb right into Molly's loving arms.

For the moment, Caeli was content to succumb to Molly's pampering administrations. To lay aside the prestigious honour of being the new Australian "Businesswoman of the Year." An award she had avidly coveted, yet an award she would now gladly surrender – along with its daunting responsibilities in the high-powered business world from which she had come, to once again wallow in Molly's tender loving care – for the moment.

"Molly is Molly, pure and simple," Mr. Shaw had stated only yesterday, intimating his high regard for her. "She never changes and I can only say thank God for that."

How true his words, Caeli thought now, observing Molly's pleasant countenance, for as far as she could see –apart from her kindly blue eyes now appearing a little faded, and her pretty dark curls now a silvery grey, she had changed very little in either looks or disposition with the passing of the years. Indeed, it could be said that the years had been exceedingly kind to her, for her pleasant round face seemed barely touched by the ravages of time – surely a reflection of her faith in mankind and her goodness within? Even her clothing appeared much the same as Caeli remembered it. A simple grey frock reaching down to her ankles, a snowy white apron, the Saint Christopher medal – the patron saint of travellers bought for a sixpence many years before in the chapel's shop and supposedly blessed by none other than his holiness the Pope, a permanent comfort around her neck.

Though Molly was by no means a "traveller," never having ventured further afield than the city of Dublin in her life and that on her honeymoon many years before with her late husband Pat, but claimed it was a traveller of life she was, and as much in need of the Saint's protection than if she had circled the globe a dozen times.

The years fell away as Caeli and Molly embraced, as though time itself stood still and they had never been apart. Their arms entwined as they walked down the hall to the rear of the house where the kitchen awaited, casting its friendly light and delicious aromas out into the hall, as though they'd popped out to welcome her in. The kitchen, the warm throbbing heart of this big cold house and Molly's domain for the past forty years that had drawn every last one of them in, simply because Molly was there. The setting unpretentious: grey stone walls and stone-flagged floor, reflecting the stark way of life of generations past. Everything appeared as Caeli remembered it: Scrubbed kitchen table, snowy-white curtains and ancient oak-dressers lining its walls, the same iron pot-rack hanging from its rafters dangling an assortment of gleaming pans and pots. The only discordant note to be struck being that of the new gas stove standing alongside the old that Mr. Shaw claimed Molly refused to use. Even the same shabby armchairs sagged before the fire, inviting one to sit and linger, with the same black kettle humming merrily on its hob, promising a good strong cup of tea with every scalding spit.

"Molly's confessional," her mother had called the setting, for many a heart had unburdened there. Where deep into the night Caeli would sit and unburden some more.

CHAPTER TWENTY-TWO
GOING FORWARD – LOOKING BACK

The howling wind of the previous night had blown itself out to a playful breeze when Caeli opened her eyes on her old room the following morning. The bucketing rain reduced to a rhythmic plip-plopping from gutters and downpipes. The fresh morning air embracing her senses, spiked with the rich earthy tang of salt and sea, while a pale wintry sun was attempting to smile through her bedroom window.

She shivered, regardless of the improvement in the weather and the radiator glowing red in the grate, her whole body in a state of shock on account of the disturbing experience she had encountered during the night.

Not the usual nightmare that had dominated her nights for years – searching for her young dead lover Danny O'Halloran, beneath a troubled sea. Last night he had been very much alive and had come to her bed, the experience too real to be a dream and still shuddered through her. Still feeling his warm moist breath upon her whispering close to her ear: *"So you've come back then, my lovely colleen…"* Still feel his hands caressing her body and his lips crushing down hers, her most intimate places aroused and on fire as though she'd been raped.

Unable to convince herself it was but a fantasy of her imagination or the overindulgence of wine shared with Molly in the kitchen the previous night, or the talk of the past that had fired her subconscious to the point of the ridiculous. Convinced she was either a raving sex maniac or a total idiot. She had to be, didn't she? For everyone knew that Danny was dead, long ago lost to a watery grave.

"No wonder I'm cold," she muttered, noticing the bedroom door ajar and leeching the warmth out into the hall, though positive she had closed it the previous night.

174

But then the house had always been cold, she reasoned. Even warm summer days seeing fires burning in the vast living rooms in a vain attempt to dispel their eternal feeling of winter. "Winters House," she mused wryly, that it should have been called "Winters House," tugging the quilt up over her nose and casting her eyes about.

The same rose-bud wallpaper and rose-coloured drapes confronted her. The same crystal and silver accoutrements adorned the dressing table in much the same order she remembered them to be. A sense of unreality swept over her then, the feeling she was somehow caught in a time warp and had never been gone from the house at all and the intervening years were the lie.

Straining to hear sounds of Molly in the kitchen below, the clang of a pot or a pan or the call of her sister's troubled child she had yet to meet, or even the bark of her father's nameless pair of dogs romping in the courtyard at the front of the house.

Imagining she could hear Meegan's timid voice calling to her back through time, *"Caeli... Caeli... Where are you, my Caeli?"* and four-year-old Josie madly pedalling her tricycle through the cold empty halls.

But the whispers of the weary old house were the only reality, hobbling through its two hundredth year. And the more chastened sound of the sea, lapping more gently the great wall of cliffs, upon which the house stood.

Yet she did hear something, she did, she did – a murmur of something deep in the house, the faintest whisper of someone singing – her mother singing, forcing her upright in the bed and straining to hear more. So absorbed in the memories of her mother and the past was she, that when a light tread sounded in the hall, her eyes darted to the door, half expecting her mother to enter. But it was Molly who came. Good faithful Molly, the stabilizing influence of the family for so long that they'd long ago taken her for granted, stepping lightly into the room carrying a tray of tea and toast.

"Ah, so you're awake then my lamb," she hushed into the gloom.

"Yes, I'm awake, Molly... Just lying here reminiscing..."

"Ah well now, I expect ye would be" Molly replied, "bein' gone for so long," placing the tray on the bedside table and switching on the rose-shaded lamp. "But bless my soul, lass!" she exclaimed as the light filled the room and fell upon Caeli. "You're as white as a sheet darlin' girl, as though ye've seen a ghost!"

175

Caeli chuckled wryly. "Well, for one freakish moment I thought that I had, for you gave me quite a start when you entered, Molly dear. My mind is so full of Mother and the past, that I imagined I was back there in time and that you actually were Mother coming in. She's been on my mind ever since I came."

"Arragh, 'tis no wonder you're so pale… But in my opinion, ye've altogether got too many things goin' on in that head of yours for your brain to digest!

"So prop yourself up on those pillows now an' get this lovely cup of tea into ye while it's still hot. It'll put the roses back into your cheeks in no time at all.

"Though I know ye slept well, for I looked in on ye lass not half an hour ago, an' it's dead to the world ye were."

"I surely did, Molly," Caeli lied. "Slept like a log, can't even remember my head touching the pillow – thanks I suspect to all that wine I consumed last night."

Feeling more than a little relieved that it had been Molly who had opened the door and left it ajar.

Stretching and yawning exaggeratedly then, unwilling to reveal just how badly she had slept or to confide in Molly the disturbing experience of the night.

Yet even if she had confided in Molly, Molly would not have been unduly alarmed, but rather relieved. For it would have confirmed an occurrence she'd been aware of for years – that there was a dark and mysterious visitor who'd been coming to the house and walking the halls of Turlough's Wing late at night. That he entered the house via the cave and the secret door that led into the master's office, having seen a light in the tower room directly above it from her bedroom window late one night. She had raced to the master's quarters in Turlough's Wing to report the intruder, only to be told he was expected and would be returning many times in the future, and that when she saw the light, she was to keep to her room and say nothing of him to no one. She had almost collided with the darkly clad figure when leaving the master's quarters one night and immediately sensed a disturbing familiarity about him. That he'd been in the house for the master's funeral a few days before, hovering in the shadows. That he was in the house still, having seen a light in the tower room again last night.

"Good!" Molly retorted, sitting companionably on the bed and patting Caeli's hand. "'Tis worn out ye were with all of that bawlin' ye were doin', but in the long run, it'll do ye the world of good, clear the cobwebs out of your head an' make ye feel all the better entirely for it!"

Caeli was feeling better already. Soothed by Molly's comforting presence and quaint colloquial ways, and she said as much.

"You are probably right, Molly dear, for I'm feeling better already.

"And Molly," she added on a more serious note, "thanks for understanding, for putting up with my idiotic blubbering last night. Crikey, if the kids could've seen me, they'd've got the shock of their lives, for they've never seen me cry. Haven't cried in years, as I told you last night... Quite surprised myself..."

"Sure now, 'tis nothin'," Molly said, brushing the unaccustomed plaudit aside with a wave of her hand and a click of her tongue. "Isn't that why I'm here now, my lamb – to watch out for me own?"

"Just the same... A grown woman blubbering like a two-year old...?"

"Arragh, 'tis only to be expected, an anti-climax so to speak, returning home after bein' gone for so long an' lookin' back on the past – an' a sad past it's been at that. But haven't I the grandest feelin' – now that your darlin' self has come home, that everythin's goin' to be alright! And who knows," she added with unfailing optimism and patting Caeli's hand again, "we might even get a call from my boy in America this very day informin' us he's found Josie... Wouldn't that be grand now? But in the meantime..." rising and placing the tray firmly on Caeli's lap, "get this tea an' toast into ye now while it's still hot! I'm off to put a lovely bit of beef in the oven for your dinner."

Molly was pampering Caeli to the extreme, as though she was her young charge all over again and Caeli was lapping it up. Admitting to herself in a very smug manner that she liked being "Mollycoddled," yes, she liked being "Mollycoddled" very much!

"Oh Molly, before you go..." she called after Molly's departing back, "has Rory returned yet, for I'm dying to meet him."

Molly turned, her hand on the doorknob,

177

"Not that I'm aware of. I'm not expectin' him back before noon when his stomach starts to growl. For I'd say he'll be havin' the time of his life off with the McGinty lads, though I can't help feelin' anxious for him."

"Oh? Why so?"

"Well, it's the first time he's been away from me since he came – though I know I have nought to worry about. The McGinty's – old McGinty's youngest son Kieran an' his lovely little wife Milly, that is, are good God-fearin' folk an' the only ones around here that I'd entrust him to. They know his story an' have sworn to watch over him like a hawk. An' besides," she added, "the outing will do the lad good – bring him out of his shell, so to speak…"

"What do you mean when you say 'the only ones you'd entrust him to and bring him out of his shell?' it sounds pretty serious stuff to me."

"Serious enough," Molly replied, re-entering the room and again sitting on Caeli's bed. "But it's all in the child's head, if ye know what I mean? Psychological, we've been told," tapping her temple as though that explained everything.

"An' best that I fill ye in now lest ye unintentionally put your foot in your mouth an' trip yourself up," arousing Caeli's interest even more.

"The poor little mite's had more than his share of trauma in his seven years of life, let me tell ye, enough to send a grown man off his rocker, let alone a seven-year-old child – or barely five as he was at the time."

'So I've heard."

"He's been to Hell an' back, Caeli! His troubles beginnin' from the minute he was born when that sister of yours turned her back on him an' gave him away. And for the life of me I've never been able to understand how she could have done such a thing – puttin' him up for adoption with his very first breath an' handin' him over to strangers she knew nothin' about – for she was always such a lovely soft-hearted girl. Then the couple who adopted him – an' from what I can gather, they really loved him – for he surely loved them, havin' a terrible accident an' gettin' themselves killed, along with a darlin' little girl they'd adopted as well.

"How fragile life is, Caeli," Molly went on, shaking her head in dismay, "that it can be snatched away from us so easily? A few moments' distraction was all that it took. A backward glance an' the car skiddin' on the icy road an' down into the river an' killin' them all instantly – except Rory that was. The poor little soul windin' up in an orphanage in that terrible 'Heathen North' with all sorts of problems to contend with, like wettin' his bed an' screamin' out in the night from the horror of it all. Then bein' tossed from pillar to post in a dozen different foster homes since an' treated none too kindly, or so I've been told, before the Blessed Monsignor discovered him an' your father actually went up there to that ungodly place an' brought him back here to us.

"It's all this psychological stuff that the doctors speak of," she continued, tapping her temple again, "that makes him believe it 'twas all his fault an' that he was the cause of his family dyin' – an' now the cause of your father dyin' too, which is utter nonsense of course – though in a way 'tis quite understandable. For he told me he was actually dreamin' that your father *was* dyin' before he actually did, an' that's what gave him the courage to abandon his bed an' go to the master's quarters that night.

"He was terrified of course; wendin' his way through the halls of Finn's all alone in the dark with no light to guide him, then up the staircase into Turlough's Wing, jumpin' at every creakin' board an' shadow. I don't know how he did it, or where his courage came from, for he's a bit on the timid side. Yet I think it was his very fear that drove him on, convinced that the dream was really happenin' an' tellin' me later that he'd seen your father gaspin' for breath in the dream an' holdin' his chest an' callin' his name – Rory... Rory... That the dream was so real that he said he had to hurry an' mustn't be a baby, that there was no time to come an' get me, that it might already be too late..."

"Ooh, spooky stuff Molly," Caeli said with a shiver.

"Isn't it, though...? Made me hairs stand on end an' me toenails curl... But it gets even spookier Caeli. For he claims he even saw the hearse in his dream that wasn't a hearse at all but the master's four-poster bed bein' carted down the drive by six men dressed in black. An' that there was an old woman there too, also dressed in black from the top of her head to the tip of her shoes an' pointin' her finger the way of the graveyard down in the valley below. That gave me the creeps' good'n proper Caeli, brought old Granny Grainne back into me mind that's been dead a good many years an' really put the wind up me.

But the thing that affected the child worst of all – an' dear God it still does – an' if I am to be honest, it still affects me, was that even though he was certain he was awake – having pinched himself several times to be certain he was, he could still hear the bell in the church tower clangin' over an' over again in his head."

Caeli could feel her own hair standing on end and goose-bumps rippling her flesh, but apart from uttering a shuddering "ugh" she said nothing more, her breath bated, wanting to hear every last detail of the night-marish story to its bitter end.

"As for the Quinlivans' accident," Molly continued, "Rory's adoptive parents that is, I can almost understand why his conscience is botherin' him so, for he told me he was bein' naughty at the time an' disobeyin' his mother, an' that the accident would never have happened if he'd been good.

"Drivin' home from Sunday Mass, they all were, his dad 'n mam in the front an' Rory an' the little girl in the back – Rosebud was her name, an' he'd wound the car window down. Apparently his mam had turned around an' told him to wind it back up, that it was too cold on the baby, but he'd ignored her. Then his dad had done the same, just taking his eyes off the road for only a few seconds an' that's when it happened, the car skidded on the icy road and crashed into the bridge and down into the river it went."

"Oh Molly, how dreadful… The poor little fellow… No wonder he's riddled with guilt. But clearly it wasn't his fault, that the ice on the road was to blame… But how come the McGintys are the only ones you'd entrust Rory to?"

"Well, certainly not that lot down there in the valley, I mean," Molly replied, her voice full of scorn. "They're an unfeelin' lot an' were unjustly cruel to your father since your dear mother's passin'. Hounded him day in an' day out, sayin' he deliberately pushed her over the balcony – all due to that blabbermouth Bridget O'Brien's blitherin' lies – as if he could have done such a thing?

"An' now they're bein' just as cruel to the child. Claimin' he's a chip off the old block an' as mad as the master.

"An' they're mad at me too, because I won't tell them in so many words whose child he is – though I only half know that meself… That he's either yours or Josie's I mean – though that should be obvious.

"They've even been layin' bets that he's a Dromgoole an' the master's grandson, yet persist in callin' him a 'Nobody's Child,' –

ye know, a child born out of wedlock to a wanton woman with no father in sight to claim him.

"They don't know that..." she bristled, "they're just ignoramuses an' bein' vicious. For Josie never was a "wanton woman" chasin' after the boys. Just the opposite, she was a darlin' girl an' a proper lady an' I loved her like me own. An' I'm certain that the terrible thing that was done to her on the night that the innocent child was conceived was never her fault.

"Perhaps they think he's mine...?"

"Oh no Caeli," Molly said, "they eliminated ye' long ago, certain if he was yours ye'd never have given him away – havin' borne an illegitimate son of your own many years before an' not abandoned him.

"Besides, the timin' was all wrong as far as you were concerned, for ye've been gone too long – twenty odd years an' more, an' rumoured to be livin' abroad. Whereas the timin' was right for Josie and the numbers added up, Josie disappearin' the night of her eighteenth birthday, eight years ago, an' the lad just past seven. But who the third party, the blessed child's father might be, none of us has a clue.

"But all that aside, I trust the McGintys. Young Kieran's a lovely young man an' as decent as they come an' does a lot for meself an' the master. Dependable he is with two lads of his own who seem to understand Rory's special problems an' treat him kindly.

"But oh, he's the darlingest little fellow, Caeli," she added, switching her attention to Rory and her mood to one of pure love, "Deep an' thoughtful like my James used to be. But he's also very vulnerable an' I need to protect him from that lot down there.

"But don't think for one moment he's slow... He's as sharp as a tack an' as quick as a lick to sum someone up. An' once he feels he can trust... Well, Lord save us all, he turns into a regular little chatterbox.

"Your father used to tease him," Molly went on, "Just like he used to tease Josie when she was his age. Tellin' him he must have been vaccinated with a gramophone needle because he talked so much, which of course made the little rascal giggle an' talk all the more. He reminds me so much of your sister..."

"Does he look like her then?"

"Aye, he does – or at least in my opinion he does. Though I can't say its altogether in the look of him, but more in his aspect, if ye know what I mean. For even though he has Josie's lovely green eyes, he doesn't have her gorgeous copper hair or her out-goin' personality; his hair is as black as a raven's wing – like yours and your Dada's was, and there's a seriousness in him that was never in Josie.

"Still, ye'll be judgin' him for yourself soon. But remember now, he's not been informed that he's a Dromgoole – your father was adamant about that. Believin' it was Josie's place to tell him if she wanted him to know." Then, with a cautioning waggle of her finger, added, "So be on your guard now, Caeli. Zipper your lips an' don't be lettin' any cats out of bags, for as I've already told ye, he's as sharp as a tack!"

"Consider them sealed, Molly," Caeli replied, pulling an imaginary zipper across her lips and mumbling, "Mum's the word."

Molly was obviously satisfied. "Good lass!" she retorted.

"As for yourself… I've told him you're Mr. Dromgoole's daughter come all the way from Australia to pay us a visit, an' that he's to mind his manners an' call ye Aunty Caeli."

Aunty Caeli… How the words jolted through her, as though being an aunt had never occurred to her before. How impossibly possessive they sounded… *Aunty Caeli…* How irrevocably connected they made her feel to the troubled child she had yet to meet.

"I've never been called 'Aunty' before," she said, sounding quite awed. "And you don't have to worry about me, Molly. I'll not be letting any cats out of bags or skeletons out of the family cupboard either! I'll be the soul of discretion, for I've only my nephew's welfare at heart."

"Good lass!" Molly retorted for the second time, sounding doubly satisfied. "That's all I wanted to hear. So I'll be away to the kitchen then an' get that bit of beef in the oven or we'll be eatin' it raw!"

Once again Molly exited the door and started back down the hall. The sound of her humming some old Irish ditty coming back to Caeli, who was propped against the pillows and sipping her tea and feeling strangely assured that everything *was* going to be alright.

As the familiar surrounds of her family home gathered about her, she began to feel for the first time since Danny had died that the injustices of the past were beginning to loosen their hold and slip away. The kindness of Molly and old Mr. Shaw contributing greatly to this, arousing a sense of belonging in her she had never expected to feel.

Even the bleak old house with its unhappy past that she'd viewed so apprehensively the previous night, seemed more endearing to her now. Admitting to herself she'd been less than a fool to think she could have returned to this magical land and sort things out in a flash and be gone from its shores without falling under its spell.

And now there was Liam Shaw to consider. The unexplored territory of this old-new friend who'd so recently re-entered her life, who, in the few brief minutes of his phone call to her in Australia, had made such an overwhelming impact on her that she'd come running halfway across the world to his feet. One look from his soft brown eyes and one single embrace in his father's office had upended her world and shattered her carefully controlled emotions and awoken in her a wild primeval need. How she hungered to hold him and taste of his passion, to hear the words as yet unspoken between them that he would say to her and she would say to him; words of some ancient Celtic love song buried in time that as yet she did not know the words to, to be poured from the depths of her being over every inch of him. For he would come – as sure as night followed day and the dawn rose up in the morning, he would come. But come, not as the shy uncultured youth of the past had come, uncertain and tongue-tied of his words, but as a strong virile man, sure of himself and ready to take her and make her his own. And she would be waiting… Oh yes, she would be waiting…

"This is all *mine!*" she now cried to the space of the bedroom about her, thrusting her arms wide in an all-encompassing embrace. "*Mine!*" she repeated, if she so wished and could bring herself to abandon her beloved Australia and the small business empire she had built of her own volition there. Thinking how irrational she'd been to claim she'd accept nothing from her father's estate, that perhaps it was here she belonged after all? Here in this house where the Dromgooles had dwelt for two hundred years. Here in this land where her roots dug deep in its Irish sod. For as much as she despised her father, she could not deny her birthright – deny that she *was* a Dromgoole born here in this house and of this heritage, whether she liked it or not. And now – if she chose, "THE Dromgoole!" the powerful mistress of Liath Caislean and the first mistress ever! Feeling strangely empowered by the thought, certain that her young sister Josie and the mother of the troubled child Rory, and the only kin she had left in the world, would soon be found. Putting her faith in the memory of a ten-year-old boy with steel-blue eyes full of knowing who possessed the power to see beyond that which other mere mortals could see. A child, who, even then at the tender age of ten had given the impression that he carried the weight of the world on his shoulders and of whom the townsfolk had whispered was no ordinary child but possessed of supernatural powers. Jamjo that child, James Joseph Joyce, and Molly, their housekeeper's son, out in the big world searching for Josie at that very moment... And that he would find her, Caeli had no doubt.

But finding was one thing, bringing her back was another. Would Josie want to come back? Would Jamjo's words wield the power enough to entice her back, or would the knowledge that the son she'd rejected at birth as a vile and shameful thing, had been found and was waiting for her at Liath Caislean drive her even further away? So many questions as yet unanswered. But the question that taunted her above all other was: Who was Rory's father? Was he someone from the immediate locality and known to all? Or was he a stranger from far away?

CHAPTER TWENTY-THREE
REQUIESCAT IN PACE

It was in Turlough's Wing, the North Wing of the house, where Caeli's sharpest memories lay, within the rooms of Turlough's that the ghosts of the past lingered longest and strongest, and in Turlough's where she'd gulped her first breath and the dye had been cast in that time of long ago to determine the course of her life. So naturally, it was to Turlough's Wing to which she was drawn and the pilgrimage to her past must begin.

It seemed colder in this wing, gloomier, neglected and unloved. The hall-runners threadbare, the paintwork peeling, the dust embedded, the dark-panelled walls laden with the equally dark portraits of her dour-looking ancestors, their mouths prissy prim, their eyes coldly dead yet as coldly appraising. "The parade of the dead," she murmured with a shiver, knowing each one by name – the Dromgoole men dating back to the time of Turlough. Turlough – Finn – Olaf – Conaire – Lief – Donagh and the rest, the portraits of their wives and children interspersed among them – bar one. The discoloured space on the wall with its rusted hammered-in hook telling part of the story – that indeed there was a story to tell, yet revealed nothing of its circumstance or the woman whose portrait had hung there, the woman so reviled by Bran Dromgoole that even her name was forbidden to be mentioned in the house.

"Eileen Dromgoole, your father's mother," Molly had whispered, attempting to satisfy Caeli's childish curiosity in a time long ago, the scant information gained from gossiping villagers tongues. "Deserted her husband and infant son – Bran – your father, they say, and ran off with "A prince of the Earth – or the very devil himself?"

She was feeling quite spooked by the time she arrived at her parents' rooms, and even more so upon entering them, for even though their earthly remains had been removed from the place, the sense of their spirits remained. She felt like a trespasser might feel upon entering a stranger's domain with no right to be there, that any deed of ownership – which was hers for the taking, brought no entitlement of admission to this deeply private place.

Fighting back tears, she entered the small sitting room of her late mother's refinement – fine French furniture and faded peach drapes. Noting her mother's magnificent portrait now hung above its exquisite white-marble fireplace that had once hung in Turlough's Great Hall, an arched doorway opposite it, leading directly into the bedchamber.

The drapes had been opened here, obviously by Molly, anticipating Caeli's need to come. Pale wintry light shafting through its narrow mullioned windows laden with galaxies of dust that had settled on the great bulks of furniture and the magnificent four-poster bed – the bed that her parents had shared for the term of their married life and in which she and her sisters had been born. Visualising her father laid out on it now as he had been but a few days before, dressed in his best formal attire. His hands crossed resignedly upon his chest, his face ashen and grim, the silken draperies that hung about him, frayed and faded plum-red. She could even imagine the womenfolk gathered about him, dark and devout in their nunnery black, rosary beads clicking, threading fingers, praying for his immortal soul to be raised above – *Hail Mary full of grace the Lord is with thee*...Their menfolk clinging to the outer rim, more likely praying for a good stiff drink before they carried their master down to "Lie in State" in the Great Hall below.

The room was overbearingly cloying still, burdened with the lingering odours of death and burning incense and the sweet anointing oil of myrrh, and the inevitable stench of melted candlewax from the dozens of candles that Molly would have undoubtedly lit.

For Molly had a "thing" about candles, according to Molly, candles went hand in hand with everything sacred? Sort of like "soul-savers" she claimed them to be and powerful antidotes of the devil, that a prayer was hardly a prayer at all without the acrid little twiddles of smoke to accompany it to heaven.

The setting as silent and lifeless as an abandoned stage now, awaiting its actor's return to enact the next scene and return it to life. Yet she sensed that the cast of the dead still lingered, and that her father was watching and strongly disapproving of her being there at all. Glancing nervously about her, daring to touch nothing, and anxious to be gone from this scene of death and return to the land of the living. Wondering again what it was he'd held against her all these years that had made him despise her so. Wondering also at her parent's marriage and if they'd been happy together, sensing often her mother had not.

"A wake to end all wakes' was what your father wanted Caeli," Mr. Shaw had said, describing the gathering in Turlough's Great Hall in great detail. "His wish was to be there in the Great Hall among us with his coffin placed on the Valhalla Stone and the sconces on the walls set ablaze as they had in days of old. Molly even had the banners cleaned and rehung and the Dromgoole Coat of Arms and the ancient weaponry scrubbed and polished. And they looked magnificent Caeli. We did him proud."
Are you saying that he wished to attend his own wake, Mr. Shaw? That's weird…"
"I am. And I assure you he gave us no trouble at all and was very well behaved. And the Mons was all for it. And we buried him quietly the following day.

How sharply his words brought the occasion to her mind, visualising the scene in all its glory: A blending of two ancient heritages – Norse and Celt! Magnificent! Stirring! Dramatic! She could even imagine trumpets in the gallery above blared. Yet try as she might, she could arouse no sense of bereavement for this man who had sired her, squeeze not one solitary tear from her well of compassion to mourn his passing or show that she cared. Only cold hard feelings would come, feelings of regret for the past and for what might have been, and she turned from the chamber with a heavy heart.

Her mother's eyes in the portrait seemed to be following her as she re-entered the small sitting room and sat in her mother's special chair, eyes full of compassion, as though she understood what her daughter was feeling. The portrait that had been painted when she had first come to Liath Caislean as a bride, its skilfully blended hues capturing her stunning youthful beauty and the true-to-life shades of her brilliant green eyes and magnificent copper hair. But it had also captured something more, a look one could only describe as

187

melancholic, as though she was mourning a great loss. The magnificent heirloom ring – a stunning baguette emerald set in a sea of diamonds and traditionally passed down to the eldest daughter on her mother's side of family for generations (which Caeli now wore), sparkling upon her right hand.

She must have been pregnant with me at the time, Caeli mused, having been told she'd been small and premature and born barely seven months into the marriage. Wearily she closed her eyes, sensing her mother's spirit close about her and calling back to her through time: *'Is that you, my Michaela, my precious girl, come home to me at last...'* Yet on opening her eyes, the sound was no more but a mere flight of fancy, an unfulfilled yearning deep in her heart. The creaks and the groans of the weary old house were the only reality, whispering their long-kept secrets not quite loud enough for her to hear.

Tears stung her eyes then, feeling impossibly forlorn as she scanned her mother's most cherished possessions. Valuable ornaments and Waterford Crystal filled the cabinets, with the cheap little vase she had bought for her mother when a very young child, proudly displayed in among them, and the harp standing in one corner, and the music box she'd so loved as a child with the dancing ballerina under its lid. Then there was the doll... The exquisite porcelain doll she'd been told had been gifted to her before she was born from someone "very special," but never told from whom, and only permitted to play with it here in this room. Her eyes going full circle then and coming to rest on her mother's bible placed on the small round table beside her.

Eagerly she gathered it to her like a long lost friend. The message inside its leather-bound leaf in the swirling copperplate of Grandfather O'Sullivan's skilled hand, *"To our beloved daughter, Maureen Geraldine O'Sullivan,"* it read, *"on the occasion of your Marriage to Bran Olaf Dromgoole, From Mother and Father with love."* Her mother's smaller, neater hand beneath it, recording the names and the dates of the births of the children of that marriage, interspersed with the deaths of the O'Sullivan grandparents and other family members. The last entry written in her father's bolder scrawl: *"Maureen Geraldine Dromgoole. Beloved wife of Bran Olaf Dromgoole,"* followed by the date of her birth and the date of her death – the twenty-sixth day of December – Boxing Day. The day after Christmas, the season she'd adored. Followed by the startling penitent plea: *"Forgive me, Mavourneen…"*

"Forgive me, Mavourneen…" – Strange words to record for posterity or the eye of a curious visitor perusing the holy book. Her blood ran cold as she spoke the words aloud, "Forgive me, Mavourneen…" How sinister they sounded ringing in the cold stale air about her. And she said the words again, "Forgive me, Mavourneen…" Forgive him for what, she wanted to know. What vile deed had he done that compelled him to beg her mother's forgiveness in such an open and undisguised manner for future generations to read?

"Forgive me, Mavourneen…" The words added a new dimension to her prior perception of what had taken place in these rooms on that terrible day her mother's death. "The tragic accident" she had accepted her mother's passing to be, now smacked of the guilt the community so steadfastly believed – that her father and their master Bran Dromgoole had deliberately pushed his wife – and their beloved mistress, into Turlough's Great Hall to her death, from the balcony outside this very door!

"Forgive me, Mavourneen…" Was the penitent plea he'd so undisguisedly penned an admission of guilt, and his half crazed mind wracked with remorse? Or was it some other indiscretion he was seeking her mother's forgiveness for? For as much as Caeli despised him, she could not believe he would have physically harmed her mother. He'd hurt many people in his life – as Caeli could surely attest to, but his weapon had been his vengeful tongue designed to cut to the core. Besides, her mother had brought out the best in him; it was only herself that had brought out his worst. He had truly been devastated with her mother's passing, and retreated into a make-believe world of his own, choosing to believe that her mother was still alive and ever at his side. And as Molly had so bluntly – yet so aptly put it: "That was the day he lost his marbles."

Purposefully now, Caeli reached for a pen, she had entries of her own to record. First entering the details of her young sister Meegan's death the year after their mother's, followed by that of her nineteen-year-old lover, Daniel O'Halloran. Recording his death as the same day as Meegan's, even though the actual date of his passing was unknown, linking them forever as one in the bible as she did her mind. For though she and Danny had never married and he therefore was not legally "family," he was the father of Kevin her son and in her opinion he had every right to be there. Then with great pride, she penned in the details of Kevin's birth and that of her late husband Malachi Morgan, entering the dates of their marriage and Malachi's subsequent demise a mere few months later, followed by the posthumous birth of his daughter, Elizabeth Morgan, eight months after that.

Then chewing the end of the pen in agonised indecision, she entered the birth of Rory Quinlivan. She hadn't even met the child, and for all she knew, Josie might strongly object. But quite frankly she didn't give a damn what Josie thought or whether she'd approve or not. In her estimation, Josie had sank to the lowest rung of life's ladder, incensed by what she had done – given her innocent baby away when she'd had the means to keep him. And she was also incensed at the injustice of the community for tagging the child a 'Nobody's Child!' He was somebody's child! He was her sister's child and her nephew and a Dromgoole! An ancient Irish name dating back hundreds of years to the time of the Viking invasion of Ireland, and for what it was worth, she believed he was entitled to his place in this family record here among them. They all had that right whether Josie or she or anyone else approved or not!

So with that in mind, she finally penned in the details of her father, Bran Olaf Dromgoole – the late head of this alienated clan, recording his lifespan of seventy-five years.

The ordeal had been draining, yet she closed the Holy Book with a sense of a task well done. Her hands trembling as she returned it to its place on the table that it slipped from her grasp and thudded to the floor, jarring something from between its pages.

It was a photograph, an old coloured photograph of a handsome young man in a blue British Air Force uniform, much frayed about the edges as though it had been handled a great many times. *"To My Darling Maureen, Eternally Yours, Michael, October, 1940."* the inscription across its lower right hand corner read.

CHAPTER TWENTY-FOUR

MICHAEL

"To My Darling Maureen, Eternally Yours, Michael October 1940..." Who was this Michael from her mother's past? And why was his photo kept hidden away? That he'd been someone dear to her mother was obvious, for why else would she have kept it ever close, concealed in the folds of the bible she had read every day?

Though certain she had never seen the photograph or met the man of its content before, Caeli felt equally certain she had, for there was a strong familiarity about him that suggested she knew him well. For the young British Airman staring out through the windows of time, had the same violet-blue eyes as her own and the same fine features and curve of smile and jet-black hair, giving her the oddest feeling she was looking in a mirror at a bygone image of herself.

Even his name leapt out at her and struck her like a physical blow – *Michael!* The masculine counterpart of her own – *Michaela!* As did the date – *October 1940,* placing her mother in London at the time of her conception, for she had been born in the June of forty-one!

Recalling Mr. Shaw's words of only hours before, claiming her mother had returned unexpectedly from London in the December of that year with what he had described as: "A deep melancholy upon her" and that she had "lost her sparkle" and that he'd more than a little surprised when she'd actually accepted his latest proposal of marriage, for she had turned him down on numerous occasions in the past.

'Eternally yours, Michael...' were obviously the words of a lover... Her mother's lover...? A war-time romance...? Then what had taken place in war-torn London back in that year of 1940 to end the affair and prevent her from marrying the man she'd so obviously adored? Was the answer to that obvious too? A casualty of war tragically removed from the scene seemed the only logical explanation for her pregnant mother's sudden return to Ireland and

the instant acceptance of Mr. Shaw's latest proposal of marriage. Yet for some unknown reason her mother had changed her mind the following day when he'd taken her to Liath Caislean and introduced her to his best friend Bran. That had been the end of wedding bells for Mr. Shaw, for she had married Bran Dromgoole instead.

The idea beginning to dawn on her then that this mystery man from her mother's past could even be her father, and that she might not be a Dromgoole at all? The more she thought about it, the more probable it became. For apart from having the same jet-black hair as Bran – the man she had always thought was her father, she would swear they had little else in common, whereas even a blind man could not have failed to see the startling resemblance between her and the man in the photograph. And if Bran had seen the photograph too, he also could not have failed to notice the uncanny resemblance between this Michael and Caeli herself, which could well explain his utter dislike and rejection of her from the moment she was born.

Then again, if she wasn't Bran Dromgoole's daughter, why had he placed her before his favourite daughter Josephine – who undoubtedly was, bequeathing Liath Caislean and the bulk of his estate to another man's child instead of his own flesh and blood? It didn't make sense. The photo creating yet another mystery she desperately needed to solve, and with a strong sense of ownership to it, she returned it to its place of safekeeping within the folds of the Holy Book, planning to tackle Molly about it at the earliest opportunity, certain that Molly would know.

Anxious to be gone from these rooms of long-kept secrets and broken dreams now, almost convinced that the mystery man in the photo *was* her father, yet failed to understand why her mother had kept such vital information from her when aware of how much Bran Dromgoole had hated her. Remembering the letter he had written to her, tucked in her handbag, the letter that Mr. Shaw had assured her she would want to read one day. Perhaps that day had come? Perhaps that day was now? Perhaps it would answer some of the questions she so desperately needed the answers to? Deciding she would read it upon her return to her room in her search for the truth. For if Dada had known she wasn't his daughter then perhaps he had known whose daughter she was and named the nameless from another land?

She likened herself to Rory then, to her sister's abandoned child she hadn't even met, and of whom the community had so cruelly tagged a 'Nobody's Child,' a child born out of wedlock with no father to claim him. Feeling like a 'Nobody's Child' herself now, with no father to claim her! That she and this unknown child of her sisters had something in common before they'd even met.

Uncertain if she wanted to continue the pilgrimage to her past, wary of other long-kept secrets she might stumble upon along the way.

Indeed, the young man in the photograph was already poking at her conscience and challenging her right to be there in the house at all!

But surely she had a right – at least half a right – being her mother's child and all? Yet sensing somewhere beyond the walls of Liath Caislean and the encompassing sweep of the sea, that there was another house with other people in it she half belonged to too – cousins and uncles and aunts, and perhaps even grandparents too? People of a different ilk and persuasion of life, who might even love her for what she was and welcome her there in among them?

Vacating the cold silent rooms of her mother and the man she had believed to be her father, with the ever increasing conviction he was not, and that the man in the photo was. The unknown British Airman of her mother's secret past, who so closely resembled herself, now the most dominant thought in her mind.

Anxious to know all about him now, to learn where he'd come from, whom he'd come from, his likes and dislikes and what his hopes for the future had been? Fascinated by the discovery of him, feeling more connected to him with every passing moment. Connected by name – Michael – Michaela; connected by looks – his incredible violet-blue eyes convincing her more than anything else that she was conceived of him.

CHAPTER TWENTY-FIVE
MEEGAN'S ROOM

Meegan's room was at the far end of the hall on the first floor of Finn's Wing and adjoining her own, the uninhabited servant's quarters positioned on the floor above. It was the wing in which her family had mainly resided, with the exception of her parent's quarters, traditionally situated in Turlough's Wing where Turlough's Great Hall was located. The portraits on the walls of happier disposition here, the subjects being herself and her sisters and the younger Dromgoole generations that were actually smiling, compared to the dark stern subjects that lined the halls of Turlough's Wing. Yet strangely, it was here in "Finn's" that her flesh began to crawl and the hair on the back of her neck to bristle, overcome with the eeriest feeling she was being watched.

The pain she felt on entering the room was worse than she'd expected, for it remained what it had always been, the room of a very young child. A shrine to Meegan was the room, devoid of life yet breathing the essence of all Meegan had been: An exquisite fourteen-year-old blossoming to womanhood, yet trapped in the mind of a three-year-old child forever. Or as Monsignor O'Leary had so aptly put it with her passing, "One of God's innocents on loan from heaven, and he had wanted her back."

The room was sweet-smelling and well-tended; the white four-poster-bed hung with fresh draperies, its quilt and pillows fluffy and pink, obviously at Molly's caring hands. Beloved treasures of Meegan's short life neatly filled its make-believe space: Children's books lined its shelves; smartly clad teddy bears partaking of fantasy tea, seated around a small table; dolls dressed in best finery lined up along the window-seat, as though awaiting their mistress's gentle return. For Meegan had been the most innocent player of all in the sordid affair played out in this house all those years before, for she, like Danny, had paid the highest price of all – paid with her life.

"O-o-oh C-Caeli… D-Dada h-has s-sent him a-away," Meegan had said, attempting to relate the conversation she had just overheard to her older sister, distressed to the point of stuttering badly and having great difficulty getting the words out. Great sobs convulsing her body, tears wet and warm seeping into Caeli's best jumper. "H-h-he's w-w-wicked, C-Caeli… Oh w-what are w-we t-to d-do?"

Meegan, who had turned to Caeli for comfort since their mother's tragic passing the previous year, had come to her then in a flutter of panic, skittering through the house like a creature possessed to find Caeli upstairs in her bedroom and throwing herself sobbing into her older sister's arms.

"There-there, little one," Caeli had soothed, speaking to her as though she was a baby, "now stop your crying my pet, and speak slowly and calmly and tell me what's troubling you. Who is wicked? And who is being sent away?"

Meegan's reply confusing, "D-Danny… D-Dada…"

"You're not making much sense, Mousie," Caeli had replied, calling her by her favourite nickname and stroking her long black hair as sudden feelers of fear gripped Caeli's insides. "Here, let's sit on the bed and you can tell me all about it," becoming more and more fearful as the incredible story began to unfold.

Meegan, it seemed, had been up in the tower-room (her favourite retreat), situated above their father's office, which in turn was in the base of the huge round tower. "Like the top of the world," Meegan would say in her timid little voice, enthralled by the sight of the endless sea and sky spread out before her. Remaining there for hours on end, loving the solitude and preferring her own company, for Meegan was painfully quiet and shy.

Well rugged-up in a quilt she had been, the adventures of Winnie the Pooh and a bagful of gumdrops awaiting her pleasure. But she must have been too rugged-up for she'd fallen asleep to be awoken by the voices of Dada and Danny O'Halloran down in Dada's office below. Their words sounding normal and un-worrying to her at first and she'd soon become engrossed in the pictures of Poo and Piglet and the honey pot, her favourite book, knowing the story by heart. But the voices had become loud and angry and alarming to her, and she realised that Dada and Danny were very upset.

"L-l-like they w-were q-q-quarrelling, C-Caeli," she'd explained. "It s-scared me s-so…" Their angry words mounting the twist of the iron stairs and echoing up into the tower room above, making her more distressed with every passing minute.

"I-I-I tried n-not t-to l-listen, C-Caeli," she said, explaining that she'd even put her fingers in her ears and pulled the quilt up over her head in her attempt to block the sounds out. "B-but I-I s-still c-could h-hear th-them, C-Caeli." Apparently hearing every last word and stuttering so badly, she could hardly get the words out. "Th-Th-they were *h-h-h-horrible* w-words, Caeli." Words she did not want to hear but run away and hide from and not have to hear them at all. But everyone knew that the only way out of the tower room was down the clattering spiral steps and out through Dada's office.

"Words…? What sort of words?" Caeli coaxed, exercising an external calm she was far from feeling inside. "Think hard, my pet, for it's terribly important that you get the words right."

The mere thought of her darling Danny caught up in some squabble with Dada did not bode well, for only the previous day they had gone to him seeking his permission to wed. Expecting his blessing, aware he thought highly of Danny and that he'd be glad to be rid of her, to be bitterly disappointed with his reaction, one of total surprise, having no inkling of the romance, followed by an outburst of unreasoning anger and sheer disapproval.

"Married!" he had roared, delighting in seeing her jump. "When did all this come about?" Stunned to learn it had been a year.

"B-before mother…" Caeli stammered, always nervous in his company and taken aback by the harshness of his tone. "I'm sure mother approved… She knew we liked each other – and she liked Danny…"

"Maureen Mavourneen *knew*?" There was scorn in his voice and disbelief of her words. "Your mother *knew… knew* that you and Danny were… But by God girl, what story is this! Your mother *knew* and said nothing of it to *me*?"

She also recalled how Danny had butted in; eager to lend his support and possessively slipped an arm around her shoulders, as though that would somehow strengthen their cause.

"Yes, Mr. Dromgoole – Sir, I'm sure Mrs. Dromgoole knew, that she was very much aware we had fallen in love, encouraged us even. We got on extremely well, Sir, Mrs. Dromgoole and I. And as Caeli has just said, she – Mrs. Dromgoole I mean, seemed to like me very much…"

"Oh did she now? And what about Zita, *your* mother – what does *she* have to say about all of this? You *have* spoken to her?" The question meant to make him squirm, and caused him to shift from one foot to the other.

"Well no, Sir, I haven't as yet – though she's certainly aware we've been courting and is delighted about that. But I thought it customary to speak to you – being Caeli's father, to ask your permission first, Sir."

A whole bloody year and right under his nose and he hadn't suspected a thing. How could he have been so blind! Even Zita had known what was going on and had actually encouraged them but deliberately kept it from him – what in God's name was she thinking of…! And likely the whole bloody village knew of it too and were laughing behind his back!

The lad was hardly ever here for Christ's sake, away at university most of the time, here some weekends and the odd week or two in between, that's all! The thought never entering his head when he'd brought Danny here to Liath Caislean that he'd fall for Caeli or that Caeli would fall for him. That wasn't the way he had planned it at all. He had brought the lad here for his own pleasure, to fill his own need to watch him, to gloat over him, to have him near – a purely selfish thing!

Too good-looking for his own good the lad was and too cock-sure of himself. Aware that every female in the village was chasing after him and that he could have had his pick of anyone of them any day of the week. It had never occurred to him that Caeli might have wanted him too. And now they were seeking his permission to wed! Dear God! The thought of them being alone in some secret place doing intimate things was repulsive to him. As for getting married… Never in a million years! Maureen Mavourneen may well have approved, but Maureen Mavourneen hadn't known the truth.

He had cut them off harshly, making half-baked excuses that they were too young or had to finish their educations and experience more of life, but offered them hope that he would consider the matter. Then, under the pretext of having urgent business to attend to, which he indeed then did, vitally urgent business regarding Danny's future, he dismissed them.

The following day he had summoned Danny to return to the house unbeknown to Caeli. Molly, aware that something untoward was up had anxiously hovered outside Bran's office door, hearing their angry voices within, but unable to decipher the words being said.

Danny was the first to storm from the office, the master close behind, their dark heads bowed and cursing with every step they took and slamming the door behind them when they left the house. While all the while timid little Meegan had been cowering under the quilt in the tower room above, unable to escape, fingers stuck in ears, yet hearing every word.

"H-h-horrible, n-nasty things, Caeli... Th-that D-Danny c-couldn't m-marry you e-ever! A-and s-something a-b-bout him b-being a-a un-g-grateful s-sod, b-because D-Dada w-was g-giving him l-lots of m-money... Th-thousands of p-pounds D-Dada said and th-that D-Danny m-must g-go f-f-far a-w-way on a b-b-boat."

"And what did Danny say to that," Caeli then asked, her voice deadly calm, her face as white as the sheets on the bed.

"Not m-much, C-Caeli," Meegan replied, her speech momentarily improving, now that the terrible weight of the quarrel had been passed to her sister. "D-Dada was d-doing m-most of the t-talking, but I did hear D-Danny s-s-say Th-that h-h-he'd l-like to k-k-kick his..." Her speech becoming more agitated again and reluctant to repeat the forbidden word poised on the tip of her tongue, looking imploringly up at her big sister's ashen face. "It's an n-naughty w-word, C-Caeli."

"It's OK, my pet. You can whisper it to me."

"B-b-buggerin'," Meegan whispered apologetically, close to Caeli's ear, "That h-he'd like to k-k-kick his b-b-buggerin' b-backside to k-k-k-kingdom c-come!"

Caeli sucked in her breath as the room began to spin and bright white lights flashed before her eyes, feeling she was teetering on some precipitous brink and about to fall off.

"Then what happened?" she whispered back

"Th-then they b-both l-left, C-Caeli, and s-slammed the d-door s-so h-hard that it m-made m-me j-jump and f-feel a-all s-sort o-of s-sick in-s-side and I-I h-hurried d-down the s-steps to f-find y-you…"

Caeli was feeling pretty sick herself at that point of time, fear overriding her normally controlled demeanour, her body shaking like a tree in the wind, no longer able to hide her distress from her frightened little sister. And they clung to each other, both trying to bestow and draw comfort from the other.

It was then; at that precise moment that Molly arrived on the scene, bursting into the room like an avenging angel, knowing something was dreadfully wrong.

"What's goin' on girls?" she'd demanded to know, "for there's the devil to pay down below! Your father an' that Danny O'Halloran lad shoutin' at each other like a pair of hooligans, your father goin' off in one direction lookin' like thunder an' fit to kill an' Danny just as bad goin' off in the other, an' young Meegan here, skitterin' about like she's got a bee in her knickers! Lord save us all, I've never seen the likes of such goin's-on in all me born days! Have ye all gone stark raving mad?"

Dada had returned the following day, grim faced and tightly drawn into himself, offering no explanation as to where he had been or what the argument with Danny had been about, yet seemingly anxious for Danny's welfare. Explaining that Danny had gone out in *Sea Nymph* – his little yellow yacht, following their disagreement the previous day and had not returned, that he'd alerted Paddy McGraw the Coastguard, of Danny's absence, for the weather was changing, the wind on the rise and an almighty storm brewing out to sea.

With everyone concerned for Danny's welfare, Meegan's absence had gone un-noticed until she was called for tea, for it was quite normal for Meegan to amuse herself for hours on end.

They had rung the bell in the courtyard over and over, warning all in the valley of an emergency and to come. The word quickly spread that this special young girl was nowhere to be found, bringing every last man of the isolated community rushing to join in the search.

Had they gone straight to the clifftop, they might have saved her, but understandably, they'd searched the house first. Searched it from top to bottom then searched it again. Searched high in the attics and deep in the cellars and even searched the shuttered and shrouded rooms of Turlough's Wing, their alarm increasing with the strength of the storm and the oncoming night. Some even searched the house again, while others re-checked the stables and outhouses of the estate with lanterns and torches blazing, the family dogs eventually leading them to the ridge of the cliffs overlooking the sea. The storm was raging and screeching like demons of the deep when at last they found her, tossed like a rag doll in the surging mass below. Fourteen-year-old Meegan was dead and nineteen-year-old Danny was missing at sea.

Looking for Danny from the top of the cliffs, Meegan was said to have been with all the concern of a devoted lover in her pure young heart. For it had been no secret to anyone that Meegan, in her infinitely innocent way, had been in love with Danny too.

Yes, the pain was much sharper here, and Caeli turned from the shrine to her beloved young sister with an overwhelming sadness in her heart. Yet in the doorway she paused and turned and looked back in, hoping to find she knew not what? Yet its pristine atmosphere remained unchanged, as did the smiles on the faces of the dolls lined up along the window seat, waxen and unmoving, their glass eyes blindly staring, offering no tears of compassion or hint of understanding, their cherry-red lips pouting as though they had something to say yet doomed to remain eternally mute. Her heart was heavy as she again turned away and tiptoed from the room as reverently as she had entered it, knowing she would never cross its threshold again.

CHAPTER TWENTY-SIX
MEETING RORY

There was only one other room in Liath Caislean that Caeli now wished to see, "The Nursery," the cosy haven of Josie, her baby sister's room, who had been barely four when Caeli had been forced from the house. Then, apart from the Great Hall in Turlough's Wing, into which her mother had fallen, there was nothing more of the house that would draw her that day. Only the rooms of the ones she'd held dear were important to her now, the rooms in which the most pertinent scenes of their lives had been acted out and so greatly affected them all, the rest just meaningless spaces of someone else's dreaming that could wait another day.

Yet on entering the room of the beloved child, she was shocked and confused, for it wasn't the room she had expected to enter at all. It was a stranger's room full of stranger's things, where nothing of the adorable four year old sister with the bouncing copper curls and sea-green eyes remained to stir up old memories and tug at her heart – save those that a raggedy yellow-haired doll conjured up. Its toys and baby furnishings banished to the attics, the small infant's bed traded for a grownup's contemporary suite. The room of the child she had foolishly thought to revisit, a memory of the past that existed no more. It was a woman's domain she had entered, a woman of which she knew nothing about. And she struggled to come to terms with the change and annoyed with herself for not having anticipated it, that the precious child of the past had long ago vacated and permitted an unknown woman to enter and take her place.

Wearily, she stretched out on the stranger's bed, feeling no connection to the child or the woman Josie had undoubtedly become, the only thing that linked her now to her beloved little sister and the memories of the past, was the bedraggled yellow haired doll.

How she wished its stitched-on lips could break open and speak and reveal what had happened in this room on that night of long ago that had caused Josie to flee from the house and never return. And flee from whom? Who had terrorised her so that she'd felt impelled to run away? For according to Molly, Josie had come up here to her bed that night, following her eighteenth birthday party in Turlough's Great Hall 'as happy as a lark' but nowhere to be found come morning.

"Simply disappeared" Molly had said, "gone, like a puff of smoke with word to no one an' not heard from since." The news was unexpected, unaware that Josie had even left, having taken it for granted she would have remained loyally by Dada's side all these years – being his favourite daughter and all.

Questions she'd put to Molly the previous night, to which the normally forthright Molly had been abnormally evasive, her answer making little sense and skirting the issue.

"The Lord only knows why young lassies do what they do, my lamb," Molly had hedged, "Or young laddies either for that matter. I've long given up tryin' to work the young folk of today out. An' if I had all the answers, wouldn't I be puttin' them in bottles an' sellin' them in the marketplace an' makin' me fortune…"

"But, Molly…" Caeli protested, certain Molly was hedging and knew more than she was letting on about. "Josie *must* have said something… Hinted at least that something or someone was troubling her and given some clue as to what she was planning to do?"

"Nary a word, my lamb, she seemed quite untroubled to me, in fact just the opposite was true – extremely happy. Had a whale of a time at her party that night, an' didn't she look gorgeous an' all an' so like your mother – God rest her soul, that it pained me to look upon her. Some even sayin' she had that special look of a woman in love, for its radiant she was.

"Yet as far as I could see, there was no one special at her party that night. No one she batted her eyelids at or paid any special attention to – though she could've had her pick of any one she fancied that night, they were all jostlin' for her attention and more than a little in love with her. An' she danced every dance with every adorin' young man in the room until the clock struck midnight that I wore meself out just tappin' me toe watchin' her do it. An' she was still dancin' an' hummin' all the way up the stairs to her bed.

"But I've been thinkin' – at least since we've learned of Rory's existence, that perhaps the blessed child was conceived against her will up in her room that very same night, that the good for nothing son of Satan that did the unspeakable deed, was already up there waitin' for her when she went up? For accordin' to me calculations – an' I've always been good at doin' me sums, the date of Rory's birth coincides precisely with the date of Josie's birthday – almost nine months to the day!"

Molly's "sums" confirming Caeli's calculations too, for Caeli had had the very same thought.

"Be that as it may, Caeli," Molly continued, "even if your sister had been taken against her will that night – an' God save us all, I pray that was never the case, she couldn't have known she was expectin' a child at the time, could she now? So for the life of me, I can't understand why she ran away at all – at least not before speakin' to me or her Dada or even to Jamjo. For as God is me witness, Caeli, I swear I had no idea she was goin' or that anythin' was troublin' her. She went off with Jamjo earlier that day for a walk in the woods with not a care in the world – for he had a birthday present to give her – a Claddagh ring, it was – a beautiful gold friendship ring, for he was unable to attend her party that night. An' I'm sure she'd have told him if somethin' or someone was botherin' her, for she always confided in him. Very protective of her, my Jamjo was, an' always has been. Like brother an' sister the pair of them were, bein' born an' raised under the same roof. Nor did I know then, nor do I know still, the identity of the good for nothing varmint that would do such a terrible thing to an innocent girl – if that's what you're askin' me, Caeli. I'm as much in the dark as everyone is about that."

But even though Molly sounded sincere, Caeli was not altogether convinced she was telling all she knew and couldn't help feeling she was holding something back. Not missing the slight hesitation before her reply, nor the uneasy flick of her eyes that would look upwards or downwards or any which way but directly into hers, but feeling too weary to press the point further that night. Yet the more she thought about it, the more convinced she became that Molly knew more than she was letting on about and determined to get to the bottom of it.

No, there was nothing remaining here in this room to stir up the memories of her dear little sister, nothing to carry her back on a wave of nostalgia to the happier days of years gone by, all evidence of the beloved child – bar that of the raggedy doll, had been swept clean away.

Abruptly, she swung her legs to the floor and sat upright on the bed, making ready to leave, unaware of how totally wrong she could be. Her sudden movement startling someone or something concealed behind the curtains. A sharp intake of breath, a rustle of silken drapes alerting her to the chilling realisation she was not alone. The horrible feeling she had experienced from the moment she'd re-entered Finn's Wing and her passage down the hall returning full might to shiver through her once more. The horribly invasive feeling she was being watched.

With pounding heart and the gruffest voice she could muster, she demanded: "Come out from behind those curtains at once, whoever you are!"

An alarmed gasp, a quick shuffle, a bulge appearing in the curtains barely three feet high – then absolute silence, as though whoever or whatever it was, was holding its breath in absolute terror and unable to let it go.

"I know you are there," she said in a gentler tone, realising from the size of the bulge that it could only be a pint-sized ogre or a young child. Concluding the latter the most likely, assuming the bulge to be Rory, her sister's son.

"If your name happens to be Rory Quinlivan," she continued, in a kindlier voice, now certain she was right, "I would very much like to make your acquaintance."

No response.

"I'm Mr. Dromgoole's daughter, come all the way from Australia to meet you,' she coaxed, "You may call me Aunty Caeli if you like."

Still no response…

"It's really quite safe for you to come out you know, for I really don't bite – at least not too often. Only when I'm extremely hungry or you happen to be a big slice of chocolate cake with icing and cherries on top."

Stifled sounds… Giggles perhaps?

"Oh well, I shall just have to sit here and wait," she said, yawning and feigning disinterest. "I've got lots of time, you know – all day actually. Though it would be a shame to miss that scrummy roast-beef dinner that Molly's got cooking in the oven… Yorkshire pudding too I believe, with oodles of gravy…"

Moments of agonised indecision dragged on for what seemed an eternity before two green eyes peeped through a slit in the drapes, making their final assessment. Apparently satisfied she was quite harmless, the slit slowly parted and low and behold, there before her stood Rory Quinlivan, the child the community had so cruelly tagged a half-wit and a worthless "Nobody's Child." Yet undeniably he was "Somebody's Child." He was her sister's child and her nephew, the flesh of her flesh and the blood of her blood.

Caeli gasped, knowing him instantly, recognising in him a Dromgoole through and through and so overcome with the knowledge that for a moment she was struck dumb.

That he was Josie's child she had not the slightest doubt, for the green of his eyes alone would have given him away. Yet his hair was black – a raven's wing black – sleek and shining, as her hair and Dada's and Kevin's and even Danny O'Halloran's hair had been, sharply in contrast to that of his mother's magnificent mane of copper curls, like *her* mother's hair had been.

But his demeanour was one of great age, of learned intellect and pain, as opposed to the bubbling untroubled child Josie had been. Distrust of everyone, and the world in general, seeped from his every pore and sparked plainly evident in his vivid green eyes. And his body was slight, as though a good puff of wind could have blown him away, as opposed to the plump little Miss, his mother had been. Fully understanding now what Molly meant when she'd said it was more in the aspect of the child that marked him Josie's son. Something intangible that Molly saw in him that was clearly evident to Caeli too, and also like Molly, a something she too could not quite define.

The green eyes stared hard at her now, as though they were taking her measure and plunging right into her soul. She felt in awe of him. In awe of his beauty and obvious intelligence and wondered how Josie could have given such an incredible child away.

With a sob tearing from her throat, she opened her arms as she opened her heart. "Come little one" she said raggedly, falling to her knees before him. "Come here to your Aunty Caeli." And without hesitation, the little one came.

CHAPTER TWENTY-SEVEN
YESTERDAYS

Miss Josephine Dromgoole had been all of three on that particular Christmas Eve, her plump little body most cosily curled into a huge winged chair positioned beside a big roaring fire in Turlough's Great Hall. The glowing embers in the massive grate had been burning for days, with the hope of instilling a measure of warmth into its thick stone walls, for the Christmas festivities were being held there the following day.

Her chubby little arms hugged chubby red-stockinged knees drawn up under her chin, a misshapen rag doll (due to its owner's most ardent hugging) with unblinking blue-button-eyes and a tangle of yellow woollen hair, squashed tightly in between. The child was unmoving, totally mesmerised by the glittering wonderland of Christmas lights and decorations bedecking the massive hall about her.

Only her sharp green eyes moved, quick as the flick of a lizard's tongue, darting here and there to feast upon the dazzling metallic chains that looped the ancient iron sconces and the weapons of Viking antiquity mounting its walls, then linger on the huge Christmas tree standing in one corner. Its multi-coloured baubles and blinking lights fascinating the child as she traced the garlands of tinsel coiled about its branches right up to the golden-winged angel on top, then plunged them back down to ponder again the mysterious packages piled under the tree, tied up with ribbons of silver and gold.

"So pretty, Miss Mopsy," she whispered to the doll, her baby voice full of wonder, her eyes returning yet again to the garlands of red-berried holly looping the mantel above where she sat, where three Christmas stockings were hung.

"See, Miss Mopsy," she explained to the doll, awkwardly raising three chubby fingers, "One for Caeli, one for Meegan, and one for me."

"But mustn't touch!" she cautioned, waggling a finger and frowning sternly at the doll. "Yukky poison, Mammy said," referring to the red holly berries. Then, spying the mistletoe dangling in the entrance, she cupped her hand over her mouth and stifled a giggle.

"That's kissy-missy," she informed the doll, as ten-year old Jamjo had informed her in his best matter-of-fact informative sort of voice, "If you stand under that you're allowed to kiss anyone you've a mind to," he had said. "So you'd better watch out Josie, for tomorrow I'm coming for a kiss."

Josie giggled some more. Jamjo was funny. She liked Jamjo.

Clutching the beloved doll tightly to her, she wriggled from the chair and crossed the room to sit cross-legged on the floor in front of her most favourite delight of all – the small clay figures of the Nativity Scene gathered about a straw-filled manger.

"See, Miss Mopsy," she proceeded to explain to the doll, "That's Mary and Joseph and the animals, and baby Jesus asleep on the hay," relating her three-year-old's version of the story of Christmas to the doll, but quickly silenced when she heard a voice calling from the foyer.

"Josie... Josephine Dromgoole, where are you?" the voice said, right outside the door. "Hmm, I wonder if she could be in here..."

Josie sucked in her breath, for she knew it was her big sister Caeli. Caeli always said those sorts of things. She adored Caeli and her little heart fluttered, anticipating the let's-find-Josie game she loved to play so much, excitedly covering her eyes with her hands, playing hide and seek the only way she knew how, believing that if she couldn't see Caeli, Caeli couldn't see her, sitting perfectly still, barely daring to breathe.

She heard her big sister enter the room and move about, saying: "Hmm," again and wondering if she was under the table or hiding in a cupboard or behind the drapes, then made her squeal with delight by suggesting she might be in one of the packages under the Christmas tree.

"There you are, you little scallywag!" Caeli cried, feigning surprise and jumping when Josie uncovered her eyes and said, "Boo!" "Right under my nose and I couldn't find you!" and bending, she scooped the laughing child up in her arms and spun her gaily around, for Caeli adored her little sister as much as Josie adored her.

She thought her gobble-up-gorgeous with her masses of bouncy coppery curls and rosy-pink cheeks and sweet rosebud mouth. In fact, she was totally enslaved by her. But then little Miss Josephine Dromgoole had everyone under her spell.

"How many sleeps now, Caeli?" the little girl asked amid squeals of tickled delight.

"Only one more sleep, my pet," Caeli replied, plonking down on the floor with Josie in her lap, "and when you wake up in the morning, Father Christmas will have been and left you lots of presents! Isn't that exciting?"

But Josie's face crumpled, her sweet little mouth turned down at the corners and her big green eyes stared imploringly into Caeli's of deep violet-blue. "Don't want presents, Caeli," she pouted. "Only want puppy."

Caeli chuckled and hugged the beloved child to her, thinking, here we go again. "So you've already told me, my pet – at least a hundred times! But surely you want other presents as well... A dolly or a tricycle or a new skipping rope... What other presents did you ask Father Christmas to bring you?"

"Nuffink," Josie said, shrugging her shoulders and shaking her head, making the copper curls bounce like springs on her head. "Only want puppy!" she repeated, pouting all the more and threatening to cry.

Caeli nuzzled into her neck and made gobble-up noises bringing forth further squeals of delight. Then, poking her in the most ticklish places and emphasising the words, said, "You're – like – a – broken – gramophone – record – aren't – you – miss!" inducing further giggles. It was then that their mother, Maureen Dromgoole, entered the room. "What's going on in here?" she asked brightly. "Sounds like the Christmas festivities have already begun!"

Her amazing green eyes – the same as her youngest daughter Josie's, were full of the fun of the moment. Her kind curve of mouth, pulled wide in a good-natured smile revealing her perfect white teeth, her delicate features lightly powdered and rouged and an eye-catching beauty still, despite having born three children and now in her thirty-fifth-year. But unquestionably her most outstanding asset, which never failed to draw the eye before anything else, was her crowning glory, her magnificent mane of copper-coloured hair, uncertainly tamed with a tortoiseshell clasp at the nape of her neck. Caeli's eyes glowed with unconcealed admiration as she took her mother in, admiring her willowy body so elegantly attired in an up-to-the-minute outfit of caramel slacks and long-line jacket, a diaphanous scarf of emerald silk a frivolous touch at her neck. Wishing, as she had often wished that she'd inherited more of her mother's fantastic good looks and outgoing personality, for though she was blessed with her mother's fine features, she was smaller of stature and serious of nature with her father's jet-black hair. But unquestionably, Caeli's most outstanding asset was her eyes. Neither brilliantly green like Josie's and her mother's, nor deep midnight-blue like Meegan's and her father's, but black-lashed pools of violet-blue uniquely her own.

"This little scallywag is still going on about a puppy, mother," Caeli said, scrambling to her feet and smiling broadly, caught up in the magic of the Christmas Season. "Do you think she's been good enough for Father Christmas to bring her one?"

"A puppy now is it?"

"A white one, mammy," Josie added hopefully.

"Well, we'll have to wait and see what tomorrow will bring, won't we?" her mother teased, planting a kiss on the abnormally serious face of her youngest and winking at the smiling but normally serious eldest. "But why would you want a puppy now," she continued to torment, "with all the grand toys he'll be bringing you…"

The look of dejection that crossed Josie's face was more than Caeli could bear, and she hastily offered the soothing words while glancing at their mother as if to say "Oh please don't tease her."

"But if you've been a good girl, and you my pet have been the best little girl in the whole wide world, I'm certain Father Christmas is tucking a fat white puppy into his big red sack for you this very minute!"

But the subject of the puppy was quickly demoted to that of lesser importance as the very observant Miss Josephine Dromgoole found a new point to ponder.

"Why did mammy wink, Caeli?" she now wanted to know, contorting her face in a comical attempt to wink herself.

"*Did* Mammy wink, pet?"

"I saw her wink," Josie insisted, turning accusing green eyes on her mother.

"You don't miss a trick, do you miss?" her mother responded, "and it's high time you had your tea and a bath and put into bed, or Father Christmas might not come at all!" Asking, as she turned to Caeli, "Can you attend to her, dear, bathe and get her some tea? Something easy, like a coddled egg and fingers of toast? For I know Molly would be grateful, for she's up to her eyeballs preparing things for tomorrow. And you know Josie... She won't eat for anyone else but you or Molly."

"Sure I will... That's why I came to fetch her..." But where has our Mousie disappeared to? I haven't seen her for ages." Mouse or Mousie, being the pet name for thirteen-year-old Meegan, on account of her affliction and being so painfully quiet and shy.

"Upstairs in her room, I believe, with the door firmly locked, at least that's where she was half an hour ago. All very hush hush, I might add. I tapped on the door several times but she wouldn't let me in – even though I called out and said it was me. But it wasn't too hard to guess what she was up to – the sound of rustling paper, giving the game away."

"The dear little pet... Do you know when I took her to the village to do her Christmas shopping, she not only bought gifts for us and for everyone coming here for Christmas Dinner tomorrow, but for every man, woman and child on the estate as well. I suggested sweets for the children and hankies for the adults, and she was quite happy with that."

A dark cloud descended upon them at the mention of Meegan, dulling their bright Christmas mood, as both mother and sister contemplated the cruel twist of fate life had dealt her: A difficult birth three months too soon had caused permanent damage to her brain.

"God love her," Maureen murmured, "And how like my Meegan," she added, while pulling Caeli to her in an urgent and unexpected hug and saying as she did. "I want *you* to remember my precious girl that no matter what life has in store for you that I've thanked God every minute of every day for giving you to me." Then she paused, as if she was about to say more, but did not. Caeli returned the embrace, understanding her mother's heartache over her young sister Meegan's unfair fate, yet puzzled at the words that were clearly meant for her. Feeling her mother had opened a door to something in her past she had wanted to confide, yet abruptly changed her mind and closed the door again.

"OK, my pet," Caeli said brightly, as she headed for the Great Hall's doors with Josie in tow. "Your bath awaits you miss…" Deciding she would tackle her mother later about whatever it was that was on her mind, that the timing just hadn't been right.

"I'll be in father's office should you need me dear," her mother called after them, Josie's parting remark ringing clearly back to her as her youngest and eldest mounted the South Wing staircase of Finn's, "But why did mammy wink Caeli, why?"
She thought her youngest offspring altogether too shrewd for a three-year-old, but what a sheer delight and Godsend to her marriage she had been.
"Miss Personality Plus!" her father proudly called her. His perfect child, so different from the others… and if one knew the child, one could only agree. For Miss Josephine Dromgoole was a bewitching little minx who could charm the birds right out of the trees, an extrovert of the highest order born to be adored on the stage of life, devoid of Meegan's heartbreaking affliction or Caeli's too serious ways. Her mother the first to admit – though only to herself, that of her three daughters, this enchanting child was the one most like herself, and not only in looks, but in personality too.

Spying the rag doll lying forgotten on the floor, she gathered it to her and wearily sank into the same fireside chair her three-year-old daughter had so recently vacated, aware it was only a matter of time before it's loving owner would come running back to seek it out – at least before she would eat her tea or settle down to sleep for the night, for the doll was Josie's most constant and beloved companion. From the feel of it, it needed a bath too, something soggy and brownish smearing its cheek – chocolate dribble perhaps? Yet its blue-button eyes looked innocently up at her and she hugged it to her regardless. For the doll seemed to fill some latent need within her, reminding her of another doll in another time and place.

Was it payback time, she wondered, feeling the guilt of what she had done in that time of long ago engulf her once more and an overwhelming dread fill her heart. Unable to explain or suppress the indefinable feeling that something in her world was about to go horribly wrong.

CHAPTER TWENTY-EIGHT
LONDON 1940

Maureen had always loved Christmas, loved the message of peace and goodwill that the Holy Season wrought; loved the exultation of attending Holy Mass Christmas morning in the ancient stone chapel in the valley below, and returning home after to fires burning in every hearth and the mouth-watering aromas of Molly's Christmas fare filling every nook and cranny of the monstrous old house. She even loved the stark commercialism and the visual trappings of it: the holly, the ivy, the mistletoe, and especially the huge Christmas tree bedecked in shimmering tinsel and twinkling coloured lights. But most of all she loved the joy of giving and sharing with their small circle of friends, and the carols they'd so joyously sing gathered around the piano on Christmas night.

The workers from the cottages would be the first to arrive. Eleven o'clock seeing every man woman and child filing up the hill from the valley below. A smorgasbord lunch of Christmas fare awaited them in the massive kitchen with bottles of Guinness and mulled red wine and homemade lemonade for the children. And there was a second Christmas tree, decorated especially for them, and hung with a gift for each and every one.

Then the Shaws would come – the Shaws always came, always the first to arrive and the last to leave; their oldest and dearest friends Eugene and Jessie Shaw and their two teenage sons Chester and Liam. And Doctor Tom, her physician and trusted confidant would come, his timid wife Ruth clinging tightly to his arm. As would the eminent Monsignor Timothy O'Leary come, folk bonded for all time with the unspoken promise of loyalty and friendship forever.

Her eyes also scanned the tinsel-draped room, as sparkling and spellbound as her three-year old daughter's had been. Also darting from tree to garlanded mantel to Nativity Scene – her favourite too, devouring every last detail as though this was the last Christmas she was ever to see.

The fire crackled, cinders shifted, sparks sprayed, miniature explosions sucked up the chimney in its draught. Her gaze intent upon the dancing embers and the scenes of the past recreated there: Britain at war… London burning… The passionate affair… The child on the way… The tragic ending… The broken heart… An old, old story, eternally new… And again she asked herself, if it was payback time?

The war had been raging for almost a year when she had arrived in London, honoured to sing for the enlisted men there. The German Luftwaffe were blitzing the city relentlessly and air-raid sirens had blared into her rendition of "The White Cliffs of Dover" at an officers' club on the outskirts of the city, when a young British Airman had approached and taken her arm.

"Here Miss," he had said, "allow me to escort you" and had ushered her down some rickety stairs to a dimly lit cellar. His arms close about her as she trembled in terror at the bombs that exploded overhead. His arms about her still when the "all-clear" sounded, for already they had sensed an awakening between them, the irrepressible stirrings of love.

His name, she was to learn, was Michael. A young British pilot with jet-black hair and a suave Douglas Fairbanks moustache and the most incredible violet-blue eyes she had ever seen.

The affair had been urgent and passionate from the start, made more so by the uncertainty of war, and she had fallen pregnant with Michael's child almost immediately. He was so overjoyed at the prospect of becoming a father that he'd impulsively purchased the exquisite porcelain doll, certain even then they were having a girl. Planning to marry the following weekend and meet his family, but his plane was shot down over the English Channel the following day.

She returned to Ireland only days after that, deeply in mourning at Michael's death and certain she would never fall in love again. Deciding she would marry for convention's sake and give her unborn child a father and a name. And who better than Eugene Shaw, the prominent Dublin lawyer who'd been in love with her forever, and had proposed to her on numerous occasions in the past?

He had met her from the ferry in Cork, and as she had expected, he'd proposed to her again. Much to his delight and utter amazement, she had accepted, but had changed her mind the following day when he'd taken her to Liath Caislean and introduced her to his best friend Bran.

She had heard about Bran Dromgoole, the master of the isolated "Liath Caislean" on the West Coast of Ireland. Heard he was a half-crazy recluse of ancient Viking blood who'd been raised by a half-crazy father whose wife had run off with another man. Heard he was rough and tumble and ill-bred and lacking in social graces. But she had also heard he was devastatingly handsome, dark and brooding and possessed of a wild animal attraction that assured him of no shortage of the company of the opposite sex. Attracted to him herself the instant she saw him, but for reasons more callous. Observing him from a distance, she had noted he bore an uncanny resemblance to Michael, so much so that they could have passed as brothers! Though Bran's eyes were almost black, compared to Michael's of a deep violet hue, and he was bigger of stature, as opposed to Michael's more diminutive state. The thought crossing her mind before they were even introduced how easily he could pass for her unborn child's father. Even his antisocial disposition and the isolation of his house cast high on the crest of the wild Irish cliffs, seemed a godsend to her, the perfect place to hide from the world and mourn her love and raise his child.

'Hi Bran, Merry Christmas, this is my Maureen who has just consented to be my wife – I've told you all about her...' She could still hear Eugene's ecstatic introduction, recall the delight on his face, believing he had won her heart at last. But she also remember how Bran had ignored him, offered no shake of hand or congratulation or Christmas tiding, his dark eyes intent only upon her. In awe of her beauty and magnificent mane of copper-coloured hair and her amazing green eyes – eyes as intent upon him and enslaving him even then. Sensing the power she had over him, a power she would use to her advantage, a means to an end.
"Welcome Mavourneen," was his bland response.
"An early Christmas present, Bran..." hers equally as bland, proffering the gift she had brought. "Black Market chocolates from London... Can I tempt you, Sir?"

"Oh yes… You can tempt me…" he had meaningfully whispered, ignoring the chocolates and Eugene and the maid offering drinks, unable to tear his eyes away from her, reaching instead to lightly caress her cheek. The die had been cast even then, knowing in that instant he was hers for the taking. That before the night gave way to the dawn he'd caress all of her.

CHAPTER TWENTY-NINE
BOXING DAY

Yes, it was payback time. Time to receive a serving of what she herself had dished out, time to pay the piper for deceiving Bran into marrying her all those years before because it had suited her needs and saved her the embarrassment of bringing an illegitimate child into the world by passing Caeli off as his. Time to face up to the truth of her suspicions as well, for she'd sensed a change in Bran that kept him away from home far too often and drew him deeper and deeper into his own private thoughts. And she was thinking the worst – another woman – that he had fallen in love with someone else. Setting the time in her mind to voice her fears and bring them out into the open as the day after Christmas – Boxing Day; the day when the Christmas festivities were at an end and their guests had departed, for her suspicions were eating away at her and she could live with them no longer.

The handsome pair of Red Setters padded into the room, a welcome distraction from her troubled thoughts. Shara, the aristocratic female, languished on the rug close to the fire, disdainful of her presence, while Dougal, the more affectionate male, devotedly sat at her feet, his noble head resting on her knee, his soft amber eyes gazing adoringly up at her, a lick of her hand bespeaking his undying affection.

"What is it, old fellow?" she had tenderly asked, stroking his dignified head. "No one's paying you any attention today, heh?"

The animal whined softly and thumped his tail on the floor, as though he understood her every word.

Yes, everyone in the household was busy that day, going about their special chores for the Christmas celebrations. How they put her idleness to shame, wasting time going over a past she could not change and nurturing insubstantial fears as though she had nothing better to do.

"You two come with me," she commanded, placing the doll on the chair and rising with deliberation and patting Dougal firmly on the rump. The dogs were up in a flash, excited, anticipating play, romping about her expectantly as she marched from the hall in the direction of her husband's office in the base of the huge round tower, for she had special chores of her own to perform.

Half an hour later finding her seated at her husband's desk in a deeply pensive mood, studying three pieces of jewellery of vastly differing values placed on the desk before her, which, for reasons beyond her understanding, she felt compelled to present to her three beloved daughters the following Christmas morning. Personal items, precious to her, more treasured for their sentiment than their hugely discrepant monetary values, each representing a special milestone in her life, and very different to the gifts she had already bought them, wrapped and beribboned under the tree. Hence the small enamelled shamrock on a silver chain of very little monetary worth, the teardrop pearl on a fine gold chain of considerably greater value, and the priceless emerald and diamond ring, all three glowing in their varying intensities in the lamplight now focussed upon them.

It was for her tenth birthday she had received the shamrock, the unique symbol of Ireland. Three green enamelled petals set in a cast of silver. "Your double-numbers shamrock!" her mother had called it and naming it thus forevermore in her mind. Remembering how excited she had been on attaining her "double numbers" birthday, turning ten and feeling very grown up as she wore the little bauble about her neck. Even now, all these years later, merely holding it in her hands made her feel warm and special inside, for it invoked the happy memories of the day she had received it. The birthday party and the birthday cake – or rather the two cakes her mother had baked to form the number ten. She even recalled the rustling green taffeta dress she had worn – for green – especially emerald green, had always been her favourite colour.

Now, with trembling fingers she returned the shamrock to its box and closed the lid, deciding she would give it to her precious little Josie the following day. For even though Josie was only three, she knew she would treasure it and demand to wear it immediately – as she herself had done. For little Miss Josephine Dromgoole was a pose-artist of the highest degree who simply adored pretty things and being the centre of attention. Yes, my "double-numbers shamrock" shall go to my baby Josephine, she decided.

The single pearl on the golden chain was the next of her treasures to dangle in the lamplight before her, a lustrous, perfectly formed teardrop pearl. It was for her sixteenth birthday she had received it, coinciding with the night she had sung with the Irish Philharmonic Orchestra in the great concert hall in Dublin. Her dress again green, the preferred emerald-green but velvet this time, shimmering and soft, reaching mid-calf, her shoes of the shiniest patent black leather with dainty two-inch heels, her mass of copper curls cascading to her waist and gleaming like newly-minted pennies under the glaring stage lights. She knew she looked gorgeous, descending the stairs of her parents' home before they had left and twirling before their gushing praise. Recalling how her father said that the dress looked too bare, that it needed something to complement it, and winking at mother, he had then produced the small jeweller's box from his coat pocket. "I think this will do the trick," he had said, proudly placing the pearl around her neck.

What a night to remember! She was sixteen! The pearl her birthstone and the world her oyster! "A teardrop of the moon," her mother had said.

"A teardrop of the moon," she whispered now, lost to the thoughts of her second daughter Meegan. "A teardrop of the moon for my precious child," she repeated, thinking how apt the gift of the pearl was for her special young daughter, for it was Meegan's cruel fate that had caused her the greatest heartache of all and over which she had shed many teardrops of her own. For Meegan had made her own spectacular debut into the world, born on her mother's birthday but three months too soon, so at the whim of Nature, the pearl had become Meegan's birthstone too.

"It's so beautiful…" Meegan had timidly observed, admiring the pearl on some occasion in the past.

"Indeed it is, my darling… Almost as beautiful as you, my precious girl is," promising that the pearl would be hers one day.

It seemed Meegan's lot in life was to be fraught with uncertainty from the moment of her premature birth. "An angel fallen from heaven," Monsignor O'Leary had said of the fragile child, who was not expected to survive the day, predicting that it was only a matter of time before the Good Lord reached down and took her back. She had exceeded all expectations and was now an exquisite thirteen-year-old developing into womanhood in all the right places, yet the tragic circumstances of her birth had condemned her to childhood forever. Her long black hair contrasted sharply with the alabaster whiteness of her skin, her blue-black eyes stared huge and bemused from her undeniably Dromgoole face – that it pained her father to look upon her.

"Mouse," the family had nicknamed her, on account of her being so quiet and shy, preferring her own company and moving about the huge old house like a shadow.

Almost angrily, Maureen replaced the pearl in its red satin box and snapped the lid shut, frustrated at the unfairness of Meegan's fate, but also at the sense of time running out she could not shake off. The insubstantial feeling of urgency that strengthened her decision that now was the time to give Meegan the pearl.

The emerald ring was something quite different. Valuable! A magnificent baguette emerald, embedded in a sea of diamonds; a treasured family heirloom from her mother's side of family passed down to the eldest daughter for generations. By right of progression, it would have been gifted to Caeli on her twenty-first birthday or her wedding day – whichever came first, but again because of the inexplicable sense of urgency that Maureen could neither explain nor dispel, she'd decided to wait no longer, but to give the ring to her fifteen-year old daughter the following day.

With a sigh of relief, Maureen closed the lid of the box with the ring inside, satisfied with her decision and the choices she had made, feeling she'd accomplished something she just had to do. Wrapping each gift with the utmost care she set them aside to personally present to her three beloved daughters the following Christmas morning.

Barely seven months into the marriage it had been when Caeli had been born and never to this day had Bran voiced the words she knew were on his mind that Caeli was not his, even though he had voiced them loud and clear by his actions towards her, and his rejection of Caeli from the moment she was born? How thankful she had been for Doctor Tom's discretion, pronouncing Caeli premature when she was not. Aware he was in love with her and would have done anything for her. And thankful to Molly too for delivering her most precious child into the world, coming to depend on Molly, like none other since that night. Feeling strangely comforted now, recalling the promises they'd made on that highly emotional night of long ago, how they'd promised to care for each other's children, should life deal either one of them a tragic blow.

Now the eagerly awaited Christmas Day had come and gone and entered the irretrievable realm of the past, leaving her feeling morbid and decidedly flat. The dreaded Boxing Day was now upon her, whisking the joyous feelings of Christmas away and replacing them with feelings of emptiness and loss. It was a day that had always depressed her, yet decidedly more depressing *this* Boxing Day. And she wondered what it was about this particular day that made her feel so dismally down, so full of fidgety fear and the intangible feeling that something in her life was about to go horribly wrong.

Perhaps that is how it is for all who are about to die. Anxious feelings one cannot pin down, vague expectations of impending doom, of something disastrous lurking around a corner? For this was the last day on earth Maureen Dromgoole was to see.

CHAPTER THIRTY
REVELATIONS

"Why did Josie leave, Molly?" Caeli asked when they'd eaten their fill of the roast beef dinner and Rory was once again off exploring the house. The pair cosily ensconced before a roaring fire in Molly's domain of the kitchen, a big pot of tea on the table before them. "Why didn't she stay and marry the man, whoever he was, or at least remained here and had the infant at home?"

"Well now, my lamb, as I said before, who's to know why the young of today do what they do? They've altogether a different way of thinkin' than I ever had when I was their age an' they're streets ahead of me."

Again, Caeli got the impression that Molly was hedging and would have none of it.

"It's no use you trying to fob me off with more of your Irish blather Molly, for I'm certain you're covering something up and know more than you're letting on about. It's written all over you. So out with it now, for I desperately need to learn the truth."

"Oh, dear me now," Molly mumbled, sounding all flustered and flushed in the face. "It's fobbin' ye off now that I am, an' coverin' up? What makes ye think that?"

"Come now, Molly, we've known each other far too long to have secrets from each other. I know when you're being evasive, that you know who Rory's father is, or at least have a darn good idea?"

"As God is me witness, Caeli, I swear that I don't. I haven't the foggiest idea who the good for nothing son of the Devil himself is, though I wish to God I did."

"But surely you have your suspicions…?"

"Nary a one lass, an' 'tis rackin' me brains I've been doin' since Rory came here among us, tryin' to work out who the blagg'ard might be an' starin' at everyone that crosses me sight tryin' to detect some sort of resemblance to the lad. But all I can see is a mixture of his mother an' the Dromgoole in him an' 'tis up against a brick wall I've come. For honest to God, Caeli, Josie had shown no particular interest in any of the lads at her party that night – even though everyone claimed she had a sparkle of somethin' special about her an' glowed like a woman in love.

"The first I knew of Rory's existence was when Monsignor O'Leary rang here twelve months ago, sayin' that he had to speak to your father on a matter most urgent an' that I was to go an' insist that he came to the phone as quickly as possible. An' I'm sure it was the first your father knew of the child too, for the immediate change that came over him was nothin' short of miraculous, as clear as the night sweeping light into the day. He was all of a dither, sayin' that he had to get dressed an' go out – which in itself left me speechless, for he hadn't been out since Josie had left all those years before! Then orderin' me to go clang the bell in the courtyard an' summon young Kieran up here to the house – three clangs for Kieran an' he would come runnin,' an' that I was to tell him to bring the car around. So I knew somethin' of great importance was in the wind, but never in all me born days did I imagine it would be a child – that it would be Rory!

"What a shock it was when your father returned with the poor little soul huddled in the back of the car beside him with all he possessed in a brown paper parcel hugged tightly to him! Dear God, Caeli, a million questions were runnin' around in me head an' there was me struck as dumb as an ox an' unable to ask a single one! All I could see was how pale an' how thin the child was, his britches hanging down about his ankles an' a jacket big enough for meself to wear, but the only things keepin' him warm! An' even before I was told who he was, I had taken the little soul into me arms an' hugged him tightly to me, for me heart was achin' for him so.

"Yet even then, before your father had said one single word about who he was or where he had come from, I already knew, the profound effect he was havin' on your father alone, tellin' me he was no ordinary child, but someone special. For a sense of your father's old self had returned. A sense of pride I'd not seen in him in many a long year an' standin' taller somehow. An' I knew there an' then that the child was a Dromgoole an' brought here among us to stay. But oh," she added, her tone softening to one of pure love, "he's the darlingest little fellow you could ever lay eyes on Caeli…" as if willing Caeli to love him too.

"So, you honestly don't know who his father is then?" Caeli persisted, not quite believing Molly had told all.

"As God is me witness, Caeli, I swear that I don't. But I'd sure like to get me hands on the good for nothing excuse for a man that would do such a terrible thing to an innocent girl. For I'd swear on Pat's grave an' a stack of bibles that your sister was as pure as new fallen snow an' had never been one to go gaddin' about with the boys.

"Aye, give me broom an' five minutes alone with the creature an' I'd've thrashed him within an inch of his life… So help me God I would!"

"But whatever possessed her to run away in the first place then Molly?" Caeli persisted, disregarding Molly's indignant outburst, "that's what's puzzling me. Why didn't she stay and tell you or Dada what had been done to her? Surely Dada, with his intimate knowledge of the local community, could have discovered who the culprit was and taken him to account…"

Molly seemed uncomfortable, looking sideways and up and down-ways and ceiling to floor-ways; any which-way but into Caeli's questioning eyes.

"For heaven's sake, Molly," Caeli cried, observing the woman's discomfort. "Tell me what you know! For it's obvious you know something. Obvious you're covering something up. Out with it now…!"

"Arragh, my lamb, don't force me to say things I ought not to be sayin' – speakin' ill of the dead that can no longer speak for themselves. I don't want to be doin' that, 'tis disrespectful an' disloyal to the family somehow."

"You, disrespectful…! You, disloyal…! Caeli gasped, genuinely amazed.

"Don't be ridiculous, Molly. How could you even begin to think that, you, who've been here with this family for forty years and are the most loyal and respectful person I have ever known! So if you've got something on your mind that might help to unravel the mystery of Josie's disappearance in any way at all – and you obviously have, best tell me about it now and get it off your chest."

"Arragh, my lamb," Molly sighed, knowing she was backed into a corner and obliged to say what had been on her mind far too long. "I never could hide anythin' from ye could I? Yet it's really no big commotion an' likely no connection to the night in question when Josie disappeared at all.

"It's just that your father had not been himself for quite a while back then, an' I know for a fact that sometimes his actions caused Josie distress – not that she ever said as much in so many words, or that your Dada was aware of it either. But I have eyes on me face an' a brain in me head an' the ability to sense certain things, an' I'd been aware for some time that Josie was more than a little bit frightened of him."

"Frightened of Dada? You've got to be kidding! God, she was the light of his life, his favourite daughter, for heaven's sake, and he positively adored her! She had only to flutter her gorgeous green eyes or crook her little finger and he would come running... Frightened of Dada... Pish...! Lord, what did he do, hit her or something?"

"Course not, Caeli," Molly replied, sounding personally offended. "Don't be ridiculous! Your father was never a violent man. A black temper on him, aye, to match that black hair on his head an' that name of his – Bran – meanin' black crow or somethin', but never violent..."

"Black Raven, Molly..."

"Aye – wasn't that what I said...? An' you're quite right, lass, he did think the world of her, even though they didn't always see eye to eye. For she was his world an' all that he had – what with your mother an' Meegan in the arms of the angels, an' yourself gone to God only knew where? An' so like your dear departed mother she was – God rest her soul... The spitting image of her everyone said, an' to me that was the crux of the problem."

"Problem...? How do you mean... I don't understand..."

"Well, Caeli," Molly went on reluctantly, regretting she had gone down this path and wishing she could turn around and go back, "your father never got over your mother's passin' – as I'm sure ye already know, an' that he pined for her until the day of his own. Terrible it 'twas, he never went out nor let anyone in – except Mr. Shaw an' the Mons an' Doctor Tom – who came every week to check on his health an' twice every day towards the end.

"I believe he preferred to live in the past, that he just couldn't face the reality of life anymore without her beside him, an' that it all got too hard for him. But he found great consolation in Josie – her bein' so like your mother an' all. He even called her Maureen Mavourneen at times, just like he used to call your mother, an' spoke to her as though she *was* your mother, which was spooky indeed an' used to scare Josie half out of her wits. So when Josie left, I think your father's brain up an' left too. It just sort of snapped an' he did a lot of strange things that a man of sane mind would never do."

"What sort of things?

"Ah well now… Ravin' through the house like a lunatic for one with one of those Viking helmets on his head, an' proddin' the live-in staff in their backsides right out the front doors with one of those long spikey spear things from Turlough's Great Hall – darned dangerous if ye ask me – all but meself that was, leavin' me the impossible task of carin' for him an' the house singlehandedly. Then he ordered me to close off most of the rooms of Finn's – just like I'd been ordered to close off the rooms of Turlough's when your mother died – as if I hadn't enough on me plate already! Thank God Mr. Shaw stepped in an' told me to bring in all the help I needed, or I'd never have coped.

"Though when I come to think of it, closing off the unused rooms of Finn's was a sane an' sensible thing to do, what with meself an' your father the only ones rattlin' around in the place. But it's me tongue that's rattlin' on now an' not gettin' to the point of the matter at all. For there were times when he got even worse than he was when your mother passed on – an' that was bad enough – as ye'd surely recall? Times when he'd tell me somethin' he'd only just told me five minutes before or forget what it was he was about to do. Or times he forgot to put his trousers on an' ran around the house in his underwear – which was not a pretty sight to behold at all. Though little things like that didn't worry me much – except the underwear bit, for wasn't I almost as bad meself? We'd even laugh about it when he was more his old self an' cod ourselves it was old-timer's disease – though I know there's no joy in havin' that!

"You mean he had Alzheimer's?"

"Doctor Tom did mention that word… though he wasn't into discussin' your father's afflictions with me. All I know is that your father always recognised *me*. But strangely enough, Josie was the one he seemed to have lost sight of. Most of the time he was truly convinced she was your mother an' called her Maureen Mavourneen – just like he used to call your mother when she was alive, an' that upset Josie terribly. But he got ten times worse after Josie left before he got better – withdrawin' completely into a world of his own an' sittin' for hours on end just starin' into space. Then there were times when he'd gabble on to the mistress as though she was sittin' right there beside him an' never died at all."

"So what happened then?"

"Well, he just seemed to give up entirely when Josie left. Wouldn't get out of bed in the mornin' nor splash a drop of water on his face nor shave his whiskers nor eat. I had to get Kieran up here to see to him every day, to bathe an' dress an' spoon-feed him like a baby. Life at that time was at an all-time low an' me patience pushed to the limit. Each day draggin' on as dreary an' uneventful as the one before, an' I was all but climbin' the walls – until Rory came that was. Rory changed everything Caeli; changed our whole world an' turned our lives around – your Dada's an' mine. He was our lifesaver Caeli, a Godsend to us that brought your Dada back into the world of the livin,' an' I mean that from the bottom of me heart, for he improved time out of mind when Rory came."

"And you've not heard from Josie since?"

"Not a word, an' that's what broke your father's heart. For I'm sure I've no need to remind ye that she was the light of his life."

The ringing of the phone in the hall brought Molly to her feet and rushing out to answer it, calling back over her shoulder as she went, "That could be me boy now with news of Josie…" Returning minutes later flushed and excited to confirm that it was.

"This modern day world never ceases to amaze me Caeli," she said, puffing and sounding utterly bemused. "To think that me very own son was ringing me all the way from London to tell me he thinks he's found Josie – an' I pray to God he has, an' he's boardin' a plane to America this very night, goin' to a place called Las Vegas – a town in the middle of a dessert, would ye believe?"

"But that's fantastic news Molly!" Caeli exclaimed, leaping to her feet and hugging Molly to her and doing a little jig at the very same time. "But why is he actually *going* to America?" she queried, putting great emphasis on the "going," "Why doesn't he just phone her instead?"

"An' didn't I ask the very same question meself," Molly retorted. "But he thinks it might not be easy persuadin' Josie to come back an' that face to face might be a whole lot more powerful an' influence her all the more – for she always took notice of him. They were the closest of friends ye know, an' he watched out for her as she watched out for him. So if his heart is set on goin' there is nothin' I could say that would make him change his mind. But he's promised to ring me the minute he finds her.

But can ye imagine it, Caeli?" Molly prattled on, overwhelmed at the events taking place around her. "Me, plain old Molly Joyce here in this quiet little corner of Ireland talkin' to me son all the way off in London, an' perhaps even tomorrow, all the way off in America? God save us all Caeli, just thinkin' about it makes me feel all fluttery an' anxious inside… But what a wonderful contraption the telephone is?"

Yet "wonderful contraption" or not, to Molly the telephone remained a mystery beyond her understanding, unable to imagine how a voice could be carried far across the sea through such a thin cord! Caeli assured her it could and that they would wait for Jamjo's call – feeling all fluttery and anxious inside together.

For Caeli was protective of Molly's unworldliness to a fault, who in all her born days had never ventured further afield than the grand old city of Dublin, let alone departed Ireland's shores! Claiming she had hated every minute of the days she had spent there – even though on her honeymoon with her beloved Pat. Pronouncing it a "Mad Hole" that was good to get away from and return to the "sanity" of quiet country life.

CHAPTER THIRTY-ONE

THE LETTER

MY DEAREST DAUGHTER CAELI,

If you are reading this letter, then it means that my last and dearest wish has been denied me – to see my beloved girl again.

I begin by offering you my humblest apologies for what I did to you and to others all those years ago, the sorrow of which has etched deep into my soul with the passing of the years and made it even harder to express in words. Sorry that I didn't have the courage to come right out and tell you the truth right from the start.

Now, my intentions are to reveal all – to bare my soul as it were – to implore your forgiveness and hope I can bring you some measure of understanding as to why I did what I did all those years ago.

You see, Daniel O'Halloran was my son, Caeli, and therefore your half-brother – reason enough to deny my consent to your marriage, as I'm sure you'll agree. I should have told you the truth there and then, but I was a coward Caeli, unable to bear the shame of my indiscretions and have you look down your nose at me. But had I known the course my selfish actions would take, I would gladly have born that shame.

I completely lost it that day when you and Daniel came to me seeking my permission to wed. I wasn't expecting it, nothing was further from my mind, totally blind to the fact that you two were sweethearts and had fallen in love. How my heart ached for you, my daughter and my son – true star-crossed lovers doomed from the start. For marriage was out of the question and Daniel had to be sent away – at least until you got him out of your system. But then I lost it completely and sent you away too, having no idea you were carrying Daniel's child at the time. I also need to emphasise here, the solid truth of the fact that when Daniel fell in love with you, he had no idea that he was my son or related to our family in any way.

Of course I told Daniel the truth, yet as angry as he was, he could offer no other solution and against my wishes planned to tell you everything. And in hindsight, I wish to God he had. But he took off in *Sea Nymph* before he did so.

You know the rest of the whole sorry saga, my daughter. The blame lies with me and I accept that – for I was the one who let him go. I thought it would do him good to sail about the bay for an hour or two and let off some steam, never anticipating for one single moment that things could go so tragically wrong and that I would never see my beloved son again. I couldn't bear it, Caeli, and was mad with grief when I unjustly lashed out at you, blaming you for Daniel's death and turning you out of my house.

How I've wished I'd controlled my temper that day and been man enough to tell you the truth. As things stood, we were all losers. We all lost Daniel, but I also lost you and our dear little Meegan and ultimately my grandson and a granddaughter too.

I've been lonely for you my daughter and when I heard you had borne Daniel's son, I wrote to you, hoping to make amends, but I believe you had left for foreign shores by then. But respectfully, I would like to point out – with no presumption intended, that your son is truly a Dromgoole and has every right to adopt and perpetuate the family name if he so chooses.

I also feel I owe you an explanation regarding Daniel's conception. Zita O'Halloran is of traveller's blood, as I'm sure you are aware, and bit of a wild one that first caught my eye when her band requested to camp on my land. She was young and bewitching then, dancing barefoot around the campfire with petticoats twirling and those big gold earrings of hers flashing as though they were on fire too, and before I knew what had hit me, we were having an affair. And I might have even married her, for bewitched I truly was, but a few weeks later, the field was empty, the vans had moved on and almost three years were to pass before they returned and I was to see Zita again. She had a little boy with her then, and her father informed me she had married Barac O'Halloran, but the marriage hadn't lasted five minutes and she was free again. But I was married to your mother by then.

It never dawned on me that the boy was my son, Caeli, until Zita contacted me many years later requesting money for his education. I was stunned of course but glad to oblige, for by then I had no doubt he *was* my son – one look at the young man he'd become was enough to convince me of that! And so I agreed, but on the condition I might see him now and again and that she'd not take him wandering all over the place again. I also bribed her with the cottage she still lives in and a fairly good income for life. But what clinched the deal was my promise to bestow a substantial sum on Daniel that would set him up for life – which I did, but anonymously of course. I also confess it was I who gave him *Sea Nymph* – anonymously again. Watched him from the harbour wall learning to master her, which I am proud to say came naturally to him and I named him "My Wild Gypsy Wanderer of the Sea" forevermore in my mind.

It came as a great shock to me to learn that I even had a son, but also a great delight, for I'd always wanted a son, and what a magnificent son he turned out to be! I was besotted by the lad as you yourself were, and hungry to have him near me, hence my decision to bring him here to Liath Caislean to do some casual work about the estate during his university semesters, never dawning on me that you two would meet and fall in love.

As for Zita... she thought it best to keep Daniel's paternity between ourselves and I agreed, both having our reasons for doing so – Zita's – I'm ashamed to say, more noble than mine. For Zita has a strong traveller's pride and believes it was better for Daniel to be a deserted son rather than bear the stigma of being an illegitimate one.

But as the months went by my pride in Daniel grew – as did my feelings of guilt for deceiving your mother, for Maureen had always been sensitive to my moods and had noticed a marked change in me. Mistakenly thinking there was someone else in my life – as indeed there was. But it was Daniel, and not another woman as your mother had led herself to believe it was. Her suspicions were eating away at her until that terrible Boxing Day morning when she confronted me and brought them out into the open.

Such a cold and blustery day it had been, yet your mother insisted we go riding. She would not take no for an answer and even had the horses saddled and waiting in the courtyard, for I think she had planned to have it out with me somewhere away from the house – in the Folly perhaps? We were both up in Turlough's in our private sitting room having a whisky to ward off the cold before we set out, when I actually brought the matter up. Confessing my affair with Zita and that Daniel was my son – none too gently, I might add, blabbing it out in my typical unthinking way. She took it very badly and we both said things we never should have said before she rushed from the room.

You know the rest of the story, Caeli, how I ran after her and tried to grab hold of her and calm her down – Bridget O'Brien was right about that part at least! But never in a million years did I push her, though I fancy the shock of my words would have broken her heart long before her neck was broken by the fall. But then my mouth and my arrogance and my uncontrolled temper have always let me down and blinded my reason, and for once I am certain I have your absolute agreement on that, having experienced all of the above on many occasions yourself.

I want you to come home, my daughter. With all my heart, I want you to come home. Liath Caislean needs you – as I am truly convinced you need it. And the little that is left of we Dromgooles needs you too. Unite the few. Build new bridges between yourselves and the community and regain the respect our grand old name once knew. This is where you were born, Caeli, here in this house on the wild, West Coast of Ireland. Your roots run deep in its sod.

And without intending to be presumptuous, I also want you to know that there is someone here whom I believe is also hoping for your return. A man who came to me many years ago when just a lad and our world was a happier place, a shy awkward lad, whom I believe you liked very much and of which I have come to realise in hindsight, was only to change when Daniel entered your life.

It is Liam Shaw I speak of, Caeli, Liam Shaw, Eugene Shaw's youngest son, who declared his love for you in the purest and simplest way in that time of long ago, confiding in me his wish to marry you one day, that you were the only girl in the world for him. I cannot speak highly enough of the man he has become, nor of the Shaw family.

Liam is also a lawyer, as his father and older brother Chester are, and a fine upstanding citizen loved and respected by all and deserving of only the best. He has never married, Caeli, and it's my belief that he never got over his love for you.

A lot of time has passed I know. Water under the bridge as they say, but I sincerely believe that true love transcends time and is forever locked in one's heart. It was my dearest wish back then, that you'd return Liam's love and marry him one day. I used to think how grand it would be if, after all the generations of friendship between the Shaws and the Dromgooles that we'd finally be united by the closer bond of marriage one day.

But let not the sentimental vagaries of your senile old Dada distract you one way or another. You, my daughter have a will of your own and will do what you will do.

That I was far from an adequate father, I'll not deny, and can only offer in my defence that if your mother had lived and been at my side, she would have guided my hand and I might have done better.

Until me meet again, I remain,
Your loving father
Bran Dromgoole

Caeli was stunned by the letter and struggled to take it all in.

Her thoughts spinning off in utter confusion, wanting to believe, yet not knowing whom or what to believe.

Horrified to learn that Dada had sired her dead young lover Danny O'Halloran with the gypsy woman Zita O'Halloran and that Danny was therefore her half-brother, conceding that was a good enough reason for Dada to deny his permission for them to wed. Yet even more horrified to learn that she in turn had borne her half-brother's illegitimate son! That she'd actually produced an illegitimate son of an illegitimate son!

The tone of the letter was perplexing to her too, too smarmy, too polite and considerate of her feelings to be the words of Dada, that words like "love" and "regret" and "beloved daughter" were alien to his tongue and did not ring true. Compassionate words, remorseful words, sentimental words that related in no way at all to the harsh hateful man she had known him to be. Even the letter itself made her suspicious, for, though undoubtedly penned by Dada's hand, it sounded nothing like him, but more like the words of the benevolent Mr. Shaw? Dada had never loved her, had never even wanted her in his house and had unjustly cast her out.

Yet at least it had answered the question she had long wanted the answer to – why Dada had been so dead-set against her marrying Danny – because Danny was her half-brother! But even that was potentially a lie, for the man in the old coloured photograph, discovered among her mother's possessions, now cast a different light on the matter. For if he proved to be her father – and she now had good reason to believe that he was, it clearly meant Bran Dromgoole was not. Could Bran have been aware of the photograph too and had the same thought, and the reason behind his antagonistic feelings toward her and spitefully conceal the fact she was not his daughter at all and unrelated to Danny in any way?

Yet even though the letter had answered one question it had created another. Why Liam Shaw and their innocent relationship of their youthful past should have been mentioned at all?

Unable to see its relevance to the matters contained therein. Feeling he been mentioned for a reason? But what reason?

As far as she could see, it only served to raise her suspicions of him and question his loyalty to her and wonder what his intentions towards her really were.

But disappointingly, as she had hoped, no reference to the photo of the young British Airman or her paternity had been made.

CHAPTER THIRTY-TWO
LIES REVEALED

Jamjo did indeed return from America and bring Josie with him, but astounding them all as his wife. Announcing they had married in a chapel in Las Vegas, explaining that they'd always been in love and secretly engaged when Josie had so suddenly disappeared eight years before. He also confessed it was he who had fathered Josie's child, making Molly bitterly disappointed in her son.

"It hurts me to say it, Caeli," she later confided, "but never in all me born days have I felt ashamed of me own flesh an' blood, an' I still find it hard to believe that it was me own son that took advantage of our Josie all those years ago. That's not the way Pat an' me brought him up to be. We raised him to be a gentleman, respectful of women, an' if I hadn't heard it straight from his very own mouth, I'd never have believed it at all!"

"Oh come now, Molly," Caeli said soothingly. "Don't you think you're over-reacting, that you're being too hard on him, for one indiscretion doesn't make him any less a good man? And he swears he knew nothing of the pregnancy, that if he had, he would have moved heaven and earth to find her and married her there and then. They were just two young people madly in love and caught up in the passion of the moment – which I myself know only too well."

"Aye, ye could be right there, my lamb," Molly replied, softening to the situation, "For I'm not so old an' decrepit that I can't recall how it feels to be young an' madly in love meself. Just the same, I expected better of me son, though I can't deny I'm over the moon at havin' a daughter-in-law an' a grandchild of me own at last."

"Then go with the flow and enjoy them, Molly, for you have to admit that Rory is an adorable little fellow and they all seem very happy together – especially Rory."

"Aye, they do at that, an' they deserve to be. An' I have to say the same about that boy of yours too," she added, nodding her head knowingly; Kevin, having arrived in Ireland shortly after learning of his mother's inheritance.

"Such a lovely young man…" Molly gushed in all sincerity. "He's completely lost his heart to the place and fits in so well that ye'd swear he was born an' bred here among us an' never set foot from Ireland's shores at all! An' if me eyes don't deceive me, he's also lost his heart to that young Patsy Shaw, an' it wouldn't surprise me one little bit if there was another weddin' in the wind. Off hand in hand they've gone, with a very excited Rory in tow."

But the feelings of goodwill were soon to change, Josie storming into the room where Caeli was alone, looking pale and distressed with Jamjo close behind her, having just read the letter Caeli had received from her father via Mr. Shaw. They were appalled at its content, at the lies it contained. Lies they had uncovered while in America but decided to keep to themselves and withhold from Caeli, aware they would cut her to the core. But after reading the letter they had changed their minds, deciding she must be told the truth, no matter how painful that truth proved to be. Josie rushed to her sister's side and grabbed her hand, making it glaringly obvious that something very serious was on their minds and about to be said.

"Caeli dear," Josie began, glancing anxiously at her new husband – now standing by the fireplace, one booted foot placed on the fender and an arm on the mantle, glancing as anxiously back. "There is something I – we – that is Jamjo and I, have to tell you. Something we'd decided we weren't going to tell you at all. Well, two things actually, as there is another matter we haven't been altogether too truthful about."

Caeli's heart sank, sensing the solemnity of the moment, and Josie coughed nervously, pausing to select her words with the utmost care, while knowing whatever words she chose or how diplomatically she strung them together, they would still convey the same devastating message and tear her sister apart. Words that would unleash a whole new meaning to words like "deception" and "betrayal," words that would reveal such unimaginable treachery that she feared they might even destroy.

"And I must warn you darling," she continued unhappily, "that what I am about to tell you isn't very nice," unaware of the tourniquet grip she had on her sister's hand turning its fingers blue.

"In fact it's an absolute bombshell," she added, "So you must brace yourself dear for it's going to shock."

Caeli could feel the blood draining from her, suddenly feeling lightheaded. "Josie… Jamjo… whatever's the matter?" she demanded to know, darting fearful eyes from one to the other.

"Surely it can't be all *that* bad? Not like the time… Oh God no… Don't tell me it's my children… That something terrible has happened to my children!"

"No dear, nothing as bad as that!" Josie hastily replied, but thinking it came pretty close.

"I can't do this darling," Josie blurted out, after several long moments of silence had elapsed, glancing again at her husband and sounding quite distressed, "I can't… I really can't… *You* must tell her…"

"Whist now, my love, you're getting yourself in a state…"

"*You* must tell her… Please darling," Josie reiterated, her voice sounding shrill. "I know it's my place, being her sister and all, but I can't – I just can't! And besides, it would sound more credible coming from you… You were there… You were part of it all… You were the one directly involved!"

"Hush now, my love. Calm yourself now and be strong for your sister's sake."

"Oh, for heaven's sake," Caeli cut in impatiently, "Will one of you tell me what's going on! The tension is killing me!"

As grave as a judge, Jamjo vacated his stand by the fire and came and sat opposite them, not relishing the task his wife had put upon him for one single moment. The task of revealing the person he'd seen in Las Vegas on the night he'd arrived there searching for her. Yet Josie was right. He *was* the one directly involved and it *would* sound more credible coming from him. Recalling the night with such clarity of mind because of the profound effect it had had on him. Going over the events once again in his mind, reliving every last detail of what had taken place in that bar in Las Vegas that night: The lights cast low, the music of Gershwin tinkling from a piano, the poker machines in the main gaming hall whirring and ringing, money wheels spinning, crowds roaring, fortunes won and fortunes lost on the toss of a dice. Deeply absorbed in his thoughts of Josie at the time was he, unable to believe he had found her at last. The life-sized billboard in the foyer confirming it was so, "The Delectable Susan St Clair" – Josie's new name, was due to appear on the main stage at ten. He had been overwhelmed at the thought that soon they would come face to face and he would hear it from her, hear in her very own words the truth of the matter, the honest-to-God reason why she had left. The reason that had caused her to flee from Liath Caislean in the middle of the night eight years before without confiding in him the terrible deed that some son of a bitch had done to her.

He'd tossed down a whiskey in the hope of calming his nerves and ordered another, imagining the ecstasy of holding his beloved girl in his arms once again. Going over and over the things in his mind that he might say to her and she might say to him, when laughter from a party further back in the bar jarred into his thoughts and drew his attention. A happy, raucous group making ready to leave, winding single file through the tables directly towards him when he had seen HIM, the obvious leader of the pack, completely relaxed and laughing so boisterously in their midst.

"As Josie has already implied, Caeli" he began soberly, "it is really quite devastating news and is indeed a bombshell I fear" – picking up the threads of the conversation where Josie left off. "Something – or rather someone I stumbled across while in America that we've all believed dead these twenty-odd years and of great significance to you and your son. So, I also suggest that you brace yourself dear, for it is, as Josie has already said, news that is going to shock."

But it was already too late, Caeli pre-empting what was to follow and already shocked! *Someone they'd all believed dead for twenty-odd years and of great significance to her and her son,* brought only one person to mind – Danny O'Halloran! Thinking at first that she'd heard Jamjo wrong or that he was mistaken, for it wasn't possible that Danny was alive. Then in the next instant, recalling the terrifying experience of her first night back at Liath Caislean. Almost convinced at the time that Danny had been very much alive and had come to her bed and made love to her, kissed and caressed her wine-besotted body and even whispered in her ear: *So you've come back then, my lovely colleen...* the experience so real that even with the dawn of the bright new morning, her body still throbbed in very private places, unable to convince herself it had been but a figment of her imagination, influenced by the talk of the past and the overindulgence of wine shared with Molly in the kitchen the previous night.

"Yet before I say another word on the matter," Jamjo's voice cut into her thoughts, "I want to make it perfectly clear, Caeli dear, that Josie and I do not tell you this lightly, that we've agonised long and hard as to whether we should tell you or not. Initially, we were dead set against it, believing no good could come of it. But now, in view of certain things that have come to our attention – namely your father's letter and the lies contained therein – or rather the lack of the truth, we have changed our minds completely and are now of the opinion that we are obliged to tell you what we have so recently stumbled upon, that the deception has gone on long enough."

He paused, bowed his head, his fingertips drawn to a twitch on his temple, obviously feeling the strain and finding it as difficult as Josie to speak the words he was now bound to say. Words that revealed such unbelievable atrocities and lies, that if they were ever to escape the boundaries of the room, all hell would break loose and undoubtedly initiate another official enquiry into the old family scandal. Aware, as Josie was aware, that no matter how glibly the pertinent words were assembled and rolled off his tongue, they were about to shatter every last one of Caeli's most cherished memories.

"Please continue, Jamjo," Caeli said, in a voice grown so small it could barely be heard.

"I'm sorry, my dear, but there's no easy way of telling you this, other than to come right out and say it," inhaling deeply before announcing, "Daniel O'Halloran is alive!"

Caeli's sharp intake of breath revealed the shock that ran through her, even though she had already anticipated what Jamjo was about to say. Challenging him now, flinging back at him with a sardonic smile and a toss of her head the frivolous denial. "However did you come by such a ridiculous notion, Jamjo dear? Danny alive… You know as well as I do that cannot be true." Adding more forcefully, jabbing her finger in the direction of the rear of the house overlooking the sea, "Danny drowned right out there in that ocean twenty-two years ago, along with our precious little Meegan!"

Jamjo was expecting such a reaction, aware before he had begun that it wasn't going to be easy to convince her of the truth. "But I saw him, Caeli," he protested. "Saw him with my own two eyes! Spoke to him even…!"

"You are surely mistaken, Jamjo dear," she patronised smugly, while falling apart inside. "You were exhausted from your travels,

238

Dublin to London then onto America, that's quite a long haul. You saw someone who closely resembled Danny, that's all."

"Oh Caeli... How I wish that were true and that I was mistaken... How I wish I could prove myself wrong and not have to breathe a word of this to you. But I am not wrong, nor am I mistaken, and at first Josie and I could see nothing to be gained by telling you any of this and we'd agreed we would keep it to ourselves and say nothing of it to you, that it would only mean more heartache for you. But on account of the abominable lies contained in your father's letter – or as I said before, and more to the point, his deliberate lack of not telling you the truth, we are now of a mind that you have the right to be told all we know. Danny was as close to me then as you are to me now in that bar in Las Vegas that night, He spoke to me even. There's no mistaking it was Danny O'Halloran alright – no mistaking it at all!"

But Caeli was still in denial. Certain Jamjo meant well, but simply unable to believe (or more to the point, not wanting to believe) that her darling Danny had been alive all these years and had not sought her out, or even worse, that he'd ignored the existence of his son. For she had been corresponding with Danny's mother, Zita, ever since Kevin was born, so didn't it stand to reason then, that if by some miracle Danny had eventually been found, washed up on some foreign shore with amnesia or such that Zita would have been the first to let her know?

"Please continue, Jamjo," she said in a voice grown dangerously calm but verging hysteria, little bits of all she was breaking away inside leaving raw open endings and cold gaping hollows.
"It was the night I arrived in Las Vegas, Caeli," Jamjo continued, realising he'd opened a Pandora's Box and was bound to continue. "Seated at the bar of the club I was where I'd traced my beloved Josie to, when I first saw him. My mind a thousand miles away from all that was going on about me, thinking only of my darling girl and what I was going to say to her to convince her of my love and return home to Ireland with me. For I knew it wasn't going to be easy – knowing by then what had driven her away.

"It was the laughter of a party across the room that first drew my eye. Ten or a dozen there must have been in the gayest of moods, rising from a table, staggering a little, making ready to leave. But it was not until they were passing the bar where I sat on their way out that I saw him. The swagger on him in their midst nudging some old dormant memory in me – you know the way Danny had of sauntering about in that devil-may-care manner and his head tossed so cockily back? A real man-about-town, surrounded by an adoring entourage of friends, was the impression I got – for didn't he just look the part; swanky white dinner jacket and a white-silk scarf so casually draped about his neck... And I swear to God, Caeli, without so much as a thought or a whisker of hesitation on my part, I called out to him as he was passing: 'Why, if it isn't Danny O'Halloran himself.'"

The effect his words were having on Caeli was more than he'd bargained for, for she'd slumped against Josie like a lifeless rag doll, every vestige of colour drained from her face. Alarm bells rang within him, sending him rushing to the sideboard to splash some brandy into a glass and take it to her, coaxing her to drink as he held it to her lips.

"Here now, sip this dear... Good girl... Goood girl... A little more now... Swallow it down..."

Caeli clutching the glass over Jamjo's hands needing no coaxing, gulping the amber liquid greedily and coughing harshly as its fiery strength caught her breath.

Yet it had the desired effect, restored some colour to her deathly white cheeks and thawed the ice that ran through her veins.

"Forgive me, Caeli," Jamjo said. "What a thoughtless oaf I am."

"Not your fault – shock!" Caeli murmured hoarsely, snatching the glass from his grasp and draining every last dreg.

"Oh Caeli... Caeli..." Josie cried, wrapping her arms around her sister. "Didn't I warn you it was something horrid and was going to hurt?"

But ridiculously, Caeli was still in denial and shaking her head.

"Couldn't have been Danny," she insisted, slurring the words from the sudden infusion of the alcohol, "Surely a look-alike. We all have one you know. The spitting image of our selves they say, just like our dear old ancestor Turlough and Dada. And besides," she added with a cynical laugh and grasping at straws and berating him gently, "you were only a child, no more than ten when Danny disappeared. How could you possibly remember what Danny looked like?"

Jamjo prised the glass from Caeli's fingers, marvelling at how it hadn't shattered in her vice-like grasp, and placing it on the coffee table before them, returned to his chair before he replied.

"I hear what you're saying Caeli, and well I remember how young I was. I was all of ten, as you say. Yet I remember Danny and the way he was as if it was only a flash of a light globe away. You of all people should never be challenging me about that! You of all people should remember the enormous effect he had on us all. The absolute charm of the man drew everyone under his spell and I no less included! But the strange thing was that over in that club in Las Vegas that night was like stepping back through the door of time, the clock in my head spinning backwards, taking me back to those days when I *was* that ten-year old boy! And lo and behold, standing not two feet before me was Danny O'Halloran, as large as life and as charming as the day he was born.

"I swear to God, Caeli, there was no thought of Danny, or his disappearing, or much of anything else in my head at the time, only thoughts of my beloved girl and the prospect of seeing her again. It was something in my subconscious that triggered an instant reaction in me at the sight of him that instinctively made me call out his name. It was as simple as that, I saw someone I recognised from the past and called out his name! There was no premeditation or hesitation on my part to gather vague notions that here was someone approaching me across a crowded room that looked a hell of a lot like that Daniel O'Halloran fellow I used to know way back in good old Ireland many years before! He stopped right there in front of me Caeli, and looked me straight in the eye, and wouldn't I be swearing on a stack of bibles now that for the briefest of moments there was a flicker of something there in his own that I can only describe as relief? That for one terrifying moment, when all of life seemed to have ground to a halt in some sort of suspended animation, that I thought he was about to come right out and admit to me who he was and laugh at me straight in my face.

"Yet his voice when he spoke was untroubled, easy, and devil-may-carish, like the Danny we knew. The brogue on him grossly exaggerated, as it always was, 'As thick as scalded cream,' me Mam used say, and his reply as casual as you like, 'You are surely mistaken sur.' And I have to admit there was doubt in me then as the logistics of such a chance meeting began to spin in my head. And even up until then, up to that point of time, to that very moment, just maybe, maybe, some swift explanation on his part could have convinced me otherwise. That he was a trick of the light or a trick of me eyes or the double whiskey in me, or that my notorious sixth-sense was galloping away with my reason.

"But it's what he said next that unequivocally convinced me it was none of these but Danny O'Halloran himself. Some big, brassy blonde from his party – which by then had moved out into the foyer, called back to him in what I perceived to be a loud Texan drawl, 'Are you coming or not, Eamon Kelly, we've got serious partying to do' – or words to that effect. Then as easy as you like, he smiled at me. The same winning smile me mother used to call his 'win-the-world' smile, his black eyes flashing balls of excitement by then, and he whispered to me in a voice so low, that I'm sure it was only myself meant to hear. "Did ye not hear, young Jamjo Joyce, that I am not me?" Then with a devilish wink and a sweeping theatrical bow, he added, "'Tis Eamon Kelly at your service, sur." Then he spun on his heel and fair skipped away like a delighted child, the white silk scarf flying out about him, and moments later he was lost to my sight, gathered eagerly into his company of friends. But by God, Caeli, I can tell you I was shaking like a leaf by then as the implications of what had occurred began to hit home. The past roaring back at me like a freight train, whistle blowing, carrying a cargo of ghosts! And I don't mind admitting I needed no coaxing to toss a third whiskey down!"

Yet Jamjo's rush of words still seemed to have fallen on deaf ears, Caeli staring blankly into space as though she'd heard not a single word.

Jamjo's heart sank. "Caeli… DO YOU HEAR ME?" he shouted in frustration, "Heed what I'm saying, girl – He called me by name! I swear to God, HE CALLED ME BY NAME!"

"He called you by name," Caeli repeated in a slurring lifeless drone.

So he had got through. "Yes, he did, he did!" Jamjo responded eagerly.

"Jamjo Joyce is what he said. It was Daniel O'Halloran all right; I'd know that low-life son of a bitch anywhere!

"And there's another thing, Caeli," Jamjo went on when the silence in the room seemed to beg for more and fired up to the point of telling all. "Something else that's crossed my mind since that can

242

only add credence to what I've just said. Something that occurred quite some time ago when I'd accidentally stumbled across a file in Eugene Shaw's office safe – at Eugene's request, I might add. He'd sent me to collect a particular document, but I managed to extract another file directly beneath it as well, which, clumsy oaf that I am, I then managed to drop and scatter its contents all over the floor. It was while I was gathering the papers up and bundling them back into their folder that I noticed what they were: A long-standing record of funds transferred from the Bank of Ireland to a bank in America. That in itself was unusual. But it was the name on the front of the file that leapt up at me; because it was a name I knew so well – the name of an old pal of mine from our Trinity days – Eamon Kelly.

"But I knew for a fact that it wasn't the Eamon Kelly I knew that these funds were being sent to. For the Eamon I know works for Doyle's in Dublin and we'd just met for lunch the previous week and he's never even been to America! Yet I'd made the connection and the name on the file stayed with me, occasionally wondering of the story behind it and who the Eamon Kelly in America was. And wondering also, I might add, why that particular file was in Eugene's private safe and not in the basement where all other such files are normally kept. But as it was none of my business and certainly not my place to question my boss – who happens to be the head of the firm and has been very good to me, I never queried it.

But now I have to wonder if Daniel O'Halloran – who, I've since learned now calls himself Eamon Kelly, is the one and the same?

And wouldn't I be as dumb as a doorknob to think they were not? That being the case, it almost certainly implicates Mr. Shaw's complicity in the matter – that he was aware that Danny O'Halloran was very much alive and living in America all these years."

Caeli could hear Jamjo's words clearly enough. Words distinctly pronounced and emphasised to bring her clear meaning. Words that entered the door of her mind and ushered her down a path she had no wish to tread. She didn't want to believe that old Mr. Shaw with his clear blue eyes was anything but honest and true and uninvolved in any sort of underhand dealings or conspiracy. She didn't want to believe that Danny was alive and a traitor to her and their son and all the horrible things Jamjo had implied he was, unwilling to relinquish the God-like image she'd created of him in her mind. Her young dead hero, placed so high on a pedestal that none other could ever hope to live up to.

And what of that son, Kevin – her son – Daniel's son, her mind rambled on, the illegitimate son so like his father that she'd never regretted for one single moment bringing into the world? Surely if Danny *had* been alive and known such a son existed, wouldn't he have moved heaven and earth and hell itself to seek that son out? How was she to explain to that son that the father he had idealised as much as she had been very much alive and living like a king in America all these years, while they had struggled on in Australia alone. A mere few hours' flight or a phone-call away, yet he had chosen to ignore Kevin's very existence since the day he was born?

And what of Zita, Danny's mother, how would such news affect her? Yet a growing unease about Zita had already begun to infiltrate her mind. Recalling the annual trips Zita had made to America since the year dot, packing her bags and winging out of Dublin as regular as clockwork.

"Distant relations," her letters had explained, and the only family she had left – apart from her grandson in Australia, who, though many times invited, she had never quite managed to come and see.

Caeli had been sympathetic to Zita's cause and encouraged her to go and had even sent her the fare when her fortunes improved.

Had Zita known all along that her son was alive and living in America and the reason for the trips?

Was the Pope a Catholic, she might well have asked? The answer, glaringly obvious to her now that Zita, like Danny and Dada and God only knew who else, had played her for a fool.

A blinding anger rose up in her then as the reality of the truth began to hit home. An anger born as much of the sense of her own gullibility as of the betrayal of the people she had trusted and loved. An anger so consuming that she screamed from the agony of it and punched into the cushions of the sofa with all her might.

As though he'd pre-empted her actions, Jamjo rushed to her side just as Molly entered the room. Molly's eyes darting from one to the other appraising the situation in two seconds flat. Wise enough to know in her forty years of living in this house with this family that nothing short of another catastrophe had again descended upon them, and again it would appear, upon her precious Caeli. Waiting for no explanation – for it seemed the girl was losing her mind, she ordered Jamjo to the kitchen for a pot of tea and her new daughter-in-law upstairs to fetch pillows and a rug.

CHAPTER THIRTY-THREE
RORY'S PATERNITY

It was some time later, when Caeli was suitably pacified that Molly was to learn the cause of her distress. Amazingly, she listened to Jamjo's incredible story without interruption, seeming not at all surprised at the words being said. Her very own son claiming that after twenty two years Danny O'Halloran was very much alive. That he'd not only seen him but spoken to him only days before while over in America searching for Josie. Inwardly, she was relieved at the news, that her long held suspicions were at last proven right, that the mysterious hooded figure she had glimpsed in the dark halls of Liath Caislean on several occasions over the years, had indeed been the self-same man and that she wasn't losing her marbles after all. "And while we're in the mood for setting records straight, Mam," Jamjo continued before she could say as much, "there's another matter that Josie and I badly need to get off our chests."
"Oh…?"
Three pairs of eyes landed on him with varying degrees of interest. Jamjo's seeking only his wife's who was sitting alone on the opposite side of the fireplace looking sad and pale and so very vulnerable, that he rose and went to her and protectively enfolded her in his arms and whispered something close to her ear. Trustingly, she looked up at him, her lovely green eyes shining in sheer adoration as she nodded in silent consent.

"But there is a condition, Mam – Caeli," he firmly stated, as he turned to face them. "Before I breathe another word, I must have your solemn promise that what I am about to disclose to you here and now will never go beyond the boundaries of this room."

"Dear God!" Molly cried in alarm, her face also paling and her hands once again flying to her chest. "You sound so grave, so serious, my son. But whatever it is, you have our word, isn't that so, Caeli?"

Caeli nodded her agreement, feeling as alarmed as Molly so obviously was. "Of course Jamjo, mum's the word – if that is your wish."

"Well then… Caeli… Mam…" Jamjo began tentatively, licking his lips nervously and holding Josie close, "you are not going to like what I am about to tell you one little bit… Another 'bombshell' I fear, and possibly even more distressing than the one I've just dropped."

Molly and Caeli glanced at each other, cynically wondering what could possibly rate as "more distressing" than the last.

"Well here goes," Jamjo said. "For starters, Josie and I haven't been altogether too truthful about certain facts of another matter we've led you to believe to be true, and we apologise profusely for that. It was never our intention to deceive you, but in all sincerity, we truly believed that the lie would be infinitely more acceptable and less hurtful to all parties concerned than the truth. But again in light of your father's letter, Caeli, we are of a different persuasion now and we wish to make a clean breast of things.

"Oh Lord… Not Dada again," Caeli groaned. "I should've known it would have something to do with him."

"Hush, Caeli, please," Josie protested. "Let Jamjo continue, for its not easy for us to tell you this. It's too shameful, too personal, too close to home. So please darling hush and hear Jamjo out."

Caeli was suitably silenced and Jamjo glanced gratefully at his wife.

"The truth of the matter is that Josie no longer wishes me to take the blame for something I am not guilty of, feeling now, because of your father's deliberate and ongoing malice towards you, Caeli, that we at least owe it to you – and to you also Mam, to tell you the truth – that Josie has protected her father long enough."

He inhaled deeply, as though the extra draught of oxygen might provide the courage he so badly needed to say what he was now committed to say, eventually exhaling on a sigh of inevitability.

"Again I will be blunt," he said, "for under the circumstances there is no other way I can be." Yet moments of silence dragged on, increasing Caeli and Molly's curiosity to near breaking point, before he finally blurted out: "Rory is *not* my son… I am *not* Rory's father – as we led you to believe – though I wish to God I was!"

"Mother of God…!" Molly gasped, the inevitable hands again clutching at her chest. "What is it you are tellin' me now, my son?" she demanded to know. "That this precious child that I've come to love with all me heart is no longer me grandson? Is that what you're tellin' me now?"

Josie intervened in a voice raining sorrow.

"What Jamjo is saying Molly dear, is that he is completely blameless; that he in no way has soiled me or shamed you, as you so harshly implied he had; that it's time you were told he isn't the bad guy in all of this, but a completely innocent and honourable party who was trying to protect me, and that he's *not* the father of my son."

Molly looked from one to the other, visibly confused. "Then dear Lord in heaven, who is…?"

Josie was also blunt. "Dada," she replied.

The room was shocked to silence. Molly and Caeli watched helplessly the hot silent tears overflowing Josie's lovely green eyes as the painful secret tumbled unstoppable from her lips, the secret that had festered within her for almost eight years. Aiming her words directly at Molly, she began to explain.

"That was the reason I left like I did Molly. Snuck away like the proverbial thief in the night without explanation to you or anyone at what had taken place in my bedroom that night. But please, don't judge me too harshly, for I was so full of disgust at what Dada had come to my bed and done, that I just couldn't face you or Jamjo – especially not Jamjo. For you see, Molly dear, Jamjo had asked me to marry him on the morning of my birthday the previous day, down on the footbridge crossing the stream in Dada's woods, and I had so joyously said yes! And we'd sealed our engagement with this Claddagh Ring, which, I might add, has never been removed from my finger since. But because of my party that night – but mainly because of Dada's particularly unstable state of mind at the time, we'd decided to keep the engagement our secret until the following day when all of the fuss and ado of the party was over and we could speak to you both alone. We also thought it expedient to keep our distance from each other at the party, knowing we'd be unable to hide the love between us and give our secret away – thus Jamjo's urgent excuse of an elsewhere story.

"But we didn't get the chance, did we? Dada destroyed our plan and stole the most precious gift I was saving for Jamjo, and made me feel so dirty and ashamed and unworthy of Jamjo's love that I just couldn't face either one of you that night. All I wanted to do when Dada had finished with me was to bathe in hottest hot water I could bear and scrub the deed away. Yet in all these years, I've never quite managed to do that and I still feel unclean to this day.

"The dirty old pervert…"

"Hush, Caeli, please… Let me finish…

"I knew I had to leave. Could think of nothing else but getting as far away from Dada as fast as I could, totally shocked and disgusted at what he had come to my bed and done – hence the early-morning-train to the north. I threw a few things into a bag and stole from the house as quietly as I could, fearful of waking you Molly, and witnessing the shame of the deed written all over me. And later, when my child was born, the same feelings prevailed and the only justification I needed to give my newborn son away.

"You were engaged… You loved my boy back then?" Molly whispered in wonder, sifting back over the words Josie had said.

"Oh Molly… loved him…? I've loved Jamjo all my life! I thought you realised that. Even as a babe – before I even knew what love was, I loved him – at least since the Christmas he kissed me under the mistletoe when I was barely three! But I think even then, with my infant perception of things, I somehow knew we were made for each other and would always be together. He was my best friend, Molly, and when Caeli left home, my only friend – not counting yourself of course, for you were always there for me and kindness itself. There has never been anyone else for me – even though I've known a few men who wished it were otherwise. It made no difference where I was in the world or what I was doing or whom I was with, I just couldn't forget Jamjo and the perfect dream we'd created and move on from there."

She gulped back the emotion that threatened to engulf her and carried on stoically, determined to purge herself clean of the past.

"Rory was the outcome of that one terrifying liaison on the night of my eighteenth birthday – some birthday present, heh? I felt so repulsed by what Dada had come to my bed and done that I couldn't even look upon my innocent babe, let alone hold him in my arms, and I put him up for adoption straight away.

"But the shamrock…" Molly queried, "How did he come to have your special shamrock that ye treasured so much? The shamrock your dear mother had given ye just before she died, if ye cared for the lad so little? For as battered as it was, I knew it was yours. I recognised it the moment I laid eyes on it."

"Ah yes, there's the shamrock, isn't there Molly…" Josie replied thoughtfully.

"Perhaps it was my mothering instinct that made me take it from around my neck and tuck it inside his shawl, or perhaps I wanted him to have something of me after all.

"Though I was surprised he still had it, for as beaten and worthless as it is, I thought it would have been stolen from him long ago by some bullying child or such.

"It sort of restored my faith in humanity a little when I saw it, for it crossed my mind that somewhere in his brief young past there must have been some compassionate people who'd watched out for him after all. But I also believe he must have fought many a hard battle to keep it too."

"Yes, I believe that too," Molly replied, "for it means a lot to him. He refuses to take it off – even in the bath – even for me! And I've promised to buy him a brand new chain to hang it on for his birthday, if he gives me the piece of string…"

"How naïve I was" Josie continued, "to think that by casting my child from me I could undo the past and pretend he didn't exist, to simply turn my back on my son and smile at the world and get on with my life in a normal manner. But giving him away was only the beginning of the guilt and the heartache and the utter sense of loss that was to follow. Acknowledging his every birthday… Wondering every day of my life where he was or how he was… Was he sick or sore or being ill-treated? Wishing with all my heart I could turn the clock back and undo the deed I'd so selfishly done and be given another chance.

"But life rarely gives us second chances does it, Caeli?" she said, meaningfully turning to her sister.

"Even so, I imagine I had it a whole lot easier than you did when you left home – or more to point, when Dada forced you out. At least I had a few belongings and a sizeable bank account. Whereas I believe, Dada cast you out with nothing, which, for the life of me, I have never been able to understand."

Caeli had never been able to understand it either, at least not until the photo of the young British Pilot had come to light. But that was another story, another bombshell she could toss back at Josie when the timing was right.

"Looking back," Josie stated, as though summing the situation up, "and believe you me, I've done that a great many times, I would like to say something in defence of Dada's actions that night, that I feel it wasn't altogether his fault, that I was also to blame."

Molly and Jamjo were horrified at such a suggestion, and protested in unison:

"Oh no, child, whatever are you saying…"

"Oh no, my love, never!"

Tenderly she raised a finger to her new husband's lips. "Please… Please, darling, hush and let me explain. I feel I was to blame because I *look* so like mother, but especially did I at my party that night.

"You see, I was proud of the fact, vain even, for you have to admit she was a beautiful woman, and I'd gone to extremes to recreate the image of her in her portrait that night, which, at the time was on view for all to see, hanging in The Great Hall between Dada and Turlough where my party was held. In my vanity, I'd even had a replica gown made – you know the lovely golden tulle one that mother is wearing in her portrait, Caeli? I'd even had my hair fashioned in the very same style – swept up to one side and cascading over one shoulder. And I know I succeeded – lord, how I succeeded! Everyone was amazed at the resemblance, commented on it all night, saying that I looked like I'd stepped down from the painting itself! So that's why I feel I was partly to blame. How stupid I was, not to have foreseen the effect it would have upon Dada, for as I recall, he was going through a particularly bad patch of confusion at the time and speaking to me as though I *was* mother – as Molly will surely bear out."

"Aye, he was at that." Molly reluctantly agreed, adding that "confusion" was hardly the word.

"All night he'd been watching me with open admiration, and idiot me, twirling before him, delighting in it and lapping it up, not imagining for one single moment what was going on in his poor befuddled head. And later, all the while he was with me in my bed, he kept whispering "Maureen Mavourneen," the term of endearment he exclusively used when speaking to mother. So in retrospect, I have to believe it was mother he was lusting after that night, and not me at all."

"Huh! That still doesn't exonerate the dirty old bugger," Caeli cut in disgustedly. "But what do you mean when you say he was confused?" sounding somewhat confused herself, "are you suggesting Dada was mad?"

"Perhaps mad is too strong a word, Caeli, but some form of dementia certainly – as Doctor Tom will surely bear out. For there were times when he seemed quite normal – at least as normal as you or I, and times when he went completely off his rocker – like the time he ranted through the house with a Viking helmet on his head and half his clothes on and muttering obscenities to himself.

"And then again there were the times he'd retreat within himself and lose the plot altogether. 'Off with the fairies' Molly used to say he was at such times.

"And what with the stories I'd heard of our dear old ancestor Turlough – Dada's mirror-image look-alike – who was also said to have completely lost the plot, I've come to the conclusion that their maladies are more than likely hereditary, and that you or I could wind up in the very same boat one day and lose our marbles too?"

"What utter nonsense you go on with Josie!" Molly admonished her harshly, as though such a thing could never come about, for even though she was constantly dabbing her eyes – evidenced by the mountain of tissues piled high on the chair beside her, she had digested every last word. "You girls are the women of the family," she added, "the strong-minded ones," as though suggesting they held the outcome of life in the palm of their hands.

"An' besides," she went on, "It only comes out in the Dromgoole men, like old Turlough an' your Dada an' a few others too – includin' your Dada's Dada – old Donagh Dromgoole – or so I've been told, who was said to have turned into a proper raving lunatic when his wife ran off with another man.

"An' haven't I been tellin' Caeli as much of your Dada's queer little ways," she went on, "for from my observations – an' 'tis practically every day of the past forty years that I've made his acquaintance, 'tis convinced that I am it was the tragedy of your mother's passin' that was the beginnin' of *his* decline. An' I'm sure Doctor Tom would agree with me at that, for in all me born days I've never seen a man go to pieces like your Dada did that day."

"The poor old soul," Josie said sympathetically. "It couldn't have been easy for him without mother…"

Caeli could not believe what she was hearing, and quite frankly her young sister's drivelling compassion for the father she despised – and now seriously doubted was her father at all, was getting on her nerves.

"You've got to be kidding, Josie!" she exploded. "How can you possibly forgive the evil old toad after all he has done to you and me and our precious little Meegan, and for all we know to mother as well? Not to mention *my* children – ignoring their very existence from the day they were born! How can you be such a blithering fool to forgive behaviour as contemptible as that?"

Josie was silent for what seemed a very long time before she replied.

"Who am I to forgive anyone, Caeli?" she eventually responded in barely a whisper, "When I can't even begin to forgive myself…"

"Come now, my love," Jamjo hurriedly intervened, understanding her thoughts and where they were taking her.

"Don't torture yourself so, for it's all in the past, and regardless of where the blame lies, you can never go back and undo what is done. Just get on with your life and focus your lovely green eyes upon Rory and me.

"For I swear before God we'll make it up to the lad a thousand times over! And as far as I am concerned he *is* my son and will always be treated as such, and no finer son could any man ask for."

Silently Josie responded to the love of this man she had adored as far back as memory would take her. Responded to his tender reasoning and wise counsel as she had way back in time when her toddler-steps had sought him out. It seemed he had always been there for her, through every ugly crisis this unhappy family had wrapped about her. There for her when her mother had died and the much publicised family scandal had exploded about them. There when Danny went missing and Meegan had drowned in the waters of Raggemorne Bay and the media went crazy and climbed the walls surrounding the house and scared her half to death. Yes, Jamjo had always been there for her, even when Caeli had so suddenly left.

Now his comforting words fell like a soothing balm upon her, seeping into her every pore, easing the guilt within her and making her feel a little less guilty and a little more healed somehow.

Turning her thoughts full focus on Caeli now, concerned at the level of hatred she had evidenced in her sister's voice when she spoke of their father.

"Yes, Caeli," she said, "I can forgive Dada. I *must* forgive him if I am to live a normal life, and you must forgive him too. For if I've learnt anything out of all of this, it's that the burden of hate is too hard for me to bear and would have ultimately destroyed me.

"Besides, the way I see it, hate would take up the room in my heart that I need for storing kinder emotions, for thanks to my wonderful husband here, I now have an abundance of those, for he's given me a second chance at love and to be a mother to my son. And as much as you won't like to hear me say it, Caeli, I say thanks to Dada too, for it was Dada who brought my son home."

Caeli sat in silence, in awe of her young sister's wisdom, wisdom that reminded her of her young daughter's wisdom. Comparing the two, aware they were related – Liz and Josie – niece and aunt, and the inherent similarities between them, the perpetual bond of blood. If not Dromgoole blood, then the blood of their mother's people, the well-bred O'Sullivans from County Kildare. How humbled and chastened she felt at her young sister's words and suitably drawn into line, and Josie continued.

"Perhaps in time we will learn to put the past behind us and let Rory grow up like any other little boy, believing Jamjo *is* his father – for I too swear before God and all of you here that he'll never hear different from me.

"Sure, not a day will go by when I'll not be reminded who fathered my son, or my shame in abandoning him, there'll be no escaping that. But hopefully, in time, the rights will somehow counteract the wrongs and balance them out and I'll learn to live with them – though God only knows my guilt will remain. But then I somehow hope it does, that perhaps I'll become a wiser and better person because of it."

Caeli sucked in her breath and looked at her sister with newfound respect, seeing clearly now the uncanny likeness to their mother. The same green eyes sparkling with an almost feverish fire, the same untameable mass of copper hair tumbling about her shoulders gleaming in the firelight's glow, the same delicate features. Suddenly understanding how her father's troubled mind could so easily have mistaken her for his wife.

Turning towards her new mother-in-law then, the beloved old housekeeper who had loved and nurtured each and every one of them unconditionally and become such an essential part of their lives, Josie announced with an uncertain brightness.

"So there you have it, Mammy Molly, the truth of it all, the whole shebang, as those crazy yanks over there in Las Vegas would say.

"Jamjo has done nothing wrong, nothing to shame you, and it's for Rory's sake we ask you to wear the lie and the gossip that will undoubtedly go on behind your back. There's a grandson here for you if you will have him, but I warn you Molly dear, he's only the first of many, and that the role of grandmothering could become very demanding and leave you little time for anything else."

Molly's answer came in a broken half-sob of raw emotion, spluttering the words, clasping her hands tightly to her chest as though devoutly in prayer...

"Have him... Have him...! Dear God in heaven an' all His beautiful saints, me prayers have been answered at last!"

Caeli could only watch the emotional scene that followed, the highly charged drama drawing to its climax on the broad stage of life. Feeling excluded – the odd one out – an unimportant observer with nothing expected of her and no part to play. Watch, as if in a dream Josie and Molly and Jamjo rising and stumbling into each other's arms and holding each other so very tight with tears of joy streaming down their faces.

For them, it was an exquisite time, a time of forgiveness and healing and hope for the future, a time of unbridled emotions and new beginnings, a time to put an inglorious past behind them and seal a pact on a glorious tomorrow.

For Caeli, it was a time of ending, of re-evaluation, of closing doors and making new decisions, feeling incredibly alone and cold inside. Even the house seemed to be mocking her now, urging her to be gone, to go find some friendlier place to huddle and hide and lick the fresh wounds inflicted upon her that day, a place where she'd known only happiness, with no unfriendly ghosts lurking in its shadows or waiting their moment to rise up and taunt her and overpower her once more. But where – where in the whole of Ireland was she to find a place such as that?

Yet there was such a place that came to her mind and dominated her thoughts in her wretchedness now. The fantasy world of her childhood, the magical place of Granny Grainne's legends into which she'd so often escaped when life in the house had become unbearably cruel. The fabled home of the "Little People," the fairy folk of Ireland; the make-believe place of storytellers and dreamers; the enchanted place of the hawthorn tree where every last wish was said to come true.

Wish inside a fairy ring and every wish to you they'll bring…
The place she had brought her handsome Danny O'Halloran to all those years before, wishing with all her heart he would love her forever.

"Our secret love nest," Danny had whispered, awaking emotions erotic and wild and uncontainable within her. The place where he'd lain her down on the sweet mossy bed of the woodland floor and taken her maiden virginity away, swearing he would love her 'til his dying day.

CHAPTER THIRTY-FOUR
GRANNY GRAINNE'S

She slipped from the room unnoticed, her slipper-clad feet treading softly the cold grey corridors of the daunting old house. The eyes of Dromgooles past looking down upon her in her passing, their sombre dark images lining the walls seemed colder and even more disapproving of her than ever before. As though they were saying she did not belong and time she was gone, that this house was not for her – that this life was not for her – that they were not for her. Pausing at the blank discoloured space where the portrait of a woman had once hung, a woman of whom she knew very little, yet a woman she felt she knew very well, that they had much in common. A woman despised by Bran Dromgoole even more than she, her very name forbidden to be spoken in the house.

"Your Dada's own mother, and your grandmother! Molly had whispered in a time of long ago, repeating village gossip and attempting to satisfy her childish curiosity.

"Eileen Dromgoole nee Eileen Barry – a beauty they say, who, ran off with a prince of the earth – or the very Devil himself."

Feeling strangely connected to this rebellious woman now, wondering again at her story and why she had abandoned grandfather Dromgoole and her infant son all those years before? And with whom had she left and to where had she gone?

Feeling rather rebellious herself at the time, cut to the core with the lies and betrayals revealed to her that day. Feeling the need to hit back, to ruffle a few feathers and break a few rules and somehow make her presence count for something here in this house.

Daring to whisper the forbidden name – "Eileen Barry…" then say it again a little louder – "EILEEN BARRY…" It echoed. It felt good. It felt better than good. Then, abandoning all restraint, she flung her arms wide and yelled it at the top of her voice, "EILEEEEEN BARREEEEEE...

Childish she knew, yet incredibly satisfying somehow. Making her feel she had stuck a blow for her unknown grandmother and let her know she was on her side. How it echoed through the house and reverberated still as she gained the sanctuary of the kitchen, Molly's domain and the only room in the whole of the house she now felt welcome in.

Exchanging the slippers for an old pair of Wellington Boots and thrusting her arms into an old mackintosh that had hung on a peg on the back of the kitchen door, she fled to the freedom of the world outside.

Instinctively summoning the nameless pair of dogs, an instinct born of a time long ago when she'd summoned her mother's dogs, Dougal and Shara. One sharp slap to her thigh, one long clear whistle with a rising whip at the end, brought the nameless pair bounding to her side as though it was a well-practised game, then dashed off before her as she opened the gate in the high stone wall.

The same windblown track of memory traced the same ragged cliff-top before her, the same open sea surged at the cliff-face in full winter's might, the same salty spray carried up on the wind and lashed at her face and stung at her eyes.

A sense of déjà vu swept over her again, as other memories brushed through her mind and brought the past back to life once more.

Hearing again Molly's voice catching up to her ears in that time of long ago: *Put some shoes on child... Ye'll catch your death of cold...* transporting her back to that time when she *had* been that child, fleeing the house and her father's spite to run wild and free. To tumble down to the soft green meadows of the valley below and follow the stream flowing babbling and cool to a place in her father's woods, the magical place of the hawthorn tree.

The image of Danny O'Halloran rose before her then, as clear to her now in her mind's eye as he was when she first saw him, one booted foot placed firmly on a rock and straddling the track and deliberately barring her way.

How magnificent he'd appeared to her then. How her heart leapt at the sight of him and the breath left her body, insanely handsome and so powerfully built.

His pitch-black hair tossed wildly by the wind, his eyes as black as a starless midnight sky that had mocked her even then, as though he had known she would come and be hopelessly enslaved by him.

How magnificent she envisioned him still. Old yearnings deep and eternal stirring within her, regardless of the treachery she had learned of him that day.

Yet perplexingly, it was not to the place of the hawthorn tree and the erotic liaisons with Danny that her feet would lead her to this day, feet that seemed to have acquired a mind of their own and led her off in a different direction entirely. Unfalteringly stepping the stones of the icy cold stream with the dogs as sure-footed as she ever close in her wake, and still hot on her heels when she re-crossed the stream at a place further in to finally emerge on a densely overgrown track. Fingers of gorse snatched at her clothing and snared at her hair, before finally arriving at a tumbledown dwelling – the remains of Granny Grainne's hut, deep in the Dromgoole woods.

It was but a shell now. A pile of crumbling stones and rotting timbers encroached with moss and bracken and mouldering back into the earth. Yet the essence of all it had been – all it had meant to the lonely child in her then – an enchanted place to escape to, remained there still.

Yet the dogs would not come near, no matter how often she slapped her thigh or whistled the wind for them to come, but padded the perimeter restlessly, ears pricked, instincts alert to something only they could sense. So she entered the ruin alone, feeling strangely reluctant yet as strangely eager, expecting to find she knew not what.

Prisms of weak wintry light filtered the gaping holes in the roof; the sheltering appendages of overhanging trees daubing its interior with ghostly wavering shadows; a thousand echoes of her beloved Granny Grainne seeped rich and full from every crack and cranny of the small crumbling space, whispering the spells and predictions that the superstitious community had come in their droves to hear, and the tales of the ancient folklore of Ireland that had fired Caeli's young imagination and left her ever hungering for more. Yet loudest of all – though if she were asked to describe it, she could only say it was nothing but the murmur of something she had almost forgotten way back in time – Granny Grainne's prophecy. The prophecy beyond her understanding then as it was now – *Beware him child… Beware the one you love most…*

So overcome by the experience was she, that she fell to her knees with the reverence of kneeling before an altar of God in some ancient sanctified ruin, as though the damp eroding walls contained a divine power to penetrate the depths of her soul and mesmerise her in all their rotting decay. Her knees landing on something solid half-buried in the rubble, and instantly she knew what it was – Granny Grainne's crystal ball! Frantically she dug around it with her bare hands and eagerly picked it up amazed it was still there, that in all the years since Granny Grainne's passing it hadn't been stolen away by some vagabond thief.

With a strong sense of ownership, she held the ball tightly to her, sensing a power shimmering through it, that the spirit of her beloved Granny Grainne still lingered therein. Feeling as though she had been meant to find it, that it had been waiting for her to come and claim it as her own? Clearly she could hear the old fortune-teller whispering to her now, repeating yet again the prophecy she had so often warned her of as a child in the long ago past, a warning that seemed fraught with a new sense of urgency now – *Beware him child… Beware the one you love most…*

Now had it all become clear, the meaning of the prophecy that had escaped her understanding for so long. Did she at last see that it was Danny O'Halloran Granny Grainne had been warning her of all along? For Danny was the one she'd loved most, loved with a passion bordering on madness, but excluded him from her reckoning long ago, believing him lying in a watery grave at the bottom of the sea.

But she knew differently now, didn't she? Learning only that day that Danny was very much alive and deliberately chosen to ignore her very existence and that of his son.

Yet as far as she knew, Granny Grainne had never met Danny. Three years in her grave before Danny O'Halloran had come on the scene.

Obvious to her now that Dada – or Bran Dromgoole, as she now preferred to refer to him as, now doubtful he was her father at all, was the mastermind behind the plot to spirit Danny away to

America. But equally as obvious – willingly or not, that Danny had been in on it too.

Yet common sense alone dictated that such a massive deceit could not have come to fruition by their unskilled efforts alone, that there had to be others involved.

Others, with the legal ability to kill off the old and create the new, to falsify documentation, add a fictitious name to a fictitious birth certificate and prove that the non-existent did in fact exist.

But who among the close-knit Irish clique and her so-called friends would have risen to the task of sinking so low to plot so viciously against her?

The accusing finger pointing first and foremost at old Mr. Shaw, the kindly snowy-haired gentleman with the honest blue eyes she used to call "uncle" and so recently regathered to her heart.

With even more questions tormenting her mind than when she had come, she vacated the ruins of Granny Grainne's hut with the crystal ball tucked close within the folds of her coat, feeling the need to hide it, to keep it a secret from prying eyes. Recalling how Granny Grainne had said that it had a line of succession and that it would be hers one day and that she was to guard it well – her inheritance from Granny Grainne… but why?

She had no kinship to the old woman. No inherent metaphysical powers to see into the future and predict people's lives, and quite honestly, she didn't believe in such things. Yet conversely, she would have sworn at that very moment that she could sense Granny Grainne's presence about her and hear her murmuring back through time.

How she wished that the crystal ball would swirl in its depths and speak to her now and give her a sign to prove Jamjo had been mistaken and that Danny had not betrayed her at all. Yet her every instinct screamed back at her that Jamjo had been right, the curious file he had stumbled upon in Mr. Shaw's Office, irrefutable evidence of this. That being the case, and Eugene Shaw *was* involved, wasn't she logical then to assume that Liam his son was in on it too? He would have to be, wouldn't he? Especially in light of the fact that he seemed to have vanished off the face of the earth, for she'd not heard from him for several days.

Clear to her now that she wasn't wanted here, that she did not belong in Bran Dromgoole's house or in his world or even in Ireland.

261

The Ireland of her past was a stranger to her now. Clear she belonged in a very different world, the faraway land at the bottom of the earth. The land of her late husband Malachi Morgan's dreaming, of scorched red earth and wide open spaces and endless blue sky.

"Well, to hell with the lot of them!" she cried, in a rare show of anger when back in her room and flinging her suitcase on the bed. "I've had enough of the whole damn lot of them and I'm going home!" Home to her Liz and her life in Australia where its plain-speaking people called a spade a spade. At a loss to unravel the web of deceit she now found herself in, to establish who among the one's she had thought were her friends, was loyal to her or not? The only thing she felt certain of, was that she was certain of nothing at all.

"And to hell with the inheritance too!" she added more forcefully, deciding she wanted no part of it, that it had proved nothing but a legacy of lies.

"Let Kevin have it if he wants it," she mumbled crossly.

"Let him bow and scrape to his grandfather's demands if he's so inclined, and become Liath Caislean's slave forever!" The bud of a thought then unfurling her mind, if that had been Dada's intention all along?

"There is nothing I want from here!" she reiterated, reaffirming the vow she had made before she had left her home in Australia and the golden carrot of the inheritance had been dangled under her nose. Yet, on second thought, perhaps there was? One thing coming to her mind that was totally unrelated to the Dromgooles in any way at all and of which she believed she was entitled to and desperately wanted to have – the photo of the young British Airman hidden in the folds of her mother's bible since before she was born, who, like herself, had no place of belonging here in this house. The handsome young man barely more than a boy who'd been in love with mother all those years before, who so closely resembled herself and so similarly named – Michael – Michaela!

But Michael who... Michael what... Michael from where... Certainly Michael from war-torn London back in the year of 1940. Certainly Michael engaged in a war-time romance with her mother, and dare she say – certainly Michael her father? Obsessed with him now, eager to claim the little she knew of him and make him her own. Sensing his approval of her and what she'd done. His violet-blue eyes seemed to delve into hers and say, "Bravo my daughter" and urge her on. Regretful she hadn't spoken of him to Molly, feeling an opportunity lost, certain again that Molly would know.

She returned to her mother's private sitting room at the crack of dawn the following morning to retrieve the photo, and casting her eyes about the room for what she was certain was the very last time, came to rest on the porcelain doll.

"Why not," she murmured, "Mother said it was mine" told that the doll had been gifted to her before she was born but only permitted to play with it here in this room. "A gift to be cherished from someone special," her mother had said, but never from whom, yet obvious to her now that the "someone special" had been the man in the photo – her father? Its touch felt electric in her hands as she picked the doll up, sensing in a time long ago that the man in the photo had touched it to; his touch, touching hers, her first and possibly only physical contact with her father?

With the doll securely tucked in her overnight bag and the precious photo clutched in her hand, she crept from her parent's private domain in the accursed Turlough's Wing and descended the stairs with the utmost care, fearful of waking the rest of the house and forced to explain her sudden departure. But there at the bottom of the stairs stood Molly.

"So, you found it then," Molly said.

PART FOUR

AUSTRALIA

CHAPTER THIRTY-FIVE
RETURN TO AUSTRALIA

"You look tired, Mum," Liz observed, eyeing her mother anxiously when picking her up at Brisbane airport, and more than a little perplexed at her sudden return. For she was under the impression that her mother had accepted her father's inheritance and therefore its ridiculous stipulation as well – that she remain in Ireland and reside at Liath Caislean ten months out of every year, and therefore had not expected her back until almost the end of the year.

"Everything OK…?"

"Everything's fine, love," Caeli assured her, though it was far from the truth. "Just feeling a bit weary, that's all. For the flight was horrendous, for I could only get economy right up the back of the plane, which I might add, was packed like a tin of sardines. It was almost impossible to get any sleep and even harder to get to the loo! Remind me to break the journey the next time I go and stopover at Singapore or Hong Kong or someplace like that for a day or two – if I ever go again, that is."

"Good idea," Liz agreed. "But you *are* OK? I mean there's nothing troubling you, is there?" Liz persisted, knowing full well that there was.

"No, not really, love. As I said, I'm just a bit weary, jet-lagged, I suppose. Nothing that a good strong cup of tea and good night's sleep won't cure. The strain of the past few months has caught up with me, I guess. Not to mention the fact that I couldn't help thinking that with every mile that brought me closer to you, it put another between Kevin and me – for I've rejected my father's inheritance outright, and it's passed to your brother."

"Ooh, drastic stuff. And you're having second thoughts about that – and a few regrets?"

"Plenty of thoughts… And yes, I guess there's a few regrets there too. Kevin is too far away from me for one, and I know I shall miss him terribly."

"And the others…?"

"Oh, just this and that," she offered vaguely, as they headed for the car park. "But I know your brother is happy in his new role as 'Master of Liath Caislean' and that's the important thing."

"I'll *bet* he is!" Liz retorted. "Who wouldn't be, with all that lovely moolah and a vast estate as well? And knowing my brother as well as I do he'll be in his element strutting about playing Lord of the Manor. It suits his personality to a tee. Though I must say I haven't done too badly myself from my unknown grandfather's will!"

"No, you haven't, my girl! And it will well and truly set you up for life, and I guess I should at least be grateful to him for that."

"So, what else is worrying you, Ma?" Liz persisted, knowing her mother too well to be fobbed off.

But pry as she might, she could draw her mother no further on the matter, and talk soon shifted to Liz's new fiancé, Anthony Laporio.

"You do like him, Mum?" Liz anxiously asked as she swung her mother's silver Mercedes through the wrought-iron gates of her mother's riverfront home.

"Indeed I do – VERY much."

"Then I take it we have your approval?" Liz further probed, as they unloaded the bags from the boot of the car, parked under the elegant porte cochere.

"Absolutely," Caeli called back over her shoulder, humping a bag up the front steps and followed by Liz humping another. "How could I not approve when you two are so obviously made for each other and head over heels in love? Don't suppose you've set a wedding date yet?"

The door was unlocked and the bags unceremoniously dumped in the hall before Liz replied, sounding cagey.

"Well… That's one of the things I want to talk to you about.

"But let's pop the kettle on first, shall we? For I'm dying for a cuppa and I'll bet you are too.

"And hey," she added, calling over her shoulder as she headed down the hall towards the kitchen, "I've got a special treat for you… Lamingtons, your favourite, filled with fresh cream… Yum! Got them from the bakery first thing this morning…"

It was over the tea and cakes in the sun-filled kitchen that Liz revealed her plans. Plans, Caeli was soon to discover, already a fait accompli and took her by surprise.

"Tony and I really don't want to wait, Mum," Liz began, waggling her cake-fork as though she was conducting a symphony. "We'd like to get married as soon as we can, for we're keen to visit the Paris and London fashion houses for the oncoming season. The Haute Couture," you know," she added grandly and tilting her nose in the air. "Tony thinks we should kill two birds with one stone, so to speak, and make it a honeymoon trip as well."

"Oh, *darling*... How *romantic*..." Caeli drooled. "Paris *and* London... Sounds *wonderful* to me... But how soon is 'soon' and 'not-wanting-to-wait'?"

Liz giggled happily. "Well, we know its short notice but... with your permission, we'd like to hold the wedding here at home in three weeks' time. Have the ceremony down on the jetty at the bottom of the garden, with a marquee set up on the lawn for cocktails and hors d'oeuvres, and have the actual wedding breakfast up here in the house.

"Nothing flash!" she added, seeing the look of alarm cross her mother's face. "Marriage celebrant, buffet – crayfish and champagne – that sort of thing, elegant but simple for our closest friends. Would you have a problem with that?"

Boy, they *had* thought it out and Caeli's response was dubious.

"No, no, not at all, my love... Sounds perfect to me – if we've got time to organise it all that is? And I must say I feel extremely privileged that you want to get married here at home, but three weeks... Yikes Liz, that's cutting it a bit fine! I'll have to get my skates on, for there's an awful lot to do!"

Liz giggled again and flung her arms around her mother.

"Yahoo!" she hollered, positively bursting with happiness.

"But you don't have to lift a finger, dear mother of mine. For I knew you'd agree, but doubted you could be here, so I went ahead and organised everything myself. The celebrant and the caterers are booked for three weeks' Saturday – the last Saturday of summer here at exclusive 'Rivergum House' at one o'clock sharp!

"And Mum," she added blissfully, "you're not going to believe the dress I've bought..."

Caeli was stunned. "If that's what you want, then of course I agree – that's if you're certain this Tony Laporio is your Mr. Right?

"Oh Mum!" Liz replied, floating on cloud nine, "I knew I could depend on you.

"As for Tony being my Mr. Right? He's all I've ever dreamed of from the moment we met and I'm absolutely crazy about him.

"You just can't imagine how wonderful he is or how wonderful he makes me feel," prattling on happily, as though she was the only girl in the world to have fallen in love.

"And what I find absolutely *amazing* Mum is that he actually feels the same about *me*!"

How Liz reminded Caeli of herself at an even younger age than her daughter was and the overwhelming feelings she had felt for Danny O'Halloran all those years before. Feelings so intense that they had roared through her being like a fever in her blood that no apothecary's potion or Monsignor O'Leary's hypocritical threats of eternal damnation, could have quenched. Her mouth twisting wryly at the thought of Danny's betrayal and his carefree life in America while she'd struggled on alone in Australia to support herself and his son. But diplomatically she held her tongue. Now was not the time to air bitter grievances or reveal Danny's treachery. Now was her daughter's time, her beautiful Liz about to get married to the man of *her* dreams, riding the dizzying heights on the roller coaster of first love, and she would not spoil it for her, quipping teasingly and faking her most brilliant smile.

"Love at first sight, eh? I do believe I've a pair of incurable romantics on my hands!"

"Yes… *absolutely*…" Liz drooled. "Isn't it just too scrumptiously delicious, mother – being in love?"

"Yes, *absolutely*…" Caeli drooled back.

But Liz's bright mood was to change in an instant, as though a dark cloud had gathered over her head and blocked out her sun.

"Speaking of weddings…" she said with a frown, "there's another I have to tell you about that's really quite staggering news. Took place on some island a few days ago and will probably shock you to the core. It sure shocked me. Gee, you could have knocked me over with a feather when I saw the picture in the paper…"

"Oh?" Caeli eyed her daughter with interest and raised her eyebrows quizzically, awaiting the "staggering" news to reach her ears. But wait she did, for it was agonisingly slow in coming.

"For heaven's sake, Liz, spit it out!" she said, when several long seconds had elapsed and it was obvious Liz was having some difficulty mouthing the words.

"Oh shivers, me and my big mouth," Liz mumbled unhappily, sorry she had brought the subject up. Reluctant to convey the latest sensational turn of events that had not only made headlines in all the Australian newspapers, but the television channels and the international press as well. Certain she was about to cause her mother a great deal of anguish, yet at the same time equally certain she had to be told.

"You're not going to like it, Mum," she warned. "It's probably going to hurt."

Caeli shrugged her shoulders and tilted her head and thought how recently she had heard those very same words. Responding on a bitter half-laugh, positive there was nothing her daughter could say to her now that could hurt her any more than she already was.

"Huh! So, what else is new? Come on love; out with it now, give me your worst!"

"Well, it concerns Sebastian Templeton..." Liz hesitantly began, reaching across the table and grasping her mother's hands, certain the information she was about to impart would render her prostrate on the floor.

"He got married last week, caused quite a stir. Hit the local rag and telly and everything."

Caeli's response was disappointing to her daughter, to say the least, not at all the shattered response Liz had expected.

"Huh! Is that all?" her mother said, "And here's me thinking something drastic had occurred – like World War Three, or a plague of locusts on Darling Downs."

"To Renni Dubray..."

"Oh."

CHAPTER THIRTY-SIX
ONE PROBLEM SOLVED

An uncertain silence spread between them, dramatically described as a pregnant pause. Soft-hearted Liz, the ever-devoted daughter, watching her mother like a hawk, expecting to see her to crumble and ready to pick up the pieces, Caeli surprisingly unperturbed, thinking there was nothing "staggering" about it, that it was as it should be. That the fussy, effeminate Renni Dubray and the dominant Greek-god of a man Sebastian Templeton, seemed right for each other somehow. The very same thought having crossed her mind on the one and only occasion she had seen them together, thinking then how naturally their opposing personalities seeming to spark and meld as one. The yin and the yang, she had thought, one sort of ending where the other began. Liz's "staggering news" had only confirmed what she'd suspected all along, that Sebastian Templeton and Renni Dubray were more than just crewmates or business acquaintances, but indeed were a couple. Recalling Renni's open and utter dislike of her from the moment they'd met, darts of unbridled jealousy shooting from his eyes so tangible that they'd actually made her flinch. But of course he could never have liked her, could he? She could see that now. To Renni she was a threat, a serious contender for his lover's affections and therefore could view her in no other light.

Much to her daughter's dismay, Caeli burst out laughing, enormously relieved it had finally come to this. That Sebastian Templeton was hopefully out of her life once and for all, and that one of her problems at least, had been solved.

"Oh Liz," she cried, through the tears of laughter streaming down her cheeks, "Is that all? Well whoopee-do and good luck to them I say!" Thinking – but not saying – and good riddance too!

But Liz felt decidedly let down by her mother's reaction and protested strongly.

"But Mum," she cried, "Aren't you totally crushed? Totally devastated? For I got the distinct impression that something serious was going on between you two and expecting to hear the big "E" announcement any tick of the clock – especially when Sebastian hot-footed it to Ireland right behind you."

Her mother's laughter subsided to an amused chuckle.

"Definitely not the something *you* had in mind my girl – at least not on my part and I'm really surprised you thought there was.

"It was never that sort of a relationship, but a purely platonic one right from the start, I thought you realised that?

"Though I have to admit that in the beginning I was hoping for more, for I felt quite attracted to the guy. For you have to admit that he's stunningly good-looking and I knew I was the envy of every other woman on the planet being escorted around by him.

"But there was always this barrier between us Liz, this no-go zone I just couldn't break down – though heaven knows I tried.

"It was really weird, for he just had no interest in romance or sex or anything intimate like that. A pleasant dinner... A bottle of wine... Intelligent conversation... but no passionate kisses or gropings in the dark, and certainly no carting me off to his bed!

"I began to suspect he was gay. My suspicions confirmed, I might add, when I met Renni and saw them together and Renni's reaction to me.

"I didn't need a crystal ball or a psychoanalyst's degree to work that one out. To me it was obvious; their body language said it all.

"Strangely though, in spite of the obvious and nothing more than an occasional hug and a peck on the cheek, Sebastian still spoke of marriage to me."

"How come...?"

"Well, it was actually the night I'd decided to end the relationship – and not because of Renni either – though that did have some bearing on the matter. But mainly because Sebastian had become too domineering and attempting to control my life and I wasn't enjoying his company anymore. You know me... I'm very much my own person and not into being bossed around. Independent too long, I guess. So I broke it to him as gently as I could after dinner that night – the night before you brought your Tony here for that memorable Sunday lunch when you announced your engagement.

273

"Boy was I in for a surprise! He got all in a huff and sprang the ridiculous thought-we-were-going-to-get-married bit on me! As you can imagine, I was flabbergasted Liz, for we'd never spoken of marriage, and quite frankly the thought had never entered my head, and I was more than a little bit irked at his out of the blue idiotic presumption, it really rubbed me up the wrong way…"

"Aw… Who'd ever have believed it?" Liz cheekily teased.

Caeli was unfazed by her daughter's remark and ignored it.

"Truly, we'd never spoken of marriage," she reiterated. "We were merely friends. For as I've already said I'd felt from day one that there was something decidedly different about Sebastian. But I just couldn't put my finger on what it was, and I guess that's because I'd never knowingly associated with any gay guys before and just didn't recognise what that something was.

"But what a Jekyll and Hyde he turned out to be," she continued, "for I thought he was joking and laughed in his face.

"Big mistake Liz, the outcome very nasty and quite an eye-opener and upset me terribly. But knowing me, and how explosive I can be when my dander is up, I gave back as good as I got and we parted that night not the dearest of friends."

Liz was intrigued, and her mother continued, barely pausing for breath.

"Sebastian followed me to Ireland to give me – as he so nobly put it, and I quote, 'A second chance!'

"Oh don't look so surprised love, it was purely an ego trip on his part, unable to accept the fact that I'd actually turned his gorgeousness down! His self-esteem was seriously wounded being scorned by a woman, and doubly so when I turned him down again!

"But ultimately he must have got the message, and came to realise it was for the best. For apparently he *did* see the light, didn't he? He actually found the courage to come out and admit to who he was and who he really wanted to be with – Renni Dubray."

"But if he was gay, Mum," Liz persisted, decidedly puzzled. "Then why on earth did he want to marry you?"

"Lord Liz, I don't know. I'm no psychiatrist! Though my guess is he was really confused and in some sort of denial regarding his sexuality."

"But he seemed to adore women, Mum, as they so obviously adored him. He attracted some of the most beautiful women in the world – like those models."

Caeli nodded her head in strong agreement.

"You're dead right there, love. But even 'adored' might be a bit of an understatement. For apart from being drop-dead gorgeous, he could be utterly charming when he chose to be.

"Drooled at his feet" is more like it! But then apparently so did the male of the species too? And I've since heard tell that homosexuals are usually the most perfect gentlemen – especially towards women. But as I've already said, I'm no expert and only guessing."

"Then why did he ask you to marry him?" Liz persevered, unable to leave the subject alone. "Apart from you having a brain in your head and being positively gorgeous yourself, I mean!"

Caeli chuckled. "You'll get on, girl. Flattery will buy you the moon and its shadow.

"But as for Sebastian asking me to marry him, in so many words he never actually did. Just made that ridiculous spur of the moment assumption I would, and I really can't imagine why such an idea should have entered his head in the first place at all?

"Perhaps he couldn't handle rejection…" Liz suggested.

"Could be… Or perhaps because he'd turned forty, he was full of the sense of time passing and re-evaluating his life? For turning forty is a rude awakening of time passing and a milestone in most people's lives.

"Or then again, perhaps it wasn't a wife he was seeking at all but a mother figure to coddle him in his advancing years – reminiscent of his own mother perhaps?

"Come to think of it, Liz, he actually told me I reminded him of his mother. Heaven forbid – that was a rude awakening for me… Never knew whether to feel flattered or affronted, for I'd heard she was a bit of a dragon.

"Then again, perhaps he saw in me his last stab at going straight and having a child – for he adored children, before finally admitting… What is that expression they use – coming out of the cupboard?

"The closet, Mother…"

"Well, coming out of the closet then, before finally admitting who he really was."

Liz was looking at her mother in stunned amazement, her jaw gaping wide, but eventually managed to remark, "Aren't you the dark horse then, keeping all this intrigue to yourself with nary a word to yours truly? Where was I when all this was going on, orbiting the moon or climbing Uluru?"

"Orbiting the moon, I suspect – or at least with your head in the clouds mooning over your handsome Tony!

"But seriously, love, I had every intention of telling you all that Sunday you came here for lunch, for inwardly I was shattered at Sebastian's attitude, at how nasty he'd turned out to be.

"But I didn't get the chance, did I? What with you two love birds springing your engagement on me and that phone call from Ireland earlier that morning, all thoughts of Sebastian clean left my head!"

Liz was quite awed.

"However did I ever read you so wrong dear mother of mine, me, who can usually read you like an open book. For I'd assumed – and quite naturally so I should think – especially in light of you phoning me from Ireland and sounding quite gaga over something, *and* because I knew Sebastian had followed you there, I thought you were about to tie the knot…"

"He was there fully five minutes before I sent him packing…" Caeli protested indignantly.

"Well, all I can say is thank goodness you did, for I'm awfully glad you didn't – marry him, that is. For in all honesty I wasn't too keen to have him for a stepfather.

"He was beginning to get on my nerves too – big time – even in small doses! And frankly, I was quite relieved when I read in the paper he had married Renni Dubray.

"But then I was worried for you. Concerned how you would react if the news were to reach you in Ireland. So when you stepped off the plane with your chin on the ground, my heart sagged there too, thinking the worst – that you were a case of the lovelorn nursing a broken heart! And there was me blaming poor old Sebastian Templeton for it. Thank goodness I was wrong."

Yet without realising it, Liz had been her usually intuitive self and hit the nail right on the head, for Caeli *had* been a case of the lovelorn nursing a broken heart. It was only the object of her affections in which Liz had erred. Unaware of her mother's involvement with Liam Shaw, or the latest shattering revelations about Danny.

Suddenly everything became too much for Caeli; the lies, the betrayals and the stress of it all, and to Liz's horror, she burst into tears and little by little unburdened the whole sorry saga from woe to go, beginning with her feelings for Liam Shaw.

CHAPTER THIRTY-SEVEN
CONFESSIONS

"I fell in love with him, Liz," she said, "passionately and true to my nature – all or nothing, and I was totally convinced he felt the same about me. We go back a long way, Liam and I, for the Dromgoole's and Shaw's have been friends for generations, and I truly believe we were on the verge of something special before Dada brought Danny O'Halloran to Liath Caislean, and that – as far as I was concerned, was the end of Liam or anyone else for me. But apparently it wasn't the end for Liam. Claiming he'd never got over me or fallen in love with anyone else. And I believed him Liz, for it appeared obvious from our very first re-acquaintance in his father's office in Dublin, that the old "special something" we had once shared, was still there, despite the many years we'd been apart. Though if I am to be honest, Liz, I have to admit I felt it way before then. Felt it over the phone, here in this house, the morning he rang me from Ireland, half a world away. And again to be honest – with no intention of deriding your amazing powers of persuasion, I have to admit that it was really on account of the things Liam said to me during that phone call – but especially the manner in which he said them, that ultimately swayed my decision to return to Ireland at all."

Liz was looking at her mother with a gob-smacked expression on her face, her mouth gaping wide, as though she would comment, but the words refused to come.

"Coincidentally, Liam arrived at Liath Caislean on the same day Sebastian did." Caeli continued. "Phew, what a shemozzle that turned out to be! Both sitting in the parlour wondering about the other; Molly hovering around, arms akimbo, wondering about them and asking them straight out what business they had there. She's amazing Liz, you'll adore her, for I plan to bring her here for a holiday if she will come... For she's always been there to protect me and mine and she seems to forget I'm not a child anymore. But I soon sent Sebastian packing, made it perfectly clear there was nothing but friendship between us. Then Liam professed his love for me – right there in front of Molly – for no way was she leaving, stating that he'd always been in love with me, which deep in my heart I believed to be true – and even confirmed by Dada in that letter he wrote me... Then he got down on bended knee right then and there with Molly looking on, and made his proposal of marriage to me."

"And your answer was...?"

"YES! Emphatically YES! That I'd be the happiest woman on the face of the earth to be his wife! Even Molly butted in and said yes for me too, but I doubt that's likely to happen now."

"So, you've not heard from him since?" Liz gently pried.

"Not a word! And almost two weeks have gone by since he left Liath Caislean and returned to Dublin. Time enough for news of the conspiracy to reach his father's legal establishment, would you not agree? His silence convincing me he's as guilty as hell, Liz," adding glumly, "God, I sure know how to pick 'em, fallen for another despicable rogue who has also betrayed me, just like the other men in my life. Though never *your* father," she hastened to add. "Malachi Morgan was the sweetest man on the face of the earth, and an absolute Godsend to me."

"Conspiracy...? Betrayal...? Whatever are you talking about, Mum? Sounds awfully melodramatic to me..."

"But of course... You haven't heard, have you?" Caeli replied, unable to hide the bitterness in her voice. "Heard that my beloved Danny – the love of my life and the father of your brother – whose death I have mourned every day of my life since he was supposedly "Lost at Sea," but of whom I have now been informed, isn't dead at all but very much alive and living like a king in America!" Proceeding to relate the details of Jamjo's chance meeting with Danny O'Halloran when in Las Vegas searching for Josie.

"All hell broke loose when the truth came out, and I refused to believe it at first. But now I am totally convinced that everything Jamjo has told me is true. That Danny *is* alive and that your conniving grandfather was the twisted mind behind the plot to take him away from me – the revelation of which, I might add, was the deciding factor that made me reject the inheritance and let it pass to Kevin.

"I felt so utterly betrayed that I wanted no part of anything connected to Danny or Dada or to Ireland, and I left the house the following morning and caught the first available flight back here.

"And to think it was that damn letter that Dada had written me that brought things to head – almost as though he had planned it that way? For until Josie and Jamjo read the letter, they'd decided to keep me in the dark about Jamjo meeting Danny in America, and to say nothing at all about it to me."

"The letter informing you Danny was grandfather's son and therefore your half-brother?"

"Yes, among other things, most of which have turned out to be lies. But more of that later…

"Furthermore" she said, "and it gets worse, Liz, for I wasn't the only one to get hurt by Dada's actions." Proceeding to reveal how Dada had gone to Josie's bed and raped her on the night of her eighteenth birthday and fathered her son.
"I feel sick to the core when I think of him now, for he almost ruined Josie's life too, and I can only thank God Jamjo found her when he did! And to make matters worse – if they could get any worse… Josie was a virgin at the time.

"'Saving herself for Jamjo' was the way she put it, which was another surprise – I mean a surprise because she and Jamjo were in love and secretly engaged, for he'd asked her to marry him on the morning of her birthday and had given her a Claddagh Ring as a token of it.

"She told me that she'd felt so dirty and disgusted at what Dada had come to her bed and done that she just couldn't face Jamjo – or Molly either.

"Soiled goods" was an expression she used. Hence stealing from the house in the dead of night like she did, not only carrying the burden of the terrible deed Dada had gone to her bed and done to her, but also the seed of his son implanted in her womb, vowing, as I did, to never to return to Liath Caislean again."

"Ugh! The rotten old mongrel…" Liz responded with a shiver, "I'm disgusted too!"

"But still there's more… And I feel totally shattered and betrayed by the whole business and wish to God I'd followed my instincts and stayed right here at home. I knew it could only mean trouble.

"For while I'm referring to Bran Dromgoole as my father, I now have good reason to believe he is not. The evidence, of which I might add, was confirmed by Molly the morning I left Liath Caislean."

"You've got to be kidding… What sort of evidence?"

"I kid you not… Pretty strong evidence, I'd say. A photograph, an old coloured photograph of a young British pilot Mother had apparently met when in London during the war – for she had a beautiful singing voice Liz, and sang for the enlisted men there. A photograph I had stumbled upon hidden between the pages of mother's bible in her private rooms in Turlough's Wing.

"That he was someone special was obvious, for why else would she have kept it in her bible for so long? And there's also an inscription that confirms as much.

"Here," she said, producing the photograph from her handbag and placing it on the table before her daughter. "See, there!" Pointing to the inscription and tapping it with her finger, '*To my Darling Maureen… Eternally yours Michael… October 1940.*'

Liz picked up the photo, the uncanny likeness to her mother astounding and spoke for itself

"Gee Mum," she said, "this is real spooky stuff. He's the spitting image of you!"

"Isn't he though, or me of him. And as you can imagine it gave me quite a jolt. For when I first saw it I instantly felt he was someone I knew or ought to have known, that somewhere along the line he was part of the family and related to me! So much so that I had the weirdest feeling I was looking in a mirror and staring back at a bygone image of me!

"So you can imagine the thoughts that ran through my head, questioning if this unknown man could be my father, especially when I read that inscription: '*To* my *Darling Maureen… Eternally yours Michael… October 1940.*'

"For everything fitted Liz. Mother's sudden return to Ireland in the December of that year just before Christmas, then marrying Bran Dromgoole shortly after that and myself being born in the June of '41 – supposedly premature.

"And Molly confirmed it, confirmed he was my father that Mother had confided as much to her on the night I was born."

"Then why didn't she say something about it to you before?"

"Sworn to secrecy... She said she never would have told me at all, if I hadn't found the photo and challenged her about it, that mother would have told me herself if she had wanted me to know.

"She said it was the typical wartime love story: Two young people – Mother and this Michael, falling in love in war-torn London and about to get married when he got killed.

"She also explained mother's sudden change of heart and why she married Bran instead of Mr. Shaw. For apparently she was engaged to Mr. Shaw; but had suddenly changed her mind when he took her to Liath Caislean and introduced her to Dada – to Bran. And because he – Bran, bore a striking resemblance to this Michael – notably the same jet-black hair and facial features – though I can't say I noticed much of a resemblance myself, she thought he would pass more convincingly off as my father than the auburn–haired Mr. Shaw ever would.

"Molly knew the whole story," Caeli continued, "for it was Molly who delivered me into the world and remained with mother the whole night through. She also told me that she and mother had formed some sort of pact for the future that night – namely, promising to be there for each other's children should some tragedy befall either one of them. I think mother must have been feeling very vulnerable at the time, for Molly also confided that Dada – or rather Bran Dromgoole, deserted her that night. That he'd taken one look at me and stormed from the room and rejected me right from the start.

So when I think about it Liz, if Dada – or Bran Dromgoole, had seen the photo – and Molly was certain he had, then he also could not have missed seeing the resemblance between us and concluded I wasn't his, which would also explain why he spent his whole life despising me. For again, according to Molly, he wasn't a forgiving sort of man, but inclined to hold grudges, and likely never forgave mother for concealing the fact she was pregnant with me and tricked him into marrying her. And I can't say I blame him for that. But a bit hypocritical, wouldn't you say, rather like the pot calling the kettle black, bearing in mind he had an illegitimate son of his own. That Danny was Dada and the gypsy woman Zita O'Halloran's illegitimate son. Born out of wedlock before he met mother true... But again according to Molly, *he* never told Mother about that."

"Ah... And so the plot thickens."

"Indeed it does. The mind boggles. And I now have to wonder if Jamjo's so-called 'chance' meeting with Danny in America was by 'chance' at all or was it a set up – that we were all set up? That for reasons I cannot yet fathom, Jamjo was *meant* to 'discover' Danny in that bar in Las Vegas that night and *meant* to find Josie – bearing in mind again that he went there following Zita O'Halloran's lead.

"And there's another thing that's been worrying me too, and I'd swear to God I heard it right. I'd said something to Molly about being relieved that I wasn't a Dromgoole after all, and she mumbled something under her breath that sounded awfully like, 'Don't be too sure about that.' But when I challenged her about it and asked her what she meant, she denied having said any such thing. Weird."

For the first time in her life, Liz was struck dumb, fresh out of words of wisdom to impart.

CHAPTER THIRTY-EIGHT
ALONE

Caeli was once again alone in her gracious old Queenslander home, nestled on a tranquil bend of the Brisbane River and feeling the depth of that loneliness like never before. The emotional highs of Liz's wedding, held in the house that day, had run their course and plunged her into the opposite extreme, emotionally drained and morbidly depressed. For it had truly turned out to be a day of conflicting emotions. Ecstatic on the one hand for her beloved daughter and her marriage to her handsome Tony Laporio, yet sad on the other because Kevin her son – now living in faraway Ireland, had not come, and sad for herself too, unable to dispel the memory of Liam Shaw from her mind and *his* proposal of marriage to her. A proposal she had gladly accepted, yet a proposal she now realised he had no intention to keep.

The last of the wedding guests, her oldest and dearest friends Joyce and Bill Tufnell, had just departed, the last to leave, yet the first to have welcomed her to this country twenty-two years before. How she wanted to rush to the phone and beg them to return, desperate for the company of tried and true friends this night.

The spick and span rooms made it hard to believe that a wedding reception had been held in them that day. The caterers departing as efficiently as they'd come, sweeping every last vestige of the magnificent occasion away. The only giveaway signs to remain, were the many vases of roses, spilling their glorious perfume and colour from every stand in sight, and the top tier of the wedding cake grandly ensconced on a silver platter in the centre of the dining room table.

Needless to say, Liz had looked radiantly beautiful in an identical gown to the one the "childlike model" in the Sydney fashion parade had worn, and also looked "too young" to be a bride. Her long golden hair wreathed in honeysuckle picked fresh from the garden

284

that morning, holding a long filmy veil in place. The "something old," the stunning emerald and diamond heirloom ring passed down from mother to daughter in her mother's family for generations and gifted to her that morning. Tony Laporio, her handsome young groom in white tie and tails fair bursting with pride at her side.

Their vows they'd exchanged on the sun-baked jetty jutting into the river, the azure sky and diamond-studded river their magnificent cathedral. The simple yet meaningful ceremony, witnessed by seventy guests gathered on the pebbly little beach, Mendelssohn's "Wedding March," joyously played by a string quartet. Kevin however, had been noticeably absent, unable to make it, much to his sister's unspoken dismay, "Commitment to Liath Caislean," his excuse, a commitment too new to avail him the time.

The new Mr. and Mrs. Tony Laporio were now en route to a speck of an island on the Great Barrier Reef on the first leg of an extended honeymoon/business trip, planned to coincide with fashion shows of Paris and London, concluding with a few days in Ireland visiting Kevin at Liath Caislean, before returning home to Australia.

Caeli showered, and wrapped in a white-towelling robe, started back down the hall feeling restless and depressed. The daylight quickly fading to dusk, filling the house with deepening shadows, the high VJ walls of the "Queenslander," rising like canyon walls about her, hemming her in, making her feel small and insignificant and of little account to anyone.

Reminiscently she paused at Kevin's vacated room in her passing, missing her son in Ireland now more than words could tell. Its door flung wide, its macho red and black interior looking horribly neat stripped of his clothing and personal belongings and screaming "abandonment" back out at her. Only his beloved Freddy-teddy remained abandoned on the bed, as though Kevin had also abandoned his childhood, in his haste to be gone?

The lingering aroma of "Miss Dior" then drew her to her daughter's room, its feminine roses and cream décor, similar to her own room at Liath Caislean. It looked like a bomb had hit it. Clothes scattered everywhere. The filmy white wedding veil carelessly draping the dressing table's mirror, the gorgeous white gown as carelessly flung over a chair, the white satin wedding slippers dumped on the floor, as though Liz had also been in a hurry to be gone.

How dramatically her life had changed since Liam's phone-call from Ireland a few short months before and how unprepared she had been for such change, and how deeply that change had affected her: Kevin now living in far-away Ireland and the master of Liath Caislean, and her beloved Liz a married woman that day and independent of her now. How empty and alone and no longer needed she was feeling, that her role of "mother" had run its course and become obsolete. Her life stretching before her uncertainly now, posing the confronting question: "What now?" What did she want to do with the rest of her life – or more to the point, what was she *going* do with it? For well she knew what she wanted, she wanted Liam Shaw. But Liam Shaw, it seemed, did not want her!

She was wallowing in self-pity and she knew it, yet incapable of pulling herself out of the depression she now found herself in, feeling her life was falling apart and desperately in need of a change of direction.

Even the business she had spent more than half her life creating and of which she was normally so very proud, seemed to have lost its appeal and become an unwanted chore. A daily grind she no longer looked forward to, and right at that moment would have gladly relinquished its responsibility to someone else.

And who better than her Liz, she thought, rashly deciding that's what she'd do – hand the business over to Liz upon her return and take time-off and travel. Just pack a bag and fly off somewhere, anywhere, it didn't really matter.

Yet on second thought, it mattered a great deal. The young British airman in the old coloured photograph again nudging into her mind, indeed had he ever left it? His amazing violet eyes contained a multitude of secrets waiting to be solved and he seemed to be saying: "Come to London, Caeli.

Come to London and find my family – your family!" Come to London, where he had been stationed during the war and fallen in love with her mother, and where she herself was undoubtedly conceived. The destination of her travels – when Liz returned, decided unequivocally then, that London, England, first stop it would be.

The remnants of the hot humid day had surrendered to a cooler twilight as she wandered outside to her high rear veranda with a glass of red in hand to wearily slump into a settler's chair.

The surrounding shrubbery, nondescript opacities now, hunched dark and mysterious in the garden below. The river, a shimmering ribbon of velvety ink by then, rippled silently on, reflecting the lights of the high-rise buildings on the opposite bank. The sun dipped huge and red to a charcoal horizon, setting the sky ablaze with brazen pink clouds and brush-marks of gold. Somewhere overhead, a lone bird squawked, sounding forlorn as it sought its refuge for the night, while others winged westward towards the setting sun, their silhouettes dark and indistinguishable as the day succumbed to a star-studded night.

"God I love this country," she whispered, scanning the newly awakened specks of stars and overwhelmed by the beauty of the scene, drawing comfort from the knowledge that somewhere up there "The Southern Cross" was also coming to light. For to Caeli, it represented the signature of home.

Her home and garden designed as a haven of peace and tranquillity and calm contemplation, but as with everything in life, solitude also came at a price. For solitude allowed her thoughts to wander, to relive yet again the cruel charade of the past.

She had found it impossible to accept the legacy Dada had left her or to remain at Liath Caislean once Danny's existence had been revealed, especially when learning it had been Dada himself who had masterminded the deceit. To her mind, he had taken his hatred of her to a much deeper level and Liath Caislean to once again become the hostile place she had always known it to be. Sensing his tyranny still dwelled in its walls and pulsed in every room about her, even though banished to his grave.

She had packed her bags upon her return from the ruins of Granny Grainne's hut, planning to slip quietly away the following morning, not knowing whom to trust anymore. Who among the sea of smiling Irish faces that had shone out so brightly in welcome was genuine friend or sinister foe?

Her nerves were as taut as towbars as the staggering events of the past few months re-ran yet again through her mind, heralding the pain that was only a whisker away. Pain fashioned by her menfolk in a time long ago. Pain fashioned anew with the ache in her heart for her beloved son Kevin, lost to her now to the powerful pull of the Dromgoole legacy and the life of bondage that Liath Caislean unconditionally wrought.

And what of the pain she felt for her beloved son Kevin's pain? Pain that all of her mother's love could not shield him from nor lift away. The pain of knowing that his father had been very much alive every day of his life and had not wanted him. Pain *he* would have to live with for the rest of *his* days.

But worst of all, and the hardest to live with of all, was the all-consuming pain she felt when she thought of Liam Shaw and the treacherous role she was now convinced he had played in the ghastly charade. A part she believed he had played exceedingly well, deserving of a Hollywood Academy Award at least. For he'd accomplished what no other man since Danny had been able to do – he'd made her fall in love with him – helplessly and hopelessly in love.

Her depression would not lift and the drink did not help, missing her son in faraway Ireland more than words could tell and filled with a mother's fear she had lost him forever. Lost him to something so powerful she was no match for: The call of Liath Caislean and the call of Ireland and the even greater call of the past.

Kevin was Liath Caislean's new master now, the lord of its lands and the staggering wealth the inheritance wrought. He had even laid claim to the family name, wishing to be known as Kevin Dromgoole forevermore. Not that she had any objection to that. Cynically thinking he had more Dromgoole blood in his veins than any of them did – unlike herself, who apparently had none? His father being Danny O'Halloran, her passionate young lover, Danny in turn being the illegitimate son of Bran Dromgoole, the man she had believed to be her father. He had even inherited the powerful physique and brooding dark looks of his Dromgoole progenitors, the resemblance between the three men escaping her before yet as clear to her now as it had been to Mr. Shaw. Three men... Three Dromgoole men... No four, counting their ancestor Turlough. Four men so physically alike in spite of the two hundred year lifespan between them, conceding that Kevin was deserving of the name, that he fitted the mould of the Dromgoole men exceedingly well.

But looks were only looks that eroded with time and as far as the similarities went, for it was on the inside where Kevin was different, on the inside where it counted and determined the calibre of the man. She knew her son to be proud and honest and good to the core, not for him to bring shame upon the Dromgoole name as his father and grandfather before him had done. Reluctantly admitting that in Liath Caislean and in Ireland, Kevin had found his place in the world, his Shangri-la. But she also believed that in Kevin, Liath Caislean had found its saviour too. For he was blindly in love with his heritage and all Ireland stood for, a love as deep and irreversible as his new-found love for Patricia Shaw. That because of Kevin, the story that began two centuries before by the crazy old Turlough Dromgoole, would continue far into the future, and that in time, the "Dromgoole" name would become a proud and respected one once more.

Inexpressively now, she regretted returning to Ireland at all, wishing, as a naïve young girl had once wished inside a fairy ring for the desires of her heart to be granted, that she could turn the clock back and return all their lives to the way they had been just a few months before. Yet knowing she might have wished for the stars to fall from the sky for all the good it would have done. That regardless of whether she had returned to Ireland or not, the outcome would have been the same. Danny's presence would have still been revealed to her, and Kevin would still have gone to Ireland and become the new master of Liath Caislean, the outcome predetermined by Dada in a time long ago?

But she *had* returned, gone back to Ireland and back to the house and back on her word, breaking her vow she would never return to the house again. Surprising herself at how deeply the return had affected her, how the mere sight of Ireland from the plane had brought tears to her eyes and stirred her Irish blood and the desire to belong. Beguiled by the beauty of the land and its sea of smiling faces and their glib Irish tongues and softly spoken words. Even softening her heart to Bran Dromgoole – heaven forbid! Swayed by Mr. Shaw's exalted praise of him, but mostly by the letter he had written to her contritely explaining many things. Almost convinced she had judged him unjustly, until Josie and Jamjo returned from America and read the letter too and revealed it for what it was – a load of good old Aussie Bullshit and the joke well and truly on her. Well, he'd got his revenge, hadn't he?

Was that what this was all about then, the elaborate hoax, the shattering of lives, the years of hate, about seeking revenge and settling old scores? Dada's final act of retribution against a blameless child who'd so innocently entered his life? Surely not, surely there had to be more? Something way back in his past that had embittered and played on his mind and multiplied out of proportion, something that related to his mother perhaps? The unmentionable woman who'd abandoned him and his father for another man. The faceless woman of the missing portrait removed from the walls of Turlough's Wing and condemned to the attics in disgrace, leaving only a rusted hook and a blank discoloured patch to eternally remind and despise.

Perhaps there were other truths awaiting her discovery too? The truth of her mother's passing for one, not quite as certain now as she had been that it was the tragic accident Bran Dromgoole and the "powers that be" had claimed it was. Perhaps Dada's wealth and position held a stronger power to manipulate the outcome and spoke loudest of all? Perhaps the community's unwavering belief of their master's guilt, was condemned to remain a backhanded whisper? That he really had pushed her mother to her grave – perhaps seeking revenge on her too?

And now she had to wonder if it had been Kevin all along that Dada had wanted to step into his shoes as the master of Liath Caislean and not her at all? That he had drawn a warped sense of pleasure casting the temptation of his wealth under her nose before whipping it away. Certain her pride and pain and disgust when she'd learnt that Danny had been very much alive all these years, would make her turn her back on the inheritance and go scampering away. And what a vicious twist it had been to learn that Danny was Bran Dromgoole's son, and that she in turn had borne her half-brother's son. That Kevin was the illegitimate son of Dada's illegitimate son! That all along it had been Dada's sick plan to put Kevin on his throne and take him from her. How simple it had been to have Liam phone her in Australia and lure her back to Ireland, certain Kevin would follow, that the strength of his bloodline was too strong to resist? The whole enactment a pointless charade of Dada's twisted mind, designed to ravage her feelings and somehow pay her back?

Obvious to her now that Jamjo had also been used, guided by Danny's own mother, Zita O'Halloran, to "discover" Danny in that particular club in Las Vegas on that particular night. That the so-called "chance" meeting had not been by "chance" at all, but a skilfully organised plan?

She had to admit she felt beaten, physically and mentally thrashed. Unable to get it straight in her mind who was for who or what was for what and overwhelmingly aware that the truth of it all might never be known and lost to her forever. Conceding that even in death Bran Dromgoole had accomplished his greatest revenge of all over her, that he'd reached from the grave and taken her son, as surely as he'd taken Danny O'Halloran away from her, all those years before.

CHAPTER THIRTY-NINE
DREAMS COMES TRUE

Settling sounds of the night grew all around her as new ideas formed in her mind. Soft rustlings high in the trees and deep in the undergrowth as unseen creatures sought their havens for the night. Cicadas chirped from secret places, frogs croaked relentlessly down by the pond. Mozzies buzzed, annoyingly biting. Rippling wash slapped gently the pylons of the jetty and shushed upon the pebbles of her private little beach, soothing sounds that seeped through her, until rudely interrupted by a loud urgent thumping upon her front door.

"Who in heavens name…" she muttered, leaping from the chair and rushing down the hall and calling out impatiently as the thumping continued, "Hold your horses mate, I'm coming, I'm coming," then opening the door safe in the knowledge that the outer screen door was securely locked.

She could only gasp at the vision before her and gasp again in disbelief, certain her eyes were deceiving her, that because of her total yearning for the man, her mind was playing games and had somehow conjured him up. Yet when she blinked her eyes and blinked them again, he was still there.

His clothing was crumpled, his hair uncombed, his appearance dishevelled, as she had never seen him before, an overnight bag tossed over one shoulder, unimportant trivialities barely worth mentioning. Only his face, his dear beloved face did she truly take in. The face she had convinced herself she would never see again, yet the face she could not dismiss from her mind, ever before her day and night.

How pale it was, how fatigued he looked, the weariness seeping beyond the physical, through to the very essence of him, his soft brown eyes so full of accusation that she could not hold their gaze and was forced to look away.

"Liam…" was all she could utter bewilderedly, desperately wanting to unlock the screen door and gather him to her, to wrap her arms around this man who had dominated her every waking moment since their re-acquaintance in Ireland a few months before; to meld her body impossibly close to his and somehow absorb him, to absorb his fatigue and pain. But she didn't. She couldn't. Unconvinced he was there and not just a figment of her yearning.

"You left," he said flatly, slumping against the jamb of the door exhausted. "Didn't even bother to say good bye…"

"Liam…" she repeated. "But I thought you were… I didn't think that you…"

"You didn't think what!" he exploded, slamming his hand into the screen door with an almighty clatter and harshly cutting her off.

She flinched at the noise and his anger, her voice faltering, "B-but I thought… I thought you were part of… Oh my darling, you came…"

"Course I came," he said wearily, his anger spent. "What else was I to do, for I wasn't about to lose you again. And if I'm not mistaken Caz, you promised to marry me, or had that small detail slipped your mind?"

Her heart was pounding so hard that she thought it might burst her need to hold him so strong that she thought she might die. Yet still she did not open the door, but remained as still as a statue cemented to the floor while everything she hungered for stood two steps away.

"But weren't you part of Dada's conspiracy?" she flung back accusingly.

"Hell no, Caz, I knew nothing of that! That was our dear old dad's doing, your dad and mine, in cahoots with that evil old devil, O'Leary."

It was then she began to cry. Hot silent tears she could no longer contain spurting from some well of hope deep within her.

"Oh Liam – Liam," she blubbered, "I thought you were part of the horrible deception and only pretending to love me."

He almost choked his reply, genuinely stunned by her words.

"Pretending… Pretending to love you… Dear God in heaven, Caz, haven't I loved you all my life!"

Ridiculously, she still did not move and the door remained locked.

"Then why didn't you write, or phone, or come to me sooner?" she demanded to know.

"Well, in the first place I didn't know you were gone, did I? Or what I was to think when I discovered you were? And then it took a hell of a lot of digging and delving on my part to get the bottom of what was going on. And all hell broke loose when Jamjo stormed into the office in Dublin and accused my dad and the firm of corruption and resigned his position there and then on the spot! And it got even worse when Dad was informed that you'd packed your bags and were already gone!

"I left for Liath Caislean as soon as I could because I couldn't believe you'd have left without talking it over with me and at least given me the chance to have my say and clear my name. And when I eventually arrived at Liath Caislean, I was well and truly confronted with a closed shop. Josie and Molly and Jamjo banding together, convinced I was up to my neck in what had gone on and as guilty as hell, and wouldn't so much as let me get me big toe in the door!

"I had to camp in the courtyard for nearly a week before they'd come out and let me in! And even then, it took a powerful lot of talking on my part, to convince them of my innocence!"

Still Caeli did not move.

He exploded then, frustrated and tired beyond belief, slamming his hand into the screen door again and shouting at the top of his voice,

"For God's sake, woman, what's a man supposed to do, must I stand here all night? Open the bloody door before I tear it from its hinges, for I desperately need to hold you in my arms…" causing neighbouring porch lights to blink on and the local dogs begin to bark.

But they were the magical words Caeli needed to hear. The desperate words of a man in love bespeaking his need and his innocence, words that compelled her to take the last step and unlock the screen door. "Oh my dearest… My darling… I thought… I thought…" Her words trailing to nothing as the metal lock clicked and he was inside.

In one sweeping movement he flung the bag from him and kicked the door shut and gathered her hungrily into his arms.

"You thought wrong, my girl!" he rasped, his voice raw with desire as his mouth crushed down on hers in a kiss that was urgent

294

and hard and devouring. Kissed the hot salty tears that trickled down her cheeks and the cool damp tussle of her freshly washed hair, kissed her eyes and her cheek, her neck and her breast, wanting to kiss all of her, gasping at the beauty of her as the white towelling robe fell away. Her legs collapsed beneath her then, overcome by the touch and feel of this man and the wild urgent need that was raging between them and would wait no longer to be fulfilled.

There would be no more talk of whys or wherefores that night, no more accusations or explanations. Tonight was their moment, the time for their bodies and minds and infinite souls to unite and meld as one. Tonight, a glorious design of Heaven made only for them.

Tomorrow the questions would undoubtedly flow, as would the pain their answers would bring. Tomorrow she would learn the whole truth – or as much of it as Liam knew. Learn that indeed there had been others involved in the ghastly charade to whisk Danny away and create him anew. The chief perpetrators being – as she had already suspected, Liam's own father Eugene Shaw, the esteemed Dublin lawyer and the man she used to call "Uncle" and believed beyond reproach and would have trusted with her life. And not surprisingly, the holier-than-thou hypocrite Monsignor Timothy O'Leary, the "Holy Man of God" with the wandering hands she had never trusted. Bran having confided in them – his closest lifelong friends practically since the three of them were born, that Daniel was his illegitimate son, born of the traveller woman Zita O'Halloran, and therefore could not be allowed to marry Caeli. But he'd failed to mention that Caeli was not his daughter, but another man's child, and therefore the marriage could have taken place. Thus the massive deceit had come into play.

Mr. Shaw and Monsignor O'Leary – Bran's loyal cohorts unto death, the main architects of the plan to spirit Danny away and reinvent him anew, true to the childhood pact they had made in the cave beneath Liath Caislean when they were lads. Placing their small index fingers side by side and Bran slicing through their fresh young flesh with a big rusty knife, uniting their blood and spittle and the unbidden tears that had sprung from their eyes as one, and swearing to God they'd come running to each other's aid for the rest of their lives "no matter what."

And not least of all – yet the hardest to accept of all, was the irrefutable truth that Danny himself had been involved, up to his eyeballs in it, willingly or otherwise. Handsomely bribed – as the secret file in Mr. Shaw's office would clearly reveal, to abandon her and the land of his birth and re-invent himself anew in America and ignore the very existence of her and the son he'd so passionately implanted in her at the place of the hawthorn tree.

Also to learn that Zita O'Halloran – Danny's mother, and Kevin's grandmother, had also been in on the plot from the very beginning, well rewarded and rehearsed in her role to reveal Josie's stage name and point Jamjo in the direction of that club in Las Vegas that night – Danny pre-arranged to be there and play his part. How simple it had been, a few minutes of Danny's time, no more, counting on Jamjo's keen observation and unquestionable integrity to do the rest?

But tomorrow was time beyond knowing, tomorrow an eternity away. Tonight was the here and the now and the only time that mattered for Caeli and Liam, as wrapped in each other's arms they entered the Gates of Paradise, to speak only the language of love.

CHAPTER FORTY
NEW BEGINNINGS

To awake to the light of an Australian dawn was a privilege Caeli had never grown tired of or taken for granted. To awake to that dawn with Liam beside her was a privilege beyond compare, and she stretched and yawned luxuriantly, feeling unimaginably light-hearted and deliciously free. Free of the nightmares that had haunted her nights far too long and even daring to believe that the spectres of the past had relinquished their hold and at last set her free and all because Liam was there? His arms protectively about her the whole night through – as though he would challenge the very Devil himself to enter her dreams and trouble her again, his arms protectively about her still in his sleep of exhaustion, as though he would hold her forever.

Gently, she slipped from his loving embrace and crept to the open French doors in steps as silent as a floating sylph, every inch of her feeling vibrantly alive and the morbid depression of her usual awakenings miraculously lifted away.

"Good morning, new day," she whispered, feeling absurdly young. The change in her dramatic, yet a change she was certain would remain with her forever.

The weather changed too, a gusty breeze fluttering the flimsy white curtains about.

The air exquisitely cooler, the last days of summer poised on the cusp of a brand-new season and a hint of autumn in the air.

Love changes everything… How profound the phrase, assuming of course it changed things for the better.

How often she had heard it, how often she had said it. But "love" in her experience – apart from giving her two wonderful children, had brought her nothing but heartache and despair.

How naive she had been in that time of long ago, she realised that now. A gullible girl playing grownups games when taken in by Danny's charms and swept up in his passion, mistaking his silver-tongued words and lustful advances for love. Desperate for love, deprived of her mother's love with her passing, and the love of a father she had never known, the love that Bran Dromgoole had never been able to bestow on her. More aware than ever with her mother's demise, how deeply he had despised her, his hatred become a tangible thing for all to see and come to a head the day of Meegan's funeral, for that had also been the day he had cast her out. How he had screamed at her like a madman that day and physically pushed her out of his house – the memory of it still tore at her heart and rang in her ears. For not only had he accused her of being the cause of her young sister's death and Danny's death too, but also the cause of her mother's tragic passing twelve months before, claiming if it wasn't for her, they would still be alive!

Even her subsequent marriage to Malachi Morgan had been little more than a farce, a selfish way out of the desperate situation she had found herself in. At least she'd had the courage to be honest with him and tell him the truth. Yet unbelievably he had still wanted to marry her, to accept her unborn son as his own and take them abroad to begin a new life together. But even that wasn't meant to be.

As for other relationships, there were none worth mentioning, brief encounters, one-night stands. Even her relationship with the drop-dead-gorgeous Sebastian Templeton that had made her the envy of every other woman on the face of the earth, had never evolved to the romantic liaison she had hoped it would be. Her growing suspicions regarding his sexuality, finally confirming Sebastian was gay.

Then Liam had come. Like a bolt from the blue, Liam had come.

What was it about Liam that changed her mind about love and men? What was it about Liam that one glorious night in his arms transformed her whole outlook on life and up-ended her world and wrote "happy ever after" in a rainbow of colours across her heart? Awaking that morning with a strong sense of that change within her and a lightness of heart she hadn't known in a very long time; aware that her instincts were keener and her mind sharper somehow, as if they'd been honed on some fine sharpening stone overnight.

Even the air she breathed and the scents of her garden seemed different to her now, purer, heady, and more exotically pungent somehow. And the strong vibrant hues of Terra Australis stretching clear to the mountains, more vividly intense, more keenly etched in the rich earthy pigments of umber and cadmium and smoky-gum-blue.

As silently as she had left it, she returned to the bed where Liam lay sleeping, overcome with the need to reassure herself he was really there and not just a dream to be gone with the night.

Eager to again look upon this man whom she'd believed was once again lost to her, the man who had dominated her every waking thought since their re-acquaintance in Ireland a few months before.

But he was also the man who had crossed half the world to prove his love and claim her and make her his own.

"I adore you, my darling," he murmured, stirred by her touch and gathering her hungrily back into his arms. "Marry me darling – now – today, for we've wasted so much time... And we'll honeymoon the world for the rest of our days!"

Her response was unhesitating, ecstatic.

"Yes my beloved, yes, yes, yes!" adding, with a light-hearted giggle, "But 'today' might be a tad ambitious, but tomorrow should be fine. As for honeymooning the world... wherever thou leadest I will follow, but first stop London, if you please?"

London was calling her loud and clear, as the young British Airman was calling, "Come to London, Caeli. Come to London and find my family – your family!" His handsome young image so very like her own, having convinced her he was her father. As did his name "Michael!" Surely their same jet-black hair and deep violet eyes and identical fine features were no freak toss of nature? Surely her mother had named her for him – Michael – Michaela... Surely the inscription on the photo: *To my Darling Maureen, Eternally yours, Michael, October 1940*, suggested an involvement much deeper than friendship and the words of a lover – her mother's lover, who had been in London at that time entertaining the British servicemen there? Informed by Mr. Shaw that her mother had unexpectedly returned to Ireland in the December of that year and married Bran Dromgoole shortly after that, making it clearly obvious to her now that her conception could only have occurred before her mother had married Bran, when in London with Michael? For Caeli had been born the following year, in the June of forty-one. Eager to begin her search now, to trace the roots of his family – her family, and discover all she could about him, and at last become a "Somebody's Child," with a father to name and claim as her own.

The photo of the young dead hero and the details thereon all she had to go on in her search for the truth – and the British Air Force records in London, the obvious place to start. Feeling strangely certain now that the family she was seeking somehow sensed she was coming, that even the Bow Bells of London were clanging out in welcome and bidding her to come?

"Your wish is my command, my beloved... But why London...?"

Proceeding to inform Liam of the photo she had found among her mother's possessions at Liath Caislean, and of her belief that the man of its content was her father, adding that Molly had confirmed it was so.

"Then London it shall be, my darling girl, full speed ahead."

For the first time in her life she felt truly loved, that this was the stuff dreams were made of. Marvelling at the incredible man in her arms and the inestimable treasure his love had brought; the treasure that had always been hers, even when blinded by Danny O'Halloran's charms.

For she had fallen in love with Danny, blindly and utterly in love, but he had not loved her, then she'd married the gentle Malachi Morgan, who had loved her enough to make her his bride and claim Danny's illegitimate son as his own, but she had not loved him – or at least not enough.

It seemed a long time ago since she had fallen in love with the dark-eyed Danny, with the handsome youth with the promise of heaven wrapped-up in his smile, the utterly sensuous Danny who had touched her in deep private places and driven her wild with his kisses and taken her maiden virginity away.

As far as she could see, the outcome of life came down to choices, to that fraction of a second one pauses to evaluate and decide which way to go – left, right, up, down, to say yes or say no.

She had said a resounding "yes" to Danny in that time of long ago by surrendering to the passion he'd aroused in her and the outcome had been Kevin, their son.

But Bran Dromgoole's decision to choose between a daughter and a son had been a far more callous and calculated one. The cold-hearted decision to choose between Caeli, born under his roof and raised as his daughter but another man's child, or Danny, his illegitimate son born of the traveller woman Zita O'Halloran? A son he would never openly acknowledge as his son nor bestow the Dromgoole name or wealth upon. And he had favoured the son.

She had no wish to return to Ireland. The men in her life there had treated her badly and shattered her trust and let her down: Dada and Danny and old Mr. Shaw, whom she had loved and respected above all other. And even the hypocritical priest, Monsignor O'Leary, her spiritual adviser, her confessor and a Holy Man of God, had let her down in more ways than one.

The land of her birth was as dead to her now as the love she'd borne Danny, its enchantment and people having lost their hold and vanished like a spell brewed in some hobgoblin's pot in a legend of long ago.

How desperately she wanted to be free of the past and put it behind her, to gather its ghosts and senseless wrongs and wedge them in some deep dungeon of her mind and forgotten forever, while all too aware that life didn't work that way.

Life was never that simple, never that kind. Too many things awaited their moment to prise the past open and relive it again: Family gatherings, old photos – especially old photos, songs and sayings and quite pensive moments, and always the season of Christmas to trigger the memories and bring them all back.

Still, there was always tomorrow. She believed in tomorrow, hung her hopes on tomorrow, but never more so than now because Liam was there.

The inspirational verse she had learnt from her mother as a very young child, again running rote through her head:

Today you come to me so new,
And with you comes the chance to do,
The things I'd not done yesterday,
Oh please don't let me waste this day…

Today was yesterday's tomorrow. So now – from this very moment she could begin life anew, stand on the brink of the brand new day with Liam beside her and fresh hope in her heart. How empowered the thought made her feel, how determined she was to take Josie's advice and fill her days with so much love that there'd be no room in them for harbouring hate. For when all was said and done, wasn't love the most important thing in life? Love, in its many different forms that made hearts soar and worlds go round?

As if choosing their moment to validate her thoughts, her daughter's wise words once again came to mind, *"Dwell on the good memories, Mum… On the people you love…"* And again she was swept up on a wave of emotion, but this time no treacherous undercurrents churned about her and dragged her down, no wicked demons raised their ugly heads to taunt her mind and terrorise her dreams. Only the calm healing waters of forgiveness would come and lap soothingly over her and all because Liam had come?

Liam had come – just as Jamjo had come to Josie. Come, when she'd believed he'd betrayed her and that she would never see him again. Two remarkable men who'd flown halfway round the world to offer their women a second chance happiness. Now Caeli, like Josie, was determined to grasp it for all she was worth and cherish it more with every new day. Then, when the chimeras of the past *did* return (and foolish she was not to think they never would), she could draw from her stockpile of happiness and confidently shoo them away.

Her voice was barely audible as she echoed her daughter's wise words: *"Dwell on the good memories, Mum… On the people you love…"* softer than the cooler breeze of the changing season fluttering the filmy white curtains about.

Yet even as the words left her lips, the breeze grew stronger and whipped the curtains high and billowing to the ceiling. And she likened them to the full-blown sails of dear little *Sea Nymph*, sailing with Danny on a breeze-filled summer's day. Seeing him now as he was then, all of nineteen and heartbreakingly handsome, flushed from the sun and the wind in his hair. Hear his strong Irish voice calling back to her through time: "Isn't she yare, Caeli, isn't she yare!" the beloved yellow vessel riding the waters of Raggemorne Bay like a sleek shaft of sunlight or a creature born of the sea, heading for harbour and bringing them home.

"Dwell on the people I love," she repeated, in a voice full of wonder, sensing the hard core of hatred that she had borne Danny melting away and a blessed forgiveness taking its place.

Knowing in her heart she would always love Danny, that the memory of him and those blissful days of yesteryear would always remain a part of her no matter what.

For Danny was her first love, her awakening to womanhood and the father of her son, and for these things alone he would always retain a special place in her heart.

Feeling confident of the future now with Liam beside her, seeing her direction stretched clearly before her and eager to embrace it, to set upon the road that would lead her to the family of the man she was now certain was her father, sensing that somewhere they were awaiting her coming and eager to greet her and gather her in.

"Dwell on the people I love" she whispered again, her voice full of wonder, as she snuggled back into Liam's waiting arms.

THE END